Giles and Julie

by
Hugh Bowen

Strategic Book Publishing and Rights Co.

Strategic Book Publishing and Rights Co., LLC
USA | Singapore
www.sbpra.com

For information about special discounts for bulk purchases, please contact Strategic Book Publishing and Rights Co., LLC. Special Sales, at bookorder@sbpra.net.

ISBN: 978-1-68181-101-7

Review Requested:

If you loved this book, would you please provide a review at Amazon.com?

Thank You

Books by Hugh Bowen

REVERSAL
WHY?
EDGE
CAVE

Table of Contents

Preface

Giles and Julie is the story of a boy and a girl growing up in WWII France. The war came upon them as *'a curse from Satan'* as Sophie, Giles's mother, says. They survive, but it must be remembered that millions perished. It was the most cruel and destructive of any war ever conducted by mankind. The two young people retain their humanity, go forward with their lives, and confront the turmoil of the postwar world. In this regard, let them stand for all people of that period, those who lived and those who died.

Some important persons of the period are represented. When I have them speak, I have used my memory, buttressed by historical documents, as a basis for what they said or might have said.

The story is embedded in the history of the period and I have maintained the chronology of the war and the early post-war period. Some of the events are described in footnotes. With the benefit of hindsight what actually happened in the war can now be seen more clearly. Footnotes also provide translations of French words, phrases, and acronyms.

The history of WWII has been copiously documented. The internet provides easy access to the record. To gain a better acquaintance with the background to *Giles and Julie*, the following books are recommended.

Horne, AlistairA *Savage War of Peace, Algeria 1954-1962.* MacMillan, London 1977 (reprints 1991, 1993)

Horne, Alistair *Seven Ages of Paris.* In particular *Age Seven* 1940-1969: De Gaulle. Knopf New York 2002

Lacouture, Jean. *De Gaulle The Ruler. 1945-1970.* Translated by Alan Sheridan. W.W.Norton & Company, New York and London 1992

Porch, Douglas. *The French Secret Services. A history of French secret services from the Dreyfus Affair to the Gulf War.* Farrar, Straus and Giroux, New York 1995

Part 1.
The Early Years of
Giles Martin

Chapter 1.

Eastern France. September, 1943

On that Thursday Giles Martin, aged 11, was coming out of the *École Primaire* in Plaignes, a small town in eastern France, when he sees *Hauptmann* Maximilian Gregor shot. White faced, he runs home to tell his mother, Sophie, what has happened. His breath comes in gasps. She can hardly understand him. She anxiously takes his arm. "Sit down, Giles. Calm yourself."

"Oh, *maman* . . . it was terrible!"

"You're not hurt?" Sophie asks anxiously.

"No, *maman*. I'm all right. It was so sudden!"

"What happened? Tell me!" she cries, fearing but already knowing that some awful thing had happened. All the time, in this dreadful war, awful things were happening.

"He came out of the house, *maman*, the house of *Madame* Picard, and closed the door behind him. He was pleased about something. I could see that, *maman*."

"And what happened? What happened, Giles?"

"He stood by his black car, putting on his gloves. The other kids and I were across the street by the school gate, the one with the iron railings. Then, suddenly, there were two shots. We all jumped. They came from the roof behind us. We looked up, but saw nothing. Just the roofs and the chimneys. The German fell to the ground and lay there by the black car, one glove half on. At first he moved. Then he

11

lay still. There was blood on the paving stones. The girls shrieked. I only stayed a second more. I yelled, 'Run! Run fast! The German soldiers will be here!'"

"*Ah, mon Dieu!* But who fired the shots?"

"I don't know, *maman*. It just happened."

"Who was there?"

"A bunch of us . . . and the teacher, *Madame* Ronde."

Sophie holds him in her arms, rocking to and fro. "The war, the war! A curse from Satan!"

Two days later, Saturday, the Germans round up the women, the children, the old men. There are no young men left. The Germans have taken them for forced labor in Germany. They order the people into the square. No one knows what is to happen, but they have dire forebodings.

The squad of German soldiers in their grey uniforms and rounded helmets stand in a line. The six hostages are brought out, their hands tied behind their backs, and stood in front of the stone wall. *Madame* Ronde is one of them; another is Sophie's uncle; both prominent people in the community. They are shot. Giles hears their cries, *"Vive la France."*

The priest, standing alone in front of the people, makes the sign of the cross many times. The square is filled with sobbing. An old woman falls to the ground, clutching her chest.

When it is done, the German officer inspects the corpses and shoots one through the head with his pistol after he had seen a slight movement. The soldiers throw the corpses, with their sightless eyes, onto a horse drawn cart.

Giles lies on his bed that night and goes over . . . again and again . . . what he had seen. Again he hears the sounds of the shots, sees the figures falling and the splashes of red blood on the wall where each had stood. It had happened in front of the school, like a lesson. The scene is etched into his mind. Everything else had been normal, like it always was. The street, the cobblestones, the windows of the houses, the church steeple, the cat sunning itself in the midday warmth, then scuttling away at the loud sounds. They all had their reality, their life, their decency. Then there was this. Why? Why did this happen? Is the life of a person so trivial that it can be disregarded? No more than an apple falling from a tree.

That was the moment Giles became an atheist. The idea of a god was absurd, unless that god was incredibly evil and treated humans as playthings, like a game of checkers. The idea of god was disconnected to life as he knew it. It didn't matter what the priests and others said. There was no god.

Giles determined to strike out on his own. He doubted that anyone he knew disbelieved in god like he did now. If he had to be unique, he would be unique.

Giles curls up in his bed, his eyes close, and he falls into nature's potion that ravels up cares and renews the self. He sleeps.

In the morning Giles awakes, again oppressed by the reality of the killing. He knows how most French people are keeping their heads down, trusting few others because of the *collabos*[1], living in a state of unease, fearing the present and, even more, the future. They do what they can to survive each according to his own devices, some with honor and gallantry, others with sullen and defeated spirits, and some betraying others. [2]

---

[1] *Collabos* was the word used for collaborationists.

[2] The German occupying forces promise, at first, that those who behave themselves peacefully and quietly have nothing to fear. They warn that any hostile act will be subject to the most severe punishment. The French soon learn that could mean torture and death. They also learn that behaving peacefully is no guarantee against being taken hostage and shot; or, if a Jew, being loaded into a cattle car of a train. Some trainmen say the Jews are taken to camps in Poland and killed there; but no one knows for sure. In the later stages of the war the Germans commit atrocities against all the people in a village. At Ourador-sur-Glane they herd the population into a church, set it on fire, and burn to death 642 men, women and children. The murders at Tulle are similar; 213 civilians lose their lives, 99

But simple survival was not for him, even though he was only 11, that was not for him. He would never be a coward, he would fight, he was French, he was born on Bastille Day, July 14th.

At breakfast Giles tells his mother, "I no longer believe in god. I'm sorry, *maman*. It's just us here, the good and the bad."

Sophie would plead with him to regain his faith, but Giles never wavered from his finding. In terms of certitude, it could be compared to the epiphany of St. Paul.

---

after torture. Those were the facts of life and death during the German occupation of France and they must never be forgotten nor forgiven.

Chapter 2.

The Maquis[3] and Life in occupied France. 1943-44.

Mec is in their little cabin, tucked away in the mouth of a cave behind trees and bushes in the craggy *Forêt du Quartier* south of Plaignes. The end of the cave leads to a shaft and then to a tunnel cut into the chalky ground by eons of water flow. After 150 meters[4] the tunnel leads to a small opening, also concealed by trees and bushes, on another hillside. If their cabin is ever attacked, they have an escape route.

---

[3] The resistance groups in France, particularly those operating in the countryside and mountains, were called the *Maquis*. Members of the *Maquis* were called *maquisards*. The word is derived from the Corsican, *macchia*, used to describe land covered by dense vegetation and bushes where criminals and desperadoes hid themselves. The Germans exploited this connection to crime by declaring *maquisards* to be killers and criminals and decreed that they should be treated as such.

[4] In this account distances will be given in the units used in the country where the story is taking place. Hence, in Europe, North Africa, etc. distances are given in meters and kilometers, in the UK and US miles are used. Conversions: 1 meter equals 39½ inches (1 yard 3½ inches), 10 kilometers equals 6.2 miles.

Mec is well aware of the gritty truth. The Germans have been systematically successful in uncovering the Resistance across France, particularly in Paris and other cities, and then torturing and killing the men and women they capture. The way to survive is by stealth in what they do and by ruthlessly exterminating the spies, "the pigeons," in their midst.

In spite of the successes of the Germans, headed by the *Gestapo*[5], and the servile *Milice* (the French police squads carrying out German orders), the number of *maquisards* secreted away in the woods and barns is growing. But no hiding place is completely secure, especially against the traitors. Some of the traitors are simply men and women who side with the Germans. Others are unfortunates who operate under threats of torture and death to them and their families. No matter who they were, Mec puts a pistol to their heads and shoots them. He has a well tuned nose for sniffing them out and has no compunction in eliminating them. They are spies, willing or not. Killing them can save hundreds of lives and safeguard their operation. Such are the exigencies of war. After Mec shoots them he dumps their bodies in front of the German *Kommandatur* in Dijon. Mario could soon be one of the corpses left there.

They have a radio transmitter that they can use to contact London. But they have no operator. The last one, a woman lent to them by another group, was discovered by the Germans, tortured, and shot. The Germans are skilled in discovering the location of a transmitter when it is broadcasting. They tune into it with multiple direction finding receivers and then triangulate its position. Radio operators have short lives. So Mec keeps the radio transmitter hidden and has forbidden its use.

---

[5] The Gestapo were the German secret police that operated outside the law and with no constraint. Their principal source of information were denunciations of persons by others. As an organization the Gestapo was ruthless, callous, and efficient. Most of its staff were office personnel coping with the stream of documents describing millions of suspected people. The field operatives, though few, were feared by all. Those who were not sadistic by nature, soon became so.

It is still too soon to attack the Germans in the open, whatever the provocation. Mec has to be calm, smart, and merciless to ensure the survival of his small group.

Mec knows what is happening in the outside world. He listens to the BBC broadcasts in French on an ordinary prewar radio. The news is good. The British under General Montgomery have defeated General Rommel and his Africa Corps at El Alamein and have been joined by the Americans in North Africa. At first the novice Americans are not battle-worthy. They have to learn the hard way what it takes to fight the Germans. The British with the Americans have just invaded Sicily. The Russians have defeated the Germans at Stalingrad and gone on to win the titanic tank battle at Kursk[6].

The Germans are retreating. But they are still strong. As a fighting force they are still the best in the world. It will not be easy to defeat them. In France, the Germans are building the Atlantic Wall to stop the coming invasion by the Allies. It will be a formidable barrier if properly defended. One of the inhuman realities of war is that the skill and bravery of the individual soldier has little to nothing to do

---

[6] The defense of Stalingrad, at a huge cost to the USSR, and the victory at Kursk, were the two crucial battles of WWII in defeating the German armies. Everywhere after that the Germans were depleted in manpower, armaments, and munitions. There was never any realistic hope they could regain the initiative or stem the tide of the forces arrayed against them. Hitler thought his secret weapons could do it. But they proved to be only pinpricks. He and others had made the crucial decision not to concentrate his scientific forces, which were considerable, in the development of the atomic bomb. That effort was always half-hearted, the Germans judging that success was too far distant and that, hopefully, they would have won the war before the British and Americans had perfected a bomb.

This decision was unknown to the Allies and caused Roosevelt to give the Manhattan project, the development of the atomic bomb, every priority in fear the Germans would get there first.

By 1943 the clear thinkers in the German General staff were realizing the war was lost. The feeling was permeating, though admitting it was far too dangerous. Any signs of defeatist attitudes in the German army were suppressed by summary courts martial and firing squads.

with the value of his country's cause. The skilled and brave German soldiers of WWII were fighting for the most evil regime that has ever existed.

Mec lights another cigarette. *Hauptmann* Gregor, before he had been shot, had uncovered three members of Mec's resistance group and been typically sadistic in interrogating and killing them. In doing so he had been following standing orders from Heinrich Himmler, head of the SS[7]. Himmler, more than any other man, had turned the German state into a murder machine.

To be caught is the risk they all run in the *Maquis*. The three had been careless. They were bound to be seen, sooner or later, meeting together behind the bakery. Everyone came to the bakery, including the *collabos*. Mec didn't know for sure who had betrayed them, though he suspected Mario Bettelli, the Italian. One of his women is a clerk in the German *Kommandatur* in Dijon. She had seen Mario's name on a page of a file open on the desk of a *Gestapo* officer.

Mec leans back in the sofa that they had carried with considerable effort up to the cabin. His mind snaps from one thought to another. The killing of the German officer had accomplished nothing and cost the lives of six good persons. The shooting had been done by someone outside Mec's group, likely by someone with a personal grudge against the German. If Mec ever found him, he would shoot him. A weakness of the *Maquis* was that each group, or an individual, could act on their own. It was difficult to maintain discipline and cohesion when hatred and fear ruled so many minds.

However, the separation of the *Maquis* squads, one from the other, is also their advantage, indeed their necessity. One squad knows little of the others. When the Germans catch a *maquisard*, the understanding is that the captive

---

[7]SS was the acronym for Schutzstaffel, a Nazi paramilitary organization, commanded by Heinrich Himmler. After the war Himmler and the organization were convicted of crimes against humanity.

tells nothing of importance for 24 hours. He may dissemble cooperation or hang tough, even if tortured. His task is to do his or her best to deceive and mislead the Germans. Whatever delay can be gained, it gives Mec and others precious time to prevent further discovery. When a prisoner eventually gives in, as almost all do, the Gestapo learns only a limited amount about a local cell.

Mec pours himself a generous glass of *Côte de Nuits*, a classic red wine of Burgundy. No need to stint himself of that pleasure! So far, so good. In spite of some success against them, the Germans have not penetrated their organization beyond some fringe persons, nor halted their undercover sabotage, nor stopped their build up toward the day for their full-blooded insurgency. That day would come. The lines on Mec's face crease into a grim grin. There would be no mercy when the time came. None. Then the swine who had invaded and occupied their beloved country, *La France*, and killed their innocents, would know the dogs of war. Oh yes! They would know the dogs of war!

Mec is a compact, wiry man from Marseilles, born and bred in the rackets there, inured to violence and living in the underworld. He is also an ardent patriot. He had been in prison in Tours and escaped in the chaos of the German advance in 1940. He had found refuge with a cousin in Plaignes. He has no papers and thus cannot declare himself to the French or the Germans. He has nothing to lose by being in the resistance, except his life. His criminal talents, combined with intense purpose, are exactly what is needed in France's desperate hour.

There are many reasons for people to join the resistance. Some join out of simple patriotism. But stories similar to Mec's are common. Being in the resistance is a way to survive, to avoid being sent to Germany as slave labor, and to have a purpose in their lives.

Mec's *Maquis* operate in the broad swath of forest and farmland between Dijon and Troyes. As yet they can only acquire information and accomplish adroit sabotage, like putting sugar in German vehicle fuel tanks. Over time the sugar caramelizes in the cylinders, making a sticky goo, and the engine seizes up. Everything from motorcycles to tanks can be immobilized. Another ploy, that bring smiles to their faces, is to place sodium chloride in the German's food and drink. The result is mass diarrhea among the German officers and men.

Mec's *maquisard* men and women are employed in the German offices and depots. At great risk to themselves they copy papers and steal rifles, ammunition, grenades, mines, binoculars and other useful items. A good part of their success is due to the low rank German soldiers, mostly older men unfit for battle, seldom admitting the thefts to their officers for fear of severe punishment. Besides, they would lose their sexual privileges with the French women. By the end of 1943 Mec has 52 German MP40 rifles, and a good supply of ammunition and explosives.

The resistance fighters are a mixed group, which makes for some friction. Many are communists who envisage France after the war as a copy of Soviet Russia. Others occupy the political center or they are right wingers, even a few are royalists; others just have a love of France. The few religious among them pray to Ste. Geneviève, their young girl saint from the fifth century. She is credited with the miracle of saving Paris by prayer and exhortation from the dreaded Attila the Hun. A wit recalls another version of the story. Attila's horde had reputedly raped 10,000 virgins in Cologne. His by-passing of Paris was due to the common knowledge that there were not 10,000 virgins to be found in Paris.

Mec smiles. In wartime, as in peacetime, sex is a major ingredient in the kaleidoscope of human affairs. It surprises him that the Germans do not seem to know that the brothels in the major cities are supplying information to the resistance and thence to the Allies. *Le Coq* in Dijon supplies up to date information about the disposition of troops in the region and the passage of troops and war materials, east and west, through the city. A favored woman at *Le Coq* is a Jew with flaming red hair. A German general protects her from being deported. Because of his intimacy with her, she is a rich source of information.

As 1943 gives way to 1944, vengeance is in the air like a pungent aroma. The rotund butcher in Plaignes, rueful about the meager meat rations consisting of offal, tripe, and scraps, tells Mec he has his knives ready. "I'll butcher them like the pigs they are! I'll put their testicles in the feeders for my birds!" It is more a boast than an actual intention, of course, but it tells of the suppressed fervor of many.

The women murmur in the market place, planning their vengeance on the *collabos*. Now, as winter becomes spring, and with the invasion of the Allies imminent, the whisperings are like the rustle of leaves before an impending storm. Giles and the other children hear some of the mutterings and are sworn to secrecy by their parents and teachers. To Giles it seems that there are two worlds, one open and ordinary, the other secretive and dangerous. He has to live in both.

Giles has been carrying messages for a year now from his home in the small village of Criselles, close to Plaignes, to places in the *Forêt du Quartier*. He knows every pathway, dip, fold, and cave in the forest. One most carefully hidden cave is half-way up a steep slope. At one time it had been inhabited by Neolithic people. The narrow entrance to the cave is between aged-smoothed rocks and is seemingly blocked by fallen trees. Mec and his men built the barricade to seem natural and impenetrable. But the fallen trees have been cunningly cut and invisibly hinged. They can be parted sufficiently to permit entrance. Mec, Giles, and the others are careful not to create a pathway to it, making a point of coming and going only when they have to and taking different routes. Mec uses the hideaway for various purposes, including secreting a downed RAF pilot. The Germans had swept the forest, but hadn't found him. The cave and its uses are another of the many lessons in deception that Giles learns. Hide well, deceive the eye, and do not make patterns for others to find.

Giles has a book about Robin Hood. Robin had defied the bad men of his time by hiding in Sherwood forest, then coming out and killing them. The book is bilingual with French on the right and English on the left. Giles is learning English from the book. He doesn't know that *Roo-been'ood* is not the right way to pronounce the name. There is no one to teach him. But that is no deterrent to believing himself a modern Robin Hood with the destiny and duty to save his country from the invader. Then, tucked away on a high bookshelf at school, he finds a tattered primer of English with a guide to pronunciation. Giles studies it and does his best to voice the sounds in the privacy of his little room.

Sometimes Giles finds his mother sitting in the kitchen with her face drawn and her cheeks wet with tears. In front of her she holds a photo of her husband, Giles's father. He had been a corporal in the army, wearing two chevrons on his sleeve. Before the war he had been a bookkeeper. He was killed near Mons in the Blitzkrieg advance of the Germans in May 1940. Giles was only seven at the time, but he remembers his father quite well. He had been a short man with a mustache and glasses, who read to him at bedtime. Not only children's stories, but serious books about history and why Normandy was called Normandy. Giles recalls his father teaching him that it was because the Norsemen from Scandinavia had conquered the land and settled there. "It wasn't as cold there as up by the arctic circle," his father had chuckled. "Everything, you see, Giles, has a reason." His father had taught him that there was a reason behind everything. You only had to find it.

Left widowed with a house, her young boy, and a small garden in the enemy occupied part of France, Sophie has kept herself and Giles alive with strong, bitter resolve.

At the start the only form of resistance possible for her is to survive. The prevailing mood is to adjust to the Germans and their decrees. Resistance grows slowly and enlists only a few. Only about two per cent of the population are ever actively engaged in the resistance. Most just preserve themselves by one expedient or another. As a Paris prostitute declares after the liberation when accused of collaboration, "*mon cul est international, mais mon coeur est français.*[8]" Indeed, providing sex to the occupying forces was a minor industry in France and other occupied countries, and a way of survival.

Apple and walnut trees grow in Sophie's garden and every apple and nut is thankfully gathered in. She toils in the garden to grow vegetables, particularly root crops like potatoes, turnips, and beets. They provide a greater return in food bulk and they can be kept for a long time in the dank cellar beneath her house. Sophie grows flowers too. Besides her son, they are the only beautiful things in her life.

She keeps rabbits in a hutch. She has a furrier come in to kill and skin them. The rabbit meat gives Sophie and her son much needed protein. The furrier pays for the furs and makes jackets out of them to sell in the outdoor markets. Some are bought by German soldiers, in some cases to send to their colleagues freezing on the Russian front.

Sophie is nervous about her son's activities. "Take care. Always have your school pass with you in case you are stopped." Sophie hugs her son. "You're a good boy, Giles. Somehow we will live through this."

Sophie finds work at a local apple orchard and has a supply of apples to supplement their own. Gradually, she and Giles rise above the level of bare existence and she is proud to achieve a tolerable life for her son and herself. Her back stiffens and she turns to thinking about *La France* and what her country - *La Patrie* - means to her; warmth like a mother and valor like a soldier.

Their circumstances change when a German officer knocks on their door. Sophie is terrified. Are she or Giles to

---

[8] Literally, "my ass is international, but my heart is French." *Cul* most often means the buttocks. However the word is also used as a euphemism for female genitals.

be taken away to an unknown fate, like others have been? Thankfully, no.

Hauptmann Leon Müller is short, plump, middle-aged, and has little of the soldier in him. He is a supply and requisition officer. By this time Sophie is keeping the books at the orchard. Müller has come to her, after seeing the orchard owner, to work out a proper method for buying the orchard's apples.

Having worked in an office alongside her husband before the war, Sophie knows how to keep books. Müller values that. With her help he provides a steady supply of first rate apples to the German military and he can show his superiors that he wastes no *pfennigs* while maintaining good relations with the often hostile French.

Leon Müller is a country man and, in a few weeks, he and Sophie are on amiable terms and first name basis. He supplies her with a modern typewriter, paper, and carbon sheets so that she can make copies of the invoices and lists. Seeing his mother use the typewriter Giles asks her to teach him to type. She shows him how to spread his fingers and learn where the keys are. In a couple of months Giles can type with few errors and at some speed. He aids his mother with the typing and thanks her and, ironically, the Germans for helping him attain this valuable skill.

Though something of a nonentity to his militaristic fellow officers, Müller is liked well enough and appreciated for finding ways to augment the officer's mess with tasty treats like *pâté de foie gras*. That he is visiting a French woman in the course of his duties and, presumably, for his personal pleasure, is overlooked. The rules and regulations against fraternization are no more effective in the German army than in any army.

Sophie finds she can relax with Leon in spite of him being one of the detested Germans. She makes the exception for good reasons. Not the least of these is that he protects her from other Germans. It is understood that Sophie is his woman and he has sufficient rank to make it stick. As important to Sophie is that he comes with small gifts of butter, eggs, a bag of flour, even some meat, plus the occasional small bag of real coffee. She feels almost guilty in accepting his largesse, but she shares the foodstuffs with Mec and his people. That is how, on occasion, the delicious aroma of real coffee, not the *erzast* stuff made from acorns, comes wafting out of their forest cabin.

Giles is a strong lad, well behaved, a top student at the school in Plaignes. On excursions into the countryside he returns with wild *cèpe* mushrooms that grow in the forested areas and, in the summer and autumn, with berries and sloe plums gathered from the hedgerows. No one knows the land better than he. He tells his mother, "don't worry, *maman*. They see me all the time and know I roam and run in the fields. You know I snare rabbits by the hedges. They see me with the dead rabbits I bring home to you. A German soldier admired me for it and bought one of my rabbits at a fair price. You remember? I brought the money home to you, *maman*."

Leon Müller becomes even more generous; he is starved for friendship and desolate from the death of his mother killed in the bombing of Germany. He brings Sophie lengths of cloth for her to make clothes for herself and Giles; he even brings her electric light bulbs. She tells her neighbors she had bought them at the start of the war. As a special gift for her birthday, Leon gives her a Zeiss camera and rolls of film, along with the chemicals, basins, projector, and paper needed for developing and printing the photos. He tells her she should take photos of the weddings and birthdays of her neighbors to earn extra money. But she has to keep to herself where the equipment came from. He would be in deep trouble, he tells her, if it was found out. He spends innocent evenings with Sophie teaching her how to develop and print the photos.

Their mutual dependence blooms to the benefit of both. Giles, complicit with his mother, welcomes Leon to their home and occasionally does favors for him, such as cleaning his boots. Giles learns the lesson: do not antagonize when amiability serves you best.

Knowing of Müller's visits to Sophie, Mec comes to her. He asks her to gather information from the friendly German captain. By doing so, she can avoid any later charge of consorting with the enemy. Rather, she will be a member of the resistance and avoid the inevitable "purification" of collaborators following the defeat of the Germans.

Müller is often accompanied by *Lieutenant* Klaus Brun. For the most part Sophie and Giles have only to listen to the two men talking between themselves. They, fortified by the hard cider Sophie gives them, relax and smoke and speak about what they are doing and what is happening in the war. They talk of their visits across the region to military installations and depots. They are dismayed that the war has turned against them and battles are being lost. They talk of their home towns and the devastation caused by the bombing. Sophie, living close to Germany, has enough German to understand what they are saying and her German improves rapidly by talking with them.

Realizing that language ability is a major asset, Giles sets himself to become fluent in German. He picks it up easily, as children will. At the same time he diligently studies his native language and reads the classics such as Phèdre by Racine and the writers of the 18th century enlightenment, Voltaire, Diderot, Helvétius. They had helped precipitate the French revolution by their resistance to the autocratic aristocrats and priests of their time. Giles finds echoes in their writings of the oppression France is now living through. He thinks too that, by his reading, he is honoring his father and his love of books and reason.

The literature is hard going for him, but Giles persists, seeing the importance, among other things, of establishing a basis for living a good, honest, and moral life now that he is an atheist. He studies English using the primer and the Robin Hood book. When the Americans and the British come to their village, as Giles is sure they will, he will greet them in their own language.

Müller looks after the welfare of his fellow officers in a variety of ways. Among the items coming under his purview as the "supply" officer, are the brothels in the region, including *Le Coq* in Dijon. It is reserved for German officers and favored *collabos*. As in all armies venereal disease is a problem. Müller goes to the Houses, along with their medical officer, to ensure the men are being serviced as safely as possible. Becoming friendly with the *madame* at *Le Coq*, Colette Saludin, Müller learns about any new girl's reputation and passes the news on to his fellow officers. The current buzz is of an exquisite girl, as Colette has heard her described by her *madame* in Paris, coming to her from the famous *Les Poulets* house. The young prostitute is the favorite of a general who has been posted to Dijon. Colette already has reservations for the girl, even before they have seen her!

Not that Leon indulges himself. He grew up in a Calvinist village in Bavaria and has been taught that sex is a sin, sadly necessary for procreation and only excusable on that account. To the extent that he is tempted, he distrusts himself to perform. His lack of experience, he is convinced, would make him a laughing stock. Thus the platonic relationship he has with Sophie is most valuable to him; not least because it is taken by all and sundry that he enjoys carnal pleasures with her.

In Sophie's kitchen Leon and Klaus snicker about the "houses" and what happens there. Giles doesn't understand what they are talking about. He asks his mother. Sophie finds it difficult to reply. For this reason, among many others, she misses her husband. A boy needs a father.

She says, "it's where men go to relax. The women there talk to them and are friendly," is the best she can say. Some of the older boys at school say it is like what the farm animals do, why his penis can become hard and uncomfortable, and why the sheets in his bed are sometimes stained in the morning. But that has hardly illuminated Giles. It is something to do with girls and "carnal" pleasure. But girls do not attract him. They are too unlike boys. He looks up carnal in a dictionary to find it means "knowledge of the body" and "pleasure of the senses." There must be something more to it. He has the sense of again catching a glimpse of another world; in the normal world things are to be seen and known about, in the other world things exist behind a screen that is hard to see through.

Giles takes the information gathered from the two Germans to Mec. Nothing in writing. Giles commits to memory whatever the information is, developing the ability to memorize timetables of trains, the number of vehicles in convoys, the disposition of guards, the count of German soldiers on sick list, and so on. He learns the trick of using mnemonics. "Twenty-one trains have no brains." "Soldiers three guard the tree."

Mec tells Giles what he needs to know about the German dispositions. Giles relays it to his mother. She, out of concern for her German friends, as she says, takes an interest in whatever is happening. Often she discovers the information that Mec is seeking.

Giles has a cover name, *Lutin* (Imp.) Indeed he is like an imp, appearing suddenly here and there as he explores around his home. People find him a bright, intelligent, likeable lad and a helpmate to his mother. Still a little small for his age, he is handsome with green-blue eyes, a good set of white teeth, and a ready smile under his light brown hair. He had come through puberty without any pimples on his face. Now his voice is starting to deepen and he is experiencing a growth spurt, growing taller by the day. Mec sees he is a natural athlete, strong and agile with plenty of stamina; a boy becoming a young man who accomplishes whatever he sets out to do with steady determination.

To the Germans he seems like the boys of the Hitler Youth. Indeed, in many respects, he is like them, except for his dedication to France and all things French. Perhaps, if the Germans had known he was born on July 14th, Bastille Day, they would have been more careful about him.

As Leon and Klaus well know, leakage of their talk in Sophie's house could put them in front of a firing squad. The disciplining of their own troops by the Germans is famously severe. They confide their fears to Sophie. She reassures them that her lips are sealed. It is the greatest lie she has ever told. She has done it for *La France.* God will forgive her.

Giles becomes aware of the life and death power of information. He also sees that a false sense of security, such as Leon and Klaus have when in their house, is a prescription for disaster.

Chapter 3.

May 1944. The Butterfly Effect.

Later on, Giles would learn its name: the "butterfly effect." In his case it wasn't the flap of a butterfly's wings that would produce the eruption, but a rail bent out of shape; not by much, but enough.

* * *

Giles carries a message to Mec about what Sophie and he have heard from the garrulous Germans. In a week's time a heavily-laden train will be carrying German troops, tanks, artillery, and munitions from Dijon to Auxerre; that is, through Mec's territory. It will continue to the German supply depot at Sens. The supplies and reinforcements are to strengthen the Atlantic Wall against the coming invasion by the Allies.

Leon and Klaus sit at the kitchen table and work out what they will need to feed 400 soldiers for the two and a half hour stopover at Dijon. The soldiers will be fed by field kitchens set up on the station platforms. Officers can restore themselves at the local restaurants or they can visit *Le Coq*. The Germans give *Le Coq* special dispensations in goods and foodstuffs so that the décor, fashionable attire of the women, the cuisine and the wines are the best to be had.

Even when nothing special is happening, *Le Coq* benefits in these ways. It is reputed far and wide among German officers for its amenities as well as for its hostesses, as *Madame* Colette Saludin likes to call her girls.

Colette models her establishment on the famous *Le Chabanai*[9] house in Paris where she had worked in the 20's and 30's The girls there, including herself, were always stylishly gowned and coiffed. The house on *rue Chabanais* was within walking distance of the top hotels, the *Opéra*, the *Bourse*, and the fashion houses on *rue St Honoré*. Colette finds it most regrettable that it is wartime and that no internationally famous people can visit *Le Coq*. When she was at *Le Chabanais* the clients included Cary Grant, Humphrey Bogart, and Marlene Dietrich. She had serviced both Humphrey and Cary and been congratulated by *Madame* for the excellence of her service to the two American film stars.

Now, in wartime, with many suffering deprivation to the point of bare subsistence, attractive young women were asking Colette to take them on. She can afford to be selective and her House gathers a high reputation. Even so, schooling new girls to the profession is always problematical and Colette hates to waste her time on a dud. Thus, with an experienced girl about to fall in her lap, Colette knows it's her lucky day. The girl coming in from Paris is a favorite of a German general who has been posted to Dijon. The general insists on the girl working at *Le Coq*. For the girl to be *une fille*, that is a prostitute, is part of her attraction for him. Colette shrugs her shoulders. She has seen it all. Men are perverse creatures, much more so than women. But men keep her in business. *C'est la vie.* It's the God up there who is responsible, not she.

---

[9] The most famous claim to fame of the brothel at 12, rue Chabanais was that it was the House that the Prince of Wales, later King Edward VII, favored in the 1880s and 90s. He was corpulent, more so in his later years, and used a chair, especially made for him, that enabled him to gain satisfaction without over-exerting himself, nor had the ladies to be acrobats to service him.

Hauptmann Leon Müller instructs *Madame* Saludin to prepare for the coming train. He cautions her to have everything well set in the lounge and dining room as well as in the service rooms. "Make sure your *filles* understand the importance of their appearance and manner as well as . . ahem. . . their work. Your maids must attend to whatever needs the officers have," he instructs her. "The continuance of your privileges depend on it."

"Such a fusspot," Colette thinks to herself. She says, "Don't concern yourself, *Hauptmann* Müller. I know how to run my business!"

Le Coq is only 100 meters from the railway station, so no transportation is required. *Hauptmann* Müller and *Lieutenant* Brun will be at the station to expedite matters. Their general has made it clear that he expects to hear an excellent account of the provisioning of the officers and men. Leon and Klaus fear, as every German soldier in France does, that a blemish on their record will send them to the Eastern Front. It is a powerful incentive.

Sophie and Giles hear all this as Leon and Klaus plan the event. Giles passes it on to Mec.

Colette Saludin is from the docks in Marseilles, giving her and Mec a special bond. Among other things, like a passion for *Bouillabaise Marseillaise*, they share the patriotism and pride that the French demimonde have for their country. No crook, in their minds, can outsmart a French crook, anymore than a foreigner can be superior in the sexual arts.

Mec drives to Dijon to tell Colette to ply the Germans with food and drink and for her girls to drain them well, so that they will board the train ready to fall asleep. But he doesn't tell her why. The fewer the people who know of the plan the better. Colette, anticipating a good profit from the event, assures Mec that she'll make sure of it and understands why Mec cannot tell her more. Indeed she has no wish to know more. That way she cannot possibly be tempted to tell anyone anything. She smiles. It is amusing that she is being exhorted, both by the Germans and the French, to have her establishment at its best and, similarly, for her girls to be fucking at their best.

But what Mec won't vouchsafe, Leon Müller will. Because of the importance of the mission, he informs Colette, there will be military police, with an officer in charge at *Le Coq*, to ensure there is no delay in servicing the officers.

"Just make sure they pay their bills!" she exhorts him.

"Of course, *madame*, of course." He goes on to relate with pride that it will be the largest transit of men and war materials so far through the region. There will be the "invincible" King Tiger tanks and elements of the crack *Schwere Panzer Abteilung 503 battalion*[10]. But he fears the tanks will be covered with canvas on the train. Probably they won't be able to see their invincible aspects, including their long 88 mm gun that will blow the invasion out of the water. Colette fills his glass again with cognac and has him go on talking. She attends closely, anxious to remember everything clearly to pass on to Mec.

Mec dares to use the radio transmitter to inform SOE (Special Operations Executive) in London of the train's schedule and cargo. He transmits in short bursts to avoid being located by the Germans and then closes down. Even though the London operators have a hard time in making sense of his cryptic and inexpert Morse code, they believe the message. It concurs with other intelligence. The information receives the highest priority. Churchill is informed of it and of the planning to neutralize the train.

London sends a SOE agent to join Mec's *maquisards*. She is flown in on a small RAF Lysander aircraft from England, hedge-hopping its way under the German radar defenses. For the return flight, the Lysander has two downed

---

[10] Some of this battalion reached the front in Normandy and were effective against the out-gunned and out-armored Sherman and Centurion tanks of the Allies. The battalion was eventually decimated by naval gun fire and aerial attacks.

American airmen on board. Two nights later there is a low-level parachute drop from an agile twin engine De Haviland Anson. Now Mec and his squad have cameras, forged papers, Sten machine guns, pencil detonators and plastic explosives, Welrod "assassination" pistols with silencers, and a variety of other guns, hand grenades, and munitions; even Player cigarettes and Cadbury chocolate bars.

The SOE agent, a French woman returning to fight for her country, has a modern radio transmitter and she works with it and the decoy transmitters. The decoys, small boxes that can be easily hidden, are timed to go on and off at random intervals in short bursts of Morse code dummy messages. Some of the decoys are stored in the Neolithic cave. At one point the Germans are near Mec's cabin. After making the cabin look like it was not in use, Mec leaves by the escape tunnel. Some German, leaving his muddy footprints by the doorway, must have looked in, but found nothing suspicious. They didn't go near the disguised cave. By now the Germans had much to do with few men to do it.

The plan develops quickly. Working with London, Mec coordinates with the *Plan Vert* resistance of the SNCF (*Société nationale des chemins-de-fer français* - the national railway.)

The attack on the train is to be done near La Gravelle, 20 kilometers southeast of Auxerre, not far from the vineyards of the Chablis region. Giles will be used to the farm fields and woodlands they will pass through, even though he has not been there before. The terrain is much the same as around his home. Their plan includes someone who can be relied on to act as instructed, move swiftly, and not be suspicious. Giles is a good choice, therefore, on many counts. Mec is candid to Sophie about the unavoidable risks. She is fearful for her son, but agrees when Mec says it will be another of her contributions to liberating France.

Mec wants Yves, a seasoned fighter, with them for the derailment. The farm to which they are going is 40 kilometers away. They will be traveling on foot and planning to make use of a "safe" farm on the way, if necessary. However they can hope to hitch-hike.

They set out on a sunny spring day. In their packs they are carrying mechanic's tools. Their cover story is that they going to farms to repair machinery. Mec will be an older cousin of Giles, teaching him the mechanic's trade. Each of them has forged identity and travel papers thanks to the combination of Sophie's camera, a colleague who is a master-forger, and a man who is a skilled printer. He has secreted his printing machine behind a false wall in his wine cellar.

Mec knows the Germans are taking strong measures to safeguard the military train. There will be a guard train consisting of an engine and a flatbed, manned with soldiers and guns, traveling at some distance in front of the military train. The engine of the military train itself will have a flatbed in front of it, also fully armed. At the station in Dijon, as at all the places where the train stops, guards will be posted around the train.

The attack on the train is planned in detail. At the station in Dijon, the engineer and the fireman will be changed. This is standard practice. However the change-over will be to two men of the resistance. The derailment site will be at a curve of the tracks. The outside of the curve overlooks an embankment that slopes down steeply to a swamp and river. Approaching the site the resistance fighters in the cab will kill their guard and lock the throttle at full open. The train will gather speed. They will jump off before the curve.

A concern is that the German reprisals are increasing in ferocity. More hostages are being shot. Mec hopes the Germans will think the Frenchmen in the cab had jumped off when they lost control of the engine or that they had been killed in the crash and their bodies not recovered. If so, the derailment could be seen as an accident.

For the same reason they decide not to use explosives that would leave a tell-tale record. Not having explosives also means that, if Mec, Yves, and Giles are stopped and searched, they will not have any forbidden materials with them. Anyone caught with explosives could count on being harshly interrogated before being shot.

They will use their tools to undo the bolts at a junction point on the outside rail of the curve. The bolts will be removed and the rail, now free to move, will be levered outward to create a gap. The outside wheels of the engine will veer off the track and, helped by centrifugal force and gravity, hurtle down the slope at speed. The cars and carriages of the train will be pulled in its wake, all finishing up in the swampy ground and river. Mec hopes that the track will be torn up to such an extent that the Germans will have a hard time figuring out exactly what had happened.

Mec plans to let the guard train pass and then open the rail. But it could be a close call. If the guard train is too close to the front of the military train, then they will have to open the rail to derail both. Only if there is sufficient gap between the two, Mec will let the guard train pass and then open the rail. To make the right choice means they have to know the gap between the two trains. Mec has planned how Giles will measure that gap. His facility for scurrying around the countryside is exactly what is needed.

Mec, Yves, and Giles set off. In their back packs they are carrying wrenches, a crowbar, various mechanic's tools, and a small welding kit. The tools provide cover to their story. A welding kit is standard equipment to repair breakages in farm machinery. On the railway they could need the kit to burn through a recalcitrant bolt too stiff for their hand tools.

They have thought through the possibilities and the risks and dangers. They can expect to be stopped, questioned, and searched. They rehearse what they will say and feel confident that any but the most suspicious German will let them pass.

Their trek across the countryside turns out to be easy. A farmer, whom Mec knows, picks them up in his 3-wheel *camionette* and drives them much of the way.

They hadn't needed to stop at the "safe" farm and just

as well. Mec had been uneasy about it and it would turn out that his suspicions had been well founded. The farmer was furtively collaborating with the Germans. So, by luck, rather than by anything they had done, they escaped disaster. When Giles knew about it, he pondered the vagaries of fate. Even though the attack had been carefully planned, it could have come to ruin and they could have been shot dead if they had gone to the farm. Chance, luck, fate, call it what one will, plays a blind hand in human affairs. It was another lesson to be learned.

They are stopped at a check point. The Germans take their papers and inspect the vehicle and their tool kits. Mec tells them the farms they are going to are out of action due to the breakdown of machinery. Unless the machines are repaired, the farmers will be unable to meet the quotas set for them by the German Requisition Authority. They act as naturally as they can. They have nothing suspicious. Their papers are good and are returned to them.

They hole up at a truly friendly farm two kilometers from the planned derailment. Giles has done his share of carrying the tools and the heavy crowbar. He had insisted on taking equal turns with the two men. Mec is impressed.

Rather than be in the farmhouse, they sleep, prepare themselves, and wait in a loft of a barn. The Germans are checking buildings in the area, looking for any sign of the *Maquis*. In the loft Mec, Yves and Giles secrete themselves in a partitioned space.

Sure enough the Germans come round, as they are doing at all the houses and farms near the railway. A German soldier climbs the ladder to the loft. Mec, Yves and Giles lie motionless under a mound of straw. They hardly dare breathe. The soldier walks around, prodding with his rifle here and there. Mec holds Giles's hand. Giles learns what fear is. He can do nothing. His stomach knots. He closes his eyes to shut out the outside world.

The soldier climbs down the ladder. They hear the word "*nichts*" (nothing), then the sound of the German car leaving.

The farmer climbs the ladder to tell them the Germans are gone. Giles feels buoyant, as if invulnerable. Mec holds him close. "Learn the lesson well, Giles. We might have been taken and killed. Bravery has many forms. When you have to, you hide and sweat it out."

The train is due to arrive at the derailment point at 11:34 that night, give or take a minute or two. Yves knows the countryside, having lived there as a boy. He reckons three hours will give them time to go there cross-country, avoiding the roads, and prepare for the derailment. They check their dark clothing and face masks and pick up their rucksacks of tools. They embrace, shake hands, and climb down the ladder. The night is dark, the moon and stars hidden behind thick clouds.

They walk to the north, hugging the hedgerows, entering the copses of trees. There are lanes and ditches to be crossed. Any time they are in the open, they bend down and hurry forward to the next place of cover, glad of the dark night. Yves has a compass that he checks from time to time to maintain their direction. He has a small flashlight that he shields under his coat to read the compass. In places it is hard going. They have to slog through a marsh with mud and water up to their knees. Yves hadn't known it was there. They are falling behind time; they are tiring; they have to stop and rest. There is a country road ahead they have to cross. Mec says, "let's catch our breath here for a minute, by the hedge, then we will cross as quickly as we can."

Suddenly, coming up from a dip in the road, a German patrol car led by a Zundapp motorcycle and sidecar carrying a machine gunner are coming right at them. It is past the curfew hour. As they know, the gunner can open fire without warning at anything he finds suspicious. They flatten themselves to the muddy ground. Giles is more excited than scared. He is sure the Germans are not going to find and kill him. No! He will kill them.

After their arduous cross-country trek, they reach the railway later than planned.

"We'll have to work quickly," Mec tells Yves and Giles.

Mec crawls up the embankment to make sure the coast is clear. He scans either way, but sees nothing. A drizzling rain starts to fall. He puts his ear on the wet rail. Sound travels for long distances along rail lines. There is no sound. He beckons Yves and Giles to join him. They lug the rucksacks up the embankment.

Mec specifies, "this is the junction we'll open."

The bolts and nuts are rusty, hard to turn. They have loosening oil and the tools for the job. But even so, they have to use the blowtorch on one of the bolts.

"*Merde!*" (shit) Mec swears. "No one better see us." They shield the flame as best they can with their bodies.

As the nuts come off the bolts, they extract the bolts from the rails. They give two of the nuts and bolts to Giles. He treats them with oil and then runs the nuts up and down the bolts until they run freely, as Mec had instructed him to do. They can be undone in seconds.

Mec and Yves loosen the rail from the crossties for two meters. They check that they can lever the rail out of position and then use stones to jam it open.

They return the rail to its original position and lock it back in place, but only using the two free running oiled nuts and bolts. They will hold the rails in place sufficiently, Mec hopes, if they have to let the guard train through before the military train.

That done, they retreat to the bushes. Mec goes over again with Giles what he has to do. Go up the tracks for 800 meters to the hill there. From there he will see a long way up the track.

"The trains come round a bend about two kilometers away and then their lights will be shining straight at you. You start counting when you see the guard train. You count: *un petit second . . . deux petits seconds . . . trois petits seconds . . .* until the military train comes into view. OK? You've got that?"

"Yes, Mec. We've been over it before."

"All right. What do you do then?"

"I count up to forty. If the second train appears before I get to 40 I run down to the rail closest to me and give it one tap. Then I pause and give it one tap again. And I repeat until the train is too close and I run for the woods."

"Good, Giles. That's exactly right. And if you count goes over forty, what do you do?"

"The same thing, Mec, except that I now tap the rail twice in quick succession, pause, and double tap again and repeat until the second train is close."

"OK, Giles, perfect. We have a good plan, but heaven knows how it will actually play out." He smiles. "It seems crazy that a couple of mud-soaked men and a boy - just look at us, all covered in mud and slime - can wreck this big heavily guarded train! But, like the acorn said to the oak, 'small beginnings can lead to big results.' Yves, come close. I'll go over it again so we all know what we are doing. Giles, if you give us one tap we know the two trains are close together. We derail the first one, the guard train, and then the military train, following close behind, will be wrecked too. If they are further apart we let the guard train through and hope it gets well down the tracks. We then derail the military train. Let's hope it happens." They shake hands on it.

They think they hear a motor engine in the distance. It is too soon for the train; their faces tighten; they put their ears to the rails. Yes! Something is coming. They hurry down the embankment to the bushes. "Lie down! Keep the masks over your faces," Mec orders. Looking along the rail tracks they see a small open car approaching from the Dijon direction. A bright light is illuminating the tracks in front of it.[11] They see that the two men standing in the front of the car are inspecting the track.

---

[11] The Germans used air-cooled motorcycle engines to power these light rail cars. The engines made a distinctive sound.

"As I thought, " Mec mutters, "they're on full alert."

The car approaches and then goes over the junction point. It holds. They breathe again. Mec grins. "*Eh, bien!* That was a good test. If we have to let the guard train pass, we can expect the rail to hold again. Giles, go now. Be quick about it. You mustn't be late. Remember! Do it right! You are as important as we are in killing the *Bosche!*"

Giles sets out at a trot, moving beside the track. He comes to a road bridge over the tracks. He sees the German sentry on it. Giles makes a detour over muddy ground through the trees. Once clear of the trees he breaks into a run. He mustn't be late. He runs up the hill. At the top, panting for breath, he looks along the tracks. He is in time. But in less than a minute, the light of the guard engine comes into view. Giles counts off the seconds. He reaches forty. Then, at forty-five seconds, he sees the light of the military train. The gap is over forty seconds, but not by much.

Giles careens down the hill, more in a series of jumps than running. The guard train is coming toward him. He crawls to the rail and, with the small iron rod that Mec has given him, taps twice on the rail. Tap, tap. He pauses, then taps again. Tap, tap. He does it again and then again. The guard train is only 200 meters away. Giles taps for the last time, then sprints for the cover on the side of the hill. A spotlight on the guard train seems to follow him into the bushes. They might have seen him. He doesn't know.

In fact the lieutenant on the guard train has seen him. He doesn't think much of it. He radios back to the military train and the command post in Dijon. "Boy seen by track in the woods. No action taken. Maintaining surveillance."

Giles, back on the top of the hill, sees the military train coming on fast, belching smoke, quickening its speed, the piston rods and wheels a blur of motion. Its speed is quickly reducing the gap to the guard train in front of it.

The two resistance fighters in the cab have killed the guard and, after fueling the fire box with coal, stuff his body into it. The corpse is quickly incinerated, its fats adding to the heat generated. Now they jam the throttle open, and jump off.

Giles lies flat on the ground as the train thunders past. He sees a soldier leaving the flatbed in front of the engine, going toward the cab. On the flatbed a soldier looks around wildly with his gun at the ready. The train speeds toward the curve. The German soldiers on the flatbeds behind the engine, keeping guard over the artillery and tanks, are standing up, hanging on to the railings, peering forward.

Mec and Yves hear the two taps signal. After the guard train has passed, they hasten to the rail and take out the two bolts. They stand up to use the crow bar to lever the rail outward and to put the jamming stones in place. But they have been seen.

The soldier at the back of the guard train opens fire with his machine gun, spattering bullets around Mec and Yves. The engine locks its wheels. At the same time the lieutenant on it radios back to the military train. But there is no one in the cab to hear it. Only the radio operator in a train carriage well behind the engine hears it. He tells the officer in charge. He orders a sergeant to go to the cab and find out what's happening.

Time is too short for the heavy multi-car train to stop before the curve, even if someone had reached the cab. It gathers more speed, now rocking and swaying on the track.

Yves has been hit in the thigh. Mec slings him over his shoulder, runs down the embankment and into the trees and shrubs. He flings Yves and himself down on the ground, then improvises a tourniquet around Yves thigh with his belt.

Giles has a grandstand view of the worst railway disaster the Germans suffered in France during the war.

The military train continues to accelerate. On the guard train the lieutenant, to his horror, sees it hurtling toward him. The guard train had been going backwards after the gunner had spotted Mec and Yves. The lieutenant screams for it to go forward again. But it is too late. The military train is coming at them too quickly.

The engine of the military train derails. Its front clips the guard train with great force, sending it toppling down the embankment. The trains, now in a tangled mass, continue down and along the slope. The following cars of the military train, continuing from their own momentum, are derailed. Fire starts in some of the derailed coaches.

There is a minor explosion of some of the munitions on the train. The explosions become more violent as they set off one another. They culminate in a monster eruption as main munitions explode. The overall effect is the best possible collision, explosion and catastrophe that any boy could wish to see. The removal of the bolts holding the rail in place has brought about a volcanic consequence: a slight cause, an enormous effect; the butterfly effect.

Two hundred and twenty seven Germans are killed, including a general. Nearly all the survivors are wounded. The heavy King Tiger tanks fall down the slope to submerge in the swamp and river. It takes the Germans ten days to move cranes and bulldozers to the site, and mobilize the manpower to pull the monsters out. The "invincible" tanks have to be drained of water, the mud sucked out of them, and repaired. Their weight, the complexity of their mechanisms, plus the damage done to them, makes recovery and repair lengthy and difficult. Some are put out of action completely. The few that make it to the front arrive too late to make a difference. By that time the Allies are racing across France, the British, the Canadians, the Free French and even a Polish regiment to the north, and the Americans to the south.

Giles knows he has to get out of there. Bits and pieces of metal and wood have fallen around him. He gets himself up, wipes some of the mud off his clothes. He finds some clear water and washes his face. He sees lights in the distance and walks toward them. Soon the countryside is filled with German vehicles. Giles knows he has to be a victim, certainly not a perpetrator!

He walks in a dazed fashion. When a French policeman stops him, Giles says he had been near the explosion with a friend. They had been night fishing, with flashlights to attract the fish. He had been dazed by the explosions and couldn't find his friend, so he had run away. Giles shivers and speaks incoherently, not all of it put on. The policeman waves down an ambulance and puts Giles in it. Three wounded German soldiers join him. They go to the hospital in Auxerre. He is examined. The elderly harried French doctor says he is suffering from *le commotionné* (shell-shock) and puts him under observation for a day.

The Germans at the hospital, after talking with him and phoning their office in Plaignes, then to *Hauptmann* Leon Müller, put him on a bus and tell him to obey the curfew laws in future. The Germans investigating the derailment conclude that the sighting of a boy by the lieutenant on the guard train, now dead, was of no significance, being too far away from the accident site.

The next time Giles visits the cabin in the forest, he is very glad to find Mec and Yves there. Yves is able to walk with a cane and is recovering well. They greet their Lutin as a hero.

The Germans suspect the *Maquis* may have had a hand in it, but what exactly that might have been is unknown. They can't account for the train gathering speed, except as a malfunction. The engineer and fireman in the cab, along with their guard, must have been thrown out of the cab and washed away in the river. The pike and other fish in the river have had a banquet of rotting human flesh. Not all the remains of men known to have been on the train are found. There was no explosion before the derailment. Had it been an accident? It was difficult to maintain the tracks in wartime. Perhaps some Frenchman had loosened a rail, but that was impossible to tell. In any case the Germans have more important things to do, namely repair the track and have their trains rolling again.

Though the local French fear reprisals, none come. The

local German commander knows Germany is losing the war and, rather than reprisals, he concentrates on his duties and having train traffic restored. He has no wish to be tried as a war criminal after the war. He sees no hope of defeating the armies advancing against them. Hitler's secret weapons - missiles, jet fighters, Tiger tanks - are having some effect, but they are too little, too late. The commander knows the *Maquis* are keeping dossiers on their activities, on officers in particular. They can expect little forgiveness or mercy. He is going to follow the French axiom *"sauve qui peut"* (save who can) and get the hell out of there before it is too late.

The Germans repair the track. It operates until June 4 when the *Maquis* attack the railways *en masse*. A part of the success of D-Day is the slowing down of reinforcements into Normandy. Eisenhower says the resistance is worth six army divisions to him[12].

The German language has a word for the feelings that Sophie and her son have, *schadenfreude*; that is, gloating over another's misfortune. Oh, yes! Giles and his mother make quite a *schadenfreude* of it! For the first time Giles is tipsy on their hard cider. At the same time Sophie is glad that their German friends, Leon and Klaus, were not on the train.

---

[12] The value of the French resistance to the allies continues to be disputed. Eisenhower may have said "six divisions" on the urging of DeGaulle. Various revisionist historians have downplayed the effectiveness of the resistance. What is not in doubt is that many brave men and women lost their lives by being in the resistance.

Chapter 4.

Fighting in France. Summer 1944

As the Allies advance through France, attacks from the air on the roads, railways, and bridges in the Troyes-Auxerre-Chatillon-Dijon region are common. Heavy bombers are overhead day and night. The American planes, bombing from high altitudes during daytime, are a formidable sight. They are alarming to the French as only a few of their bombs hit the target and when the pilots fail to find their target, they jettison their bombs wherever they happen to be[13]. Across some fields outside Plaignes, a stick of bombs falls harmlessly, except for two cows and a cow shed.

Mec is now emboldened to use explosives on railways and roads and to ambush German patrols. Though *Lutin* is the youngest member of Mec's squad, he is as much involved as a any of them. Being born on July 14th, Bastille Day, gives him a special standing.

---

[13] Standing orders for the American bombers were to jettison their bombs as soon as the pilot was convinced he couldn't find the designated or alternative target. For the French this happened with alarming frequency, particularly over north-eastern France. The British bombers, while aiming more accurately as their experience grew, even though they bombed predominantly at night, were ordered to jettison bombs only over the sea.

"You are undeniably totally French," Mec tells him.

"I suppose so," Giles agrees thoughtfully. "People sort of have to be, don't they? Even the Germans have to be Germans, whether they like it or not."

"Luck of the draw, my boy! Just count yourself lucky to belong to the best people in the world!"

For the time being, Giles was content with that, as young people are all over the world.

Mec trains him to shoot with the German MP40 rifle and soon Giles is deadly accurate with it. It is a good rifle and Giles kills a German sentry at 200 meters. He feels nothing for the German who sags at the knees and then falls down in a heap. Giles only feels pride and satisfaction in knowing how to set the sights for range, lie prone for maximum accuracy, use his elbows and chest to make a tripod, tension the strap round his left arm, wait for a gust of wind to die down, breathe out and relax as he lines up the target, steady himself, and squeeze the trigger smoothly with no jerk. It all comes to him naturally, like snaring rabbits. No emotion is involved; just gratification in doing the job right.

Mec teaches him how to fire a pistol, holding it in both hands, sighting along the barrel.

Mec tells him, "I keep both eyes open, like the shooters did in the wild west of America. I think that best. Some close one eye, but that cuts into your field of view and takes away from how well you see distance. Try it both ways and do what suits you."

In the woods Giles practices, aiming at tree leaves. Mec's mention of the wild west in America makes him practice drawing out the pistol from its holster and shooting quickly. No time to close an eye! Soon he is fast and accurate. There are lots of birds in the woods and he practices on them for moving targets. He even hits a few.

Mec tells him. "It's like bicycling; once you've learned it, it stays with you. You'll be a good shot all your life. Perhaps you'll have to be one day."

Giles continues being a top student at school and helps out in the orchard with pruning and tending the apple trees. The Germans don't suspect him in the slightest, in some part because he has an effective shield in Leon Müller and Klaus Brun.

The two Germans carry on talking freely in the house. Giles and Sophie learn from them the German plan to use a *château*, situated on a nearby hill, as a last ditch bastion. Müller and Brun have been ordered to provision the place to support the 100 men left there to fight the oncoming Americans, and they themselves were to stay with the garrison to the last. That terrifies them.

In this way SOE in London knows about the concentration at the *château* and its location. That the beautiful *château* has to be sacrificed is an exigency of war.

To gather the provisions, Müller and Brun scour the countryside for food stuffs. The French are increasingly hiding their grain and root crops, even their livestock and vegetables. Giles helps to hide sheep and goats in a deep glen in the forest.

The two Germans talk about their scavenging plans. Giles conveys the information to Mec who warns the farmers. As a result Müller and Brun have small pickings for their efforts but, at the same time, the two Germans are being protected by the *Maquis* as they make their rounds. They are a too valuable source of information.

In some places, to weaken the resistance, the Germans arrest people on bare suspicion as much as any evidence. Near to Plaignes they turn a large farm house into a detention and execution center. The SOE agent sends an urgent message to London and is told to expect an evening raid in two days. The RAF is expert at low level attacks on French prisons.[14] The raid will be confirmed by a radio

---

[14] A major raid was carried out by a squadron of RAF Mosquitos on February 18, 1944 to open a prison at Amiens. 99 resistance fighters were

message: *un oiseau dans la main vaut mieux que deux dans la haie.* (A bird in the hand is worth two in the bush.)

Mec gathers his forces. The message comes: *un oiseau . . .* and then is repeated.

The *Maquis* are in the ditches and under the bushes half a kilometer from the farm house. They wait. A stream of heavy bombers is flying eastward overhead. Antiaircraft batteries open up on them. One comes down in flames. A crewman parachutes from the stricken plane and lands near them. A German patrol car with four soldiers is dispatched to pick him up. Mec and a squad of his men arrive first. They shoot the Germans - *pff't pff't pff't pff't* - with their silenced Welrod pistols; then return with the thankful British airman, the captured car with its maps, and the weapons and wallets of the dead Germans. They take the money and throw away the wallets with their pictures of home and family. "That will teach *les salauds* (scumbags) to make war on us," one of them says.

The SOE agent tells them, "we can expect Mosquitos at low level."

Giles is close to Mec. The farm is illuminated by the setting sun. Giles has the sharp ears of youth. "I hear something," he tells Mec.

Then they see the five Mosquito fighter/bombers, with the RAF red/white/blue roundels on their wings and fuselage, coming in low and fast over the fields. Mec sends up the pre-arranged red flare signal. The pilots know they are on target. The flight circles round to the south, then turns and comes in at 150 feet. The Mosquitos open fire with their rockets, followed by their four cannon guns carried in the nose, and then with strafing fire from their four machine guns. Two of them circle and drop bombs. They are death dealing machines, the most effective attack aircraft the allies have. They punch holes in the outer walls, destroy the outer

---

due to be executed the next day. The attack came in as low as 50 feet. 225 prisoners escaped through the crumpled walls.

perimeter of barbed wire. The noise is deafening, the concussions flatten cheeks to skulls. The Mosquitos fly off at speed, they are capable of 450mph.

Few hear Mec cry *"En avant, mes maquisards, en avant!"* (Forward, my *maquisards*, forward!), but they see him out in the open, waving them forward with his Sten gun.

The Germans have put their prisoners, including three downed American fliers, in the cellar of the farm house. The German garrison, such as it is, has been taken completely by surprise by the sudden onslaught from the air. Now the *maquisards* are in the remains of the farm house, shooting the surviving soldiers and the two Gestapo agents, a man and a woman.

Mec roars, *"Aux armes, mes français! La vengeance est douce!* (To arms my Frenchmen! Vengeance is sweet!)

"Tuez les Bosches! Tuez!" (Kill the Germans! Kill!) is the cry and the Germans are killed in a frenzy of shooting, stabbing, cutting, and bayoneting, hands up or not.

In terms of a military operation it is brilliant. Not a single prisoner in the cellar is killed, only a few have light wounds. Mec and his men move them outside. Then, having thrown the Germans inside the remains of the building, either completely dead or wounded, they set fire to the place. The house burns fiercely. No German escapes. A 100% massacre.

The *maquisards* feel only a sense of justice; justice for the French who have been murdered by the Germans, those who lived nearby and the others, perhaps 100,000, across France. Mec addresses his squad. "The Germans kill men, women, and children indiscriminately, without mercy. They can expect nothing but retaliation! Now, *mes maquisards*, we, you and I, are our vengeance weapon! *Vive la France!"*

Mec and his men and women retreat back into the forests and their safe places, exultant, with a cadre of new recruits, the ex-prisoners, to add to their number. Now they have the strength to take on small German units face-to-face.

The Germans mount a futile and short-lived search for them. They have their hands full with the mounting insurgency of the *Maquis* squads throughout France and the rush forward of the Allied armies, now from the south as well as the west. Furthermore, the Germans are becoming aware of the consequences of brutality. The *Maquis* have put out the photos they have taken of firing squads. They print some of the photos, name names, and announce that members of firing squads will be killed. On the door of a church in Tonnerre the *Maquis* put up a sign: *"Les tortionnaires seront torturés. Les meurtriers seront assassinés."* (The torturers will be tortured. The murderers will be murdered.) The signs are pulled down by the Germans. But the message is out and fuels their fears.

After the strike and massacre at the farm house, Giles, taking a round-about route, goes home. He has killed at least two Germans with his rifle, maybe more, and one at close range with his pistol. He is proud of it and calmly tells his mother what had happened, what he had done, and how he feels about it; a job well done.

Sophie bursts into tears. Her boy has become a cold blooded killer. The war, the awful war.

"It has to be done, *maman*. They have no right to live."

She tries to find words to express her abhorrence of killing. "But there are Catholics among you, and them too, and the Lord said, 'thou shall not kill.'"

Giles has to smile. The Catholics are as fierce as any. They declare it is a holy war against the anti-Christs. Much the same is said by the Communists. It is their holy war against Fascism led by their demigod, Stalin. The historically-minded among them remember the Franco-Prussian war of 1871, when Parisians were reduced to eating rats as the Germans laid siege to the city, then the German annexation of Alsace-Lorraine; then the horrors of World War I that had killed, *en masse*, France's young manhood; then, the defeat and occupation of France by the Germans in 1940. There is much to revenge.

The annihilating strike against the farm house has warned the local German commanders of the folly of concentrating troops. But they are operating under the orders of their high command, directed by Hitler himself, to defend their positions to the last man. The concept is to leave behind armed bastions that the allies have to take at much cost and that will slow their advance. In light of what the allies have proved they can do against such concentrations, predominantly with air power, it makes no sense. It is simply wishful thinking and a waste of troops.

Müller and Brun have the good sense to be the cowards they are. They have the excuse, to gather supplies, to be outside the *château* and its perimeter of defensive positions, until the last moment. As they hoped, they are away when the attack is made. This time a RAF Mosquito squadron attacks, dropping bombs and strafing with their rockets, cannons, and machine guns. They suppress the little anti-aircraft fire the garrison has within a minute and the destruction of the "bastion" is accomplished in five minutes. The last of the Mosquitoes drop magnesium fire bombs so that the ruins become an incinerating inferno. The few Germans who stagger from the wreckage are shot by Mec's men and women.

Not only the *Maquis* are tuning in to the BBC in London, but all who can, including the Germans. Everyone knows the Germans are being routed. After the halt following the Normandy invasion, when the Allies build up and slowly overcome the Germans encircling them, the whole Allied force breaks out, like a firebird out of its egg, and heads east through France, in the general direction of Paris. The British under Montgomery lead the attack along the coast and to the north of Paris. Patton's army marauds to the south. The less ardent Germans surrender. The hard core Nazis retreat to fight another day.

In August the American 3rd Army comes roaring through the flatlands around Orléans and Chartres and is pushing eastward into the country south of Paris toward Sens.

Giles is so excited he can hardly contain himself. Sophie and he tune in to the BBC. "*Maman*, listen. The Resistance is fighting in Paris. The British are clearing our northern coast, the Americans have taken Sens and captured hundreds of Germans and all their supplies and vehicles."

"Oh! Can it be true? Can it be true?" Sophie weeps.

Chapter 5.

Tonnerre. Eastern France.

Mec has stopped off at their house to tell Sophie and Giles that American tanks are in Joigny. "They are less than 100 kilometers away. If they keep coming like this, they will be here in two or three days. They may already be in Tonnerre."

Mec has left by the time Müller and Brun drive down the lane by the back of the house and stop their German *Kubelwagen*[15] patrol car there. The two Germans hurry in. Sophie begs them to leave. If they are found in her house by some marauding *Maquis*, she could be shot as likely as they. They are ashen-faced as they plead with her. She takes them down to the cellar and gives them blankets to wrap around themselves.

Sophie paces the kitchen floor, remembering the many kindnesses the two Germans have shown her and, though unwittingly, how they have been important in guiding the *Maquis* to their successes. Now they are two very ordinary

---

[15] The *Kubelwagen* was the German equivalent of the Jeep. It had been in use before the war broke out in 1939 and made an effective light-weight patrol vehicle. Some 14,000 were made in a number of versions, including a swimmer that could navigate lakes and rivers.

men, petrified with fear, powerless to do anything for themselves, dependent on whatever mercy she can find for them.

The German army is retreating, slouching through their village. Most are on foot, their tunics in disarray, their faces tired and glum, but not yet beaten. They are using horses to haul their carts along. Only a few officers are in cars. Giles doesn't see any tanks or armored cars among them.

He runs home. "The Germans, *maman*! They are going! We've won!" He looks at the anxious face of his mother. "What is it? Is something wrong?"

"May God forgive us all," she cries. Struggling to control herself, she tells Giles that Müller and Brun are in the cellar.

"Oh, *maman*! They must leave."

"But they will be killed! If the *maquisards* come here, they will kill them. Leon and Klaus are not bad men. I do not want them on my conscience for the rest of my life."

Giles thinks for a moment. "Mec will know what to do. I will find him."

"Mec has no love for the Germans. I don't know . . . "

"What else can we do, *maman*? We cannot keep them here."

"Yes, yes . . . I suppose."

Giles has found a bicycle and pedals as fast as he can to Plaignes.

Mec has set up a command post in the grocery store. On hearing what Giles is telling him, he says, "OK. We'll make an exception. They were almost as much victims of the Nazis as we were. They did little against us; in fact, they helped us!" He laughs. "Surrender them to the Americans," he tells Giles. "You said their patrol car is by your house?"

"Yes. At the back."

"Can you drive?"

"I don't know. I can try."

"Your mother has a French flag?"

"Yes. It's hidden in the attic."

"Find a pole and tie it to the *Kubelwagen*. Fly the flag from it. Understand?"

"Yes, Mec. I understand. It will be great to fly our flag!"

"OK. Müller and Brun. Have them in their uniforms. Tie their hands behind their backs. Tell them to stay out of sight by lying on the floor in the back of the *Kubelwagen*. Cover them with a blanket. Drive to Tonnerre. The Americans are there."

It is the first time that Giles has driven anything. He teaches himself how to use the gears and clutch, the accelerator and brakes, by trial and error. Plenty of error! He drives up and down the street by their house until he can control the little car. Then, with the French *tricolere* flying and the Germans on the floor in the back, he drives to Tonnerre. As he goes by, the people cheer the boy at the wheel with the *tricolere* flying. The road has been torn up. Wrecked German vehicles are blocking it. Giles has to take to the fields and farm lanes. He reaches Tonnere. The town is full of American soldiers, dirty and battle-worn, but cheerful and smoking cigarettes. "Hi! Boy!" they shout.

"P-l-eeze - - I haf pree-son-ers Ger-man. I haf need of off-ee-zer," Giles pronounces carefully.

A British liaison officer, attached to the American 3rd Army, Major Charles Marlis, happens to be there. He has hitched a ride forward with the American 737th Tank Battalion, at the request of an American colonel. Charles' mother was French. He lived in France before the war and knows the country well. The American soldiers call him over.

"Hey, major! This French boy turned up with two German officers. Some kid, eh!"

A sergeant has pulled the two Germans out of the vehicle. He salutes Major Marlis in the casual manner of the fighting Yank. "What shall we do with them, major?"

"Let's see who they are first, sergeant."

He turns to Giles. *"Bonjour - qui êtes-vous? Comment vous-appelez-vous?"* (Good day - who are you? What is your name?)

Giles comes to attention, as best he knows how. "I am Giles Martin, captain, a member of the *Maquis*. I serve under Captain Mec. I have brought two prisoners of war here. They are *Hauptmann* Müller and *Lieutenant* Brun, requisition officers."

Marlis is impressed. The boy has given a good military report. "Bravo! How old are you?"

"I am twelve years old, captain."

They have been speaking in French. Charles turns to the sergeant. "What do you think of that? This lad is only twelve and he's brought in a couple of German officers; requisition officers, he tells me."

"Yeah - a smart boy. He speaks a bit of English too."

Marlis turns again to Giles. "You speak some English? Did you learn it in school?"

"No, *capitaine*. Eengleesh not teach in school. Not permit. I myself have teach myself."

Charles Marlis looks at the boy and can only imagine the life he has led. His son, Geoffrey, a Lieutenant in the Coldstream Guards, would have been 21 that week. He had been killed in Italy in the advance on Florence. This upright French boy reminds him of his son. He looks up at the sky, not wishing the Americans around him to sense his feelings.

The sergeant asks again what he should do with the Germans.

"There's a holding area for prisoners somewhere north of the town. Detail a couple of men to take them there."

Giles is saying *"aufwiedersehn"* to the two Germans, telling them they will be all right and they are thanking him, *"danke, danke."*

Charles is hardly surprised. The boy is smart and must have heard a lot of German. "So you speak German too, Giles?"

"Ye-ess, ja, vas mein need," he says mixing the languages he still hardly knows.

Charles puts his arm round Giles' shoulder. "You're a brave lad. I will speak to you in English. That way you will learn the language better. There's an officer's mess in a restaurant in town, just by the bridge. We will go there. They might have something better than K-rations!"

It is the first time that Giles has heard English spoken, other than on the radio. He doesn't understand a word. But that doesn't matter. He knows it will take time and study.

Chapter 6.

France 1944-45.

The *épuration*[16] happens all over France. Vengeance mixes with justice. Neighbor denounces neighbor, some to settle old scores. A new terror descends on France. Men and women are held in prisons without charges or documentation; some are brutally treated, some killed. Women have their heads shaved and are paraded naked through the streets. Sophie lives anxiously, fearful that her liaison with the German officers will be denounced. Mec has left, though saying he would be back. He is working up his carting business. Mec would shield her. But he has to be there.

It takes time for the worst to be over. Now the chiefs of the collaboration are on trial in the *Palais de Justice* in Paris. Marshall Pétain, the head of the puppet French government at Vichy during the war, is exiled to an island in the bay of Biscay and dies there. Laval had been responsible for rounding up French Jews and sending them to the death

---

[16] *Épuration* (usual meaning, purification) was the word used to describe the vengeance taken on those who had collaborated with the Germans. While it lasted, the *épuration* was as horrific for the French people as the German occupation.

camps. He is found guilty and, after a failed suicide attempt, is strapped in a chair and shot by a firing squad.

The conditions in France are dreadful: deprivation, bitterness, strikes led by the communists, political turmoil, a fiercely cold winter. Country people at least have food. They survive by selling their produce, some legitimately, some on the black market. Sophie and Giles see how the Americans, so welcomed and honored at the time of the liberation, have become leaders in the black market. They use their military vehicles for transport and, producing their endless supply of cigarettes and nylon stockings, barter for whatever they want. Stories abound of how the arrogant and pampered Americans live high on the hog, like the Germans before them, while the French have meager food and little if any coal to heat their homes and offices. Under these conditions, morality and honor are scoffed at and anti-Americanism builds up. The French call the Americans being there the "second occupation."

There is political and industrial unrest. The communists grow in power. Thorez, the head of the French Communist Party returns from Moscow with the message that France must become a communist state. Otherwise, he claims, the country will be controlled by the baneful influence of the corrupt Americans aided by the upper classes of Britain. Parisians even talk of the Russians invading and having Cossacks in the cafés on the *Champs Elysées*, as happened in 1815 after the defeat of Napoleon.

May 8th 1945 is VE[17] day in Europe. The Germans have surrendered. Across France fervent demonstrations celebrate the end of nearly five years of defeat and occupation and the violent course of the liberation.

Little noticed on that same day is the first murderous act of insurgency in Algeria, across the Mediterranean from France. Algeria - *Algérie Française* - was at that time a department of France, though in reality more a colony than

---

[17] Victory in Europe

a part of the mother land. The attack happens at Setif, a dusty town, not far from the coast, 250 kilometers east of Algiers. An increasing number of incidents by the Muslims against the *colons*, as the European settlers were called, had happened. Graffiti had appeared, "Muslims Awaken!" and, more threatening, "*Français*, you will be massacred by the Muslims!"

The Muslims march in large numbers in an unformed mass at Setif for their liberation, at first peacefully. Then gun fire starts, possibly the first to shoot are the vastly outnumbered *gendarmes*[18], though most of them are Algerian themselves. The madness lasts five days. 103 Europeans are killed, including children. Many more are wounded; women are raped and mutilated. The Algerians are seen as savage beasts by the French.

The French authorities, headed by DeGaulle and his first government in Paris, respond with a merciless blood bath. About 6,000 Muslims are killed across the country. The French are seen as savage beasts by the Algerians.

News of the Setif massacre and the French retribution is suppressed successfully in metropolitan France. DeGaulle would dismiss the incident as being "snuffed out by the Governor General." Very little appears in the French press. Thus, later, when Giles and most of the French people learn the facts, they are deeply shocked. The realization sinks in that barbarity is not confined to one's foes, but is committed by one's own.

In the post-war period, external affairs are of little importance to most French people. The government, the administration, and the army must take care of things while France recovers. The country is bankrupt. The Germans took away 80% of its industry. Many wish to believe that, in time, France will resume its rightful place as a world power with its own far flung territories. Even the communists

---

[18] Police

applaud the suppression in Algeria. DeGaulle never stops talking about the "*gloire*" (glory) of France.

Sophie is mindful of herself and the events that concern her. She busies herself with her house, her garden, and the start of her apple and cider business. She falls ill. After two days of stomach ache she and Giles take the bus to Tonnerre for her to see a doctor. He diagnoses acute appendicitis and puts her in hospital. Giles holds his mother's hand as long as he can as she is wheeled to the operating theater. He sits in a waiting room, stony faced, wiping away the anxious tears that wet his eyes. What would he do without his mother! It is a new kind of fear.

After the operation a nurse tells Giles that his mother is doing fine. She also tells him that she's heard that enquiries are being made about a boy who had been in the Resistance. Hadn't he been in the Resistance? Perhaps it is him. She advises him to go to the town office and find out about it. Giles walks there and discovers that a Colonel Marlis is looking for him and has left an address at the British Embassy in Paris. Giles remembers the British officer who spoke French. He sits down and writes a letter in French. He gives his address in Criselles, and signs off in English: "Very sincerely - Giles Martin." A secretary at the office gives him an envelope and stamp.

On returning to Criselles, Giles and Sophie find a letter waiting for them. Charles Marlis tells them he will be traveling through Plaignes and would like to meet them. He will come to their house on Wednesday at 10.30 and trusts that will be convenient.

Sophie is in a stew. She opens and closes the letter, only half believing it. "*Mon Dieu*! He is coming here, Giles, to our little house! You must attend to the garden while I clean the house. Oh! So much to do. I cannot do it all. The doctor said not to strain myself. I will ask Marie from the orchard to help me."

"Calm yourself, *maman*. He is an English soldier I met for a few minutes in Tonnerre. That is all."

"We must represent our country to him, Giles. Be at our best. From the embassy of *Grande Bretagne* in Paris! A diplomat! A general I'm sure," she surmised, not bothering about the minor detail of his colonel rank as written in the letter. "A very important person, Giles. We are honored! You understand - honored! Who should we tell? The mayor in Plaignes? We must! He is sure to be insulted if we do not tell him. I will offer the English officer the best apple brandy and I'll bake my almond biscuits."

The news spreads rapidly due to Sophie telling Marie and the mayor, the mayor informing the town council, the councilmen telling their wives, the head mistress of the school informing her pupils, and Giles answering questions about the British general. Soon, everyone in the surrounding area knows that they are to be visited by a British general to honor their resistance to the Germans.

At the British Embassy in Paris, Duff Cooper, the ambassador, reads in his daily briefing that a British general is about to pay a visit to a resistance hero in Criselles. He calls in his Military Attaché, Colonel Charles Marlis, and shows him the report. "What do you know about this, Charles?"

Charles Marlis has to laugh. "It seems I have been promoted, sir. I was going there to meet up with a boy I met in Tonnerre when I was liaison to the American advance through the area east of Auxerre. This bright lad had somehow captured two German officers, tied them up, and put them in the back of a German Jeep with a French flag flying above his head. He drove to Tonnerre, where I happened to be. On his own he had learned a bit of English. He was quite remarkable, I thought, and, as I was going down that way to attend the War Games in Dijon, I thought I would stop by and see the boy."

Duff Cooper chuckles. "Excellent. Why not? Well, look here. You need all the prestige you can get to impress those chaps in Dijon. If it's permissible or not, I'm not sure, but I'm going to make you an acting temporary major general - if there is such a thing," he laughs. "Take the Rolls to ride down there. Fly a general's flag. Meet your boy and make it a goodwill visit to ... where?"

"A village called Criselles, just outside of Plaignes, between Auxerre and Chatillon."

"All right. Get your hat and uniform fixed up. The French love a show ... a bit of glitter ... as we all do. Take an ADC (*aide-de-camp*) with you. We may be struggling to build ourselves up again, and our coffers may be bare, and we may have to placate the Americans by endlessly telling them they won the war, but we can still put on a jolly good show! Don't you agree?"

The Rolls, with its corporal driver, is at the door at 7 a.m. The ADC, Lieutenant Jeremy Boxer, is standing by the car's door and salutes. "Good morning, general, " he smiles.

"All right, Jeremy. Don't look so amused. We're here to give the French, as Duff says, a jolly good show."

They are on the Seine's left bank in Paris where Charles has had the good fortune, aided by his friends from before the war, to find an apartment with operating plumbing and heating and with a small dining room. He and his French wife, Joey, as everyone knows her, are able to entertain, as all diplomats must, in what Joey calls *"grand intimité"* (grand intimacy.) She suggests to Charles, "why not bring the boy back here and let him see Paris and give him some of our best English food. I bet he's never had Spotted Dick[19]!"

"That would likely destroy a French stomach," Charles grins. "Keep to French cuisine."

Charles and Jeremy, having crawled through the chaotic Paris traffic, turn south-east to Auxerre. "Jeremy, one of the unintelligible things in life is cause and effect. A considerable reason why I'm a general today, more or less,

---

[19] "Spotted Dick" is a British "pudding" made with dough, suet, currants, and sugar formed into a roll and steamed. It is served sliced with treacle (light molasses) or hot custard.

traveling in France with all this pomp, is because I met a boy of twelve in Tonnerre. Now I'm going to meet him again. I know almost nothing about him, yet I have a sense that somehow we were destined to meet and that, in some weird way, I have the responsibility to seek him out."

Charles falls silent as the Rolls-Royce traverses the flat landscape. He's not given to introspection, but knows very well why he has searched for the boy. He had lost his son.

They stop at Chablis, an outlying town of the Burgundy wine district, and pick up a carton of the classic white wine made there. Coming into Plaignes they see bunting and flags flying ahead of them. "It must be a fete or something," Charles imagines.

Jeremy scans ahead. "Sir, I doubt it. It looks more like a reception. Driver, slow down."

Charles looks ahead at the scene down the road. " I think you're right, Jeremy! Goddam! They must be expecting us. I bet this is Duff's doing, the rascal. He's always looking for ways to promote us to the French!" He laughs. "Ah, well! We're in for it. Put on your hat and we'll do the *entente cordiale* (mutual harmony) bit."

Two *gendarmes* on captured German BMW motorcycles lead them to the center of town where a dais had been placed. There the mayor stands in his robe and chain of office. With him is everybody of importance from miles around, including an Army Colonel and Mec, representing the *Maquis*. By the Mayor's side stand Sophie and Giles Martin.

Considering it is more or less impromptu, the occasion goes off remarkably well. The little band plays "God Save the King" and everyone joins in the Marseillaise with gusto. Lunch is set up in a marquee in the town square. The town hall is still in disrepair after the Americans shelled it to get some stubborn Germans out. It is a warm day and the alfresco meal goes off just fine. A great deal of wine and hard cider is drunk. Sophie shows off the camera given her by *Hauptmann* Müller and describes how it had been used to make forgeries of German documents for the *Maquis*.

Charles gives a speech extolling everything French and the courage of the French people during the occupation. That courage was exemplified by the men and women of the *Maquis*. "Please stand up *Capitaine* Mec." Great applause. "And by *Madame* Sophie Martin and her son Giles Martin." More applause.

The cars drive from Plaignes to Criselles. Sophie invites the general and mayor to enter her house and have tea with her and her son. She serves them her almond biscuits.

Giles shows Charles his bilingual Robin Hood book and English primer. Charles teaches him how to pronounce Robin Hood and sympathizes with him about irregular verbs, both English and French; "they are so hard to learn." Charles is impressed anew by the boy. He is bright, intelligent, and not at all diffident about speaking with him. Giles tells Charles he hopes to travel to England and America.

Charles speaks with Sophie. "I will be returning from Dijon this Saturday. Would you consider allowing Giles to come back with me to Paris? My wife and I would be delighted to have him stay with us in our apartment for a few days. We would show him around Paris, have him meet people, and take him up the Eiffel tower."

Sophie hardly knows what to say. Giles jumps in. "*Maman*! *Maman*! Please! Oh, please!"

Sophie turns to the mayor, "do you think it would be all right?"

The mayor is grave at first, then smiles. "I don't see why not. It is very generous of the general. A great opportunity for your boy. What he did with the *Maquis* shows he is courageous and full of good sense. Yes, I advise you to let him go to Paris with the general."

Sophie does her best to smarten up the few clothes Giles has and packs a small cardboard suitcase for him. She gives him the little bit of money she can spare. "You must behave yourself at all times, Giles, and do what the general says. Remember, your mother will love you always. I am proud of you and proud that we are French and have survived." She holds him in her arms and kisses him. "Now you will learn about Paris and come back and tell me all about it. I have never seen the Eiffel tower! Bring back pictures. Here is my camera. There's no film in it. Perhaps the general will help you find some."

Giles climbs into the Rolls-Royce and is in awe. He has entered a different world! Nothing has prepared him for the ambience of the rear compartment of the luxurious Rolls-Royce. This is what he will aspire to in his life!

That aspiration is only reinforced when they arrive in Paris and go into the apartment on *rue St. Dominique*. To Giles it is regal with its high ceilings, parquet floors, paintings on the walls, soft sofas with high backs, and both delicate and plush furniture.

Joey greets the boy, speaking their native French. "Charles tells me you speak some English. I'll help you with it. Come along. I'll show you your room. Would you like a bath? The bathroom and the toilet are just here. Then we'll have dinner."

Joey returns to the salon where Charles is looking through his mail. She announces, "the first thing that boy needs is some decent clothes, Charles. Who do you know?"

"Who do I know?" Charles raises his eyebrows. "Clothes are not my department, my dear. All I know is that it's still damn difficult to find decent clothing. I suppose you have to 'liberate' some. That seems to be the current phrase for the black market."

"I know," Joey agrees, "it's how I found the *escargots* for that last dinner party we had."

"They were delicious, too. Well, I have to report to Duff about Dijon tomorrow. I'll ask him. Perhaps his wife can help."

The *Madame Dionnelle* Fashion House is on *rue St. Honoré*, the fashion street in Paris, near the British Embassy. Like the other fashion houses, *Madame Dionnelle* kept going through the war by dressing the wives and mistresses of high ranking German officers. She is a friend of Duff Cooper, the ambassador, and his beautiful wife, Lady Diana. Now *Madame Dionnelle,* after a word from the embassy, comes to the rescue. A tailor measures Giles. Then comes the choices for shirts, shoes, a jacket, a pair of trousers, underclothes. Nothing out of the ordinary, Joey tells the tailor.

The people there are discussing Dior's New Look, the communists and their beastliness, and the scarcity of everything, unless one is "in the know" *(au courant).* None of this is lost on Giles. He absorbs it like a sponge. To get ahead in life one has to be *au courant.*

When Charles sees the clothes he exclaims: "Good grief, Joey! He'll be the best dressed boy in France! Don't you think you've overdone it a bit? What will his mother think? And the people there?"

"Well, I suppose some jealousy, for his good fortune. I think the boy can handle it. He's told me he wants France to become a great power again. He's a sort of a budding DeGaulle! Anyhow, Charles, it should be quite obvious to both us that our son's death left a hole in our lives. Not that Giles can fill that hole. But at least we can help him be on his way to grow into a good man, like Geoffrey was doing." Joey sits down and wipes her eyes.

Charles holds her hand. "All right, Joey. I'd like a drink. Thank goodness the embassy gets a quota of Scotch. Would you like a splash?"

"A glass of that delicious Chablis you brought back, dear," she says softly. "We know when we need some comforting, don't we? A glass or two to hold back the tears."

For Giles time flies by, one thing follows another, leaving him bewildered and gleeful that life's chances have brought him, not only to the top of the Eiffel tower, but to Charles and Joey who bring a new kind of affection into his life. An affection directed to his future and what he needs to know to become more than a poor boy from Criselles.

Charles takes Giles to the Embassy and introduces him to the ambassador. Then Charles takes him to "Operations" in the basement. A technician teaches Giles about his camera, loads it with American Kodak 35 mm film, and gives him tips about taking pictures, how to adjust the aperture and shutter speed according to the light conditions, and how to set the focus. Giles is entranced. It is wonderful to know these things. In no time he has mastered the rudiments of photography.

Joey takes him to restaurants and teaches him how to use a napkin, read menus, choose wines (no English nonsense about being underage), the table manners of using knives, forks and spoons. They walk in the *Bois de Boulogne*, go to the *Luxembourg* gardens, climb the hills in *Montmartre*, step into art galleries to see the latest strange styles in painting. They spend a morning in the *Louvre* among the paintings of historic Europe. Giles likes the impressionists best with their depictions of everyday events and people.

Joey delights to find that Giles is a bright, well-mannered, boy. Yet that arouses the pain of Geoffrey's loss. When alone she dabs the tears from her eyes.

Giles does not tell her of his experiences in the *Maquis* beyond that he had run messages. He has seen that holding his tongue is as important as expressing himself in forming relationships with people, even those close to him. That he had shot Germans at his young age had to be his own private information.

As Joey tells him, there is so much, far too much, to see and learn about in Paris. "You'll have to come back, Giles; the city is inexhaustible. Besides the grandeur it has its little places. You'll read books by the American, Ernest Hemingway, and I'll take you to where he lived with his young wife at the top of *rue Mouffetard* and nearly starved for lack of money. That was when he was unknown. An American lady, Gertrude Stein, who still lives here, helped him, believing his writing was important."

The French military learns that the young *Maquis* hero is in town. Giles meets a general and is given a *Maquis* medal. A lieutenant takes him to the *École Militaire* and shows him one of the famous taxis that ferried French troops to the Marne in 1914 to stop the German advance at the start of the Great War. Giles wants to ask why that had not happened in the last war; but decides it would be impolitic. He would have to find out for himself.

Joey puts him on the train to Auxerre. From there he will catch a Chatillon bus that stops at Plaignes. Returning to the apartment, Joey bursts into tears.

Charles tries to comfort her. "What is it, darling?"

"It . . . it . . . was like seeing Geoffrey off to school at Euston in London. Geoffrey was 12, like Giles is now, so bright and good looking. Oh, God! Why . . . why . . . do young men have to go to war and be killed? Why does the big life out there understand so little about the personal lives we lead? Is there an answer?"

Charles holds her tight and feels his own tears coursing down his cheek. He murmurs the Shakespeare line from Romeo and Juliet to her. "Partings are such sweet sorrows." He adds, "But we will see Giles again, my dear. I'll make a point of it."

Chapter 7.

England 1946.

After some heated conversation between the Foreign Office and the War Office in London, the promotion of Charles Marlis to the rank of major-general is confirmed. He is now the youngest general in the British army. The news item in the London Times is read by Rupert Brewster, the headmaster of Olton school, the public school[20] that Charles Marlis and his son, Geoffrey, had attended. Charles is an OO, an Old Oltonian, and he donates annually to the school fund. The school has a Cadet Corps where Charles had learned the rudiments of military operations. Brewster writes to General Marlis, thanking him for his donations, and invites him to visit the school. Would he address the school in the Great Hall about his wartime experiences and the outlook for the future?

---

[20] In the UK a "public school" designates a private, elite school. Before state funded schools existed, certain groups, often guilds, founded schools that were open to the public; that is open to anyone able to afford the school fees. That meant the schools were limited to the upper classes and prepared boys for the higher posts in government, the professions, the army, church, and, later, in finance and industry. The best known of these schools is Eton, founded in 1440, with its connection to royalty.

The invitation is fortuitously well timed. Giles has stayed with Charles and Joey in their Paris apartment twice more and Charles and Joey have been down to Criselles and come to know his mother. Charles broaches the subject of Giles' education to Sophie and talks about the kind of education a boy will need for success in the second half of the 20th century going into the 21st.

"It may seem a distant future to you with your boy just coming up to 13. But he must prepare for a world very different from the one we knew before the war. It will be a world where a good education will be of vital importance, a world where a knowledge of science and technology will be as important as literature, art, and languages. Already we are in the start of the new age: the atomic bomb, plans to use nuclear energy to make electricity, the invention of the electronic computer, airplanes driven by jet engines, and the clash of ideas between the democratic countries and the communists. There will have to be well informed men of character and broad knowledge to steer humanity through the coming age."

Sophie is a simple person with only local knowledge, but she understands very well that her boy, sharp witted and ambitious as he is, will benefit from more than she and the local schools can give him.

"What might you advise for Giles?"

"*Madame*, my thoughts are these. English is becoming the language the world speaks. Already every pilot who flies internationally must speak English. A man who knows English as well as his own language will be at an advantage. That does not mean that French is not a rich and beautiful language, always to be spoken by the French and others around the world. It just means that fluency in English will be a great asset. My proposal is this, *madame*. I will enable Giles to go for a year, to start with, to one of the best schools in England. My son and I went there. It provides a philosophical, scientific, and practical education and is a place where boys develop their social moral character. The boys go on to important positions in every profession. You see," and Charles spreads his arms with a broad smile, "I went to the school and have not done so badly!"

Sophie smiles back, "I think you are a good man, general, as I wish my Giles to be." For a moment her face falls. "Oh! Oh! Giles would go away! I would not see him? He is the only child I have."

Charles sees her distress, tries to comfort her. "No, no, *madame*. Giles will come home to you for all the holidays; certainly for a week or more at Christmas and Easter, and the long summer vacation. I will make sure of it. He will write to you once a week or more. If you so wish, you will visit him at the school. My wife and I would be pleased to take you there. We will be living in London though, at times, I may have to be away on duty. My wife will be ready at a moment's notice to go to the school and see to your son's wellbeing. She will be his guardian and the first to know of any problem. Then she will tell you and have you come to London, if that should be your wish."

Sophie is silent for a minute. "And he can come home if he wishes?"

"Certainly. If he doesn't like it and wants to leave, he does just that. He would return to you and be educated here."

Sophie hesitates again. "I have little money. What you are proposing must be expensive."

"That need not concern you, *madame*. My wife and I have agreed, we will pay the costs of the school and the travel involved. I will give your son an allowance so that, like the other boys, he will have money of his own." That was what he had done for Geoffrey. He would do no less for Giles.

"That's very generous of you."

"One more thing, *madame*. Giles must consent to it of his own free will. You will talk with him. Then you will tell me of your decision."

"When would he leave?"

"Soon, at the start of August, to be ready for the term starting in September. He would stay with us in London. I need to have the boy formally accepted at the school. But the headmaster has told me there will be no difficulty. So I have to ask you to decide in the next week."

So now Giles, glowing with excitement and nervous with anticipation, is in the Marlis house on Eggleston Road in Belgravia, a fashionable part of London. The house provided lodging for the Marlis family and their friends as they came and went during the war. It had survived the blitz and the doodlebugs, the V1 unmanned airplanes launched by the Germans against London in 1944. A few pock marks from bomb shrapnel had been made on the front of the house. "Honorable wounds," Charles says with a grin. In the post-war world, the house has the advantage of a private garage that opens onto the mews at the back of the house. A much coveted amenity in central London. Over the garage the rooms, once the servants' quarters, give extra space to put up visiting family and friends. The rooms at the front of the house, while needing some sprucing up and modernizing, have the amenities and charm of a traditional London home.

With the help of a tutor, and Charles and Joey being with him every day, Giles is learning as much as he can about England, the English, and the peculiar language with adjectives placed in front of the nouns. You don't know what is being described until you reach the second word. Bizarre! And the expressions! *Go for a spin* means a ride in a car. Giles had thought it meant becoming dizzy. How would he ever learn it all? He has to get used to greasy English breakfasts too. But he is determined to fit in, so he downs the fried eggs and bacon.

Charles and Joey drive Giles to Olton school, located in Northamptonshire, in their Humber Hawk. Charles has told Giles that the car is the new model of the one General Montgomery had used during the European war, the one he called "Old Faithful." Giles is sure all English boys know General Montgomery had a Humber car when he was fighting the war in northern Europe. He must know that, and much else too.

At Olton school Giles walks with Charles and Joey around some of the school buildings and the extensive sports fields before meeting with the headmaster. Giles doesn't have to say much, thank goodness! The head asks a few questions about his education and his home in France to which Giles can give quite good answers in English. The head smiles and says he will have Giles help the master teaching French. During the war, the master has had small chance to speak with French people, so his French is a little rusty. On the way back to London, Charles talks about his experiences at the school when he was a boy there. He tells Giles that it is a Christian school and all the boys, no matter what their private beliefs, attend chapel service every Sunday. "I don't suppose that will be a problem for you, Giles. You were raised a Catholic, I imagine, like most French children."

"Yes, I was raised a Catholic," Giles says, without saying anything more.

For the purchase of Giles school clothes, Joey goes to the Daniel Neal store on Oxford Street. The school has given Joey a list of what is required. Clothes rationing is still in force and Giles will have one year's supply of 48 coupons[21]. Not that that will be enough for all he needs, but the clothes from Paris have given him a basic wardrobe in shirts, underclothes and socks. Now he needs a school blazer (8 coupons), cap (2 coupons), grey shorts (3 coupons), grey longs (6 coupons), and grey jacket (8 coupons), the clothes common to all the public schools. These are necessities and add up to 27 coupons. Joey holds the remaining 28 coupons in reserve for whatever else Giles might need. A school requirement is that everything has to be marked with the boy's name. Joey orders name tags and hires a seamstress to sew them on the clothes.

---

[21] In the UK clothes rationing continued to March 1949 and food rationing for some essentials until 1953. There was a considerable black market in clothes, used clothing stores were popular, and those who could went over to Europe and even to America to fill out their wardrobes. The extended rationing was one aspect of the austerity and near bankruptcy that Britain suffered after the war.

Now comes the big day, the start of the Michaelmas term. Giles has on his grey school clothes. The rest of his belongings and his personal things are in a small trunk, including a woolen scarf Sophie has knitted for him to guard him against the English cold. Charles has given him pens and pencils, notebooks, and a foot long slide rule with a built-in magnifying glass. The tutor has shown him how to use it to do multiplications and divisions, find square roots and other mathematical functions. Giles is fascinated. Charles has placed him in his old house at Olton, Linsley House, headed by the rather crusty old housemaster, B.K. Bingham, who is nearing retirement. It is one of the oldest houses of the school with a reputation for having strong Rugby players and rowers. Charles thinks that Giles, with his relatively small size, could make a good Rugby scrum-half and a cox for the House four. However he is strong too, and possibly could make a good bow man in the boat.

The school LNER (London North Eastern Railway) train leaves from Euston station and goes to the school, first on main lines, then meanders along a single track through small towns and farmland. At Euston the platform is full of boys, ranging from 12 to 17 in age, most with parents to see them off. Many boys are wearing the school cap and Giles is wearing his. The scene is unnerving to him. Everyone is excited, and speaking and shouting English at such a rapid rate that he can hardly understand a word.

Amid the din Charles is telling him, "when I did this as a new boy, I was quite terrified. My father found some other new boys and we went to the train together to find a compartment. I'll try to do the same for you." He looks around and sees a couple of young boys about Giles's age. "Come on, Giles; let's see who they are."

Charles approaches the parents of one of them and is rather astonished to hear a voice from the other side of the Atlantic. "Are you American?"

The tall man says, glancing at Giles, "no, Canadian. You have your youngster going to this school? It'll be a first for my boy in an English school. I'm Pierre David from Quebec. Please meet my wife, Marie."

Introductions are made. Marie tells Joey they are with the Canadian Embassy in London and have been advised to send their young son to Olton. "Excellent education and not too snobbish, I've been told," she tells Joey.

Joey tells her, "my husband went to school there, and he would agree with you. We have something in common, Marie. Charles was working in our embassy in Paris. We knew some of the people in the Canadian embassy there."

"It's a small world, isn't it? We'll have to get together. Our Robert is going to Linsley House."

"So is Giles!" Joey exclaims. "I'm sure they will be friends. My husband and I are appointed as his guardians by the school. His mother lives in France; his father was killed in the war."

"How sad. We lost too many of our young men too. So the boy is French?"

"Yes, he is."

"I'm so pleased. We are French Canadians and our boy, Robert, is bilingual. The boys will be able to speak French together."

"I'm not sure the other boys will like that," Joey grins. "They all seem terribly English."

Giles and Robert meet each other guardedly. Giles has, of course, been warned about not embracing when meeting people, so they just shake hands before boarding the train together. The compartment is full with two other new boys and some older ones. Once they are on their way, the boys exchange names, talk about where they came from, and their experiences during the war. Giles says nothing about what he'd done with the *Maquis*. He is not ashamed of it in the least, but senses it would be inappropriate to say anything about it.

Giles and Robert join with the other new boys in being anxious about their new school. Giles is told by one of the older boys "not to be snotty" and do as the prefects say. As far as Giles understands this advice, he must not have a dirty nose. These English are peculiar! He wouldn't have a dirty nose in any case.

"I was told," a new boy says anxiously, "that new boys are caned by the prefects as soon as they arrive. You have to fag[22] for them and, if they don't like what you do, they cane you."

"That's not done any longer," another new boy retorts, "that's what my father told me. I hope he's right."

Giles and Robert are seated together. Robert says, "Dad told me to speak English with you all the time when with other boys. We had better do that. If you like, I will help you with your English. It must be difficult for you, just coming over from France."

"Thank you. I will try with your aid."

"It isn't 'aid,' it's 'help.' You say 'with your help.' And you have to say *th*. Press the tongue forward behind the top front teeth and then release it. I know it's difficult."

Giles was thankful to have made a friend so quickly.

---

[22] A "fag" is an under-school boy who acts as a servant to prefects and older higher-form boys.

Chapter 8.

Olton School.

The experience of being a French boy at an English public school is an exciting and disturbing experience for young Giles, in small ways and big. Unlike in France no one dresses in blue, none of the workmen, no one! And the bread is always stale! No fresh baked baguettes! Then there is history! English people think Napoleon was a tyrant! Even the history master is vague about Austerlitz and Napoleon's military genius. The English heroes are Nelson and Wellington who defeated Napoleon. In these ways and many others it is a topsy-turvy world.

Without any intention of doing so, Giles quickly makes an impression. In the cadet corps the boys are trained in shooting using a Lee-Enfield Mark 4 rifle, with the bore reduced from .303 to .22, with open V and blade sights. The same sights the German rifle had. Giles listens to the instructions of the ex-army sergeant-major and lies down. He adjusts the strap around his left arm, as he had done when shooting Germans. He fires one shot. The sergeant-major sights it. "The rim of the bull's eye at two o'clock." Giles then fires nine shots through the center of the bull's eye. The sergeant-major has never seen anything like it.

He takes the target to the headmaster. "That's major competition shooting! It was no fluke. He did it again with a different rifle, allowing for the error in the sights. The boy learned to shoot in France during the war using a German NP 40 rifle. You will remember, sir, we are signed up for the Aldershot rifle competition. This boy, Giles Martin, young as he is, must be on the squad."

When the news gets around, Giles finds himself in difficulty. Robert takes him aside, under some trees near the rugby field, where they can speak privately in French. "*Mince alors!*" (*Crikey!*) You had a German gun! Tell me! Did you steal it?"

"No. Others did. My captain, Mec, taught me how to shoot."

"Your captain? What do you mean?"

"Mec was in charge. I helped him."

Giles feels embarrassed. How can he tell Robert and the others what it had been like, what he had done? He is proud of himself and feels no shame. He is learning that truth has to be dissembled. His own truth is too brutal. It has to be shaped to suit the sensibilities of others.

"I don't know how Mec came to have the rifle. He was a great patriot and thought that everyone should be prepared to defend their country. He taught me how to shoot. Then the Americans came through our part of France. We cheered them on. They gave the children candy and they had nylon stockings and cigarettes for the older girls."

Giles quickly realizes he has said too much. Robert shares the story with other boys and many soon know why Giles is such a good shot. One surmises, "he was shooting the Germans." When they ask Giles, he improvises. "No, but I would have done if I'd had to." It is only a half-lie, he consoles himself.

Giles has difficulty with the English language and expressing himself. To the other boys, he is often inscrutable. The English boys think that, being French and talking about the Americans giving nylon stockings to French girls, he must know about girls. Giles finds this another embarrassment. He knows nothing about girls. When he goes home for Christmas, he will find out, by some means or another. Perhaps he should go to that house in Dijon that Leon and Klaus talked about.

Giles fags for a prefect, Julian Lynches. Giles makes his afternoon tea. "Well, Giles, you are a good marksman, but don't let it go to your head. That doesn't go down well here. The important thing here is to be a good sport, don't tell on others, and do the best you can. I've heard you are keen to play rugby, is that right?"

"Yes. It is played in the southwest of France. I would like to learn how to play."

"Very well, you shall! You're not all that big, but you may grow. Perhaps you would make a good scrum-half. We'll see, eh?"

"Thank you, mister Lynches. What is a scrum-half?"

"I'm not a mister, Giles. As a new boy you don't have to call me anything. But I'll allow you to call me Julian, as long as you behave yourself and don't get in any trouble. A scrum-half? He is the player who scurries around at the back of the scrum, finds the ball, then throws it back to the stand-off. He's like a rat, scrabbling for the ball," Julian laughs. "But he is also the lynch-pin of his side."

Giles finds a book on rugby on the shelves of the day room and reads about the game. He tries to memorize the words describing each player and what they do. He looks up lynch-pin in his dictionary and finds it is something that holds things together. The next day he tells Julian, "I want to be a lynch-pin, a scrum-half."

Giles goes back to the Rugby book and finds that the "hooker" is the man at the front of the scrum who hooks the ball back with his feet. He then thinks to look up the word in an English dictionary and finds that a "hooker" means a prostitute, more an American word than an English one.

Giles realizes he has to be careful in his choice and use of English words and that means learning the language really well. Multiple meanings happen in French, also. After all, *"une fille"* can mean a girl, a daughter, or a prostitute depending on context. Giles writes down the words and others in his private work book. He likes language and begins to think of himself as a writer.

For a reason he does not understand, but suspects because he is French, the house master, B.K. Bingham, dislikes him. Robert and he had gathered a few things to make a simple picnic to have with their walk in the neighboring fields and woods. They are emerging from a side door of Linsley House when Bingham comes up to them. He demands to know what is in the bag that Giles is holding. He answers it is a picnic for their walk. The housemaster raises his hand and hits him across the face so hard that Giles falls to the ground. The housemaster grabs the bag and tells the two boys they are restricted to the day room. Then he stalks off, red faced with anger, though for what reason Giles does not know then and never discovers.

The other new boys are too scared to say anything when Giles tells them what had happened. They believe him, but are afraid the prefects won't. He concludes that life is unjust at Olton; just as it was for the hostages and, as far as he can make out, just as it had been everywhere for as long as people had been on the earth. The history he is learning in class seems to prove that.

So Giles accepts the event as one more lesson in life: those who have power exercise it arbitrarily, often unjustly, and for their own reasons. Robert says it is Kafkaesque. That is how Giles is introduced to Kafka and his arbitrary world. His interest aroused, he reads Kafka's books in the library and finds many parallels to the world of occupied France and the capricious way the Germans oppressed and treated the French. But, he realizes, ruefully, that when the Germans had gone, the French turned on themselves in the *épuration* and had been as unjust and vicious as the Germans had been. He has read in the Daily Telegraph, an English newspaper, that there is unrest in Algeria. He supposes that it was like what had happened elsewhere in France, a part of the *épuration*.

In the history class they are studying the Tudor dynasty. That is how Giles knows about Thomas Moore and his book Utopia; Utopia, where all things are for the good. Just a fantasy. For his beliefs Moore had his head cut off at the command of King Henry VIII. Giles is also learning that history never repeats itself, but that patterns, based on the ebb and flow of power, recur again and again. "Civilizations have never stood still. Change is the eternal constant," the history master declares.

Giles knows he is learning important things and he is lapping it up; but yet, at times, he wishes he wasn't. At times he feels overwhelmed, that he is learning too much, and that he will be too different from others, like his mother and Mec. And the complexity of things seem beyond human reason. Then he wakes in the morning and feels he has only to strive for everything to be revealed, meaningful, and understood.

Chapter 9.

An Exeat in London.

The focus of Olton school is on itself. Its collective mind is concentrated on scholasticism and, almost to the same degree, on rugby, cricket, rowing, and fives. Few people outside the confines of British public schools have ever heard of "fives." It is a form of handball played in a court with four walls and a floor, hence "fives." The players wear gloves and hit the small rubber ball with either hand. It is a very fast game and, to excel, takes much practice.

With these concerns the top priority at school, Giles is unaware of the global tensions involving France nor that they are about to intrude into his life.

Charles is in Paris. His stint there as Military Attaché with ambassador Duff Cooper has made him a primary choice of the Foreign Secretary, Ernest Bevin, for following the chaotic French military and political scene and report back to him personally.

Charles quickly renews his acquaintances in Paris. High society has come back with a roar. Sartre is thrilling the intelligentsia with his doctrine of existentialism; "we are left alone to exist with no excuses." But some think him more a *poseur* than a philosopher. Most people talk of little else but the shortage of everything, the *haute couture* of the *couturiers* Dior and Fath, and the astronomical prices, obscene in bankrupt France, that some Americans are paying for their Parisian dresses and gowns. "Only the Americans profited from the war and they suffered the least." The French ambivalence about America is ever present, a confusing mix of admiration and amity on the one hand and envy, fear, and distaste on the other. The boorish behavior of some of the rich visitors from America is a topic of smirking conversation at cocktail parties and is a way the French reassure themselves of their innate superiority. DeGaulle's thinly veiled distrust and distaste for all things American is well known. At the same time, young Americans traveling on "a-dollar-a-day" plans are welcomed. Many hope that bodes well for the future.

Charles is with Duff Cooper again. Duff, while as erudite and charming as ever, is at odds with the Labour government in Whitehall and is on his way out. His aristocratic leanings and his revolving door gallery of American and French mistresses do not sit well with the Labour party puritans at home.

The French government and public opinion are in disarray, leading to governmental dysfunction, and the country's attitude toward the rest of the world is paranoid. Perfidious Albion, as French patricians term Britain, is distrusted. Long French memories recall that Germany is either at your feet or at your throat. However the immediate concern is what the French fleet is doing at Haiphong, a port city in northern Vietnam. Léon Blum, the premier, is peppered with advice from every quarter.

French warships are there. The city and the port are under the nominal control of the Viet Minh government whose long term goal is independence. But their control is paper thin. The French people in Haiphong - the "*colonials*" - are demanding that France take control and re-establish its rule. The die-hards will not accept that it is the beginning of the end of the colonial era.

Bevin and Attlee, the prime minister, are opposed to continuing the regime of colonies. Anyhow Britain can't afford theirs anymore. In their view there has to be a steady progress toward independence. The French violently disagree. For one thing it would undermine their position in Syria where they have regained control under a UN mandate; in effect they rule the country and have a small, but vital, police and military presence in the chaotic but critical Middle East. In Algeria, their prized possession, there is unrest among the Muslims. DeGaulle and all French patriots are not about to let go of their rightful place in the world, as they see it. *La Gloire de France* (The Glory of France*)* is at stake.

Joey is receiving nightly phone calls from Charles in Paris. He is telling her that the situation is ridiculous, dreadful, dangerous, etc. Joey is stressed, torn between loyalties, to her homeland, France, and to her British husband. She hopes Charles can mediate some sort of *détente* (literally *the drawing of teeth*) before anything drastic happens. It is possible that the French and the British could come to blows again, as they had in 1940 and 41.[23]

Joey is refurbishing their London house for the social position that Charles has acquired through his promotion. Now she is choosing curtains for the house. The front rooms have high windows and whatever she chooses will be expensive. She better choose right; she goes for modern, but not controversial.

---

[23] In July 1940 the Royal Navy destroyed or severely damaged seven battleships of the French fleet at the Mers-el-Kébir anchorage in Algeria for fear the ships would fall into German hands. With the Vichy government in France cooperating with the Germans, there was a real danger that the ships would be taken and outlying parts of the French empire would side with the Axis powers. In 1941 the British forestalled them in Syria, then a French mandate, and elsewhere in military operations. In Syria, British and Australian forces defeated the local French forces. Though a necessity of war, some French have never forgiven Britain for these actions.

Having gone to Harrod's and chosen the curtains, her thoughts are again riven by the international situation and the disastrous political situation in France. It makes her glad to be living in London and only surrounded by the British raucous, but stable, politics.[24] In the Times of London she reads how Léon Blum, the French prime minister, is confronted with a critical situation in Haiphong. Besides the French, British and Americans warships are in the water there. God knows what might happen. The worst possible thing would be for them to start firing on each other. Tensions are that high.

Joey sighs. It is all too much. The war had been bad enough and now, instead of a calm peace, everything was . . . well, at "sixes and sevens.[25]" She smiles. How long it had taken her to learn the innumerable idioms used in the English language! Poor Giles! He has to be learning them now. She feels most responsible for Giles, but knows she mustn't overdo. She isn't his mother, though she has all the feelings of a mother. Her sister, Marianne, on a visit to London, tells her, "maternal milk is flowing in your veins again, Joey." Well, it probably was. Joey looks at her watch. Hey! She'd better get going. She has to pick up Giles at Olton school.

At Olton it's the half term *exeat*, a long weekend out of school. Joey drives the Humber to Linsley House and up the gravel drive to the front door. Never mind what the rules

---

[24] In France the Fourth Republic has come into being amid furious dispute. DeGaulle has washed his hands of the whole thing and retired to his country house to await being called back to rule the unruly French. The communists had nearly prevailed in taking over the government. They have been turned back by the socialists and Léon Blum, a socialist, has been elected prime minister.

[25] The British idiom to be at "sixes and sevens", describing a situation of confusion and disarray, is probably derived from a dice game called "hazard." Six and seven were the riskiest numbers to bet on and those who tried for them were considered careless or confused. However Chaucer in 1380 in *Troilus and Criseyde* uses the phrase to "set the world on six and seven" meaning a risky situation. It probably referred to a game, now unknown.

and customs are, she does what is natural and drives up to the house. Bingham, the housemaster, standing in his window and seeing her impertinence, fumes. Doesn't she know to park on the road? The information has been given to all parents. These damned French! What cheek!

Giles jumps in beside her. Joey embraces him, French style. "There!" she smiles at him, "we've just done what is known here as a PDA - a public display of affection. Tsk, tsk, eh! Sometimes it's hard to be French and live in England, Giles. The English are supposed to only allow a show of affection for dogs and horses. It's not really true - except for a little bit. But, we'd better not break too many of their customs. Your house master might expel you!" She pulls Giles to her in a conspiratorial way and then pushes him away into the passenger seat with a grin. "We both have to mind our P's and Q's."

Giles didn't understand. "What does 'minding P's and Q's' mean, Joey?"

"It means being proper. I had to learn these things just as you have to, Giles. It's an idiom. An idiom has no apparent meaning until you find out about it and where it comes from. Actually the expression is bilingual. For me, being French, it means mind your feet *'pieds'* and your wig *'queues'* when you are learning to dance. It dates from the 18th century and the court of Louis 14th, our Sun King. The courtiers had to be careful of their feet and wigs or the king would dismiss them from his court. But, if you are English, the P's are pints and the Q's are quarts. A pub keeper has to be careful with his pints and quarts. So it doesn't matter which country you're in, you still have to look after the details. It's a useful lesson, Giles. You know what they say, 'the devil is in the details.'"

The drive to London is taking some time because the roads, after the wear and tear of wartime military traffic, need rebuilding. Joey asks Giles how he is getting on in school. "Oh! Jolly good! But it's sometimes hard to understand what's being said."

Joey nods her head. "Oh! I know that! But you have picked up some essentials. You said 'Jolly good!'"

"That's not so difficult. We say *'C'est du jolie!'* It means much the same. In the English class we are reading Macbeth by Shakespeare. We have to know what words and expressions meant then, in the 16th and 17th century. The play is so dramatic. I love the witches."

Joey navigates her way onto the A1 road. All these damn lorries! She misses the long stretches of straight roads in France. You are forever turning on English roads.

"Good. I'm glad you are studying Macbeth, Giles. We don't much like the leading people in it, but there is much to learn from them. You'll finish the play by the end of term. It's worth a lot of discussion. We will talk about it when you are home for Christmas."

Giles looks at her sharply. "Oh, you said I was going home to my mother for Christmas."

"Of course, of course. So you are." Joey corrects herself, turning her head away, wincing. "But we'll have a few days together before you go back to school."

She falls silent, concentrating on the road. First, she must control herself, then find the proper role to play with Giles, something like an aunt. She changes the subject. "I want to tell you, Giles, about what we're going to see in London. Have you heard of the English pantomime?"

"Pantomime? No. What is that?"

"Well, it's a stage show, humorous and sometimes a little vulgar, with *double entendres* that the children in the audience are not supposed to understand." Joey grins. "But these days, children understand so much more than I did when I was their age. If you don't understand something that's said, Giles, make a note of it and I'll explain it to you later. The pantomime is really aimed at the child in all of us. I enjoy them. They are very English. We have mime shows, but no pantomimes in France. The one we'll be seeing is based loosely on the story of Cinderella." Joey smiles. "When

I say loosely - well, you'll see what I mean. It's really just a comic invention with people playing roles that have been established for a long time, even going back as far as ancient Greece. The prince will be played by a girl and the wicked sisters by men. The girl who plays the prince will be in tights and show off her feminine curves. A couple of hundred years ago that was very sexy and the men loved it. You see, it doesn't make much sense. And there will be a cow or a horse played by two men in an animal suit. Don't ask me why. It's just a theatrical tradition. So, let your hair down, Giles, and enjoy!"

"Let my hair down?"

"Oh, my! Another English phrase. What would we say? *Se laisser aller* or *se défouler*. But nothing is quite the same from one language to another, as I'm sure you realize by now. But already you are speaking English well. And your accent has improved so! Soon you will be taken for an Englishman. Keep at it."

"I try hard and Robert and the other boys help me."

They are on a detour around Stevenage because the main road is torn up. Joey has to concentrate on her driving. "We'll get there sooner or later. That's all right. I had planned on dinner at home this evening. As I told you, Charles is in Paris. There have been developments in Vietnam with the French warships there."

"Oh? I don't know where Vietnam is. It's out east somewhere, isn't it?"

"I think we will all know soon enough exactly where it is. Our French fleet is there to defend the French people who live in Haiphong. I personally think we should leave and let the Vietnamese look after themselves. But," Joey shrugs, "I'm not living there. You know we French, like the British, went all over the world. Now we have to live with what we created. It's not so easy."

Over dinner, Joey tells Giles that the night after they have seen the pantomime they are going to see something entirely different, a Greek play, a classic tragedy, *Oedipus Rex* by Sophocles. "It's a matter of contrast, Giles. We laugh, we cry. We live, we die. It's all part of life and the classics are classics because they express the truth about life. That's why I am taking you to see this play. You may remember it for the rest of your life."

Unexpectedly, shortly after six, Charles comes in the door, tired and anxious. "I got a lift on a plane to Hendon. Have you heard? It's a mess. A French cruiser, the *Suffren*, opened fire on Haiphong. Whether they had permission from Léon Blum or not, nobody seems to know. There are thousands of civilian casualties. Goddam the bloody French! Oh! I'm sorry, Joey and you too, Giles! I love France and the French, but sometimes they act like bloody fools and really mess things up." Charles takes off his hat and coat and slams them onto the hall rack. "Turn on the BBC, Joey. Let's hear the latest."

They listen to the radio. Six thousand casualties in Haiphong. The Viet Minh government has skedaddled to the hills. French forces are in control. Vietnamese are being shot down in the streets.

Charles claps his hand to his head. "They don't understand. They don't understand. The colonial era is over. I know that. Why don't they? I'm afraid it may take an awful long time for us humans to come to our senses. Jefferson was right in his words, however wrong he was in his actions as a slave holder, when he wrote: 'all men are created equal.' I'll be dead before that is even approximately true. Well, let's have dinner," Charles manages to grin, "and let the world take care of itself for a while."

That was, in its own way, Giles introduction to diplomacy.

They sit down to dinner. "Giles! What's been happening? How's your *amo, amas, amat*?"

"Actually, sir, I'm not studying Latin. You don't have to any longer."

"That's a change. I suppose for the better, though I enjoyed Latin. It gave me a foundation for many things. So what are you studying?"

"I like calculus. It's the math of motion, so I think it's very true. Everything is in motion, isn't it?"

Joey is thoughtful. "That's right, Giles. Everything is. We know it, but we don't think about it. More fool us."

"And the Tudors in English history. *Nom de Dieu!* It was hard to stay alive with them!"

"For some of them," Charles agrees, "that was all too true. But, at least, they didn't kill people wholesale by the millions like some of us supposedly civilized people have done. But enough of that. I believe Joey is taking you to a pantomime. May I come too?"

The next day, Saturday, the papers are full of the Vietnam story. After a quick visit to the Foreign Office, Charles is back and they go to Shaftesbury Avenue off Piccadilly Circus where the pantomime is playing. It is good fun and Giles laughs with everybody else at the antics on stage. It gives him a new insight into the staid British character. When they let their hair down, they sure let it down!

Joey takes him to *Oedipus Rex*. What a contrast! The play is an unmitigated tragedy with the cursed-by-fate Oedipus killing his father and marrying his mother, all unknowingly in a horrible set of blunders. Then he has to live with the consequences and atone for his guilt. In the play he tears out his eyes, with gushes of blood, and curses the gods.

Giles feels himself trembling, his heart beating. The theater is deathly still, then he hears the stifled sobs. Giles had never felt anything like it before. He shifts uncomfortably in the seat. Joey has tears in her eyes, but his are dry.

In the taxi taking them home, Giles sits with a studied expression on his face. He says, "my father was killed because he enlisted in the army and then was killed by a bullet that happened to fly into his heart. Life seems to be just like that, half your own action, half just chance."

He can't cry about it. Just as he couldn't cry when the hostages were shot, nor when he had killed the Germans. His feelings had not been engaged. He had to protect himself. It was what gave him strength. He remembers a passage he had read in Diderot, "one must engage the mind."

Yes! Reason was the answer! Emotions are a snare leading to delusions. That play, it wasn't real. It had no meaning for him anymore than the pantomime had. His father is dead and his mother is sacred. Giles falls asleep, but has a disturbed night with difficult tense dreams.

Part 2.
The Early Years of
Julie Rossinger

Chapter 10.

Northeast France 1939-40.

When France declares war against Germany on September 3, 1939, Julie Rossinger has had her fourteenth birthday, on July 14th. "You are a true French girl, "she is told, "being born on Bastille day." Not that birthdays are much in her family. Pleasure and affection are only occasional events. Her grim father assures her that Satan is always on the lookout to take advantage and that pleasure and sin are often the same.

Julie is the youngest of four children. Her father owns a drapery and clothing store in Avier, a village in northeast France, in the department of Aisne, close to southern Belgium. Julie helps out at home with the chickens and rabbits her mother keeps. She can kill a chicken or a rabbit and prepare the meat for the stew pot or the spit. To do it without any fuss or second thoughts is part of her reality. Flesh is just flesh. Just as her body is her body. She does not bother to think about things like that. That would be silly.

The war has little effect on their lives and it hardly seems a war at all compared with the Great War twenty years ago. People are calling it the "phony war." Some of the younger men are called up to serve in the army. They see airplanes in the sky, but no bombs are dropped. French and British planes drop propaganda leaflets over Germany. One time a strong wind blew some of them back over Avier. Julie's mother and she picked them up and used them to kindle the coal fires in the fireplaces of their house.

In her father's store Julie gains a sense for cloths and fabrics as well as for the selling and buying of goods and services for cash. In the village almost all transactions are in cash. She rings up items and makes change at the cash register. She gains a sense for money. Her father hires a seamstress who adjusts ready-made clothes to fit the customer, but she can also make a dress from start to finish. Julie watches and tries her hand at it.

The school does little to open vistas to Julie. Education is a drill. Julie finds that the serious things in life are all like that. Things are to be learned and done and not questioned. Her parents and the other adults know what's right and wrong. It gets her into trouble if she disagrees with them. Her father has used his belt on her backside to keep her from "sin." But she hadn't felt at fault. All she was doing was thinking her own thoughts. Like . . . why did God allow his son to be tortured to death? To think like that, as far as she could tell, was the "sin" she had committed. So she gives up thinking those kind of thoughts and just gets on with her daily life.

Growing up, Julie knows little beyond the village, its people, the nearby fields, and the river where she swims with the other boys and girls. She sees that boys and girls are different between their legs. For her it is another fact of life with no further meaning. She runs for the joy of it, picks the wild flowers, and eats the wild strawberries. Someone calls her an imp, "*lutine*", the feminine form of the word. Some of the kids pick it up and she acquires the nickname, Lutine. Having long legs she runs with ease; in another time and place she could have been an athlete or a model. But nothing like that enters the limited world Julie grows up in.

Entering her teen years, Julie's body is shapely, her breasts budding, but keeping small. People remark on her beauty and her long golden hair, as soft and luminous as silk. She has her first flow of blood; her mother tells her it is something that happens to girls as they grow up. A girl tells her it is to do with having babies. Not enlightened, Julie puts it aside. Her spirits are naturally bright. Her father thinks her precocious and tells her she will come to no good unless she fears the wrath of God and repents. One evening, as she goes to bed, she asks God what she should do, but gets no answer. So she puts God aside and gets on with being herself.

In May 1940 the tanks and mobile infantry of the German 7th Panzer division, commanded by General Erwin Rommel, come storming along the roads and across the fields from Belgium. Nothing stems them. Because there is some resistance at Avier by a retreating French unit that fought bravely, the Germans flatten the place with shell fire. The houses burn. Julie sees her parents killed. A shell lands at their feet. One minute they are there and in the next moment they are gone. Only a hole in the ground is left. Her eldest brother, Robert, 12 years older than her, flees. Her other brother and sister disappear, she knows not where.

A German soldier has sex with her. Julie has little idea of what is happening. She's in shock from the explosions and the violence happening around her. He uses butter so that he can slide more easily into her tight passage. He is not violent. It's sort of friendly. She lets it happen and kisses the soldier back. It seems to be the safest thing to do. She has only the vaguest ideas about "virginity." She doesn't know she'd lost it.

Later, looking back with a smile, Julie recalls how ignorance and naiveté had saved her. Other girls had been violently raped, smothered, shot and killed because they struggled and spat and screamed and wouldn't give up their bodies to the soldiers.

Julie now has no home or family or, indeed, anyone or anything. They are all dead or gone, she knows not where.

People stumble by, but she does not know them. Her house is a charred ruin. She sits on a low wall, desolate.

A German sergeant, a big tall blonde man from Marburg, asks if she is all right. She says *"oui"* and kisses him. Her attitude charms him and he and the men of his squad are gentle with her and smiling. The sergeant tells her she can come with them. So she rides with them in a half-track.

The soldiers give her food and shelter and tell her she is *schöne.* They all laugh as she tries to say German words and they French words. She keeps herself washed and clean, using the water from the streams they pass by.

In the towns the soldiers, especially one called Ernst, a slight man with a gentle manner, find things for her in the shops they ransack. They are a cheerful lot, victorious soldiers. They bring her cosmetics, perfumes, silky lingerie, corsets, black stockings, dresses, jewelry, adornments, chocolates and candy, with little discretion of what might suit her. It all delights Julie. She has never known such plenty. She'd only had drab clothes. The chocolates are yummy.

She frolics. The men encourage and applaud her. They make her happy in spite of the horrors going on around them. Every now and again a tank comes speeding past and fires its long barreled 88mm gun. The road is full of refugees and debris. The Germans tell the refugees to stop. They have nowhere to go. The Germans have conquered France. Some of the French jeer at the young girl riding with the Germans. Julie shouts back. She pities them in their plight, but she is alive and she intends to stay that way.

The cosmetics are all new to her. Her father had told her that cosmetics were the temptations of the Devil. Well, all that was in her past. Now she was in charge of her life. Ernst had been in the theater before the war. He is not soldier-like at all; though he has to try to be or he'll be shot. He knows about her having had sex with a soldier and that makes him extra gentle with her. Coming from near Alsace, he speaks some French and sometimes he calls her *la douce* (soft, gentle, beloved) and then uses her nickname *Lutine*, that she has told him about.

The German officer lets her be. War has its customs. Acquiring camp followers is in the long tradition of conquering armies. As long as the men maintain good discipline, they can have their girl. She's something pleasant in all the mess, a trophy of their victory over the French, a "spoil" of war.

In the evenings they bivouac and make a camp fire. Julie helps the men with their uniforms, washing and mending. She cooks and does other small things, being happy and friendly.

A soldier catches a chicken. Swiftly and deftly Julie knifes off its head, holds it upside down to drain the blood, disembowels it, plucks off its feathers, and chops it up to cook over their campfire. The men watch and admire her for it, cheering her on.

After dinner she sings the French songs she knows, *"Alouette, gentille alouette - Alouette je te plumerai . . . "* She doesn't know that its ditty, though a children's song and about a bird, a lark (*alouette*), having its feathers plucked, is sung by soldiers for its *double entendre* of a girl's deflowering. The German soldiers know it, but keep it to themselves behind their smiles. At this early stage of the war, with most of the German soldiers still fresh from civilian and family life, most of them behave decently. They pick up music on the radio, some of it from London, and Julie hears English for the first time. It is incomprehensible to her. Julie dances with them to the music.

The sergeant takes Julie as his girl. It stops the men from going after her and quarreling and being jealous. They stop at a house with a bedroom. The sergeant also uses butter as a lubricant and enters his large stiff member into her slowly. From what she has told him he is sure she had been a virgin. He makes love to her rather than just having sex. She responds. Her body takes over.

At first she thinks she is going mad as she is

overwhelmed by the rush of feeling, the strength of the man, her own body heaving, his cries and her cries. Then the volcano erupts. Julie has her first orgasm. She changes from a girl to a woman.

Being there, with the men, with the invincible German army, becomes her normality. The men like her and she likes them. The days are warm, but the evenings and nights are cold. Ernst, ever mindful of her, commandeers a lynx fur coat with a matching muff and toque hat from a deserted house. Julie sports herself in them in front of the men. The furs keep her warm at night.

Her shoes have given out and Ernst returns from foraging with a sack full of them. They all have high heels! Not very practical, but Julie adores them. She has only seen shoes like these in magazines. Sometimes she is barefoot and sometimes she wears the shoes. They are so difficult to wear! She has to walk in dinky little steps, balancing herself, laughing a lot. "You have to get used to them," the soldiers tell her, "or else you'll never be in 'high' society." They laugh at the *double entendre*. Not that she understood the German, but she gets the idea, grins with them, and even smokes one of their cigarettes. It makes her cough and she doesn't like it.

She's been with them for a week. The sergeant takes her into a house, along with Ernst. Miraculously there is a working bathroom in the house, with the hot water coming from the kitchen stove. Ernst soon has it going with the coal he finds in the cellar and Julie has a hot bath with soap. Ernst tells Julie to wrap a towel round herself and shows her how to shave under her arms with the razor he has found. "It's something that smart girls do, Julie. They shave their legs too. Some girls even shave higher up, around their slit. You hardly need to do that. Your little bit of blonde fuzz is too pretty to shave off. You are going to be on your own and your best chance is to be up to date and attractive. Everyone likes an attractive girl."

Julie absorbs these basic facts. Ernst makes things explicit, tells it like it is. She likes him a lot.

The sergeant gets in the bath after her, washes and uses the razor, emerges clean and shaven. He clasps the young girl to him and kisses her. She kisses him back. His erect cock reaches up and slides up into her again. It happens easily and is exciting, makes her feel wanted. She has no sense of being violated. It's all new, unexpected; an act of sharing, it seems to her; a bit puzzling but not frightening. Something adults do. Now that she is an adult, she should do it too. Her loins return his motions. She's dizzy. He spurts his milk, as he calls it, into her. After he withdraws, the milk oozes out. He tells her to taste it, gives her a towel. It tastes salty and has a particular odor that she hasn't smelled before. "Wipe yourself up, Julie." He calls Ernst over. Ernst had been watching from the doorway.

The sergeant had told Ernst to bring along the clothes and other things purloined for the girl. "We will have to let her go, Ernst, in Paris, tomorrow. Dress her. You know how to do that and you have the clothes now. Teach her some sophistication. That will be her best chance. Make her attractive, so she can get a job. I don't care if you approve or not that I've been having sex with her. It's wartime, dammit! Things are different. My wife is so damn proper! She puts the light out when I have to have it." He laughs wryly. "This chippy is a live wire. She could go on the stage with the way she puts herself out there, dancing and singing. You've been in the theater. So you know how to do her up. You're not a homo for nothing! Anyhow, I'm your sergeant and that's an order!" The two men smile, in spite of their difference.

Ernst had found a short, off the shoulder, satin dress colored sky blue, with matching long gloves. He wishes he could wear it himself. But that was an impossible fantasy for a soldier in the German army. But now there is a chance for him to express his nature, at least for an hour or two. The girl has such beautiful long eyelashes. With the eyelash brush he makes them darker and longer. Julie is fascinated. She likes being made up and being taught how to do it. If her father could see her now he would have a fit; could die of it! She loses her smile. He is dead. Her mother too. She suddenly feels desolate again and throws her arms around Ernst's legs and holds onto him as if to never to let go.

The sergeant is sitting in a lounge chair in the dressing gown he's found. He watches at first. Then he drinks from one of the beer bottles they've scavenged. He closes his eyes. His breathing deepens. Making war is wearying.

Julie asks Ernst every question that comes into her head. He is glad to enlighten her. He sees that she'd been kept as ignorant as a dumbbell. He tells her she could become pregnant and have a baby inside her if she lets the sergeant have sex with her as he has been doing every night. "You know about that, don't you?"

"I . . I'm not sure. Is it the milk he puts in me?"

"You should have some protection. That's what it's called. Girls put the thing inside, like a stopper, to prevent the 'milk', as you call it, from going up too far. I really don't know too much about it. You should find an experienced woman to explain things to you."

Ernst combs out her long blonde hair, then uses a pomade to make the hair sleek over her head. It's one of the fashions of the day in Germany. From the neck down he fluffs out her hair with a brush until it is full of air and wavy. Oh, God! What is he doing being a soldier! He would curse Hitler, except that that would get him shot. The style doesn't damage her beauty, but it does make her seem older than her 14 years.

"How old do you think I am, Ernst?"

"Oh, my! I really don't know, Julie."

"Well, I think I'm quite grown up now. Sort of going on seventeen, perhaps," she giggles.

"Sure, Julie. You're quite a girl."

Ernst does her nails, paints them bright red, as is the fashion. He tells her of his ambition to own a Beauty Salon devoted to making girls and women beautiful and sexy.

"What is sexy?" Julie asks.

"What a big question!" Ernst exclaims. "I'll try to explain. You move like a snake, you breathe like a soft wind, you smile with a smile that might mean almost anything, you dress to tantalize, you are bright, even a bit noisy, then you are sultry and quiet, you open your lips, you bejewel yourself, you glance at men, the rich and the famous. Do it right and a king may snap you up! It's happened! Oh! If I were a girl I would do it so well!"

He plucks her eyebrows, making them more arched and thinner. He applies a foundation to her face, uses a black eye-liner and paints her eyelids a powdery blue, then follows with rouges and lip stick. He is careful not to overdo it. He aims rather to bring out her natural beauty. He explains that to her. He shows her how to use everything and has her do the applications herself. He is a good teacher. "Be meticulous, Julie. You know what meticulous means?"

"No, I don't think so."

"Meticulous means taking care to do things right, being a bit fussy. When things have to be done right, you do them right and you are unhappy unless you have done them right. The saying 'the devil is in the details' is absolutely true for a girl's make-up."

"Oh! I want to do things right!"

"And be the best you can be, too, Julie."

"Yes! I'll do things right and be the best I can be! Oh! You are just great, Ernst! I love you! Can I stay with you? You are my best friend."

Ernst winces and wishes he could re-assure her. But the sergeant had told him they would be coming into Paris and have to let her go. He doesn't quite know what to say, so he goes on teaching her.

"To finish, Julie, you use a powder puff, like this." Ernst shows her how to use the big puff. "The powder sets the make-up and gives your face a softened look. Practice in front of a mirror. It's what they say - practice, practice, practice.

Understand? I'm sure you do, you're a smart girl. You can use the powder puff all over your body. The showgirls in cabarets powder their whole body! I've helped them. Being pretty is a girl's asset. Perhaps especially now and especially for you, Julie. This is a dangerous time. Men are attracted and generous to pretty girls. Be nice to them and they'll protect you. It's just the way it is. We all have to fit in as best we can." Ernst sighs. He doubts he will ever fit in.

Julie is quite nude as Ernst directs her in pulling on the silk stockings, the first stockings of any sort she's ever had, keeping the lines on the back of her legs straight. He shows her how to put on the frilly, lacy garter belt, and attach the pretty little clips to the top of the stockings. In one of the shops he has found some G-strings as well as panties. Julie tries on the G-strings and decides on one of them. Ernst tries to tell her that they are not the things girls normally wear. "I don't mind, Ernst. I think they're cute. And who is to know, eh!" and she puts a finger in the elastic band of the G-string and snaps it with a bright smile. Ernst grins. "You are some girl, Julie!"

Julie doesn't need the bra, it's too big for her small budding breasts. She draws the satin slip over her head. Seeing herself in the mirror, she likes the sight. Everything is different, her whole world, including how she looks.

Ernst brings her the blue dress. It fits her almost perfectly. She takes a needle and thread and makes small adjustments. Ernst is impressed. "You are talented, too!" he exclaims.

"The seamstress in my father's shop taught me how to sew," she tells him.

Ernst has picked up earrings, necklaces, bracelets, broaches, even a gold chain anklet, as they came through the devastated towns. He didn't think of himself as a thief. Everything was in disarray. Many of the houses were in ruins, some on fire. The good stuff, he told himself, should not go to waste.

The two of them have fun with Julie trying on the jewelry. She loves a pair of long dangly earrings with amethysts. Ernst exclaims, "Oh! Those are very daring, Julie! Perhaps too fast for you."

"I don't care. I like them," Julie cries, bobbing her head, making the dangles glint and dance. She has no idea what "too fast" means. She has a new confidence in herself. The sergeant obviously likes her and has been, in his own way, protective and kind to her. She has liked being intimate with him and is determined not to care about what anyone else may think. Ernst is her friend. There is no one except herself to make decisions for her. So she will make them. But she wants to make the right decisions, even in small things. She seeks Ernst's advice. "What shoes should I wear?"

After looking over the collection, Ernst chooses a pair with three inch thin heels, and pretty little ankle straps. When she stands up she is so tall! Ernst puts the gold chain round one of her ankles. It's so pretty there! As he does so he tells her that she should have her ears pierced. The dangles she has on are clip-ons; but every fashionable girl, he tells her, has her ears pierced and there are better fashions in pierced earrings than in clip-ons.

Julie goes to where she has put down her fur coat, muff, and toque hat. She puts them on. Ernst lifts her long blonde hair over the back of the fur coat. It falls in a bright golden cascade almost to her waist. She is such a doll! He loves it. That's how he would be if he was a girl.

The sergeant stirs, opens his eyes. Julie is standing before the mirror, posing herself, now with the muff over her hands, then twirling it and opening her arms out wide.

"Goddam!" the sergeant mutters, feeling his cock stiffen again. "Julie," he calls to her, "come here." She stands before him. "My God, you are beautiful! OK! Ernst has been teaching you things, hasn't he?"

"Oh, yes! He's taught me a lot, it's wonderful!" Then she adds, a little shyly, "and about being sexy. Am I sexy?" she asks, posing herself again, quite gracefully, but a little awkwardly.

The sergeant grins. He is not a bad man; just another human being caught up in the maelstrom of war. "Damn right! You are sexy, Julie. I'll teach you something. Come here and kneel between my legs."

He opens the bathrobe to reveal his stiffening cock. "You have had it in your body, Julie. Now you take it in your mouth. Put your hands around it. Kiss the end of it. Put your lips over it. Now suck it into your mouth. Let it go all the way in."

The sergeant talks in short breaths as the delicious feeling of the girl's mouth about his cock swamps his nervous system. His wife would never do such a thing. "What? Suck that dirty thing? Oh, no!" she'd cried. The sergeant likes it, too, that Julie is dressed and in furs and toque hat. A girl like Julie seems to know or, at least, is learning that sex is, first and foremost, for pleasure, not babies. Something his wife had never learned. Well, that's what girls like Julie were for. That she is pleasuring him, in this time and place, with the killing going on around them, their own lives in danger, restores a balance to things in his mind. He murmurs to her, "I like you as you are, Julie. A pretty girl, in fine clothes, doing what girls do. You please me, Julie, you do."

Julie by now understands that, for all his nice words, she has no choice. The sergeant is her protector, at least for the moment, and she only has thoughts for the moment. She must please him. It crosses her mind that other girls might not do what she is doing. Her father, she's sure, would have beaten her. But he's dead. She's on her own. It doesn't matter what other girls do. They aren't here. Anyhow they might do exactly what she's doing. The sergeant is telling her to bob her head up and down, use her tongue, rub the base of his penis with her fingers, still in the gloves. He says, "those are pretty gloves you have on, Julie. I like that." He strokes her face, her hair, the fur around her shoulders. "It's a nice fur, Julie. I'm glad you have it. You are beautiful in it."

Sucking the sergeant's stiff penis doesn't amount to much, Julie thinks. It's just something, she supposes, that girls get used to doing. His penis grows and stiffens in her mouth. His body convulses and heaves. He holds her head tightly over his loins, his penis down her throat. She would have cried out, but she can't. She can hardly breathe. His gush comes. The milk pulses down her throat. She swallows desperately, dizzy and gagging. The sergeant withdraws, then holds her to him as she struggles for breath. He tells her, with a broad grin, that she has given up her second virginity. "Just one to go!" he says, but she doesn't understand. She shudders and trembles, but then smiles. The sergeant was so strong! She has pleased him, that's obvious. She is glad to be learning that. She has to survive. If she has to suck men's cock to do that, then she will suck men's cocks.

They enter Paris from the northeast coming down the road from Meaux in the early morning of Monday June 17. The Germans have been in Paris for three days and have restored some order.

By ten in the morning the sergeant and his squad are passing *Le Bourget* airport in their vehicles. There are many wrecked planes and some new German planes on the tarmac, mostly three-engined Junker 52 transports. As they come nearer to Paris they see more and more German soldiers. The sergeant and his men are exuberant. No one had expected such an easy conquest of France. Only Britain remains and they will soon be invaded or, if they are sensible, sue for peace. Then they can all go home. That's what the sergeant tells Julie.

Julie is excited too, especially when the top of the Eiffel tower comes into view. She is wondering what she might do. Perhaps someone in Paris will help her. The sergeant has told her that they have to let her off before they go on to their designated arrival point in the *Bois de Vincennes*. As best the sergeant can tell from his map, they will go along *Boulevard de Sebastopol* to the river *Seine* and then turn left to reach the *Bois*.

Ernst had been in Paris as a boy. When the sergeant asks him the best place to leave the girl off, he suggests near *Porte St. Denis*. "There are many bistros and shops and clothing stores around there. She's quite a seamstress and she could get work there, or as a waitress or a shop girl. Sergeant, I feel so sorry for her. Perhaps we can find a French woman we can give her to."

"Maybe. But we can't take her any further. Our officer has forbidden it. So we'll let her off where you suggest and hope for the best for her."

Julie had undressed that night to sleep. When she wakes up she puts on the dress and clothes she'd had on the night before with the sergeant and Ernst. Ernst had scavenged a small suitcase for her, large enough to contain the few things she now has. She does her make-up, repeating what she'd done with Ernst. Perhaps she has overdone it, she thinks, looking in the car mirrors. It can't be helped. She'll do better next time.

They are riding in their half-track. When they reach *Porte St. Denis* they stop. "This is it, Julie," the sergeant says. "Here - here's some money for you. It's not much. I hope it will see you through until you can find a job."

Ernst is almost in tears as he helps Julie arrange her fur coat and toque hat. He tells her he thinks it best if she keeps her hair inside the coat. "Not to draw too much attention." He looks around to spot someone who can help the girl. But there are few people about and they are scurrying along, head down.

Ernst is realizing, with some remorse and thinking himself stupid, that a pretty young girl in a fur coat in this part of Paris will draw eyes like a magnet. "Walk quickly to that bistro over there," he tells her; "buy a drink and some food and ask about jobs." He hugs her and says "*bonne chance*" then backs away, feeling bad, wishing it could be otherwise.

The sergeant tells him, "Come on, get on board, Ernst; we have to go; the girl will be all right. She's a survivor."

They all wave goodbye as she stands on the sidewalk holding her little case.

Julie takes a deep breath. She thinks: "Well, here starts my new life." She sets off to the bistro 50 meters away with quick little steps in her high heels.

Entering the bistro Julie sits at a table. The place is almost deserted. Only two older women are seated at the back. They look at her and nod their heads. One puts her finger to her nose and says something with a knowing smirk. An elderly waiter comes over to Julie. She tells him she would like coffee and a croissant.

He eyes her, surprised and curious. "You're a stranger here? I have not seen you before, have I?"

"No. I've just come in. I'm looking for work, perhaps as a waitress," Julie tells him, tense, trying to keep calm.

Bernard, that's the waiter's name, continues to look at her as if she is some sort of apparition. "So, *m'amselle*...you can be thankful it's early. We have some croissants and coffee. God knows what is going to happen to us with the Germans here...perhaps I'll kill myself..."

"Oh, no! Don't do that!" Julie cries.

"No, I won't, not really," Bernard gives her a crinkly smile. "Don't worry. I fought in the last war and came through. We must survive, somehow. We do what we have to do, you know. It's nice to talk to a young French girl like you. I'll fetch your croissant and coffee."

Risé Mayon enters the bistro and seats herself at a table. Bernard greets her as a person well known to him.

As soon as she has sat down Risé's gaze fixes on the startlingly pretty young girl in a fur coat and cocktail dress with her face overly made-up. Being in the business she's in, she has to investigate. Chances like this do not come along every day! And what a day! The first work day in their conquered city. Already there are decrees and curfews being imposed. They all have to be sharp. The Germans say they will be well behaved. Well, that was to be seen. *Mon Dieu!* That she should live to see this day!

Bernard brings Julie coffee and a croissant and talks to her again. When Bernard comes by Risé, she stops him. "Who is she, Bernard? Do you know her?"

"No, she just came in. Seems a country girl to me, in spite of her looks. She's looking for work as a waitress. You employ waitresses, don't you?"

"Yes, we do, Bernard."

Risé allows herself a moment of amusement. What a waste to employ such a gorgeous creature as a waitress!

She goes over to Julie. "*Bonjour, m'amselle.* May I sit with you?"

"Yes, please."

"Bernard, the waiter, tells me you are looking for work. I am Risé Mayon and live near here. Your name?"

"Julie - Julie Rossinger. Would you be able to help me?"

"Oh, yes! I think so. Am I right in thinking I saw you saying good bye to those German soldiers?"

"Yes. I was alone. Everyone had been killed or fled. It was terrible, *madame.* The soldiers were kind to me and brought me here with them."

"I see. How long were you with them?"

"A week, I think. I sort of lost track of time."

"Your parents?'

"They are dead."

"Have you any papers to show who you are?"

"No. The house had fallen down from the guns and was on fire. Nobody could get in. I ran away."

"You said the Germans were good to you. Did they give you these clothes?"

"Yes. They were very kind. I helped them too. I can sew and I mended their uniforms."

"I can tell you are a very nice girl, Julie. Tell me, were you private with any of them?"

"Private? I suppose. I had two friends. Ernst who had been in the theater. He wasn't like the others. Sort of gentle. He taught me about make-up and clothes."

"And the other?"

"Oh, yes, the sergeant. He made me his special friend, I suppose you can say. I understood I had to please him. He was in charge."

"And you did please him?"

"Yes. He seemed very pleased. He gave me some money just now. He was a nice man. But not so nice as Ernst."

"I see. And you have no one here to go to or who you know?"

"No. When I left everyone had gone. Perhaps they are dead, like my parents. I don't know. It doesn't seem to matter to anymore." Julie's face began to crumble. Her shoulders slumped. She wiped away the tears in her eyes.

Risé put her arm around the girl. "It's terrible, Julie. But you are here now and you have to make the best of it."

Julie nodded. "I know, *madame.*"

"Cheer up, Julie, we are both in luck." Risé smiles at her. "You've found me and I can help you. My house is down the street here. We can walk to it."

Until Risé actually had Julie in *Les Poulets* she couldn't be absolutely sure of her good fortune. The girl was almost too good to be true. Risé blessed her habit of leaving the house in the morning, when most were asleep except for the house staff, to have a few minutes away from it all at the Bistro. She was the *sous-directrice* (assistant manager) at *Les Poulets*, working for *Madame* Céline Guyton, the owner and *La Directrice*.

Risé had long been in the business, starting when she was 17 in a house in Bordeaux. Then a customer had married her, but he proved to be a no-good and landed in prison. She divorced him and went back to work in the commerce she knew best, as a manager this time. After being in the naval town of Toulouse for a while - naval towns and ports are the sure-fire sites for establishments - a customer had told her there was an opening for an assistant manager at the famous *Les Poulets* on *rue Blondel* in Paris. She came to Paris and was hired on. In her two years there she had become well established and, with her business acumen and good rapport with the girls and customers, had increased the trade considerably. So much so that *Madame* Guyton had bought the next door building. They needed the extra rooms to house the girls and for customer service.

That morning, like Risé Mayon, Céline Guyton had been an early riser. She had to know what was happening. She was not one to ride against the times she found herself in. The Germans had informed her that *Les Poulets* would be reserved for officers, officials, and others of sufficient rank. The men would be German, Italian, and men of their war time allies together with higher class Frenchmen who collaborated and were in good standing. The German officer said she could expect, therefore, an increase rather than a decrease in her commerce,. They grinned together over their glasses of cognac.

It would be no great change, Céline Guyton thought. *Les Poulets* had serviced the upper tiers in society - diplomats, military officers, visitors who stayed at the upper class hotels, etc. - for many decades. They were used to Roll-Royces, Minervas, Mercedes-Benz, Cadillacs, Daimlers driving up the narrow *rue Blondel* to their door and discharging men. They had never lacked for men of distinction, even royals. *Les Poulets* had its doormen to usher the guests in and out and to maintain security. Unacceptables were dealt with by them, strong armed when necessary. The Germans, she was sure, would cooperate in maintaining the standards of her establishment. It was in their interest to do so. The German officer had assured her of that. It was good news to put with all the bad.

Céline Guyton's immediate difficulty was that some girls had fled, leaving before the Germans came. She had tried to keep *les nigaudes* (the nincompoops), but some girls, as she said to Risé, have no brains and answer only to their fears. They would be short handed until she could find replacements. So finding new girls was a top priority.

Risé had been on the lookout, but she had to contend with the upheaval of everything and the panic on the streets. Now, she had found one girl to replace those she had lost, at least she hoped so. The signs were good. Heavens! This new one already had "the look" in her theatrical make-up, dress, and expensive furs, and she was a gorgeous, shapely, golden blonde! From what she'd said a German soldier had been teaching her how to look and act as *une fille*[26]. From the girl's own account, as far as Risé could make out, she had been having sex with the sergeant and been given the clothes and paid money for her services.

Whatever difficulties there might be with the authorities could be overcome, Risé is sure. She'd have the girl registered. It was one of her specialties. Another specialty was having a girl adjust to her new circumstances. Risé could never tell for sure until a girl had actually been put to work.

These thoughts race through her mind as she pays for Julie's coffee and croissant. Julie shows her the compact that Ernst had found for her, containing mascara brush, rouge, powder puff, and lipstick. "That's very nice, Julie. Use them now. A girl does that after eating and before she goes out. Take it from me. I know. That's right. Now the lipstick. Your friend had good taste in choosing your things for you. Powder your face. There, that's right. Now you are a Paris girl! Beautiful!"

---

[26] Prostitutes have innumerable names in France. The politest and most common is *"fille."* It is short for *"fille de joie."* The word also means daughter and any girl in general, so its particular meaning must be extracted from context.

They would be seen going to *Les Poulets* and Risé was ever aware of marketing. This girl was a "looker." The news would spread. If all went well, being seen now would give the girl a good start.

Outside the door of the bistro Risé tells Julie, "put down your case and let me see your hair." Risé lifts the torrent of golden tresses out over the back of the fur coat. "Lovely, my dear!" She arranges the girl's hat on her head. "I will carry your case, Julie. Put your hands in your muff and walk beside me daintily, taking short steps. Keep your hands in the muff. It's more stylish and you want to be a stylish girl."

Julie does as she's told. She won't displease the woman who is helping her. And, she supposes, all Paris girls walk with short steps in shoes like the ones she has on and keep their hands in muffs, not like country girls running around in the fields and throwing their arms every which way. There were no fields here.

They cross the road at *Porte St. Denis*. The huge stone gateway impresses Julie. She feels she's in an important place. They start down *rue St. Denis* and shortly turn left along *rue Blondel*. Five story buildings are on either side, overhanging the narrow street. Daylight filters down into the chasm above their heads. Risé holds Julie's arm. She is not about to lose her find, even if the girl does not seem in the least reluctant. There are a few men standing around and they gaze at Julie appraisingly. Julie notices some saucily clad girls lounging on the narrow sidewalks and in the doorways. One greets Risé. *"Bonjour - tu as une nouvelle, Risé, eh? Bonne chance, petite!"* (Good day - you have a new one, Risé, eh? Good luck, little one!)

They pass under a canopy that hangs over a shiny red door with polished metal fittings. By its side is a brass plate with *Les Poulets* inscribed on it, along with an etching of a dancing girl with a cute little chicken at her feet. The door is rimmed with glowing red panels. By the side of the door a notice board reads, *"Ouvert à midi. Officiers militaires bienvenus. Prix reduit 12-18 hrs. Belles filles vous attendent, messieurs."* [27]

For Julie it's just another bit of the jumble that is around her and she hardly notices it. They continue on. Julie's lush lynx coat sways about her lithe body as she negotiates an unevenness in the narrow *trottoir* (sidewalk). The men and girls nearby look at the young blonde chicken. They all know what's happening. It's normal.

Risé spots some German soldiers at the end of the street. She's tempted to go up to them and, if they are officers, make a sales pitch. But no. First she has to get the girl inside and close the door behind her. But it was good to know that Germans had found their way to *rue Blondel*. There would be plenty more, she was sure. They were men away from home, natural customers. The soldiers would be having the street girls, while the officers would be welcome in *Les Poulets*.

In a few more paces they come to an iron door set at the foot of a high windowless brick wall. Risé takes out a complicated looking key from her bag and puts it into the cruciform lock. "It's part of our security, Julie. Our girls must be safe."

They enter a short, passageway that leads to the front of the main house and *Madame* Guyton's office. They enter a small salon. "Sit here, Julie. I won't be long. I'll see if the *directrice* can see you right away." Now that the girl is safely inside, with the door locked behind her, Risé starts to treat the matter as *un fait accompli*.

Julie has never been in a room like this. The walls are covered from floor to ceiling in a patterned maroon damask. There are no windows. Gilt mirrors and electric lights in bronze sconces are on the walls. The furniture is curvy and gilt; the seats of the chairs and high back sofas match the damask on the walls. On one wall is a large picture of a beautiful nude girl posed languorously on a fancy couch.

---

[27] "Open at midday. Military officers welcome. Reduced price from 12 to 6. Beautiful girls await you, gentlemen."

Julie seats herself on a sofa and steadies herself by taking deep breaths. What is this place?

A man enters through a doorway, made to look like a part of the damask wall. He is a waiter carrying a tray with coffee and patisseries. "*Madame* Guyton will be with you in a minute, *m'amselle*," he tells Julie. "Do you wish anything?"

"No, thank you," Julie says, still looking around. "Please tell me where I am?"

"You will be told. You may take off your coat, *m'amselle*. It is not cold in here."

He is being friendly toward her and Julie is grateful for that. She feels vaguely anxious, but not intimidated. She must make the best of whatever is happening.

Madame Guyton enters, Risé trailing her. She is a lady of fifty, dressed in a loosely tailored suit, smart, manicured, rather imposing, but friendly too. She is immediately effusive.

"My dear girl, how beautiful you are! I am so glad *Madame* Mayon found you. Paris is in a terrible state! You could have come to so much harm. Your name, dear child?"

"Julie, *madame*. Julie Rossinger."

"Ah, yes, Juliette. Juliette is such a pretty name. Now! You have been with some German soldiers. First our nurse and then our doctor will examine you to see that you have come to no harm and are not making babies! Though it is too soon for that, isn't it? At least I imagine so." She smiles. "The doctor will be here this afternoon. We practice good health and hygiene here. My girls are always clean. You wish to say something, Juliette?"

Julie summons up her courage, though already sensing that there is no way out. It feels like being back in school and having to do what she is told. "Yes, *madame*. I don't know where I am. Is it some sort of school? It's all new and strange to me. I've never been in a city before. I've lost all my family. My German friends let me off here. I feel lonely and . . . and . . . " Julie begins to cry, her tears coursing down her rouged cheeks.

"Oh - - my angel girl," *Madame* Guyton cries as she comes to Julie and sits beside her. "Quick! A handkerchief for the girl, Risé!"

Madame Guyton soothes Julie as only she knows how. She has comforted many girls in her lifetime in the business. It's part of the job.

Julie recovers. *Madame* Guyton holds her hands. "Dear girl, everything is in a state with the war and the Germans coming in. No one knows what will happen. Some Frenchmen are still shooting and the Germans are shooting them. The streets are dangerous, especially for a beautiful young girl like you. Girls are being raped all over the place! You may thank the good lord that you have found a refuge here. I will look after you and see no one harms you. Understand?"

"Yes, *madame*, and thank you. Please tell me what I am to do. Will I be a waitress?

"No, not exactly. You are too good and beautiful to be just a waitress. I am very plain with my girls, right from the very start, so that there will be no misunderstanding. You have been having sex with your German friends. Is that not so?"

"Yes, *madame*, I think so. With the sergeant. He was kind to me, they all were."

"And they gave you food and drink, looked after you as best they could, found clothes and pretty things for you and gave you money."

"Yes, Ernst and the sergeant did."

"There we are then! You continue doing that here. You will be looked after and rewarded for having sex with the men who come here. You were right in thinking that here it is something like a school. We teach you how to look after yourself, how to dress and use cosmetics, how to be charming and attractive, how to please men and have sex with them. Some men say we are like a finishing school for girls! I think that's exactly right!"

Julie nods her head. What *madame* had said made sense. Well, if she has to do this sex thing, she'll do it. It is obviously a well established form of work and seemed to be a good money business from what she had seen so far. Ernst and the sergeant had actually been preparing her for the job, whether they realized it or not. Well, thank you both! She is thankful to have found work so quickly.

Madame continues. "It's the way of the world, Juliette. I can't explain everything, no one can. To couple is a law of life. All the animals do it and we do it too. We all know that coupling produces babies, but sex is much more than that. It's one of our greatest pleasures and, therefore, men pay for it, like they pay for going to the theater. Actually it's a necessity for men. They go mad and do bad things without it. So what we do is a public service, we help stop bad things from happening. Well - enough of that. You're here now and we must set about getting you started."

Julie thinks she should say something. Ah! What about being paid?

"*Madame*, please tell me about being paid. I know people are paid for working."

Madame Guyton smiles. "I am glad you asked that, Juliette. Yes. You are paid. First you are paid in kind. That is you live and sleep here as your home and you are fed good food. We provide you with basic clothes and after that you buy your own clothes from the women who come here with the clothes for you to wear. As to actual money. For every service you provide to a gentleman you are paid an amount depending on the particular service provided. All the gentlemen who come here know that it is customary to tip the girls and some are very generous tippers. That money you keep for yourself. Do you understand?"

"Oh, yes! I worked in my father's drapery shop and was the cashier sometimes. I know about money."

"Good girl! You will fit in here very well, I'm sure. I will be as plain as I can with you. Life is real, not a fairy story.

Your opportunity is to work here, be well looked after, fed and clothed, and be safe. If you go out there, on the street, most likely you will be mauled and raped, maybe finish up in the gutter. Your choice is to stay here and be a success. You are an intelligent girl and you have seen enough to know that what I say is true and that I only wish the best for you. We won't talk about it anymore. We have to move on."

Madame Guyton stands up. "Give her room three in the attic, Risé, pair her up with Michelle. Take her to the nurse. Make sure the doctor sees her this afternoon."

"Yes, *madame*. She's clearly underage and has no papers. That actually makes it simple. We invent her and her age!"

"You know how to do these things, Risé. Get going. I suppose the police and city offices will be open. Who knows! In the meantime get her ready, teach her what she needs to know, have her meet the other girls, find her clothes to wear. But give her time to adjust. With any luck we have a keeper here. OK?"

They are talking as if Julie isn't there, arranging a business matter between themselves.

"Yes, *madame*. I will have her ears pierced too."

Well, that's what Ernst had said should be done, Julie recalls. Not that she needs any more persuasion. What *Madame* Guyton has been saying is clearly true. She would be lost outside.

Chapter 11.

Les Poulets, Paris. 1940-43.

Madame Guyton chooses *Juliette LaPerle* for her name. She had thought of *Juliette La Douce,* but that had become too hackneyed. The girl's fair skin and golden hair reminded her of a pearl and she had thought that Botticelli would have liked her as a model. She frowns as she thinks of the Italians invading southern France, like hyenas after the scraps left over from the German victory. She supposes some swaggering Italians would be coming to *Les Poulets.* Such is war. No matter. She will make them pay top price.

Risé creates Julie as *Mademoiselle Juliette LaPerle,* aged 18, with her birthday the 14th of July, Bastille day. The name Rossinger must be erased completely to avoid any possible tracing of the girl. She will come on the scene as if from nowhere, without a past. Risé keeps the birthday as a selling point with Frenchmen and, indeed, she is planning to have Julie's first sale, her *Début,* on that day. She will hold an auction for established customers, all older men, of course, who can afford a good price. Older men are much the best clients for *Les Poulets.* Almost all have family and other ties to the outside and visit the house for recreation. There is very little danger of them falling "in love" with a girl in a serious way. They may, of course, develop a particular liking for a girl, but that is all. Anything more is exceptional, almost an aberration, even though it happens occasionally.

For the début occasion, the girl is to be a virgin. Risé will use the old trick of a rubber O-ring for the hymen and a quail egg filled with blood from the kitchen. She'd had it done to herself when she was starting out and, since then, has created virgins of any number of well used girls. The egg is put into the girl's vagina, then the O-ring. The man can feel the "hymen" give way. Then he will break the egg by his thrusts and the blood will flow. Very convincing! Gullible men believe what they want to believe! Risé is always charming to the men, of course. God has made them slaves to their testosterone, not her. Thank you, Lord! She's made a good living off men.

So Julie will be, officially, three years older than she actually is, and therefore of age to work in a brothel. Juliette has no place of birth because, on the instructions of Risé, she doesn't know where she had been born. Yes, Juliette will say, she has lived only in France. They had always been on the move. She'd seen her parents killed by German gun fire.

In a few days Juliette has her identity certificate and her "papers", "papers" being essential in France. After seeing the registrar in City Hall and being registered, Risé takes her to the police station where Juliette is further registered and certified as a prostitute at *Les Poulets*. Juliette affirms that she is there of her own free will and that's that. The only cost, outside of some government fees, is for the registrar and the police official to each have a free evening pass to *Les Poulets*. That procedure assures that Risé will not have any trouble in registering a girl in the future. Risé laughs with them about the steps they take to not let their wives know, inventing "official business" for those evenings.

At Juliette's auction *Madame* Guyton shows off the virgin to half-a-dozen older men. Such a delicious young beauty! *Madame* has her lightly gowned in a see-through pink negligee and nothing else. The men will be tantalized by the suggestive sight of her svelte body and budding breasts. *Madame* draws the negligee aside to display the light golden fuzz surrounding her plump slit. That draws a new burst of delighted gasps and bids from the half-dozen men there. Julie plays her role to perfection. She is shyly provocative, as if she yearns for a wonderful man to relieve her of her "chastity." It drives up her price. *Madame* couldn't be more pleased.

The high bidder of the auction has his appointment with Juliette on July14, a Sunday, her birthday. *Monsieur* Melech, a regular at *Les Poulets*, is 51, married, a broker on the *Bourse*. Being ruthless on the exchange, skirting the law as necessary, has its rewards. One of which is fucking prize virgins at *Les Poulets*. His routine with virgins is: affectionate foreplay, instruction, then lust and thrust.

Madame Guyton has no difficulty with him being a Jew. Jews are welcome at *Les Poulets* as long as they are not Hasidic or similar fundamentalists. Those Jews, in her experience, besides being first class hypocrites, wear smelly clothes and don't wash properly.

At *Les Poulets* Melech can be sure the girl has been registered as a prostitute and therefore is willing and of legal age, even if the girl is actually underage, and that no harm can come to him. *Madame* Guyton is strict about registration, he knows, and that is all that matters.

His wife thinks nothing of his forays to *Les Poulets*. It is a part of French life; something that French women put up with. Michelle, Julie's roommate, with five years in the business, grins. "If and when I am a wife, I suppose I will put up with it too! And so will you, Julie!" They laugh at the thought, however distant it seems.

For his average build Melech has an out-sized cock, some 10 inches long and over an inch thick when fully erect and engorged. It quite startles Juliette. He takes his time with her, enjoying the slow build-up and eventually is fully lodged up to the hilt in her young body. She is rather amazed she can accommodate the thing. But nature has, over some four million years, prepared the female body for such invasions.

Melech fucks Julie in a number of positions. He has her kneeling on the bed so he can do her "doggie" fashion while he puffs on a cigar and sips a glass of brandy, being served to him by the maid who attends to his needs.

"You're a bitch, a fucking lovely bitch!" he cries.

Then he has her on her back to pump her with long strokes before eventually ejaculating into her with loud cries. Following Risé's instructions Julie also is crying out with "Ohs!" and "Aaaaghs!" and moans and sobs, her mouth wide open. Then she weeps real tears at the climax. Not that it really hurt her. It is just a relief to get it over with and realize she is still OK. No damage done.

Quite against his principles, for Melech believes he is proof against falling for a "chippy", he cries out, "I adore you, Juliette! I must have you again!" He pants and waits for his breath to return. "Good, Juliette, very good! Now that you are no longer a virgin I will send men to you and then come myself again. I certainly like virgins, but I also like a well fucked girl. You are a peach, a strawberry, a glass of vodka all rolled into one! When *Madame* tells me you've had fifty men, I will have another *rendez-vous* with you."

"Thank you, Melech," Julie says, not knowing what else to say.

Madame, intermittently, has been looking in and is well pleased with the new girl. The novice has been well fucked and taken it with no apparent problem. She sees a bright future for her.

"As I thought, Risé, she's a natural. It's strange how some girls are and others would rather die. She's a money girl, I'm sure of it!"

Melech tips her a f100 note[28]. Julie is amazed, struck dumb, at its size. It is far more than she had expected. It is more than her father's drapery store profit was most weeks and he worked long wearisome hour. At the same time Julie has no trouble understanding what is happening. People pay for what they want. Selling sex is no different from selling clothes and the better she does it, the better off she will be. Far better off! But she keeps her head. For Melech to give her that much money must be normal for him. So she shouldn't act totally surprised.

"Oh, thank you, thank you, Melech!" she enthuses, giving him a parting kiss; then tucking the note into the top of her stocking.

Thus, being the sensible girl she is, Julie puts aside any thought of leaving *Les Poulets*, something that she has considered, but only as a possibility. Any thought of leaving seems altogether stupid, especially now that the Germans have begun to shoot hostages in revenge for the shooting of German soldiers. Who knew who would be taken hostage and shot? With French resistance becoming active, the Germans have started to think that every French man and woman is a potential resistance fighter. Not that it is really the case, but some German commanders are paranoid about it. That's what *Madame* has said when she tells her girls to watch themselves when talking with their German customers or, even, the French who are collaborating with them. Best to not say anything about what is happening outside to avoid raising the slightest suspicion that they approve of the resistance, whatever their feelings might be. Actually that is hardly a problem. In their line of work, the girls dissemble all the time. So, Julie decides, she will do the

---

[28] The franc was worth about $2 US at the beginning of the war. Thus, Julie's tip would have been about $200 which, in 21st century money, would be worth about $800. So it was a handsome tip, but not unusual for girls to receive in the best houses from rich clients. It was said that King Edward VII of England tipped the girl who served him at *La Chabanais* with a f1000 note. Whether true or not, it was widely believed.

work as best she can, like Ernst had told her, not think about it very much, and earn lots of money.

Juliette's "teething period," as Risé names the first week or so of a new girl, goes easily. *Madame* Guyton tells Risé to take care not to rush her. Nothing should spoil her beauty. In her first week Juliette serves 14 men and does as well as any start-up girl that *Madame* Guyton recalls.

In a couple of months, with Juliette now wearing the cabaret style clothing with flair, with her hair and face done in "proper" brothel style, and performing all the sex stuff well, men are charged top franc for her.

Sundays are always busy days at *Les Poul*ets and it sort of amuses Julie. In her former life going to church on Sundays was something she'd had to do. She thought back, as she gazes at the ceiling while a man pumps her, to the time when she'd been "confirmed" with other girls in white dresses and told she was now an adult in the eyes of God. After it had happened, she didn't think about God anymore than she had before. She supposed there was a God, everybody said so. But outside of church no one paid much attention, so neither did she.

"Oh! Ooooh - chéri! That was so good! You are such a lover! Such a man! Be sure to come back and love me again - darleeng!" Julie has quickly learned the basic words and techniques of the successful prostitute.

Julie has one day a week off when she can stay in her room or find her way by the back stairs to the kitchen and be a scullery worker for the cooks. *Madame* at first disapproves, but soon sees how much the girl enjoys being with the kitchen staff. The cooks tell *Madame* that Julie deals with the rabbits and the chickens when they arrive as well as any of them. She peels potatoes and dresses the asparagus spears with a deft hand. She has to wear kitchen gloves, of course, to protect her long painted nails and her fair skin. Julie catches up her hair up in a napkin and wears no make-up, letting her skin sweat in the kitchen heat. She is sure it is healthy. She plays and laughs with the others there and is always a little sad when the day ends. But she well understands that she isn't paid nor receives tips as a scullery maid.

Madame Guyton tells every girl she is *"une professionnelle"* and not to forget it. She does not keep girls who do not perform. Men complaining that a girl has not "put out", not given the satisfaction they have paid for, means a girl is heading for the exit. Following her decision to stay, Julie like everyone else sees ever more clearly that, in the midst of the war, with shortages in everything, and the German and French police treating people brutally, to lose her job at *Les Poulets* would be a disaster.

Hence, after her day off, Julie is a luxurious *fille*, costumed, coiffed, eye-lashed, rouged, painted, powdered and perfumed, and available for "love" with any man who comes in, has the money, and is "acceptable." For a man to be acceptable includes no sign of skin disorder or symptom of venereal disease. The girls are instructed in what venereal disease looks like. Also to be acceptable, as *Madame* Guyton says, "the man must behave himself, even if he is drunk. Men meet other gentlemen here, not ruffians!"

Julie's name there, as far as her work is concerned, is Juliette. No problem. But she has let out that her nickname was Lutine and the girls and others are calling her that. *Lutine* suits her. She is quick and bouncy, ready to laugh, enjoying the games they play in the attic, like Blind Man's Bluff. She is popular, a friendly sort, always ready to share, having no snobby airs like some of the girls, while being exceptionally good at the work.

Risé had thought there might be trouble with the 15-year old because of her age. Well, one or two men indeed have upbraided *Madame* Guyton for employing underage girls like Juliette. *Madame* shows them the girl's police identity certificate and tells them, with a straight face, that she is fortunate to have a girl who seems so young. A religious hypocrite, who had fucked Juliette like the others, tells *Madame* it is a sin in the eyes of God! She tells him to stuff it in no uncertain terms and she and Risé laugh about it over their glasses of brandy. In any case he had paid the fee, just like the rest.[29]

Julie takes up sewing. It is something to do between sessions as they wait on slow afternoons. Her specialty is satin G-strings. She makes them for herself and for the other girls and charges ten francs each for them. They are in every style; some plain, some with tassels or beads. She works too on her costumes. By looking at photos and the sex magazines she soon has an excellent idea of what appeals to men. The costumes range from the barely covered, to the feathery and sparkling creations of the *Folies Bergères*, to the elegant cut-away evening gown. She develops a positive addiction for long shoulder length satin gloves to go with her long satin gowns with a narrow waist and revealing *décolleté*. She has also developed quite a passion for furs. The furs remind her of the rabbits they had raised, how Ernst had clothed her in her first furs, and how the sergeant had liked her in them and told her she was sexy. She is too much of a practical girl to think about "why." She follows where her nature takes her and where she sees her fortune to be.

Juliette studies each phase of brothel work. She wants to be the best girl there, though she doesn't say that out loud. The work starts each day in her room when she wakes up, goes to the bathroom and then the "Beauty Salon."

---

[29] Up to that time it was not unusual to have teenage girls in brothels. An album of a Paris bordello in the early part of the 20th century advertised "*Dodo, 13 ans, en presence de sa tante.*" (Dodo, age 13, in the presence of her aunt.) (Fille de Joie, Grove Press, New York 1967.)

The identification of pedophilia as a psychiatric disorder and its legal standing as child abuse emerged in the 1920s and 30s, but was not fully recognized until the 1950s. In France the underage regulation existed, but had little effect until after the war. Pedophilia was well know in ancient Greece, mainly in the form of homosexuality and was considered desirable, the man teaching the boy masculine values, how to be a warrior, etc. For the next 2000 years pedophilia and child prostitution remained a constant in both advanced and primitive societies and, indeed, remains so in contemporary times. Teenage and younger girls are treated as erotic objects on the internet. In Thailand very young girls are readily available to tourists.

In the morning two maids bring *le petit déjeuner* (breakfast) up to the attic where the girls have their little rooms, barely separated by flimsy partitions. The new building, that had been next door and that is now connected to the main building, has a small elevator. That makes it much easier for everyone to cope with the five levels of the house and the kitchen and store rooms in the basement.

Some of the girls are habitually sleepy in the mornings, always yawning and slopping around. Others may have spent the night downstairs with a man. When the man is sexually aroused and has a succession of erections, they do not get too much sleep.

Madame Guyton has rules when the man is to have breakfast in the room with the girl. The girl, helped by a maid, goes to the bathroom by the room, does her hair and make-up and perfuming, dresses in stockings, slippers, and a flowing negligee. In ten minutes she must be done and greet the man in her restored beauty when he emerges from his bathroom. Along with having breakfast with him, she will respond to any sex wishes he may still have. As Julie discovers, virile men have erections almost automatically in the mornings. They can wake up at five or six with an erection and need the fuck. They go for their piss and then go to sleep again only to wake up three or four hour later with another erection. So a girl is often busy. But she makes extra money too.

As far as *Madame* Guyton is concerned, men can go elsewhere to find disheveled girls or girls in the nude without any style. Not that she rules out nudity. That can happen as appropriate and according to the man's wishes. But she has built her business on being stylish and her girls have to be just that, stylish. That becomes ingrained in Julie's mind and becomes her own standard for herself. She learns the word "*chic.*" She will be *chic.*

After breakfast the girls do their bathing and shaving. Some girls are waxing to be even more baby smooth. Men have their tastes; some like baby smooth, others a bush. The nurse, Béatrice, is very good with skin care and can help a girl with a skin problem, often better than the doctor. Her chief injunction is, "wash your face last thing at night before you put the night creams on. Else you will be nasty and pimply and no man will take you!"

When a girl needs a vaginal douche, Béatrice does it; and when a girl is having her period, Béatrice instructs her and, if necessary, see that she has time off. She helps any girl who feels ill or needs the doctor. But she has a sharp eye for malingerers and will laugh at their pretenses. "Get on with you, girl! This is not a sanatorium for your ladyship! Just think of those rich men you might meet!"

The girls go to the "Beauty Salon." That's what they call it, but it isn't much. Crowded along the walls of the small attic room are make-up tables with lights and glass counters. It's where the girls can attach their long eyelashes and do their make-up. It's always a squish and tempers can flare. On the other hand the girls help each other, talk out their thoughts and feelings, often laugh about the men, and relish the "love" affairs that are happening. They share things among themselves, like rouges and powders and such; but they also try to respect privacies. Living so close together requires a respect for privacy.

Then they dress, maybe there or in their room. *Madame* will designate certain girls to be ready for the house opening at midday. Those girls have to be in the Salon downstairs, on time, looking voluptuous in their dresses and costumes, always adorned with feathery boas to make them the chickens of *Les Poulets*. Some may wear feathered hats or use feathers in their costumes in imaginative ways. *Les Poulets* is famous for it.

Many days men are gathered by the front door waiting for the house to open. Risé is usually in charge of opening the doors and ushering the men in. She will see they pay at the *caisse* (cashier's desk) before they go to the salon to meet the chickens (*poulets*.) At lunch time she will have the chickens stand up and have the men choose between them.

Later in the day, men circulate among the girls who are seated or standing or at the bar. The girls must not be pushy. They must let the men choose them, not the other way round. However a smart girl, without being too obvious about it, can lure a man who takes her fancy or looks rich, with her extra smiles.

A man may go straight to a service room with his choice and she will be fucking with him in a minute or two. Some men can't wait. However, a man may sit with a girl in the salon and be served wine and *hors d'oeuvres*; or a man may opt for lunch served at a table at the end of the salon. Some men enjoy having lunch in a service room where he can have the girl sit with him with her clothes off, with bare breasts with her nipples rouged, even nude except for her stockings and shoes. *Madame* Guyton makes a point of catering to all tastes. Whenever possible she greets the men and may have a glass of wine or brandy with them. She can throw down a snifter of brandy as well as any man.

A room in the cellar at *Les Poulets* is fixed up as a medieval dungeon. *Minerve*, the dominatrix of the house, is severe with the "bad boys" there. After being astonished at what some men want, Julie persuades *Madame* to let her help *Minerve* in the work. *Minerve* soon has the intelligent girl properly corseted, booted, and costumed and treating the cowering men as they wish. Julie, putting aside her tender feelings, uses the leather whip much in the same way as her father had whipped her. She enjoys it, especially when the man is a big Prussian officer, who has a desperate need to be disciplined.

For their looks in the salon the girls take the fashions of the day, usually some form of draped look, and make it more revealing and sensual. As *Madame* tells them, "the men who come here don't want to meet their mothers, wives, sisters, girl friends or daughters. Remind the men of them and they will never choose you! No! They are here to meet '*les filles de joie*.' You must be their *fille de joie*; first for their eyes, then for their senses and finally for their bodies. That is your profession! Go to it, *mes poulets*!"

The skill of a girl lies in understanding a man's needs and tastes, responding to them, and carrying through to ecstatic fulfillment. A successful girl is exuberant, sultry, amusing, passionate, sympathetic, even a little shy and modest, at one time or another. It takes little time for Julie to understand this and to respond to the many tastes of the clientele of *Les Poulets*. The men come away from being with her in a dreamy delirium. Many can only think of returning. At the desk they set up another appointment with her for the next day, the next week, or when they will next be in Paris.

Juliette LaPerle becomes a star at *Les Poulets*, sought after for her blonde beauty and by her reputation for being charming, thrilling, and satisfying. The men are universally happy with her vagina. It has just the right tightness for entry and then she has the technique of pulsing her "cat" (*chatte*) around their cocks. She practices it to make it more perfect and thrilling. German officers hear of this in remote outposts, phone to make appointments with her days, weeks, even months in advance and spend precious leave time traveling to Paris to have their hour, or super-expensive evening, of pleasure with her.

Madame Guyton is careful not to overextend her prize girl and keeps the maximum number of services Juliette does in a day to five. More often it is two, three or four. Over all, *Madame* keeps Juliette to about 20 sessions in a week and not above 100 in a month. It could easily be more. But *Madame* understands her business and sets up Juliette's reputation as being exclusive and available only for favored men. Thus, Juliette is much sought after and damn the cost.

Julie has been at *Les Poulets* for a year and a half. She has never left, in fact. She looks out a window and sees *rue Blondel* below. It's always busy with soldiers and all sorts. As far as she can see from the window, the commerce of sex is all there is in the outside world! With the war the number of girls taking to prostitution has soared. The street girls on *rue Blondel*, when it is warm, will be on the *trottoir* in scanty clothing, some with little more than a gauzy covering and a

G-string. She sees that the successful girls mix startling glamour with suggestive disclosure in their costumes, hair styles, painted faces and high heeled boots and shoes.

Julie finds nothing shameful in it. The girls and their customers simply do what they do; just like the people in her village did what they did. Now, in January 1942, it is cold and they must wrap up. A few have furs. Julie thinks to give her lynx fur coat to one of them. But there are so many. It would be unfair to select one. Each has to earn her own fur, Julie thinks, like she had to. Though it was easier for her. She smiles. How naïve she was then! She turns away from the window, away from the outside world, thankful she is safe, but wondering, too, what will become of her.

As the days, weeks, months go by, Julie becomes increasingly aware of herself. She looks after her health, her attitudes, her life force. She brushes her teeth religiously twice a day. Even though she is subject to the inevitable ups and downs, successes and failures, happy days and gloomy ones, that are the lot of all human beings, she is determined to have a sense of ascent in her life, of moving upward.

Each day and each man must be attended to, very like how she sews the G-strings and is praised for them. With practice her G-strings are more beautiful and more practical for the girls to use. That is how she thinks of her service to the men; she has to be more beautiful and more expert in knowing how exactly to do things to please.

Men pay top price for her. Most give her generous tips. The other girls look up to her, ask for her advice. *Madame* gives her whatever privileges are going. And there is the bottom line for Julie. She is becoming rich beyond anything she could have imagined as a village girl. *Madame* has put her money away in a private bank out of sight and reach of the authorities. It's all in cash under lock and key. *Madame* has recently sent half of it to a Swiss bank. It will be extra-safe there. There is a lot of that going on.

On June 22, 1942 Germany invades Russia. The initial rapid advance has slowed and now has been stopped by the

Russians. In some places the Germans have had to retreat. The German officers and soldiers in France are shit scared they could be sent to Russia and die in the wasteland there. In fact many are shipped off, especially the younger ones. Julie lives through weepy farewells with the officers, some of whom she really liked.

German manpower is over extended. More and more the German troops in France are older men, some from the countries the Germans had conquered early in the war. Slave labor is being imported into Germany from these countries, including men and women from France. For the slightest infraction of the rules, or for no reason except that Germany needs the slave labor, French people are being sent to toil and die in the factories. Young French men have become an unusual sight in France.

The clientele at *Les Poulets* reflects these changes. While there are a few young German officers who come to *Les Poulets*, most are middle aged or older. Julie is servicing men 20, 30, 40, even 50 years older than herself. In some ways it is easier. They have less in common with her and neither she nor they become personally involved.

However one older man is a considerable compensation for her; General Max Edelman, aged 58. His left leg had been torn up at Smolensk in Russia and he wears a leg brace. In other respects he is healthy and vigorous and he has a strong, almost insatiable, sex drive. He has been assigned to the staff preparing for the allied invasion in Europe through France. He knows France well, speaks French fluently and loves Juliette. "You make up for this damn war, *chérie*," he tells her.

His love for Juliette has two important consequences. The first is that, before he was wounded in Russia, he had his requisition unit send all the furs they could find to a depot in western Germany. They were to be used to make warm clothing for German soldiers in the next winter there. His men discover a fur store house filled with the best furs Russia has, the finest in the world. Max has these furs carefully packed and sent to a depot under his name to be reserved for special use. Looting was happening wherever the German army went. Plundering of the occupied countries, particularly their art and luxury goods, was conducted on a wholesale basis. The Germans did not just conquer other people, they did everything they could to rob them of their culture and identity, to make them slaves and nonentities. Among their many crimes this also must never be forgotten or forgiven.

One of General Edelman's "special uses" for his furs is to drown his young love in them. They both like fox furs, silver fox furs most of all. They are so plump and sexy! And, as they both know, silver fox furs have the reputation of being the whore's fur. "Well," Julie says to Risé, "I am a whore so I should have all of her privileges!" She primps and swishes in them for all she is worth for her customers. It is another way to enlarge the money they give her. An intellectual German officer tells her that the English poet, T.S.Eliot, wrote, "Birth, copulation, and death - that's all there is - birth, copulation, and death." In her down moments, Julie thinks that this is the literal truth. She is just the "copulation" between birth and death. But that mood passes, thank goodness!

Juliette now has her own service room and her own maid, Marie. *Madame* has had the room redecorated in a sumptuous style and Julie likes to have fur throws on the bed and over the chairs and *chaises longues*. Max likes to have sex with her when she is draped in lush furs and she becomes skillful in being sexy and romantic in the furs. She remembers well how the sergeant had told her she was sexy when wearing the lynx fur coat. So it has turned out that, in part due to him, she understands that some men want to fuck her when she is wearing furs. Thanks sarge! Extra money!

Max takes her out on the town, especially to Maxim's. He buys her the top line in evening dresses, favoring the house of *Madame Dionnelle* on *rue St. Honoré*. Max has

Juliette's hair coiffed at an elegant Salon in Paris. He buys her shoes and jewelry and gives her many presents, but he requires her to keep working at *Les Poulets*. He wants a prostitute mistress. That fulfills his particular erotic need and is also a cover. It keeps his liaison from being too conspicuous; after all, he has a wife and children in Germany.

The second consequence is that Julie is approached, carefully and discreetly, by the resistance. They want to know anything that Max lets go about the planning for the coming invasion. She would be doing her part in defeating the Germans and freeing her country from their occupation. *Vive la France!*

Madame Guyton warns her to be very careful. But the same is being done by many people in France. When someone is caught the penalty is awful. Torture and off to the firing squad or sent to the death camps.

Juliette is torn. But she is a French girl, even with all the German friends she has had. So she passes on the snippets she hears from Max. He tells her about the huge amount of concrete being used to build the coastal defenses. "But once the Americans and the British get in behind them, they will be useless." He shakes his head and tells her that he doesn't think they can ever repel a full scale invasion. The countries around the world are massing against them. It's just a question of time. "Germany is losing the war, Juliette. But don't tell anyone I said that or else we'll both be shot before it happens." He laughs. He has absolute trust in her. Such is love, even perverse love.

Time passes. Another cold winter goes by, then the summer, then another winter. The German armies are retreating everywhere. The brutalities in France increase. The resistance is growing, but being discovered more often. The German are merciless. Whenever the *Maquis* exposes itself, the Germans are swift to respond. Overall they are winning the conflict between the Resistance and themselves. Paris is suffering from every kind of shortage and deprivation. People are starving and freezing to death on the streets. Among the privileged spots are the top Houses. German officers will not let their pleasures be sacrificed. So Julie and the girls never experience the severe shortages of food and heat that others are enduring. "Sin" has its rewards, as *Madame* Guyton says.

General Edelman has been working feverishly in the planning for the defense of France. He falls ill. His wound is sapping his strength. General Runstedt, the Commander in Chief, relieves him and details him for the Dijon command post. There he will do what he can to prepare the deep defense in France should the allies break out and come sprawling across the country; like the Germans had in the other direction four years before.

Max doesn't mind. He's had enough. He will be nearer Germany when the inevitable happens. But his love for Juliette, however strange, is genuine. He tells *Madame* Guyton that he is taking her with him. He will compensate her for taking away her best girl with money and another load of furs, but that is how it is going to be. *Madame* gets in touch with the *Le Coq* in Dijon where Juliette will go.

Soon Paris will be a dangerous place to be in. It's leaking out, down to Max's level, that Hitler plans to demolish Paris when the allies are threatening to take it. He tells Juliette she is fortunate to be able to leave.

Julie finds it hard to say goodbye to everyone at *Les Poulets*. It has been a genuine home to her, where she has grown up, and she loves nearly everyone there, including all the kitchen staff. *Madame* Guyton closes the house for an evening so that they can all join in a grand party to send off Julie - their *Lutine* - to her new house in Dijon.

The next morning a general's Mercedes-Benz drives up to the red front door. Beside the driver is a corporal armed guard. They put the many trunks and cases of Juliette's wardrobe and possessions in the back of the large car. Juliette and her maid, Marie, whom she insists has to come with her, ensconce themselves in the back seat.

They set off. The corporal tells them he hopes their car will not be strafed by marauding enemy planes. Big German staff cars are being attacked in the hope of killing high officers. If they are attacked, they will crouch in the ditch beside the road, he tells Julie.

Julie has dressed well and fervently hopes it won't come to that. She intends to arrive at *Le Coq* in Dijon as a top courtesan with her personal maid. She has put on a little black dress, a Coco Chanel, and long gloves with expensive bracelets on her wrists, a gold anklet with a diamond heart, and a pearl necklace with a diamond drop about her shapely neck.

Juliette's knowledge is narrow but deep. To her, men are like children, wanting their candy. She likes them, up to a point, but seldom respects them. She is proud and sure of herself, far beyond her years. She is an accomplished actress, she has to be. She has imagined all sorts of stories about herself that she tells the men. Some men have liked her playing out dramas with them. She has played Lili Marlene, the iconic prostitute seen in the glow of a street lamp. She created a little stage in her room at *Les Poulets* and stood under a lamp while singing the song. She would do it for one man or a few. *Madame* Guyton charged extra for it.

Julie wonders what *Le Coq* will be like. She hopes it will be as classy as *Les Poulets*. Her mind wanders. She looks at the trees flowing past the window and reclines in the capacious seat. She reflects. In spite of or, rather, because of her calling, she is a privileged person, the mistress of an important man. She and her maid are being driven in style, with an armed guard, leaving a danger zone. Ha! Not many girls of her age can say that!

She is still a teenager, 18 coming up to 19, though nominally 22 according to her papers. She has that polished veneer that young women develop when living in life's realities and privileges. Julie relaxes to be more comfortable in the plump fox fur coat loosely wrapped around her. Her face is artfully made up. Her long eyelashes waft above her rouged cheeks, her perfume scents the air. "They are going to meet a top *Les Poulets* girl when I arrive," she tells Marie. "We'll show them! Right?"

"Oh, yes, *m'amselle*! We will do that!" Marie replies. Seeing her charge is sleepy she puts a pillow by her head. *Juliette LaPerle's* golden blonde hair flows over it. The car hums along the road through the pastoral countryside. Julie dreams of the girl who is running in the fields, picking flowers and eating wild strawberries.

Marie Roden is thankful to be with Juliette. She is twice the girl's age and tends to her with every care. Looking after the girl's welfare is her welfare too. She is paid as a maid but, better than that, the men tip her. Her *Mademoiselle Juliette LaPerle* makes sure they know that is expected. Marie would defend her young mistress to the death, if it ever came to that.

Marie is a Jew. By being a maid at *Les Poulets* she has avoided being put in a cattle car and taken to Auschwitz to be gassed. When *Madame* Guyton was asked if she employed any Jews, she said, "Of course not! What do you take me for? A lover of Jews! I don't allow Jewish men in here, if I know who they are! They're a dirty lot. But then, these days, so many are circumcised. You know how it is, I'm sure." She quite charmed the German officer.

From the start, Céline Guyton has done what she could to hide and protect her Jewish friends and customers. Not that Jewish men can be her customers anymore, they are in hiding. When pressed, she uses the dingy cellar room next to the dungeon as a temporary haven until safer quarters can be found for them. It gratifies her that high ranking German officers are being insulted and whipped within the hearing of her Jewish hide-outs.

Marie fervently hopes that *Le Coq* will be another safe place for her. As best she knows, she is the sole survivor of the Rodenberg family.

Julie and Marie had confided their stories to each other. Marie was as horrified to learn of the loss of Julie's family in the 1940 German invasion as Julie was to learn of the deportation of Marie's family. Now they had that bond in common. Julie would defend her maid to the death, if it ever came to that.

Part 3.
Paths Cross

Chapter 12.

Olton School. 1945.

The honor code at Olton is the standard one. A boy must not lie, cheat, or steal or allow others to. Giles lets a half-grin crease his face. What about killing? He would lie about that if he had to. But the code is, nevertheless, a good thing. It fits his conscience. He will live up to it and be an honorable Olton boy.

Giles sees plainly that being educated at Olton is important for his future, it gives him the cachet of being a gentleman and he will make friendships and acquaintances at the school that may last his lifetime. One of the other boys, David Ottinger, whom Giles likes, tells him that his father says that the important thing is to be in the network and, therefore, always have someone to call on when necessary. "Can you believe it, Giles, but the Home Secretary and his wife came to dinner at our house! Now that's networking!"

Giles thinks of Mec. Mec had educated him in the brutal truths of life and death, far distant from the niceties of the Olton honor code. It will be good to see Mec again when he goes home for Christmas. He has many questions to ask him. Like girls. They had just been there when he was growing up, a part of the landscape, like old people and trees. And he hadn't liked them much with their high pitched squeals. But then they grow up to be something quite different, like his mother. It is a puzzle.

In his study the housemaster had talked, in a round-about way, to the new boys about "private" things. He says the boys are too young to think about girls and that during term time, they must not meet any girls or even look at them. Why not? The question is left unanswered. The housemaster tells them that finding a stain on their bed sheets in the morning is natural and not their fault. But helping that to happen is a sin.

Some of the boys say it is all about "girls." He will ask Mec. Mec will give him straight answers. Perhaps Mec will take him to *Le Coq*. From what his mother had said there must be nice girls there.

Then, quite by chance, something happens that gives Giles a peephole into what happens below the surface of everyday life. At the same time it puts him into a quandary.

On this Sunday afternoon Giles takes off by himself to walk and run in the fields, copses, and lanes. It releases him from the closeness of being with the other boys all the time and is a continuation of what he had done to win France back from the Germans. He runs full pelt across a field to gain another hiding place, freezes in position, then moves on again. He sidles stealthily forward, as if there is a hostile ahead. Perhaps there will be another war and, in that event, he will have perfected his stalking skills.

He comes upon an old disused quarry laid out in a curve below a forested path. The rock face has notches and indents in its walls. Boulders are strewn around the quarry bottom. He will be a commando and climb down noiselessly and cunningly. At the bottom he will use the boulders to screen his advance against his foe.

He performs excellently, without disturbing any loose stones. No one would have heard him. Now he is behind a boulder and about to look into a cove at the bottom of the rock wall. A hostile could be lurking there. He keeps himself low, taking care to remain hidden.

Actually it isn't necessary. Reverend Walker, assistant housemaster at Linsley House, is too intertwined with the girl. Giles is taken by surprise, quickly followed by curiosity. He has seen dogs humping and Reverend Walker is doing about the same except he and the girl are face-to-face. He is lying between her legs, with his bare buttocks moving up and down. Then they move more quickly, like a pumping machine. Giles catches glimpses of her face. She is much younger than Reverend Walker and, it seems to Giles, rather disinterested in what is happening, perhaps mildly enjoying it.

Reverend Walker lets out groans and cries, then collapses. Giles, watching intently, tries to understand the scene and the reason for it. Though he can't quite piece it all together, it is obvious that Reverend Walker is acting secretively with the girl; doing something he does not wish to be known. Otherwise he wouldn't be in this remote and not very comfortable spot in the quarry doing what he is doing. From what little Giles knows and has guessed about sex, it seems that this is sex. It has, obviously, to do with girls. Giles connects it with the house master's stern warning against having anything to do with girls. Well, that didn't seem to apply to the assistant house master - or did it?

Reverend Walker stands and pulls up his trousers. The girl arranges her dress. Now Giles can see her clearly. She is one of the maids who serves in the dining room at Linsley House. Reverend Walker smiles at her and gives her an envelope. They walk to the end of the quarry where a rough path leads down a hill to a road by a village. Giles follows close enough to see Reverend Walker mount a bicycle and pedal down the road. The girl goes into the village.

At first Giles hardly thinks about it. What Reverend Walker and the girl do on a Sunday afternoon is none of his business. Giles doesn't want to cause any trouble for him. He is sure, somehow, that if he spoke up, Reverend Walker would be censured. So he lets it pass and gets on with meeting the steep challenges of his study-room assignments

He doesn't see much of Reverend Walker, a quiet reserved man who speaks gently and never finds fault with a boy. How Walker comes to be suspected is never stated. The house master has the boys come to his study one by one. He asks each whether he has seen Walker with a woman and, if so, did he recognize her. After only one or two boys have been interviewed, the word comes down from the senior prefect that you mustn't snitch, even if you have seen or know something. So Giles has to lie.

It troubles him. He has avoided telling people the complete truth about himself, but has never outright lied when asked questions. Furthermore the house master had told each boy that he must not lie. In the dining room after dinner, he had given a homily on the necessity for truth. But he had not mentioned how a person resolves a conflict between two imperatives: not to lie and not to snitch.

Giles is spared any more soul searching. Reverend Walker resigns. So Giles learns something about sex and something about the difficulties of truth. Each is a valuable part of his education.

Giles realizes he has been lucky to avoid a confrontation. He had only to remain quiet. He wouldn't tell Charles or Joey or his mother about it. Mec would be the one to share it with and help him understand what goes on below the surface.

By chance, in the school library, Giles finds a book, a very large book. It is Frazer's *Golden Bough*. The title intrigues him. What is the book about? He opens it and begins to read, at first turning from page to page, looking at the illustrations. He is fascinated. Later he would learn that The Golden Bough was, on its publication at the end of the 19th century, a profoundly influential anthropological study of the ways, rituals, beliefs, and religions of people around the world, particularly native peoples. The images and the accounts of what happens excite Giles, mentally and physically. He feels the rush in his body as he reads about puberty rites, sexual coupling, cruelty and pain, passions and brutalities. There are worlds and practices and feelings he knows nothing about, never even imagined. They bear no resemblance to what he knows of the people of France and England. Yet the people were human beings, like himself. Their experience of life is utterly different from his.

He doesn't tell anyone of his finding. Everyone at Olton thinks, it seems to him, each in his own way, that he is the heir of total and irrefutable truths. Little do they know!

Giles is now a skeptic, not only of religion, but of the social establishment around him. However, he is sensible enough not to say so.

Chapter 13.

Autumn 1945.

A tradition at Olton school is that everyone sings, even if they can't. Music was an important part of school life and Giles has to participate, like all the boys. First he has to suffer the embarrassment of going to the music school to be tested. Music has been absent from his life. When the music master strikes a note on the piano and asks him to sing it, Giles, literally, does not know what to do.

"Won't you try, Martin?"

"I do not know how to try," Giles tells him.

The music master impatiently puts him down as hopeless and assigns him to the "non-choir." When the whole school sings in the Great Hall or in the Chapel, Giles, to his relief, finds other boys who don't, won't or can't sing. On the other hand, he likes listening when the hymns and other songs are sung by the boys who can sing. On his walks, so no one will hear him, he tries to sing, very softly. If he raises his voice, it just doesn't sound like a song. So he sings more in his mind than with his voice. Perhaps Mec knows how to sing. He has a lot to talk about with Mec.

Giles hardly notices the passage of time. He has so much to learn and there are so many difficulties to overcome, starting with the language and mannerisms, the things to do and not do, how to address senior boys, the masters, the matron in the house. Then there is the undercurrent of some of the older boys making intimate friends with the younger boys. Robert tells him he must never allow an older boy to become personal, "you know, touching." What did it all mean?

It is Christmas time. Charles and Joey come to collect him. Charles has done well in the negotiations in Paris and been promoted. Now his car is designated a military vehicle, with a corporal driver. But Charles prefers to drive himself whenever possible.

"So how has it been, young man?" Charles queries after they had embraced warmly, rather to Giles's discomfiture. It was called, he had learned, "public display of affection" or PDA. Not something that well brought-up English people did, as Joey had intimated to him before. Giles smiled to himself. Charles had spent too much time in France. Giles replies, "Very well, thank you. I won a prize at shooting."

"That's great, well done. That comes from you being with the *Maquis*, I imagine?"

"Yes. That's right." Giles quickly changes the subject. "Robert and I are helping the master who teaches French."

That master had declared that France had been the crucible of modern civilization. Giles is happy to hear that from an Englishman and it makes him proud to be French. He is happy, too, of his good fortune to have been adopted by Charles and Joey and to have the mother he has and how she had shown courage in adversity. He has learned Shakespeare's saying "the world is your oyster." Now the oyster is his to open and find the pearls within. But, he knows, having eaten oysters in Paris with Joey, they seldom contain pearls. Some can be gritty with sand and a bad one can make you ill. Nothing is wholly good and, conversely, nothing wholly bad. With the earnestness of youth, Giles resolves he will live his life from now on with that understanding.

Charles and Joey see Giles off to France at Victoria station. He will travel on the Night Ferry boat train running from London to Paris via Dover and Dunkerque. Providing Giles with the First Class sleeping compartment on the train was one of their Christmas presents to him. At Dover the coaches run onto rails on the ferry boat and passengers have no need to get off for the whole distance from Victoria Station in London to the *Gare du Nord* in Paris.

The train arrives at Dover in the late evening and Giles watches his carriage and the others being loaded onto the ferry boat. It is so clever! He returns to his compartment and thinks himself the luckiest boy in the world as he tucks himself into the bed and falls asleep. Being a sound sleeper, the next things he knows is that they are an hour out from Paris and the steward is serving him a delicious *petit déj*euner (breakfast.)

At Paris, after taking a taxi cross-town, Giles rides the train to Auxerre and then the Chatillon bus that stops at Plaignes.

Giles is on his own, showing his passport and tickets to the officials, paying for his food and drink and the taxi, finding the bus at Auxerre, talking to people first in English and then in French, and being, in sum, his own man. It is, he thinks, rather like a rite of passage similar to the ones he has read about in The Golden Bough. He can now look back at what he had done with Mec and the others, killing Germans, as part of growing up and preparing himself for the world. Now he has a further and steadily growing necessity. He has to know about girls!

Chapter 14.

Christmas 1945.

Sophie meets Giles at the bus stop in Plaignes and quite astonishes him by leading him to a Citroën 2CV. Giles had read about the super-inexpensive car that will help the French economy get going again. It has a small air-cooled engine and, everyone agrees, ugly looks. But it is affordable, even for the poor of France and neighboring countries. At first the car is rationed according to need. There are long waiting lists. Inevitably a black market arises. Used 2CV's are sold under the counter for a higher price than new ones.

"*Maman*! You have it? It is yours? You know how to drive it?" Giles cries out.

"Yes, Giles. I can drive it. Get in. You can help me by pulling the starter cord[30]. It is a little heavy for me."

The car starts and they drive off. The small engine, while using hardly any fuel, can only push the car along at a

---

[30] The first 2CV models were started by pulling on a handle inside the car attached to a cable that turned the engine. It was soon discovered that the strength required was too much for many women and an electric starter was installed. Even though this increased the price of the car, and broke away from the idea of the simplest possible design, the low-powered fuel-economic little cars sold like hot cakes.

slow speed. Sophie is sitting up to the steering wheel on a pile of cushions. "You see Giles. I can drive. I call her *Ma Petite Souris* (My Little Mouse.) I like it going slow. Then I can stop quickly and avoid any danger."

They chug along the road to Criselles. "*Maman*! It's stupendous! I love it! But how did you get it? I heard there is a long list of people waiting for them and you have to prove a special need."

Sophie puts a finger to her nose. "Ah! You must know people, Giles. You remember Mec? He gave it to me. Very generous of him. That man, he knows a thing or two. I am a war veteran and I need the car for my apple business. That's what he told the magistrate. Also he gave the magistrate a fine-looking shot gun he'd salvaged from the war." She laughs. "He is kind to me. We are good friends. He comes and helps with things around the house. For his living? He does what he does with his vehicles, transporting stuff around. Now I am a merchant in apples. I buy them from the orchard and supply the shops all around here in my Little Mouse."

"You are a marvel, *maman*!"

Suddenly he is seeing his mother in a different light. She no longer cringes at anything. She is now a strong independent woman, confident in herself.

"And you, Giles! Such a young man now! The English school is good for you, eh! So we are both doing well. Let us forget the war. It does no good to remember. Except I think sometimes of our two Germans." Sophie smiles. "How frightened they were at the end! But they survived, thanks to you, Giles. I had a letter from Leon. He is back in Bavaria and tells me he is training to become a pastor in their church. Well, well, the world turns, eh! You must tell me about your school and the general and his wife. But not now. I can wait. Now you are coming home to be with me and on Christmas day you will have the best roast goose you have ever had. I've invited Mec to join us. He has no family, poor man. So I tell him we are his family!"

Giles is delighted to be back in his own room and to re-acquaint himself with his personal things, his clothes, his books, the few toys he had in childhood. The view from his window is just the same. He can see rabbits eating the grass along the hedgerows. Suddenly, almost like a shock, he feels entirely French again. Every thought is in French. Every feeling and understanding is French again. When he goes down to his mother in the kitchen, he hugs her as if never meaning to let go. She kisses him and holds him in front of her. "There, Giles. How tall you've grown! Tell me. Have you met any English girls?"

Giles blushes, which makes Sophie smile. "Oh, no, *maman*! We are not allowed to even speak to girls at school."

"That must be dreadful for you. It's unnatural! We'll see what we can do about it!"

Indeed she has already set things in motion. Marie, of the apple orchard, had lost her husband in the war, but has a daughter, Angelica, 11 years of age. Sophie has invited them over to join in the Christmas meal and festivities. She had asked Mec, too, to take Giles to Dijon. Mec will show Giles around, they will meet his friends and there will be some women and girls there.

The roast goose on Christmas day is the best. Mec is in a new suit that doesn't fit him very well. It makes him look like a square peg. Giles will be 15 come July and feels that Angelica is still a child. She is reticent, being at that difficult pre-puberty age when her body is stirring and everything is changing. Neither of the young people know how to relate to each other. So it ends up in them hardly talking to each other.

After the meal Mec tells Giles he is going out to the garden to smoke a cigar, a Cuban cigar he'd bartered from an American. "Sophie doesn't like me smoking in the house. 'You stink up the place,' she says. So I do as she says. She's a strong minded woman. The sort of person France needs. I admire her. You won't mind me saying that, will you?"

They come to the old well-worn bench. Mec sits down. "OK, my boy. Have they caned you yet at that English school? That's what I've heard. Then the boys grow up and, for their pleasure, want a girl to cane them. What do you know about that?"

Giles has no idea what to say. "No . . . Mec . . . , " he's blushing.

Mec rumbles derisively. "Those schools. I have heard about them. All boys and no girls. They keep you in ignorance and then are surprised that the boys, when they are men, like strange things. It's absurd!"

Giles, though feeling hot and edgy, is determined to ask his questions. "Mec . . . I need your help. It's just that . . . " Giles finds it difficult to continue.

"It's about girls, eh?"

"Yes . . . it is, Mec. I can't ask my mother. It would embarrass her, I'm sure. I feel so stupid. In some of the books I've read they talk about sex and I know that's how babies are born, from a man and a woman coupling. And I think I have seen it." Giles tells Mec what he had seen in the quarry. "Sort of like what animals do. The man had to resign from his position at the school. What had he done that was so bad?"

Mec draws on his cigar. "That's what's different between those Anglo-Saxons and us. We delight in it and they hide it away. It seems most of them only know enough to have children! But then they come to France and, with some luck, find out about life. OK, my boy! It's not your fault. But we need to do something about it. It's something between us men, eh! Boys must grow up to be men. First of all, sex is not bad. It's good. It is built into us. It is natural. Our bodies are designed that way. You have a penis. It becomes stiff. The woman has a vagina, a tube between her legs. Oh! It has many names, like *la chatte*, the pussy. It becomes greasy, like a well-oiled bit of machinery. The penis and the vagina are made for each other. The man puts his erection into her pussy. They both like it. It feels good. The man ejaculates his sperm into her. One of his sperm, a little wriggly thing, finds one of her eggs and may fertilize it. There is nothing bad about it as long as they both wish it to happen. Yes . . . and it may produce a child in the woman's womb. So, you see, you do a pleasurable thing in order to have children. But you or she or both of you can take precautions to prevent pregnancy. You use barriers to stop the sperm from fertilizing the egg. That way you can do the pleasurable thing for its own sake. Just for the pleasure, like eating a good meal or . . . ," Mec paused, " . . . killing Germans! That was pleasurable, wasn't it?" Mec grinned. "Now you shoot your gun, but not to kill Germans. Whoof! Off it goes! As you no doubt know, it's called fucking. A man fucks the girl. Ah, yes! The secret of life! Without it we wouldn't be here. Think of that, young man."

Mec is driving Giles in a "captured" German staff car to Dijon. It has a powerful engine and is a big car, but not glamorous like a Rolls Royce.

They are halfway down the road to Dijon, seeing snow on the higher ground and smoke rising from the chimneys of the houses and cottages. Mec tells him, "Now we are going to a place, Giles, that was important during the war, *Le Coq*. I want you to know about it. The women there entertained German officers and others and passed on much valuable information to us. Now the young ladies continue to entertain men and we are going there to meet *Madame* Colette Saludin and, I believe, one of her loveliest young ladies.[31]"

---

[31] In 1946, by the law of Marthe Richard, with the backing of Communists and Christians who shared a streak of puritanism, French brothels were closed. However prostitution itself continued to be legal. Among the many consequences was that the streets in Paris and in other cities and large towns had many more prostitutes on them, now out in the open in the neighborhoods, but with no medical or other forms of supervision. Venereal disease became a major problem. Supervised brothels were replaced by *maisons de passe* and *hôtels closes*. Many of these were hotels, some with restaurants on the ground floor, with rooms above for the

"Oh! I think I've heard of the place. Those German officers talked of it. Do I have to do anything?"

Mec sees that Giles is tense, understandably. "No, not if you don't want to. I am known there and Colette and I will make sure your visit is enjoyable."

For a while Giles is silent. Then, with a veneer of bravado, Giles says, "*Zut*, Mec! This is like when we were going to blow up that train! I didn't really know what was going to happen and then there was that huge explosion." Giles grins remembering how it had been. But he still feels unnerved; he will be entering another unknown world. It has happened to him all along. His life has been like reading a book, a book so varied in content that he couldn't possibly know what was going to happen on the next page.

Mec parks the car by the station and they walk to the nearby *Le Coq*. Now it is a hotel with a well-appointed restaurant on the ground floor that has earned a star rating. No mean accomplishment in France; even one star ratings are not given out lightly. Mec is known to the *maître d'* and, after exchanging a few words with him, Mec leads Giles along a passageway behind the bar to a door with a spy hole set in it at eye height. Mec knocks and after a moment's pause

---

prostitutes to ply their trade. The houses were, in many cases, little different from the former brothels. The establishments were well known, any taxi driver would take you to one. The effect in terms of suppressing prostitution was minimal. The law made prostitution more risky and more likely to be run by criminals. The basics of sexual demand and supply had not changed.

The new "houses" existed with the connivance of the police and other local officials. That set up a system of pay-offs, corruption and crime. Marthe Richard was cursed by almost everyone: the prostitutes, the medical services, the police, some politicians, the tourist trade, and many ordinary people. It was widely seen as a retrograde step leading to worse and more dangerous conditions for the prostitutes and their customers. Graffitti scrawls, such as *"à bas Marthe Richard"* (down with Marthe Richard), were to be seen on walls all over France. In some houses, like *Le Coq* in the story, little had changed from before. A number of films have been made depicting what happened; a famous one is *Belle de Jour* made by Luis Bunuel and featuring Katherine Deneuve.

the door is opened by a swarthy man who bids them enter. He tells them, "*Madame* Saludin is expecting you in the *salon de réunion.*

The *salon de réunion* (meeting room) is not very big, quite intimate in fact, with red walls, elegant light fixtures, a parquet floor and a small bar. It leads to a somewhat larger salon where the men can dine with the girls, with the food being sent up from the restaurant below.

The barman in the *salon de réunion* is a tall older black man from Sierra Leone, called Blackie, a popular figure at *Le Coq*. At the bar, besides *Madame* Saludin, there are three men, one of them smoking a cigar, the others cigarettes, and two young women in skimpy clothing. They are chatting, smiling, and laughing. In the background one of the new tape machines is playing light French music.

Colette catches sight of Mec. "Ah, Mec! Good to see you! So this is our young hero! Let me shake your hand, young man. You certainly are as handsome as Mec told me!" She looks to Mec. "How has it been for you, Mec? Your business goes well?"

"Oh, I go along very well, Colette, as I hope you do.

"No complaints, Mec. What is it? Moving stuff around?"

"I have a dozen vehicles now, Colette, to move the goods the Americans are sending over to help us. It's good of them and it's a poke in the eye to the frigging communists. Well - - some cases have a bad tomato or two, so the whole case is bad and tomatoes have a good price!" He laughs. "Tell me what you want and maybe something could fall off the truck!"

Colette taps him on the shoulder with the fan she often carries. "You were always one to find a way, Mec. Now young man, we shall sit down on this settee. Your name again?

"Giles - Giles Martin, *madame.*"

"You are a soldier's son?"

"Yes. My father was killed at the start of the war."

Colette tells him, " I have asked one of my loveliest girls to join us. Her name is Juliette. She will be here in a minute."

Colette had told Juliette that she wanted her in the Salon shortly after the young man arrived. "Arrange your *rendez-vous* so that it happens, *ma douce*. The young man, Giles is his name, is 17 and a sort of adopted son of Mec. Mec says he is a virgin and quite innocent. Maybe all you should do is be with him. I don't want you to press him. Mec thinks he will be a bit out of his depth. So be nice to him. If he wants to go with you, that's fine. Maybe you'll pick his cherry! Probably not though. Mec imagines he'll want to think about it. He is that sort of boy; brainy, you know. Then, most likely, with Mec guiding him, he will return. We'll see. Like a good father, Mec will pay for him. So don't be concerned about that."

Julie had raised her plucked eyebrows. She had never "cherry picked" a virgin boy! Her game was older men, anywhere up to 90! One 90 year old man couldn't get a decent erection, but she had managed to frot him up with her fingers and suck him up to a small ejaculation. Quite an achievement! It was almost unbelievable how grateful he was! Almost like stealing to take the generous money he gave her. Hey! Perhaps the money would be as good for initiating the boy. Mec was paying and he was always generous.

When Juliette enters, Colette beckons her. "Ah! Juliette! Come and meet Giles Martin."

Giles looks over his shoulder and sees a vision. The girl's gauzy peignoir floats around the red silk corset that adorns her curvaceous body. His startled eyes dart around her.

Colette tells Juliette to sit beside Giles. She seats herself gracefully to face the young man. "You are handsome, Giles. I am so glad you have come. Where do you live?"

Giles clears his throat. Her voice is as silken as her golden hair, her smile enchanting. Her scarlet lips open to him to show her glistening white teeth. She opens her mouth a little more, enough to show her red tongue just behind her lips. Even such a minor dalliance is a part of a professional girl's repertoire.

"Uh - in Criselles," Giles stammers. He pulls himself together, takes a breath. "My home is there. But I have been at a school in England."

"Oh! England! I have never been there. I hear it rains all the time." The soft mounds of her breasts are just in front of him; the black lace trim rimming the top of her corset barely covers her lightly rouged nipples.

"Oh, it doesn't rain all the time. Just sometimes." Giles thinks he must seem an idiot to her. Her flowery perfume assails his senses.

Colette regards the two young persons, not surprised at the jolt the young man is feeling on encountering Juliette. Juliette changes her pose, crossing a long shapely leg over the other.

Giles, glancing down, sees that her shoes have high soaring heels, maybe five inches high. Extraordinary! He had never seen anything like them.

Juliette touches her golden hair. Her arms are sheathed in satin gloves, reaching to her shoulders. Her fingers are bare, her inch long nails painted scarlet to match her lips. Juliette has had many men in a dither and is not surprised that this young man hardly knows which way is up. He has a good body, shapely, lightly but strongly muscled. It could be nice with him! "If you so wish, Giles, we can go to my room. That is, if you would like that."

Giles looks at Mec. Mec has the expression on his face that it was up to Giles to decide.

Giles feels out of place, unprepared. He doesn't feel right about doing something just because it's done. He knows nothing about Juliette. What would they do together? He supposes she would touch his private parts, like Robert had warned him about with the older boys. He doesn't want to disappoint Mec. Giles is uncertain; questioning himself.

What is the right thing to do? Stay or go? Neither seems quite right to him.

Sensing his quandary, Juliette looks up at *Madame* Saludin. Colette nods her head and gestures toward the bar. Juliette smiles at Giles. "Another time, Giles. I will be happy to see you again," she tells him sweetly. He is relieved. "Thank you," he says, blushing.

Julie leans over and gives Giles a peck on the cheek with a small insouciant laugh. "Just return when you are ready, Giles. I like the name. It's sweet. Giles - Giles." She leaves. She does it perfectly, like a colorful tropical bird flying off with a flap of her wings.

Juliette goes over to a man at the bar. She is relieved, too. The youth is so young, so inexperienced, but intelligent and charming, with good manners. For a fleeting moment he had made her recollect the time when she was a young innocent girl. He deserves something better than a meeting in a bar. She notices Blackie nodding his head in approval and flashes a smile to him. What Blackie doesn't know about men and women is not worth knowing and he has a kind heart. All the girls love him and his quiet ways.

Madame Saludin sits with Giles. "Dear boy, now you have been here and that's all that matters. We are nice people here and we never make anyone do what they don't want to do. Young men, like you, learn bit by bit what happens in this world and now you have learned a little bit more."

Colette stands up. Giles does too. *Colette* takes a rose from a vase and gives it to him. "Here is the card of *Le Coq*. Phone when you wish to return. And if any young English friends of yours wish to come here, be assured they will be welcome."

Since the war there had been a sprinkling of foreigners coming to *Le Coq* and Colette would like to build an international reputation. It was beginning to happen now that the wine trade had recovered and foreign buyers were coming in from all over. She had plans to branch out into the

Escort business. That would make her entirely legitimate and win open approval from the city. One had to move with the times.

As for the young man, Colette is satisfied. From her long experience she would be surprised if he didn't return. Mec has suggested the kind of scene Juliette should play with the young man. "The boy will respond to drama, Colette. I'll take him to Paris. I go there often, you know, and let him see how things are."

"But don't disappoint me, Mec! We'll start him very well here."

Mec smiled. "I plan on that, Colette. Don't worry. His mother is on our side. She's smart and a traditionalist. She knows what French fathers are expected to do for their boys. I'll keep him for your girl. Juliette is a talented beautiful girl, the best, and I'll give Giles the best!"

Colette agrees with Mec about Juliette. She is most satisfied with her. The girl is remarkably proficient and goes about the work with goodwill and no discernible resentment that fate has made her a prostitute. She is quick, sensible, intelligent and beautiful. She is favored by the wealthiest customers of *Le Coq*. She even likes being tightly corseted, something that many "modern" girls find difficult. Some men go absolutely nuts over a tightly corseted beautiful girl. Another blessing is that Juliette has a "thing" for furs and wears them with flair. She brought marvelous furs with her, gifts from the German general, and that too makes her a favorite with many men, particularly older richer ones.

The German general survived the war and is back in Germany with his wife and family. He went into the wine business, helping to put the German wine growers back on the map. Every three months or so he comes to Dijon and takes Juliette out on the town before returning with her to *Le Coq* to spend the night. So that situation had worked out as well as could be expected. He is, of course, on *Madame's* "most favored client" list and is given every deference.

Colette knows well that her business can be advertised and advanced in many ways. Having Juliette being seen outside makes plain to one and all that *Le Coq* has girls of beauty and sophistication. The general takes pleasure in having Juliette beautifully gowned, furred, and bejeweled on his arm. In a minor way she has become a feature of Dijon. Forget about Marthe Richard! Actually the wretched woman has admitted it was a mistake to close the houses. But, as more than one *politico* has told Colette, it would be political suicide for most politicians to vote to open the houses again. Beyond going out with the general and some other men, Colette has Juliette go out in Dijon in the daytime, with her maid, brightly *maquillagée*[32], dressed stunningly, properly high-heeled and bejeweled, with a fashionable hat, wearing her furs. She goes to the best shops and buys what she likes, on *Le Coq's* account. It's effective. Men see her, that's all it takes. A priest in Dijon said in his sermon that such sights should be made illegal as temptations of the devil! He reminds Julie of her father and how he used to rant on.

Mec and Giles have a good meal in the restaurant, complete with a bottle of Beaujolais. Mec tells him, "don't worry, Giles. There is no need to rush things. As Colette told you, you know some things now you didn't before. I'll tell you this. There are all kinds of girls in this world. Juliette works as a hostess in *Le Coq* to earn her living. She will stay awhile and then go on to other things. Maybe she will be loved by a man and marry and have children. One never knows. Nor do you know, Giles, what lies in your future. Don't concern yourself. For now, your task is to learn and experience the world as it is and to put that alongside your book learning. Later on I will take you to Paris. I have an office there and I drive in often. I'll show you the town. It's all part of a young man's education. After you come back from England next time we'll go."

---

[32] *Maquillage* – make-up. Often *maquillage* implies a meticulous, special, or dramatic make-up.

"I will have finished school then, Mec, and be going on to university in September. So I'll have - Oh! - about two months in France."

"Good, my boy. You'll become a good Frenchman in that time. We'll spend time together."

Back home in Criselles, Giles remembers what he had read in the Golden Bough about what young men are taught and what they do at this time of their lives. Evidently there was a commonality between those rituals and what is expected of young Frenchmen as they pass into manhood. Having lost his father as a kid, Giles is utterly grateful to have Mec to guide him in the ways of the world. Mec provides the other side of his education, in counterpoint to what Charles and Joey and the schools and universities can teach him.

A couple of days pass. Images of Juliette intrude into Giles's mind. He examines his penis. Thinking of Juliette makes it stir. He rubs himself up to an erection. He has masturbated before and not gone blind! He knows that's what some puritans believe. "Juliette! Juliette!" he cries out as the pleasure sensation surges through him. He ejaculates. Semen shoots out. For a few moments he is dizzy. He is amazed at how much it is and how far it goes. Thinking of Juliette has juiced him up. Yes, he is ready! "Juliette! I'm coming! Juliette! Juliette!" he cries out to his empty room. It's a burst of vitality, inexplicable by any laws of physics, that suddenly and unexpectedly comes over him. It's both pleasurable and fearful, a step forward into the "sex" unknown.

* * *

Before he leaves to return to school Giles meets Angelica again and, this time, he talks with her confidently, as a man of the world. He realizes what a lovely, charming, intelligent, if innocent, girl she is. No less, it seems, does she like him. She asks if she may write to him and tell him the news from Plaignes and Criselles.

Thus, during the next term at Linsley House, a pink envelope with a French stamp, the address written in girlish handwriting, arrives every week for Giles Martin. In the closed maleness of Linsley House he is an object of envy. He lets an aura of knowledge about the other sex accumulate about him, while saying very little. "Oh, yes!" he would mention in confidence, "a hot number will wear fishnet stockings!"

Unexpectedly another envelope appears, colored a pale blue, with a French stamp. The envelope contains an art card with a print of Manet's Olympia. It's the famous picture of a prostitute reclining nude on her couch, her body outlined with a thin black line, attended by her black maid clasping a bouquet of flowers. It is sensuous, but not explicitly sexual. On it Julie had written, *"Je t'attend, Giles, avec pensées chaleureuses, Juliette."* ("I await you, Giles, with warm thoughts, Juliette.)

Giles stares at it and reads the few words again and again when alone in his study room. He puts his hand to his cheek and it is hot. His study mate comes in. "Giles! What has happened? You look as if there had been an earthquake!"

Giles tries to collect himself. "Oh! It's just something from France . . . from . . . . well . . . from my mother. I'll see about it when I go home."

Giles puts the card in his small lock box and turns the key. The card is his, his alone, to keep secure and savor forever.

Though *Madame* had mentioned to Juliette that she might send one of her notes to Giles, like she did to other men, Julie had done it on her own. Young men like Giles were few and far between at *Le Coq* and, even though a couple of the older men professed eternal love to her, she hankered for a young man, to sense his innocence and, perhaps, his genuine affection for her. Mec had given her Giles's English address. She had licked the stamp and given it a little kiss as she put it on the envelope. She stood up and said to Marie who knew what she was doing, "what a hope!"

"Oh! I don't know, *m'amselle.* Strange things happen in this world. We're both here, for one thing. Many people would think that strange, after everything that's happened."

"I suppose. Well, if the young man comes we will treat him well."

"Of course, *m'amselle.*"

* * *

When Giles goes on another *exeat* to London, he broadens his knowledge by finding a copy of *Madame Bovary* on a shelf in Charles's study and, after that, copies of *Lady Chatterly's Lover* and *Justine* by the *Marquis de Sade.* Oh, boy! Extraordinary things go on in the civilized world, not just with the savages of The Golden Bough.

In the late 40's, perhaps particularly in middle-class England, all things sexual were considered at least naughty, somehow reprehensible, and best left unsaid, except in a whisper. Thus most boys eagerly lapped up whatever information they could about anything even mildly erotic and, no less, any information about the notorious French.

"Is it true, Giles, that there still are those houses, you know what I mean, in France?"

"Well," Giles informed them in a man-of-the-world manner, "those houses are now illegal. But that makes no difference, if you are in the know. My uncle is an experienced man and he has told me about them."

"Could you find out more?"

"I suppose. You fellows are positive sex fiends!" They laugh to cover the feelings, in some the fevers, growing within them.

Chapter 15.

England and France. Spring 1950.

The school had competed at a rifle meet at Sandhurst, the British Military Academy, the previous spring. Giles had led the team in scores and the team had done well, placing third in the Cadet Corps competition. They had mingled with teams from around the world including the French team of cadets from the St Cyr Military Academy. The French cadets were older, of college age, but Giles soon set up camaraderie with them and the two teams introduced themselves to each other.

Both teams struggled with the other's language, but in good humor, at least for the most part. The distraught political situations in both countries set up a crisscross of tensions and attitudes. British politics were polarized between the socialists and the conservatives, with continuing austerity and bleakness of outlook, plus the loss of standing in the postwar world, now dominated by America and the USSR. France and England were facing the loss of their colonies and their standing in the new world of nationalism. The French government was a revolving door of the top few, none of whom were able to put together a stable government. Yet, at the same time the economy was picking up remarkably well due to the French acceptance of the Marshall plan plus the unofficial wheeling and dealing of the black market. In that respect the French were doing better than the English, who were stuck in the respectable ways of doing things; with the result that the whole French economy was recovering faster than the British.

Although the British press and radio contained little news of France, Giles was aware of his country's condition. DeGaulle was thought by many to be an aspiring dictator. He had resigned and stalked off to live in his country house in a village with two churches. Yet a party in his favor had emerged and had considerable political strength. The communists permeated everything and acted more in loyalty to the Soviet Union than to France. Factions in the military and in the intelligence services fought among themselves. Everyone was aware of the French political malaise and proffered their solutions, to little effect.

The Indo-Chinese war was threatening France's eastern empire. The European Coal and Steel Community (the precursor to the European Common Market) was mixing the commerce of France with its neighbors and NATO (North Atlantic Treaty Organization) had immersed France in the policies of America, Britain and others. Some saw France surrendering her sovereignty again, suffering a bitter reprise of her surrender to Germany in 1940. Such times engender extremists and France was no exception.

Giles had pangs of home sickness when with the French cadets and felt, in many ways though not all, a strong empathy with them. He was now a mix of French and English, feeling allegiance to both countries. But, overall, he still felt more French than English and, though he now sang God Save the King with the rest of the school in his poor singing voice, he preferred to sing the Marseillaise.

A major decision had to be made. The shooting competition was to be held at the St Cyr Military Academy in northern France and would include pistol shooting. Pistol shooting had never been done at Olton school. They either had to become proficient at it or not compete. Giles had been elected captain of the shooting team and there was no doubt in his mind that they should compete. Mec had taught him how to shoot pistols. He showed the other team members how it was done.

"You stand with your feet apart, one foot behind the other." He shows the boys the proper stance. "Make yourself firm by bending the knees slightly. You can turn either way. Both hands are on the pistol like this. You sight with both eyes. Two eyes gives you better depth perception than one eye. You look along the barrel to the target and squeeze the round off. Keep your arms slightly bent. That helps absorb the after-shock."

Giles asks the sergeant at the firing range for a practice pistol and demonstrates the standing position and firing. He shoots bulls eyes.

"Goddam!" the sergeant exclaims. "You learned that during the war too, I suppose."

"Yes, from my captain," Giles says proudly.

"All right, we'll teach the team together, provided the Head approves."

The Head Master has little chance to disapprove when General Charles Marlis comes to the school, on Giles's urging, and starts a fund to teach target shooting. The gift is relatively small, but large enough to buy the regulation firearms and to bring in an outsider, an ex-Olympic shooter, to coach the team. Thus the team is going to St Cyr in good shape to compete in rifle and pistol.

The team has light blue blazers and caps, with the school crest on them. They are a group of six shooters, selected by the shooting competitions held at the school. Robert, Giles's Canadian friend, had competed, but had not made the team. However, he would come with them. It would be his first time in France. The Olympic shooter, their coach, has generously offered to travel with them at his own expense.

The trip has to be paid for. Giles feels he must not expect Charles and Joey to pay all the cost or, indeed, should he be totally dependent on their generosity. He feels strongly that he should be as self-reliant as possible.

With this thought in mind he goes to the French Embassy, Cultural Department, behind the Victoria and Albert museum, in London. After a long wait he is shown to a woman who is in charge of translators. He talks with her in his best French and then slides easily into the well-spoken English he has learned at Olton. The woman is impressed.

"Have you done translation work before, Giles?"

"No, *madame*, except with the boys and masters at Olton school and then outside when we meet with French speaking people from around the world. I have met with Haitians in London," he smiled, "but their French is terrible! I had a difficult time with them."

"Well then, it seems you have done some translation. You are still young. But that may be an advantage. We have French families coming over with their children needing to learn English. And the other way round, English families needing to learn French. But how can you manage it while you are still at school?"

Giles thinks for a moment. "I could start by translating texts."

"It's a possibility. They would have to be typewritten. Can you type?"

"Oh, yes! My mother taught me. She worked in an office and still does. With practice, I'll improve."

"You impress me, young Giles. Stay here. I need to talk with someone."

Giles looks around the office while the woman is away. It is sparse but well appointed. In the book case are a number of serious volumes about consular work. But tucked in between them, Giles discovers, is the novel *La Folle de Maigret* by Simenon. He had found a copy of it on a shelf in the Marlis house in London and read it, loving it all the way.

The woman returns with a consular official. He sees the book. "You like Simenon, Giles?"

"This is the only book of his I've read so far. I think it marvelous!"

"It's a favorite of mine too. The story is remarkable. The old woman found some things in her apartment in Paris just moved a tiny bit, nothing taken or otherwise disturbed, and then she was murdered. Simenon set up a great plot. So, Giles; you are looking for work as a translator. As you may guess we have quite a few on tap. Do you have anything special to offer?"

Giles is a bit nonplussed. What is special about him? Come on, he says to himself, you are a special person. That's what you have to offer.

"Well, as a boy, I fought with the *Maquis* in eastern France. I know what happened. Perhaps someone has written a book about it. I would start with a big advantage as someone who was there. The *Maquis* had their own way of speaking. I was a runner; that was called a *lapin*, a rabbit. My cover name was *Lutin*, an imp."

"Fascinating! That opens up possibilities. Anything else?"

"I am interested in the 18th century Enlightenment and have read Diderot and others. At school I am interested in mathematics, among other things. Now we are doing differential equations and Boolean algebra. You know, the mathematical foundation of the computers to come."

"*Ma foi!*" (Well, indeed!) the consular official exclaims, "you are an enlightened young man!"

Giles thinks for a moment and then picks up the French novel. "Has it been translated into English?"

"I really don't know," the consular official says.

"I think I could translate it," Giles says. "I know Paris quite well and my captain in the Maquis came from Marseilles. He could advise me about that part of the book."

"Well, we would have to see who has the publishing rights here. I could set that in motion for you. Tell you what. Translate the first two chapters of *La Folle de Maigret* so you'll have something to show a publisher. I'll see what I can do." And that is how Giles began his career in letters.

Joey, learning about it that same day from Giles, goes out and buys a typewriter along with six reams of paper and carbons. They read through the first chapter of the book together, translating as they go. "Always try for the English expression that is equivalent to the French. Stay away from literal word for word. That will end up as terrible English. And see here. *Ravauder* means to mend, as you know. But Simenon uses it to mean mending socks. In English to mend socks is to darn them. The more usual French word is *repriser*, but Simenon didn't use it. That's just an example of what you have to look out for."

Giles wonders if he had taken on too much. Joey gives him a reassuring hug and tells him to go to it!

He had killed Germans, gone to school in England, met a beautiful courtesan and received a personal invitation to meet her again . . . sure he can translate a book!

Chapter 16.

France 1950.

Travel had been limited since the war and none of the English boys had been to France. They are excited about it and study earnestly in their French classes at the prospect. The coach has assured the parents he would act as *locus parentis* to the boys and see that they don't get into any trouble.

Consequently, the coach has asked for Giles's help in alerting the boys to the dangers: fast cars driving on the wrong side of the road, contaminated tap water (they should only drink bottled water), the temptation to drink too much wine, and - *ahem* - sex and disease that can ruin their chances of a good marriage, if not kill them.

The boys of the team listen. Then one of them tells them his father was in France as a soldier in WWI and said carousing in Paris had been more dangerous than being in the trenches at the front. Wow! That was exciting!

"I'll do what I can," Giles assures the coach.

Two of the boys have their parents' permission to travel with Giles to his home and meet "real" French people away from the cities. Giles would introduce them to his mother and the mayor and his uncle Mec. It would be a great chance for the boys to learn about French culture and improve their ability in French.

But Giles is troubled, both for them and for himself. The two had been invigilating him, following up on what he had said before about "those girls" and "those houses." But only for curiosity sake they said. Giles had been noncommittal, but he could see how intrigued they were. He would do nothing to aid them; whatever they did had to be on their own.

But talking about it had aroused him, whether he wanted it to or not. Images of Juliette career through his mind. He recalls how he had masturbated and told the air in his room he was coming to her. She had invited him to return. Mec had said he would pay for him. But was she just a courtesan? Not anything more? Had he seen something more in her? Or was he deluding himself? But even if she was just *une fille*, why deny himself? He must gain experience and she was the obvious way to do it.

The debate goes on in his head, swinging first one way and then the other. He would be in Criselles with his mother for a few days. But how could he go to *Le Coq* after being with his mother? She would think him depraved! Especially when there was that pure and lovely girl, his pen pal, Angelica waiting for him at his home. Though she had not written for a month. He wondered what had happened. He knew his mother thought of Angelica as his intended and Angelica was so obviously right for him, the sort of girl he should marry.

Giles tosses and turns in his bed, holding his penis, sometimes rubbing it up to erection, sometimes ejaculating. How was it possible to live when he was torn by such contradictory yearnings, impulses, and thoughts?

Then the next day comes and he is calm again and involved in all the proper things in life.

They cross the Channel in a ferry from Portsmouth to St. Malo. The sea was rough and some of the boys had been seasick. St. Malo puts them close to the St. Cyr Academy at Coëtquidan in Brittany. They take a short train ride to Rennes and then a bus to St. Cyr. A French Army bus takes them to the barracks where they would stay. To the English boys everything was French, new, exciting; though some of the boys, being very English, made silly remarks about the French being too French.

The next day is spent in becoming used to the range and practice shooting at various distances with their rifles and pistols. In the evening, all the teams assemble for dinner in a big hall and are officially greeted, in French and some English, to France and the shooting competition.

The next day the competition begins. It is a hot summer day in July and, by midday, the air is shimmering from the heat. That makes shooting more difficult at the longer ranges and the scores suffer. All the teams are rather disappointed and the coaches have to shore up their morale. There are a few spectators, mostly from the local military. The security measures are directed at anybody stumbling onto the range and into the line of fire and for the shooters to strictly follow the range rules, like keeping their weapons pointing down-range at all times.

It happens on the second day of the competition, when the Olton team is shooting pistols at the range on the right-hand side of the field.

A man in soldier's uniform stands on the bluff overlooking the end of the firing line where the Olton school cadets are firing. He seems to be a soldier observing what is going on. Giles is at the end of the line, standing with the coach. Some of the team are firing. The coach suddenly grasps his thigh and lets out a cry. Giles looks at him. The coach crumples to the ground. Giles drops down to kneel beside him. A bullet kicks up dirt by his right knee. Giles looks up and sees the soldier on the bluff coming down toward them with a machine pistol in his hand. He stops and is lifting his weapon to fire along the line of the Olton boys.

Giles does not hesitate. He has his pistol in his hand. He jumps to his feet, releases the safety, raises the pistol with both hands, steadies himself for a split second, and fires. He hits the left chest of the man, severing the aorta. The man dies within a few seconds.

Giles takes charge. Are there more shooters? "Squad!" he yells, "On the ground! Pistols at the ready!"

Holding his pistol in front of him, he rapidly checks each direction around him. He sees no further threat. He shouts, "Stay down. John Rank - here - on the double!" John Rank is one of the team and a fast runner. Giles bends down and applies as much pressure as he can to the coach's thigh. It is bleeding profusely. The bullet has cut through the femoral artery. Giles rips off his belt and makes it into a tourniquet. When John Rank is beside him, he tells him, "Run to the next firing pit. We need medics and French soldiers. Go!"

As the coach said afterwards, "It was as if that boy had been born to command. He took one look at the situation and did exactly what had to be done. He killed the shooter, saving the other boys' lives, and then saved mine. Without him there, using his belt as a tourniquet around my thigh, I could have bled to death before the medics arrived."

The British ambassador in Paris is told to send consular officials to St Cyr at "all possible speed" to care for the boys. The British press, especially the tabloids, picks it up and makes it into an international brouhaha. It is an item on the agenda of the Prime Minister's meeting in the cabinet room at 10, Downing Street. Was it a terrorist act? Have MI6 (Foreign Military Intelligence) investigate, the PM orders.

The St Cyr military confirm the coach's judgment. Giles Martin acted in self-defense and to protect his companions.

Soon it is discovered that the gunman is an ex-soldier and a rabid French nationalist, hell bent to remove foreigners from French soil. He had walked onto the base in his soldier's uniform and nobody had thought anything of it. He had deluded himself, according to one of his companions, into believing that the foreign shooting squads were a threat to France and that the foreigners would go out from the base and shoot people. It made no sense, but extremists seldom make any sense. The inquiry would find that the man had a history of paranoid schizophrenia.

The commander of the base is fiercely angry and arrests the officer in charge of the firing range. The commander is called to Paris and told that the British government had expressed their extreme dismay at having young British citizens put at mortal risk by, as the Brits see it, dereliction of duty and proper care on the part of the French military.

General Charles Marlis is sent to Paris. He is to make clear that Her Majesty's Government is most disturbed at the threat to the lives of British citizens and, at the same time, soothe French feelings. He manages to do both with his well-honed political tact.

The French press discovers that Giles is a French citizen and a young hero of the Resistance. They take possession of him and acclaim his French intelligence and bravery. Giles's mother, Sophie, is brought to Paris and put up at the Bristol Hotel, a place more lavish than she had ever imagined to exist. Joey joins them from London. They all go to the Elysée Palace to meet the president at that time, René Pliven. He is only a few days in office, unused to the intricacies of French bureaucracy, and disturbed at finding himself in a spat with the British. He expresses his dismay to General Marlis and assures him that the French government is intent on the safety of British nationals in France.

Pliven summons the internal affairs secretary and asks him who is responsible for preventing a mad shooter entering a military base intent on killing the guests of France. The secretary, a professional bureaucrat, is calm and smooth.

"That would be the *Deuxième Bureau*, sir."

"All right. Tell me about the *Deuxième Bureau*. Who in particular would be responsible?"

The secretary was perplexed. He had been a government bureaucrat for a long time and was not prepared for the ignorance of this politico. "Well, sir, the *Deuxième Bureau* does not actually exist, at least not as the *Deuxième Bureau*. Before the war it existed, but it was disbanded."

"So why are you telling me about a bureau that doesn't exist?" Pliven expostulates.

"Because *le deuxième bureau* is now the collective name given to the security and intelligence services. May I explain, sir?"

The premier waves his hand. "Yes, yes." The secretary proceeds to describe, at length, the curious arrangement of the numerous French security and intelligence services and how it almost never happens that they collaborate with one another.

"Why not?"

The secretary hesitates briefly, then vouchsafes, "as a matter of pride."

"I'm too old for this kind of nonsense!" Pliven explodes. "Tell me who these proud gentlemen are who head up our services. Then I'll want them here at 9 in the morning to explain themselves. So, who are they?"

The secretary goes through the various services and their functions. The services are: *Sécurité Militaire* (SM), taking care of subversion in the ranks and at defense installations; *Service de Renseignements* (SR), collating intelligence from sources and counter-intelligence, the running of agents, spies, telephone taps, and the analysis of foreign newspapers and periodicals; *Service de Documentation Extérieure et de Contre-Espionage* (SDECE), responsible for foreign intelligence. The secretary continues, "then there are other agencies that can be involved, sir, the police, of course."

Pliven has listened, holding down his impatience. "All right. Who would be most responsible among them? I would think the *Sécurité Militaire*, at least by its name."

"Possibly, sir. But this man was only dressed as a soldier, actually in the uniform he had kept after being in the army. So he was a civilian. The military would think, I believe, that *Service de Renseignements* would have the main responsibility. Then, again, the man might have been abroad or been influenced by foreigners and come under the realm of *Service de Documentation Extérieure et de Contre-Espionage.* And then, of course, there would be the police. So it is not entirely clear, sir, who we might think has the chief responsibility."

The premier slaps his hand on his desk in irritation. *"Sacré nom de nom!* ((Damn and blast it!) Sometimes it amazes me that this country ever functions at all! Bring them all in! Tomorrow morning, 9 am sharp. I want the top men from this alphabet soup in here facing me and prepared to explain why they are an ignorant bunch of paper shufflers!"

The various chiefs, after their meeting with the premier, collectively say *enfer et damnation* (hell and damnation.) They repair to an expensive restaurant with an exquisite *cuisine* on the side of the *Bois de Boulogne* and agree on a press release regretting the incident and that they support the commandant of the post in admonishing the officer in charge of the range.

They invite Charles Marlis to meet with them. Charles, having an understanding of the intricacies of the French bureaucracy, tells them that he will report to his government that the steps taken so far are satisfactory and that the prime minister will expect to receive a full and detailed report on the matter, including whether terrorism was involved.

Meeting with Giles later that day, Charles describes how the French Intelligence Services are both incredibly smart and often at odds because of poaching on each other's turf. "The result often is, Giles, that they get all the details right, but are too compartmentalized to see the bigger picture. The government at the top level should step in and straighten things out, but these days the French political scene is so divisive that it is almost dysfunctional. This administration is very weak, like all the others that are coming and going like a game of musical chairs. Ah, well! Somehow France manages to carry on. But she is a burden to herself and the rest of the world. Let us have another glass of wine. Thank God France still makes the premium wines of the world!"

The hubbub dies down. Giles says he will go to his home with his mother and if his two friends would still like to come, as planned, then that would be fine. Robert, his Canadian friend, asks if he can come with them and Giles agrees. He can help the two English boys with any language problems.

Charles and Joey drive them there. Their arrival is a second triumphal entry into Plaignes. The mayor and everyone else of importance, including Mec, are there to greet their native hero. The mayor insists the general, his beautiful French wife, Giles's companions, will all put up at their little hotel at the town's expense. The next day after a brief march through the town, Giles is awarded a medal and a scroll. Finally it is over. In the evening Mec takes them to a restaurant in nearby Chatillon-sur-Seine.

It was then that Sophie has the chance to explain to Giles that Angelica's mother, Marie, one of her best friends, has married again and gone to live near Perpignan in southwest France, about as far away as they can be and still be in France. That is why, she supposes, Angelica has not been writing to Giles. It is all very sad. She hadn't liked the man. But he was well off and had lost his wife to cancer. Perhaps things would work out. She didn't even know their new address.

Mec and Giles sit outside their house. Mec is in fine fettle. "Show me what happened, Giles. How did you hold your gun, my *Lutin*. Like I taught you, eh? Did you have to turn?"

"Oh, yes. But I had good balance, like you taught me. He was raising his gun, getting into firing position again. I looked straight over the pistol and fired. I didn't think about it. I just did it. Like how I had killed Germans." Giles pauses. "But now, Mec, you know, I think it terrible to kill anyone. I am changing, I suppose."

"Don't trouble yourself, Giles. There is no right or wrong out there in the void for us to suddenly bring down to earth. No, you do what is right and wrong at that time, in that place. Almost anything that is right at one time in one place will be wrong at another time and in another place."

It is a serious thought. "So it is up to us, Mec, as individuals, to decide as best we can?"

"That's my thinking, Giles, and I have a clear conscience about it. As far as I can make out that man in Paris, Sartre, is saying the same thing. You build your life around your experience and do what is right, as you see it. Of course, the priests say just the opposite. They claim to know what is absolutely right and wrong as if things never changed. Absurd!" Mec chuckled. "All right, your girl friend has moved away. A young and innocent one. Did you love her?"

"I don't know. What is love, Mec?'

"Oh, if I knew that, I would be the greatest thinker of all time!" Mec laughs. "I'm a bad person to ask. I suppose I feel something like love when I'm helping your mother with things in the house. Then I go to *Le Coq* and find excitement and a fleeting affection, just for an hour or two, with one of the girls there. Both seem to be necessary and built into us, like a birthright. Well - it suits me, Giles. What about you? Have you thought of going to *Le Coq* again?"

Giles flushes. "I suppose so."

"Good. As I've told you before. First you gather experience. Then you make decisions. Don't do it the other way round. Don't decide about things first. That way you never learn anything."

That night, as Giles lies in his bed, he mulls it over. If he had only known it, he was in an "approach/avoidance conflict." That is he wants to do something while, about equally, he does not want to do it. He has had no chance to study psychology and has no experience to guide him on how to deal with such puzzles. He tosses and turns and goes to sleep without deciding anything.

The next morning he awakes early, before his mother is up. He dresses quickly and sets off walking and running over the fields, finding an elation in recapturing the pleasures of being alone, with the earth and sky, and the sights, sounds, and smells of nature. He thinks of Jean Jacques Rousseau and his portrait of the noble savage; a man of nature, innately moral and good. Yes! That's who he is!

He pours his vitality into his footsteps and shouts "halloa" to a red fox that ran across a field in front of him and into the woods beyond. He doesn't need anything more. This is enough and it is pure and innocent, like Angelica, his lost girl friend. Not only would he not betray her, but he would not betray himself by going to *Le Coq* again. He smiles, rather wryly, just to himself, as he walks slowly back to his home. Is life really that simple? He would like to think so, but he doubts it.

So, as it turns out, Giles has nothing to do with the two English and one Canadian boy being taken into Dijon by Mec. They have money enough and even treat Mec to a grand banquet afterwards. Mec calls Giles and says, "Hey! What about it for you, you goddam virgin!" He'd had a bit to drink.

The next day Giles leaves to return to Olton school.

Chapter 17.

Olton Graduation. 1950.

At Linsley House the old housemaster has retired and a new young married housemaster, Alan Sternberg, a Jew, installed. That selection signifies a new outlook for the Christian school and is remarked upon by everyone. The headmaster, Brewster, has a time in convincing the governors that it is a good thing and that it shows the world that British institutions can rise above the prejudices that have been so destructive. "The roots of civil society must be nourished," he had exclaimed to them.

To further proclaim that the school was meeting the challenges of the postwar world, Brewster appoints Giles Martin, who is already the head prefect of Linsley House, the Head of the School. For a French boy to be thus promoted in a quintessentially British institution raises eyebrows. In his letter to all and sundry, Brewster says Giles Martin had demonstrated exceptional character and is a star student going on to Clare College, Cambridge where he has won a scholarship. He is on the school Rugby Team and leads the Rifle and Pistol team. He is also an oarsman, selected to row three in the school boat. His British wards are General and Mrs. Marlis and his mother in France has been decorated as a member of the Resistance. He had saved the lives of Olton boys at the firing range in France by quick intelligent action. And so on. So no doubt about it.

When Giles learns all this he sits down and says, "Good grief! *Merde alors!*" (Oh! Shit!) He is with Joey and she laughs. "Better not say *merde alors*, Giles!"

"What about, holy shit, then?"

"Giles, behave yourself!" she scolds him. "You're an important person now."

"I know. Isn't it awful! I'm almost more excited by the letter from McMullen Publishing. They really liked my first two chapters of *La Folle* - The Mad Woman. They want me to finish it and have sent me £100 cheque. You'll help me some more, I hope, Joey. I'm still not sure of all the English phrases."

Joey gives him a hug. "You're doing just fine, Giles. Give me the text as you go along. I'll be your editor, in red ink! But you're the author. You have the final say. And to receive your first payment as a writer! I couldn't be more proud of you, my darling boy!"

Charles Marlis visits the school, being driven up from the War office in a staff car. He brings with him the Military Attaché from the French Embassy. He introduces the young French colonel to the headmaster.

"Head, I've brought Colonel Ystaing along because the French government and military wish to make amends to you and the boys of Olton school." Charles turns to the French colonel. "Please give the message to the headmaster, colonel."

"*Merci, général.* Yes, if you please, Headmaster. I am instructed to tell you that the French Ambassador to Great Britain wishes to acquaint himself with British education and it would be a great honor to be invited to Olton school to learn of your system. I am further instructed to say that the French government will fund an annual scholarship for an Olton boy to study in France for a year."

"My word, colonel! Let us sit down," the Head says.

Later that day the Head communicates to Charles, "General, neither you nor I had any idea, I think, that taking in a French boy at this school would have engendered all this. If I know anything about boys and men, young Giles Martin is destined for a remarkable life."

The Union flag and the French *Tricolere* are flying side by side in the crisp autumn air when the French Ambassador arrives. The small town of Olton had never been much on the map. Now it is. The head master has on his colorful gown of scarlet cloth and grey silk from Balliol College, Oxford and all the faculty sport their gowns. The town is represented by the mayor and the police chief. Besides the 652 boys there are local people and parents making up the big crowd. Standing beside the head master is the Head of the School, Giles Martin. He greets the French Ambassador on behalf of the boys, first in English and then in French.

It is a long day for everyone. The ambassador is an older man and he and his party are staying at the local Malbot Hotel, an Elizabethan coaching house, complete with ghosts. He invites the Head and his wife and Giles to dine with him.

After dinner the ambassador takes Giles aside. They speak in French. "France is proud of you, young man. I am proud of you. You will be leaving the school at the end of this academic year. What are your plans?"

"I already have been accepted at Clare College, Cambridge, ambassador."

"Very good. Have you thought of returning to France and studying there? At the *Sorbonne* or the *Ecole Polytechnique*. I could assure you of entry. France needs young men like you in these difficult times."

Giles feels uncomfortable, as if the ambassador is hinting he isn't a true Frenchman.

"I think, sir, that France will need men of wide education and knowledge of the world. As I read history, many of the ills of the world have been due to people of restricted vision, people who are too wrapped up in their own narrow views."

"Well, I think I agree with you. As an ideal. But ideals take you only so far. The world is a messy place, at times a pig sty." He laughs. "There, my boy. Continue as you are. You have great talents. Make good use of them. And don't forget your country, *la patrie*."

"Be assured I won't, ambassador."

Chapter 18.

The Other Paris. 1950.

On this Bastille Day Giles will be eighteen and will celebrate it in Paris with Mec. Mec slaps him on the back as he promises Giles, "we will be in *La Place de la Bastille* waving my *tricolere* flag and singing the Marseillaise along with everyone else. Then you'll feel completely French again!"

They had been sitting around the kitchen table with Sophie and talking about how this birthday would be Giles's coming of age, leaving school, and going on to university. Mec was relaxed, enjoying his coffee and cognac, feeling at home with Sophie and Giles in the snug kitchen. Mec was saying, though with a big grin, that the university was in that "backward, perfidious" Anglo-Saxon country of England. "That's what we French say because we cannot forget all that long ago history when we were forever at war with England. Times change. Those Tommies and Churchill fought hard for us this time around just as they had in the Great War. We owe them a debt of gratitude. I know that. DeGaulle should be grateful too. But all he does is pick his nose and find fault with our friends. Stupid pig!"

Giles had thought of DeGaulle as the great hero of the

French and was shocked to hear Mec's words. But then the British had not re-elected Churchill after the war. Life was not simple. There was no one truth about events or people. It sometimes seemed to Giles that life was like walking in an English pea-soup fog. Only the things close to you were real. All the rest was misty, hard to see or to bring into focus. You had to make decisions, but always uncertain if they were for the best or what the outcome would be. In London, in one of the really dense fogs, he had walked into a lamp post! He would not do that again, he hoped, either in reality or metaphorically.

Giles has been at home with Sophie, glad to leave the pressures of Olton school and to be going on from there, though mildly nostalgic for the crucible where much of his adult mind and character had taken form. He would be "going up" to Clare College, Cambridge in September and would be "reading" (that is, studying) "PoliSci" (Political Science) as his major subject along with mathematics, history, and psychology. In the liberal tradition of a great university a student can do that.

For Giles mathematics is a natural focal point. Mathematics is at the pith of reason and logic. Without mathematics science, discovery, and commerce cannot exist. Mathematics has universal application, with one of them being cryptography. Once he had found out about cryptography and its uses in secret communication, Giles had been getting up on its history, particularly in France. The "cabinets noirs[33]" of the 19th and early 20th centuries in France had led the world in encryption and had relied on the mathematics of their day to succeed. Now the mathematics are much more complex and, Giles is sure, will rely on the new computers to create indecipherable codes. He has to be computer-wise. He had learned the importance of secrecy and deception as a boy and anticipates that his understanding of the black arts of espionage will be

---

[33] A *cabinet noir*, in ordinary usage, is a walk-in cupboard or closet. Its special meaning is a "black room" dealing with secret matters.

important in any diplomatic post. He has visions of being the French Ambassador to Washington or, perhaps, Moscow. He is sure he can learn Russian in a few weeks if he has to. At his age, anything is possible.

In the mornings, Giles is completing the translation of Simenon's book into English. Now it is mostly a matter of catching typos, correcting punctuation, and making sure the sense and tone of Simenon's writing is conveyed. He sends the scripts to Joey. She suggests changes but, she reminds him, he must make the final choice. In the age of President Truman with his "the buck stops here" Giles is much aware of the responsibility for making his own choices. He's also thinking about the first book he will write. His thoughts leap about, not settling on anything, but circling around writing a novel about a boy in the *Maquis*.

He follows the news of the day in the papers, on the radio and, when he sees it, on television. He notes that France has officially recognized the "independence" of the State of Vietnam. But, as some commentators say, it is no more than a sop to try to stop the insurgency in the rural areas. When he has talked to Charles Marlis about it, Charles has told him that, out there in the Far East, France is sitting on a powder keg. "They'll soon be fighting a full scale war, now that China is supporting the rebels. They have to give more to the Vietnamese. I'm afraid that what they've done so far is too little and too late. It's not a good outlook. In the long run, those countries will be ruling themselves. It's just a question of time. If they have to fight us, they will."

Giles listens, but somehow can't bring himself to believe that the wisdom and might of France will not solve the matter in some just way for the native peoples. The world will again look to France as the seat of civilization, as DeGaulle declares, and take its rightful place in the world. In this, Giles would throw his allegiance to DeGaulle. Yet, in his tendencies toward socialism, he is fearful of DeGaulle's hierarchical, almost tyrannical, concept of government. Giles sees that the governmental system of the Fourth

Republic is failing France. The electoral system splinters the vote so that there are many parties and factions, with no one of them sufficiently popular or powerful to rule and govern the country. The result is short-lived administrations, each made up of competing groups, producing dysfunction at the top. Would the government, the constitution of France, have to be replaced by a Fifth Republic? Life is not simple.

In the afternoons, Giles relaxes by roaming around the countryside he knows so well, saying hello to the trees and the rabbits, the ones he used to trap and eat. He no longer will do that. They are part of the natural world, just as he is. He cogitates about the difference between his mind, his feelings, forever coming and going, often in confusion, and his body, the basic, undeniable physical body. They have to combine together to make him a whole person. Each has its own imperative. Truth is the imperative of mind, honesty the imperative of feeling, action the imperative of the body. These imperatives - truth, honesty, action - are the guiding principles, he decides, of how he will live his life. He walks on, deep in thought. Yet, deception during the war had been a necessity. Churchill had said that truth is so precious it must be surrounded by a thousand lies. No, life was not simple.

At the very moment of thinking these thoughts, and being puzzled by them, Giles is aware of the danger of being too much of an intellectual, too much of a "turkey" in the new expression. One must keep one's life in balance. Too much thought leads to inaction; too much feeling to hysteria; too much action to emptiness.

Giles suddenly is aware of the incompleteness of words. A word is not the thing itself. It's a horrible limitation! The reality is always greater and more complex than the word. Giles smiles. He supposes that all thinkers had realized this and he is just a late comer to the realization.

Giles stops every now and again to look at the landscape of rolling fields and copses of trees. It is beautiful. At Olton school he loved the physicality of rowing and he will seek out the Rowing Club at Clare College and be diligent in maintaining his physical skill, strength, and bodily health. That is more a British value than a French one, but one he has incorporated deeply into his psyche. His body has its requirements that no intellectualism or moralizing can deny. The new house master at Linsley had discussed in his "Values" seminar the axiom of the Roman poet Juvenal - *Mens sana in corpore sano* - a sound mind in a healthy body. It is the ideal of the stoic for whom achievement by toil is the ultimate good. Giles feels it an important guide, but not an overriding one. Life has to be fuller than that.

Giles shifts his thought to what he is doing then and there, wandering around his old countryside haunts. It is pleasurable, a pleasure for its own sake. There is no reason or rational need or utility for him to do it. It is an inner need, outside of reason. Its bottom line is, it feels good!

Giles smiles, he mustn't let the serious side of him take over too much. Without his intention, the thought leads on to the image of Juliette at *Le Coq*. Giles doesn't feel guilty about it. It just is. A part of nature. And she is a part of that same nature. In any case he knows the sex drive is a universal imperative and therefore natural. That is what Mec has been teaching him. Let nature take its course, while embellishing it into a form of art. In that frame, Juliette had done exactly that. Of course he must see her again. What he would actually do is another matter. Something he has yet to decide on.

Giles wanders on, picking some wild flowers, studying their form, feeling their beauty. He thinks back to the Enlightenment and its opening up of the mind. Jean-Jacques Rousseau, one of Giles's heroes, saw morality growing directly out of the state of nature and that it was good, not evil. Huh! The doctrine of original sin that Christians hold to is evil in itself! Giles rejoices in finding in his atheism a higher moral good, a natural good. At the same time he is frustrated that his thoughts are incomplete. He won't be a recluse! He will engross himself in the life of his times. But his social life hardly exists! That must change. He will go to

Paris with Mec. Meet all sorts. He will visit Juliette. He will go to Cambridge; be a scholar and an athlete. He will be a man of his times.

Mec has been at the house often. He and Sophie have become an item as well as business partners. In the house Mec installs modern plumbing, drains, electric wiring, and radiators to keep the house warm in winter time. Sophie can hardly believe it! What Mec doesn't do himself, he has his men do. He has the dank cellar cleaned out, drained and waterproofed. Sophie can now use it as a store room for the apples and other produce she is providing her customers. She has become the wholesale grocer for stores and shops in the area and, increasingly, for restaurants and cafes. Some are in Dijon and she supplies directly to some of the restaurants there. Mec has joined his business with hers and is moving her merchandise in his vehicles. Sophie's 2 CV car is now just for her own use. Except in an emergency, like when she took flowers from her garden to a sudden wedding of young people. Well, the girl was rather obviously pregnant.

Mec is a great partner for her. He knows everyone in the region and he, or more usually now one of his men, go around advertising and marketing her merchandise. Her business is flourishing and, for the first time in her life, Sophie has a bank account with a reserve of money. She can now afford new clothes, some new furniture for the house, and can employ an old man to look after the rabbit hutch and tend to the vegetables and flowers in her garden.

Mec is extending his long distance transport of goods to include: food stuffs, factory goods, clothing and textiles, household appliances, automobile parts. He will transport whatever needs to be delivered, no questions asked. French commerce is on the move. Because all roads in France lead to Paris, Mec has set up an office on the first floor over a dress shop on *rue Aboukir* in the 2nd *arrondisement* in the *Beauborg* district. The lady manager and he get along well and Mec takes pleasure in looking at the *coquine* (sexy, naughty) lingerie and clothing she sells. The office is just across from *Les Halles* food and flower market on the one side. On the other side is the clothing district around *rue St. Denis* that merges and overlaps the red light district. There, sex is on sale from early morning to late at night.

In the upper stories of the clothing buildings, vogue fashions are turned out. Mec brings in bolts of cloth and boxes of buttons and transports the finished goods to destinations across France. He doesn't hesitate to employ drivers with dark records. "If you steal from me, I will shoot you," he tells them, "like I did with the *Maquis* men who turned traitors." He makes an example of one and that is enough. For the clothing industry, he becomes a reliable transporter of goods at a fair price. He is doing well, though he has to grease the palms of officials to do it. But that is business. He sends his men to the girls he favors and they thank him for the business.

Mec spends his time between Criselles and the Beaubourg, feeling equally at home in both, despite the great contrast between them. That includes his natural man-to-woman affection for Sophie and his erotic satisfaction with *les filles*.

On the morning of July 13, a Wednesday, Mec drives up to the house. Sophie and Giles hug and kiss as she bids him to mind his manners and have a good time in Paris. Though she doesn't say so, if he has sex with *une fille* there, all the better. It's about time. Mec would see that he doesn't get into any trouble.

Giles was no stranger to Paris by this time, at least no stranger to the tourist and "proper" Paris. But he hadn't been to the *Les Halles* market, the first place he and Mec go to after Mec has parked in an underground garage. They arrive in the evening after the hustle and bustle of the early morning and daytime hours have passed. The famed bars, bistros, restaurants and some of the shops in the age-old buildings are open. Giles is entranced. It is a world unto itself. At the *Brasserie Loup* on *rue du Louvre* just by the market, quite a few of the people greet Mec. "Here is my boy," he tells them, without any further specification of who Giles is. They start with the best onion soup Giles has ever tasted. "What now, Giles? It's on me. Some fish and then some meat. A lobster perhaps."

"I've never had a lobster, Mec . . ."

Mec threw up his hands with big grin. "That's it then. Another item in your education!"

Giles sleeps the sleep of youth on a cot in Mec's office/apartment. Over coffee and croissants the next morning he tells Mec, "we must go to the *Jeu de Paume*. It has reopened. They have brought back many of the pictures that the Nazis stole from us. I read about it in the papers."

"Yes. We can do that. You know, nearby is the entrance to the Paris sewers. I've heard you can go down them again now. The Resistance had running battles with the Germans down there. Our men knew the sewers better than the Germans and opened up old disused tunnels, camouflaged them, and hid in them when the Germans were pursuing them. Then they ambushed the Germans. The German corpses joined the rats in the sewers and were eaten by them. A good way to dispose of German corpses - rats eaten by rats!"

They had to wait in a line, but not for too long, to enter the *Jeu de Paume* museum.[34] Once inside they gaze at the

---

[34] The *Jeu de Paume* (literally Game of the Palm) museum is one of the treasures of Paris. It started life as one of the many indoor hand-ball and tennis courts built in Paris in the 18th century. The tennis played in these courts was the precursor of lawn tennis. However the game is more complex and is heavily dependent on the players aiming their shots accurately. The game is still played, though it is more popular now in Britain rather than in France. One of the best courts in Britain is at Cambridge close to Clare College. The *Jeu de Paume Oath* of 1789 was taken at the tennis court in Versailles. The name and the oath is famous for being the first act in the French Revolution. The participants swore to stay as an assembly until a constitution was written acceptable to them.

Before WWII the *Jeu de Paume* museum was the home of Impressionist and Post-Impressionist art. During the war it became the transit point for collection of Impressionist paintings. Giles knows some of them, he has seen them in art books. But to see them for real is a new and thrilling experience. He goes from picture to picture, gazing with his mind as much as his eyes. Mec let him be. Mec enjoys the Renoirs best. Nothing like beautiful women!

Giles halts in his tracks. He is looking at Manet's Olympia. He hadn't known it would be there. Mec comes up beside him.

"You know the painting, Giles?"

Giles remains staring at it. "Er . . . yes, yes, I do." As happens with young people awakening to the riches of the world, Giles's being is in a turmoil. Even - and he thinks it shameful! - his cock is involved, straining in his underpants. That girl in the picture, staring at him with such confidence, with sensuous insouciance, makes him tremble. And she is the chosen messenger from Juliette in Dijon. For the moment Giles is overwhelmed.

Mec is fuming. "The bloody German stole it! Goering had it, the fat bastard. But now it's back. You know, Giles, I'm not an educated man, but that painting . . . well . . . it transports me. A genius, a French genius, painted it. The Germans stole our young men and women. They stole whatever they wanted. With our art, they tried to steal our soul. I'll never forgive them, never!"

It so happens that a man and his wife are nearby, speaking German. No doubt they are some of the first tourists coming back to France to see its wonders, the wonders that

---

the art the Germans were looting from the Paris museums and from private collections. Goering kept for himself over 500 paintings. Some pictures were declared degenerate and some were burned in the *Jeu de Paume* courtyard, including a number of Picassos. Happily much of the art that was stolen, has been found and returned. Starting in 1947 the *Jeu de Paume* was again showing the art of Manet, Monet, Degas, Renoir, Toulouse-Lautrec, etc. Since then, the art has been transferred to the *Musée D'Orsay* and the *Jeu de Paume* is now the exhibition forum for contemporary art and photography.

had survived the bestiality and thievery of the German occupation.

"Fucking hell!" Mec mutters. "Looking at them! Oh, no ! They were never Nazis! Oh, no! They hated Hitler, but could do nothing! Oh, yes! They are nice decent people who had Jewish friends and knew nothing about the concentration camps and the gas chambers! See this, Giles." Mec shows him his pistol in a shoulder holster. "I could kill them right now. I wish I could have killed more of them." He puts his hand on his pistol, glowering at the German couple.

Giles is startled. He cries out hastily in a low voice. "No! No, Mec! You mustn't. We must make peace now. The war is over."

Mec growls, "not in my heart, it isn't. I'll never forgive them."

Giles puts his hand on Mec's arm. "Close you coat, Mec. It will only make things worse if we go on shooting each other. I stopped that mad French man from shooting the English boys. We must not shoot each other."

Mec's eyes lower, his chin falls to his chest. "I know. I know. Take me out of here, Giles."

Giles has tears in his eyes as he leads Mec outside to the balustrade that looks over *La Place de la Concorde* and up the *Champs Elysées* to the *Arc de Triomphe*. The war is over, but it never seems to end. His champion, Mec, is as much a victim of it as anyone. Damn the war! Damn!

They lean over the balustrade together. The traffic circulates around the obelisk in the center of the *Place de la Concorde*. For a while they stand together, saying nothing.

Mec breaks their silence. "So, my young friend, life continues, whether we like it or not, eh?"

"Yes. We have our lives to lead now. Let's go on, Mec. You told me about the sewers. They should be interesting."

They go down the sewers and see the pockmarks in the walls where bullets had struck. Giles had no idea that the extensive sewer system existed. There is no sign of it aboveground. It is new knowledge to him; another item of reality to ponder and understand. When he excretes, this is where the shit goes, into a man built warren of stench; as much a necessity as the art they had just seen. Life is a many layered thing.

Mec takes him to the *Marais*. "*Marais*, as you know, Giles, means a marsh. Once all this ground was a swamp, with streams of water running through it. The streams are still there, underground now. You can't avoid history here. But you can find all that out for yourself, my smart young man. Look around at some of the splendid buildings and the *Place des Vosges* and see for yourself."

As their footsteps wind along the narrow streets, Giles does look at everything. He sees the imposing *Hôtel de Sens* with its conical slate roofs over its little towers. It is one of the leftovers from the time when the *Marais* was the affluent part of town with royal residents.

Mec is telling him. "Nowadays, the Marais is the melting pot of Paris. The Jews are coming back, this was their traditional home in Paris. So are the Chinese. You'll hear every language under the sun here. *Les Halles* and my office are just to one side of it. And now there is something else, the fags - *les pédés* - have moved in. Not that I mind. Many are talented people and work in the fashion trade. Some of them, between themselves, call each other *filles*, girls. Sort of girls in a man's body, I suppose. What the hell! It takes all sorts. Learn that Giles. You are one sort and others are other sorts. Not one better than the other, just different. And each of us, each of them, can be a good person or a bad one. That's how I see it. Except for the Germans," Mec grinned, "they are all bad! All right, Giles. I'm imperfect. Who isn't? Well, it's evening now. Let's go and look at *les filles*."

They stroll along the not-very-wide *rue St. Denis*. "Can you believe, Giles, this street was once the grand entry road to Paris, the Paris that was still centered on the islands in the Seine. They had big parades down this street. It was even narrower then than it is now. The houses overhung the street and people threw their slops out of the windows onto the street. It must have been disgusting!"

Once they had crossed *rue de Turbigo* they begin to see *les filles* standing in the doorways along *rue St Denis*. "Along here," Mec explains, "*les filles* are mostly colored girls from Africa, coming in from the African west coast countries that speak French. Prostitution has a long history there. We, the French, have been very much a part of it. The French Foreign legion is based in Algeria and is half made up with Frenchmen and half with Germans, Italians, and who have you. The legion always had their own brothels near their parade grounds. It is the same today as it has been for more than a hundred years, that is since France took over Algeria, whether the Algerians liked it or not. One of the first things the French did after they had arrived, was to set up their brothels in French style, though there had been native brothels and dancing girls from time immemorial. Most of the girls in them, then and now, are Africans but, like the Foreign Legion itself, some of the girls are Europeans. That's the same for the brothels in Algiers and the other major towns that the *pieds noirs*[35] use. How the white girls get there is another matter. There has always been a white slave trade and blondes have always been the most coveted and fetch the highest price. Once there, well guarded and closed off behind the brothel walls, there is not too much a girl can do. She will have no European clothes and will be clothed, decorated, painted, bejeweled, and perfumed in Arab brothel style. If they somehow escape and are caught, the police bring them back and they are punished by the brothel owners in some not nice way, as a warning to the others. Her best bet is to become a favorite of one of the white customers and persuade him to buy her out."

Giles is hearing this as they stroll along, often being

---

[35] *Les pieds noirs* (the black feet) is the name given to the white settlers in Algeria. Like the Foreign Legion about half were French, the other half drawn from European countries, a few from Britain and America.

solicited by *les filles* as they pass them. Mec says, *"pas ce soir,"* (not this evening) in a pleasant voice to them. "No need to be rude, unless they are rude to you, Giles. And you should know that this is not like it is in Algeria. A girl can go to the police and she can just quit. Of course, most of them have their men, their *maîtres, ponces* and *maqs*, with whom they have a relationship. And no doubt some get their black eyes. But, you know, that is not all that different to the battered wives out there. Yes, that happens. Some husbands beat up their wives. It is not so rare. We live in an imperfect world, Giles and we have to make the best of it."

"I . . . I . . . hadn't known . . . ," Giles stammers, caught between his astonishment at the glamour-sexy prostitutes he is seeing and his introduction to some of the facts of life that he had known nothing about.

"Another fact of life, Giles. Some 5,000 years ago some puritans in Babylon tried to eradicate the prostitutes from their midst. Guess what? They failed. The Babylonian prostitutes were known far and wide for their beauty, their dancing and singing, and their good service. In the Louvre museum you can look at the coins that were used in their brothels. They were one of the first currencies in the world."

They walked on until they came to *rue du Ponceau* and turned up it. "As a rule this is the best street in the *quartier*, Giles. *Les filles* use the hotel, it's really a brothel, up toward the end of the street near the *Métro* station. *Les filles* line up more on the south side of the street at this time, as you see, to avoid the evening sun. It is just a little chilly and again, as you see, many of them are out in their furs. The top girls all wear fox furs, especially the silver fox. It's called the whore's fur here."

A glamorous blonde *fille*, in a rich silver fox fur coat over her lingerie, emerges from a doorway. She says *au revoir* to the man with her. He nods his head and goes off. A young man, who had been waiting across the street, hastens to her. Mec grins. "He sure didn't want anyone to get to her before he did! That's the sex drive, Giles. For that young man then and there, an absolute imperative. She's Yvette, a constant here. She knows her business. She will have the young man pay her and be servicing him in quick time. As the girls say here, time is money."

Mec and Giles stroll and stop on the north side of the street mingling with about a dozen men doing the same thing.

"Look and learn, Giles. Neither you nor I are going to choose one of them this evening. For you, that is another part of your education."

They watch some more. A stunning Chinese girl, most saucily dressed, wearing a black shiny monkey fur jacket, takes her place in the line-up of *filles*. Mec acknowledges her with a smile and a wave of his hand. He mouths, "*pas de soir*" to her. She smiles back.

Mec decides it is enough. "Now, young Giles, you've seen what happens. More facts of life to put in your knowledge bank. It's enough for now. We'll go and get something to eat."

Mec takes him by the arm. As they walk away, Mec tells Giles, "that was Sirene. She has a good man, Jacques, who takes care of her, sees she goes to the doctor. She has a small apartment in the hotel, with a maid, too. Being a prostitute is her profession and, then, you see, she has her private life."

That clinched it. Giles makes up his mind. It has to be done. The erection in his pants is an aching iron rod. Without Mec there, he would have chosen a girl. "Thanks, Mec. Thanks for everything. Are you still on for me to visit Juliette at *Le Coq?*"

Mec slaps him on the back. "Ha! Certainly my boy. You will need a present to give to Juliette. Have you any ideas? Paris is full of things. We can find practically anything here."

"I don't know, Mec. Can you suggest something?" The distraction softens his penis.

Mec cogitates. He knows Juliette has a wonderful wardrobe of clothes, so that would not be special for her. They continue on until they come to *Le Grand Colbert* restaurant. As they are being seated Mec says the inside of the restaurant reminds him of a jewel box. "A box, Giles!" he cries out. "She likes tea. A tea caddy! We will look for one."

The next day they find a Turkish tea caddy in silver and polished wood in an antique store. The owner says it has just come in. He has cleaned it up but, he admits, he knows little about Turkish tea caddies and cannot read the Arabic. Mec talks him down to a hundred francs and the man wraps it up in newspaper and puts it in a brown paper bag.

"We have to have tea for the tea caddy, eh, Giles!" They walk to *Marriage et Frères*, the best tea shop in Paris, where they buy packets of Indian and Chinese tea. In the evening they drive back to Criselles. Sophie hugs her son and then embraces Mec. She eyes Mec. He shakes his head, with a grin. They understand each other. "But it is arranged, Sophie."

When they are alone, Sophie tells him, "thank you, Mec, thank you. You are quite the best father my boy could have. I don't need to know the details. I like Colette Saludin at *Le Coq*. We got on very well during the war and she buys some of my goods now. Give her my greetings. And Mec, you will make sure that Giles does the right thing by the girl, won't you?"

Mec grins. "I'll do that, be assured."

He tells Giles that he should send Juliette a bunch of flowers. "Sort of the same as you saw in that Manet picture at the *Jeu de Paume*."

When Giles is alone in his room he cleans and polishes the tea caddy meticulously, until the silver shines and the grain of the wood stands out like new. He notices the inscription and some other marks on it, but has no idea of their meaning.

* * *

In the morning Julie is chatting with her maid. "Marie, the young man will be here at five this evening. I've told you what Mec said. I couldn't have chosen better than to send him that Olympia picture and that Giles - that is his name,

Giles - saw the original in Paris and was quite overcome." Julie smiles. "Isn't that lovely?"

Marie smiles too. "Yes, *m'amselle*. Lovely."

"I have shown you the picture, Marie. I will help you make-up the couch so that it will be just like the one Manet painted. You will be the maid in the picture, Marie, with a bunch of flowers in your hands, and be dressed like the maid. Though she was black and I won't ask you to do black-face."

"No, I don't think I would like that. Thank you, *m'amselle*."

"You know the girl was quite nude except for a flower in her hair, a silvery choker with black trim around her neck, a bracelet, and silvery shoes. I want to do it exactly right. Have the man who knows how to do the lighting up here to check everything and then have him here to throw the switches. But remind him to keep out of sight. Right?"

"Yes, *m'amselle*."

"*Mon Dieu!* This rain! The men are staying home because the roads are flooded. *Madame* told me we are only doing half the business we normally do. I hope it doesn't stop the young man from coming. He lives eighty kilometers away, I believe."

Chapter 19.

The Occasion.

Mec drives to Sophie's house in plenty of time. He is glad to see that the house, situated on a knoll beside the road, is not threatened by the flood of water falling from the heavens. It has been raining for three days now. Houses on lower ground are being flooded. The ditch by the road outside the house has water gushing down it like nothing he nor Sophie have ever seen. Mec has read that a scientist thinks the unusual weather could be due to a warming trend in our climate. Well, if it makes the winters less cold, he's all for it.

"I'm certainly glad we water-proofed your cellar, Sophie. I hope it's dry."

"Absolutely! Not a drop. I can't thank you enough, Mec. There's a lot of goods down there waiting to go out and they've not been touched."

Giles comes downstairs from his room and joins them, putting down the suitcase he is carrying.

Mec reminds Sophie, "we will be staying the night in Dijon, see some friends, perhaps go to a movie. Are you all set, Giles?"

Giles is intent on appearing normal, though his nerves are on edge. He had bought some expensive gift paper and had spent half an hour carefully wrapping the tea caddy in it. As he was going to give it to Juliette when they met, he had decided not to write a card. Anyhow he really didn't know what to say. He didn't want to ask Mec. He loved Mec dearly but, now that he was a man on his own, he would decide things on his own.

"Sure, Mec. I'm all set."

Giles goes over to his mother and gives her a hug. "Don't worry, *maman*. Mec knows the road well."

"I'm sure he does, Giles," she says with a smile, while giving a knowing nod to Mec.

At the door Sophie bids them goodbye. "You two have a good time. The radio is now saying there will be thunderstorms this afternoon and evening. Can you believe it!"

On the road Mec is glad he has allowed plenty of time to reach Dijon. They have to make two detours where the road is flooded. In one spot a torrent has uprooted trees and work crews are dealing with the trees fallen across the road. The wind and the rain make their work even harder.

At Olton school, in the English Literature class, Giles had learned about the "sympathetic fallacy." Authors make the elements be in "sympathy" with the moods and passions of their characters. The idea is that a storm outside responds to the storm inside the person; or, as the English master pointed out, the storm outside may excite the latent storm in the person and make it come out. It is called a fallacy, but perhaps it is not.

Giles certainly is aroused by the rain and the wind as he goes toward his first sexual realization. Will it be the storm that writers rave about? He is flipping between the prospect and the fear of making a fool of himself. Suppose he can't get it up? The problem with too much intelligence is the ability to foresee every eventuality, including the awful ones.

"Do you think we'll be in time, Mec?" Giles asks, somewhat anxiously. He will be almost as pleased to have to postpone the event as to actually get there. By this time he knows what an approach/avoidance conflict is and recognizes that he is in the grip of one. He has done what Mec had told him to do, sent a bunch of flowers. So, at this point, all he can do is wait it out as they go toward *Le Coq* and whatever fate holds in store for him there. Perhaps it is just the weather, but Giles has a premonition that something extraordinary will happen.

Mec is peering through the windscreen with the wipers going at maximum. "Jesus! I have never seen such rain! But we'll get there. I wouldn't have you miss it just because of this damn weather!"

Colette has told Mec it will be expensive. "So what, Colette! First times only happen once. They should be good."

In the terms Mec understands, he is doing precisely the right thing for the boy. He hopes that being a sort of honorary father to Giles will advance his relationship with Sophie. He is getting older and wouldn't mind settling down to married life. Perhaps Sophie feels deprived of sex, as well as a regular married life, and all his needs can be met with her. She has hinted at it and he has felt her warm kisses.

Mec stops in the next village and phones Collette Saludin. "We are on our way, Colette. This storm is a bitch. Flooding everywhere. We may be a bit late."

"No problem, Mec. Just do the best you can. We will wait for you. The rain is terrible here too. Take care."

They arrive and Mec parks the car at the railway station. Putting on their coats they scurry to *Le Coq* through the drenching rain. They are only fifteen minutes late when Mec rings the bell at the end of the passage way. "Hey! I've got you here pretty well on time, Giles. So now it's up to you!"

Giles face is set. Dammit! Why doesn't Mec just shut up. "You don't have to tell me, Mec, for heaven's sake! Just let me be."

"Sure, sure, Giles. Best of luck," Mec says, backing off.

After Giles has taken off his raincoat and cap and been to the men's washroom to pee and tidy himself, *Madame* Colette Saludin herself leads him to Juliette's *chambre*. The *chambre* is quite a long way down a corridor at the end of the building. It was in the neighboring house that Colette had bought and it now formed an annex to the main building.

Colette opens the door. Juliette's *chambre* is barely lit. All Giles can make out, coming in from the light, is an illuminated chair.

"Sit here, Giles," Colette says, leading him to the chair. "Juliette has a scene for you."

Colette leaves. She is confident that Juliette will entrance the young man. She goes to the bar in the small salon and tells Blackie to give her a snifter of brandy.

"We'll just have to see, Blackie. If she can't cherry pick the young man, nobody can!"

Blackie is polishing a glass with a cloth. "We have a saying, *madame*. Man chooses, but God disposes."

"That's about right!" Colette agrees. "You're a wise fellow, Blackie."

Colette falls silent as she downs the brandy. That Giles Martin has been at the upper-crust school in England, that the other young men had been to, is most satisfactory. Having high class young men from Canada and England come to her establishment gives an added distinction to *Le Coq*, impresses her clientele. No doubt Giles Martin will take his place in the upper reaches of French society. Not that there can be any certainty that he will return to *Le Coq*. Young men can be as fickle as young girls. But with Mec guiding him it is likely that he will follow the conventional track of young men destined for the *haut monde* in France. He will reserve a place in his life for erotic pleasure.

In Juliette's *chambre* a waiter appears next to Giles, as if from nowhere. The man murmurs, "*Monsieur*" and sets a *coupe de champagne* on the small table by Giles's side, then fades back into the shadows.

Delicate lute music starts to play and the slowly increasing light discloses the scene; at first colorless, then becoming colorful, the scene is Manet's Olympia. The maid, holding the bouquet of flowers Giles has sent, stands behind the nude reclining girl.

All is still, a tableau[36]. Then Olympia softly raises her fan and starts to sing in a light beguiling voice. Julie had found the wistful song in an old book of songs of the Auvergne and a man had told her that Edith Piaf had once sung it.

Je suis un soupir dans le vent

qui est porté en mouvement

jusqu'ici, jusqu'ici et

en le même vent viendra

le beau jeune qui me tiendra

toute ma vie, toute ma vie. [37]

As she sings she slowly turns her head until her eyes rest on Giles. She poses as Manet had painted her, gazing at the onlooker. Manet, as she knew, was a regular visitor to the better houses in Paris, at least when he had the money. He died of syphilis while still quite young. She is sad for him. She feels he understood very well the girls who worked for their living in the sex business.

The music continues. The maid enquires of her mistress, "shall I bring the *jeune monsieur* to you, *m'amselle.*"

---

[36] An important feature of the better Houses in France was the décor in the service rooms. These rooms are described in *"La Vie Quotidienne dans Les Maison Closes"* by Laure Asler, Hachette, Paris 1990. From page 23: "Cunningly ornamented, the room with its perfumed drapes is the theater, the throne, the altar, the work tool of the woman."

[37] *I am a sigh in the wind*
that is flowing
up to here, until now and
in the wind will come
the handsome young man who will hold me
all my life, all my life.

"Yes. Bring my lover to me. I can wait no longer! My soul is open to him."

Julie is vaguely remembering the words from some romantic novel she'd read. They are over-dramatic, but why not? The words sounded good as she said them and it was possible she wouldn't be disappointed by the young man. Perhaps he would show his soul to her. It happened, but only occasionally. In her limited experience of young men, almost all were either over-impetuous or crushingly shy, sometimes both. They had big stiff "young" erections, but that was about all they usually brought to the "love" scene. Well, she would find out soon enough. She wanted to please Mec. She really likes and admires him. That's why she is doing her best to give his boy a good send off. She wafts her fan so that her perfume is in the air about her. Marie brings Giles over.

Giles is stunned by the special scene set before him; far beyond anything he had imagined.

The only possible thing to do is to immerse himself into the scene and let whatever happens, happen.

Juliette holds out her hand. He bends over to kiss it, saying, "*Bon soir, mademoiselle*. I am very glad to be here. Your Manet scene is most beautiful . . . as are you."

She smiles. "How gracious you are, young man. I am glad to see you again." She turns her head, "Marie . . . bring us *coupes de champagne* and *petit fours*."

Giles is standing by the bed. She tells him to sit on the chair. "I can tell you are a gentleman, Giles. This is the first time you have been with a girl like me in private?"

"Yes, it is," he admits. He glances first at her face, then let his eyes roam momentarily over her beautiful body. He flushes and looks down. Where should he put his eyes?

She rescues him with a tinkling laugh. "Don't trouble yourself, Giles. There has to be a first time for everything. Let us talk a little. Look at me and my body. You find me beautiful, yes? I think young beautiful women are God's gift to men. Do you agree?"

Giles is nonplussed by the question, but glad she is taking the lead. "I don't know . . . I suppose . . . but I think beauty and seeing what is beautiful lies within us. You see . . . I don't believe in god; it's just us here . . . doing the best we can." Giles smiles, still uneasy. He had rather imagined their bodies would be engaged right away, not their minds. Now they are discussing god! Has he offended her?

Julie does not wish the conversation to lead off into anything remotely serious, not, at least, yet. But she is pleased that the young man has a mind of his own. First she has to have him fuck her and have his first ejaculation of the session. Young men like him recover quickly and are ready to get it up for their second ejaculation in an hour or so. She is tempted to skip the condom with this virgin boy, but that would be a bad precedent to set for him. He has to be fully aware of the downsides of fucking.

Juliette raises herself to sit on the side of the couch. She takes Giles's face in her hands and kisses him on the lips. "Kiss me back, *chéri!*" she intones. "Open your mouth, darleeng! Don't be shy. You are here to let yourself go! So kiss me deeply!"

Their embrace deepens and Giles is trembling from the sensations coursing through his body. Ssuddenly, a loud thunder clap makes the building shake, including the couch they are on. It takes a second for Giles to disentangle what is happening inside him and what is happening outside. Bright flashes of lightning are coming through the curtained windows. Hail hits the tiled roof above their heads in a drum roll.

"*Ça alors!*" Julie exclaims in surprise. Even more to her surprise she finds herself sliding off the bed. As the bed and the floor tilt, she lands on top of Giles. They grasp each other, amid the pillows and cushion sliding off the couch. Marie, crying out in alarm, slides past them on a rug over the parquet floor, as if she was on a sled, and crashes into the room's wall below them.

Julie cries out to her. "Marie, Marie! Hold on to something! Hold on tight! I'll help you."

Giles grabs the frame of the couch. He clamps Julie's nude body close to him to keep her from following her maid into the wall. Julie is scared out of her wits. What can be happening? Is it the end of the world? She's glad the young man is holding her tight. "What's happening?" she shrieks.

Giles is as startled as she. He realizes the building is shifting on its foundations and falling to one side. The lights are still on and he sees cracks, then gaps, opening in the walls.

"We have to get out of here," he tells Julie tensely. "The building is collapsing. Which door or window should we make for?"

The floor is tilting more and more. Giles can feel the couch starting to slip. They mustn't be crushed by it. He must do something. Not stay there. They can't wait.

"Here we go, Juliette! We'll slide down to the window, next to Marie. Hold on!"

As Giles pushes off from the couch with his strong legs, it slides off over the floor and lands against the far wall but, thank goodness, well to the side of Marie. They slide over the floor and end up next to her. Her face and chest are covered in blood. Her nose is bleeding from the impact of crashing into the wall.

Still holding Julie firmly, Giles scans around, his mind at full pelt. Maybe the heavy rains have something to do with it. Perhaps there has been a landslide. Whatever it is they have to get out of there.

Giles thinking is right on. The river, Suzon, passes through Dijon, mostly underground. Dijon is an old town, the Romans called it Divio, and it has Roman and other brick foundations and empty spaces under the modern town. In this severe rain storm the underground Suzon has finally eroded some Roman bricks and caused a massive sink hole. The building containing Julie's *chambre* is above the sink hole that is forming and is about to be engulfed in it.

Giles accepts, without thinking about it, that the two women are his responsibility. For the moment the motion has ceased, but he senses they are balanced precariously.

They are under a window covered by its curtain. "Sit up, *mademoiselle*, and hold on," he tells Julie. "I'm going to stand and open this window."

"Can I help?" she asks tensely.

"Look after the woman. She needs your help."

"Yes, yes. Of course." She sidles over to Marie who throws her arms around her. She is terrified. The blood from her nose goes all over Julie. *"Oh! M'amselle!"* Marie moans.

Julie is still nude. Giles tears down the curtain. "Here, put this around you."

Giles unlatches the window and opens it. He looks out to a wall of mud, the side of the sinkhole. He hangs out of the window so he can see up. Fifteen feet above him is the edge of the sinkhole and there are people there at ground level. The building slips down a few more inches. He has to be quick.

Giles sees firemen at the top of the sinkhole. "Get a rope ladder down here as quick as you damn well can. We are slipping. Hurry! We don't have much time."

A fireman runs to the truck and returns with a rope ladder. He lets it unroll to where Giles is by the open window.

Giles looks down to Julie. "Bring the woman here. Be quick. I don't know how long we have."

Julie drags Marie to where Giles can grab her. He hauls her up and puts her hands on a rung of the rope ladder.

"Climb up!" he tells her. But Marie can't.

"Pull her up, men!" he shouts up to the firemen. Giles manages to put her feet on a rung of the rope ladder as they pull it up.

Once they have her up, they send the rope ladder down again. Julie climbs up it, in the process losing her window curtain covering. Colette is there and takes the nude girl in her arms. "Give me your coat!" she shouts to a woman. The woman gives up her coat and Colette wraps Julie in it. Colette tells the woman to follow them. She will get her coat back.

At the same time, Giles starts to climb up the ladder. The room, he now sees, is hanging on the edge of a wall of some ancient foundation; but its bricks are giving away. Giles grabs the next rung. Everything slides way beneath him. He is splashed by the spray of muddy water. He climbs up the ladder to the cheers of the small crowd that has gathered there.

"That was close!" he says as the firemen help him stand at the edge. They look at the turmoil of water, mud, bricks and debris below them in awe, with few words being spoken.

On the front page of the Dijon paper the next day the headline is, "That was close!" followed by a picture of Giles and then pictures of Juliette and Marie. The reporter had written an account of what had happened and the rescue of the two women and the young man. One of the firemen had a camera and shot the scene. The next day the rescue was in the papers and on TV.

Mec was at the top of the sinkhole. He tells people proudly, "that's my boy! The bravest fellow you'll ever meet! A war hero of the resistance!"

Once more Giles is famous and heroic, quite to his dismay. The reporters hold back on saying, "escape from a brothel!" Rather the headline is "Escape from hotel *Le Coq*." Giles reads it thankfully.

Mec takes Giles to the car and then to the restaurant of *Le Coq* to warm up and have some food and drink. The restaurant is well away from the sinkhole and unaffected. People crowd around. Cameras flash.

Giles asks, "where's Juliette? Is she all right?"

Someone tells him, "she's fine, thanks to you. So is the other woman. They are both in the hotel, quite safe."

A voice in the crowd asks, "is she your girlfriend?"

Mec stands in front of Giles. "Giles Martin is my boy. I'm his uncle and captain of the *Maquis* squad in which he served with bravery and skill. Naturally he has girl friends. That's all. Giles needs to be let alone to recover. Please let us have our food and drink in peace." Mec's air of authority does the trick. The crowd disperses.

Mec can hardly wait to ask. "Well, Giles, did it happen?"

Giles blushes. "No, not really. We'd only had time to kiss before the room began to fall apart."

Mec laughs uproariously and slaps him on the back. "Only kissed! Oh, my! Don't worry. It'll happen the next time."

"I don't know if there will be a next time, Mec," Giles grins. "That poor girl was terrified! She might think I'm bad luck for her."

"Ah! But you saved her. That's the important thing. We'll let a few days go by and then see what's what."

Colette Saludin is not about to turn away from the publicity. *Mademoiselle* Juliette LaPerle is a hostess in the hotel. She had brought refreshments to the room *Monsieur* Giles Martin was occupying. No mention is made of her not having any clothes on, of course. The maid was there too, seeing everything was in order. She, Colette Saludin, the proprietor of the hotel, welcomed the honor of the young resistance hero choosing her hotel. In her opinion he should be decorated again for the bravery and skill with which he had saved the lives of her two women and his own, too.

Locals went along with the story, though virtually all Dijon knew it was a fiction.

The mayor of Plaignes was not about to miss the opportunity of having another gala event, even though a smaller one, to honor their young hero once again. The mayor felt he should invite the two rescued women, even though they were working in a brothel. Well, he had been there and it was a damn good brothel!

The story even made the London papers. Charles and Joey read the account and wired Giles their congratulations.

Giles entertains a wild medley of thoughts, feelings, and emotions in the following days; but, overall, he is more relieved than anything else. He has to laugh at himself for not attaining "the big event." It seems now almost trivial compared with the fact that their lives had been at stake. Though he had not been particularly scared. Somehow he knew it would turn out all right. He seems to live a charmed life. However, not in all respects. He has a problem. Juliette wants to date with him outside *Le Coq*, as an ordinary girl, as far as Giles can make out. She said as much when they had briefly met in Plaignes during the gala to celebrate "Miraculous Escape from the Dijon Sink Hole", as one headline had it. Mec grinned when Giles told him of it and exclaimed, "Why not?"

By some miracle the tea caddy in its gift wrapping has been found intact. So Giles has an excuse to see Juliette again. He would do it somewhere other than *Le Coq*. So he sets up a date with her at the restaurant *Le Pré aux Clercs* in Dijon, noted for its outstanding cuisine and its intimacy. It is near *Le Coq*, convenient for Juliette. Mec knows the *maître d'* there, of course. Mec knows everyone of any importance.

Giles sets about cleaning the caddy again and again wrapping it in expensive gift paper. This time, he hopes, he will actually be able to give it to her.

Chapter 20.

Julie prepares.

Julie is musing at her toilette. Her room falling into the sinkhole, and she and Marie being saved by the young man, had been the first truly exciting thing that had happened to her since the Germans had come into Avier. She would like to find Ernst and thank him for what he had done for her. She smiles, a little wryly, knowing that most people would think it odd that she should thank anyone for guiding her to become a prostitute. But, the fact was, that being a prostitute had served her well. At least until now.

Julie grimaces. Her life has become repetitive and rather boring. She has been thinking about breaking away. She might become an actress. She wonders whether Ernst had gone back into the theater. She hopes he has survived the war. So many Germans were killed. Yes, being an actress is a definite possibility. After all, being a *fille* is really just a lot of acting and she likes doing scenes, like the Manet Olympia and Lili Marlene. She can sing a bit and she has read quite a few books, though none of them very serious. She likes the romances of Gabrielle Colette best.

Julie touches up her nails. Some of the men are well educated and talk about current affairs, their professions, and tell her interesting things happening in science and literature such as: it was being said that Albert Camus, the French writer, was going to be awarded the Nobel prize in literature. And she hadn't even heard of Camus! That riles her. She is becoming aware of what she lacks. However, to put against that, is Colette telling her she has "worldly wisdom" and that, in their world, is what counts. Marie tells her that "worldly wisdom" is the posh way of saying "street smarts." Well - sure. But there is more out there, a lot more. And she wants it.

Perhaps she could be an extra on some film set and be "discovered." It has happened, she knows. At least money would not be a problem. She has socked away, first from Paris and now from *Le Coq*, what seems to her a fortune, much of it in Swiss banks, where it is earning a small but steady interest. Most of it is in government bonds, to be safe, but some she has put in market stuff, especially plastics, computers, and cars, like Subaru and Toyota. Those Japanese shares are dirt cheap and she thought the names were pretty. She worked with a Swiss broker who had been her customer when he visited *Le Coq*. All the papers, properly signed and documented, are in Colette Saludin's safe, with duplicates in the bank in Geneva.

Hey! She is a woman-of-the-world now, in charge of her destiny. A lot of her young life had passed in a blur, with one day just following another. Now it is coming into sharp focus. She would be a modern young woman, taking care of herself, finding her own life and living it.

A shiver races through her body. Yes, the future is daunting. *Le Coq* is a safe haven and Colette is the closest thing to a mother she's ever had. She'd never been close with *Madame* Guyton in Paris. Her own mother had been under the thumb of her father and his "wrath of God" stuff. Julie thought back. The war had been good for her. If she had grown up in Avier, her prospects would have been dismal. Now, if she is brave enough, the world was open to her. She would take Marie with her. Perhaps Marie felt like she did, wanting to break away. If she is not mistaken Marie and Blackie, the barman, had something going on between them.

That young man, Giles Martin, had been so strong! Good looking and rather sweet, too. She could go for him! When they had met in Plaignes at the gala to celebrate their escape from the sink hole, she had invited him to see her again. But how to follow up? She didn't want him to come to *Le Coq* again. She must find a way for him to discover that she is more than just a brothel girl.

Happily, the problem is solved for her. Mec brings her a letter from Giles Martin. He has written to invite her to dine with him at *Le Pré aux Clercs* restaurant in Dijon and suggests the following Thursday. That is in two days time. He hopes it will be convenient for her. Mec takes the short note she writes back accepting his invitation.

Now, ridiculously, she is nervous about it. His invitation had been written in a rather stilted way and then he had ended it - "*with my warm thoughts.*" Julie showed it to Colette, who said it was quite charming, but an unusual way to sign off. "Very personal, Julie. Maybe it's something the English do. Though their reputation is to be stiff about these kinds of things. You'll have to find out for yourself. I'll have Blackie drive you there in my new Citroën sedan in his chauffeur's uniform. Have you seen the car? It's their top-of-the-line model with a powerful engine and front wheel drive. It turns round corners very well and goes like the wind when I want it to! Every now and again when I'm on a straight road I like to drive fast. Let it rip! Makes me feel young again! Now . . . may I give you some advice?"

"Yes . . . please."

"Don't dress too sexy. Be stylish, certainly. Think of yourself as a princess. It's time you met a young man, a proper young man who will find you the nice bright girl you are." Colette gives her a hug. "Enjoy yourself, *ma petite.*"

Colette knows from her years of experience that she is about to lose Julie. A bright intelligent girl like her is bound to want to go out into the world; and, anyway, it doesn't pay to make a girl like Julie stay on. If she did stay, she would become dull and listless and no longer the charmer men desired. The clientele of *Le Coq* liked young fresh blood. That's just the way it is.

In spite of laughing at herself, Julie can't help but be nervous that Thursday morning. It is good that the house is busy and that she has two appointments in the early afternoon.

As usual Julie attends to her body, does her showy make-up with care, has Marie dress her golden hair. She pulls the sheer nylon stockings up her long slender legs and attaches them to the straps of her lacy garter belt. She puts on one of her sexy little jet-black lacy dresses. It zips down all the way so that she can strip-tease it off easily, at just the right moment, to disclose her breasts, body, and genitals and give her body to her customer. Marie kneels to put her feet in the tall stiletto heels and buckles the straps around her ankles. Julie doesn't take off her shoes. That is something *Madame* Guyton had taught her a long time ago, when she had started at *Les Poulets*. "You are *une fille de joie*, Juliette. A girl takes off her shoes for her lover, not her customers. Always remember that time-is-money for *une fille*."

Julie paints her plump lips with a bright scarlet lipstick and pulls long satin gloves up her arms. She checks her looks in the mirrors. Marie had created a sleek and frothy abundance of her hair.

"Marie! I remember the first man who is coming likes me in a little hat. Not too much of one." Marie produces just the right thing, a fascinator with feathers and helps Julie secure it to her head.

Julie checks it looks right, then picks up a long white fox fur scarf and trails it over her black gloved arms. Julie never wants to go out to her work not looking her best. That is something Ernst had taught her and it was the best piece of advice she'd ever had: "Be the best you can be."

"*Eh, bien, Marie!* Am I sexy and beautiful?" she grins to her maid, jinking her hips.

Marie casts a searching eye over her young mistress and grins back. "*Oui, m'amselle. Parfait! Tu es belle.*"

As Julie has come to expect, the sight of her arouses the man. She sees the bulge in his trousers grow. She is coquettish, charming, flirtatious and then, on the satin sheets of the wide oval bed, under the UV lights to make her a lustrous sight, she is hungry to have his penis in her mouth and then have him thrusting into her body. That is what her vagina, her money box, is for. She cries out, "Fuck me! Fuck your whore! Jesus Christ I want you! I'm a whore. So fuck me, you devil!"

Julie had found long since that calling herself a whore excites most men. It gives them license to satisfy themselves in her to the full. Then they tip her well and make return visits. It is business, nothing more.

Julie makes good money that afternoon, but that is not what is on her mind. As the first man leaves and the next one arrives she is thinking how she will dress to meet Giles Martin that evening. It is cold outside so she will certainly be wearing furs. Well, if Giles is to be her "boy friend" he has to get used to her wearing furs. She just isn't herself without them. Perhaps he will find them sexy, as many men did. Her lynx furs will be right. Young women are wearing them, she knows, from seeing pictures in the fashion magazines. They are not her original lynx furs, the ones Ernst had found for her, but new ones that she had bought and had styled for herself. Wearing lynx would remind her of when she was young and innocent, riding with the Germans. Julie smiles to herself as she remembers it; and before that, she recalls, she had run in the fields with her golden hair streaming behind her.

The second man of the afternoon is finishing his ejaculation in her. She smiles at him as he groans his last groan. He is a nice enough man, about 50, a wine merchant in the town, married with children, who comes once a week to have sex with her. They are friendly together and he sure does get aroused, shouting and groaning, as he comes to his climax. He says, as other men do, that it is essential for his health. Perhaps it is. She occasionally thinks of the wives. Why can't they do as she does and satisfy their husbands? Perhaps, when she is out in the world, she will figure it out.

She says *au revoir* to him at the door and finally clinches in her mind what she will wear for the evening. It will be her Dior cocktail dress, white and black with a boat-neck, narrow belted waist - she will use a waist-cincher to give her the right look - with a slightly bouffant skirt reaching to mid-calf. She will wear her new pair of slender shoes with the new higher heels. Marie will do a quick fix of her hair with a chignon and a loose tress over her left shoulder. Her cute little roundel hat with white pearls will echo her white pearl necklace and earrings. She will wear just one ring, a big ruby set in diamonds. Marie will help her put the look together, from head to toe and with the pocket of the lynx muff holding what she needs and her cosmetics.

Her tips had been in cash that afternoon, quite generous, though she hadn't counted them. She puts the notes in the purse of her muff as her "mad money." OK. She is all set for the evening. She takes a deep breath. It is quite a challenge to be a fashionable mid-century girl, when her knowledge of life barely extends beyond life in two brothels.

Chapter 21.

Giles prepares.

Giles dawdles over the simple lunch he is having in the kitchen at his home. His mother has driven her Mouse to visit with a friend that morning.

He has completed his freshman term at Clare college, Cambridge. It has been a challenge to mind, body, and spirit. He is "reading" - that is studying - PoliSci (Political Science) along with mathematics, philosophy, and psychology. His tutor warns him not to try to do too much, but he is avid for knowledge and "wisdom." Though, he realizes, wisdom comes only with experience. Well, he grins, some of that experience could be lying in wait for him with Juliette.

His central field of study is the French political system from the mid-19th century to the present, with the specialty of studying French intelligence and security services. He intends to write his master's thesis on the topic. The Dreyfus affair is his starting point. His tutor agrees that modern French history cannot be understood without taking Dreyfus into account. In December 1894 a Jewish army officer, Captain Alfred Dreyfus, was accused of espionage for the Germans. It was a trumped up charge to cover the real spy and contaminated with anti-semitism. Dreyfus was found guilty, sent to Devil's Island, and imprisoned under harsh conditions. Emile Zola, the writer, accused the government of wrongful imprisonment and a cover up. People took sides passionately. Belief in the army was hard to shake. The matter was prolonged over years, the army and government refusing to concede anything. Anti-semitic demonstrations were fueled by the affair. It was a national scandal on a grand scale. But eventually the truth came out, the real spy identified, Dreyfus exonerated, and the sins of the army and government laid bare. The affair impacted every corner of French government and society. But, in the end, it spoke to the underlying strength of French culture, able to survive and correct the devastating scandal. In learning of the affair in detail, Giles was forced to recognize the past failings of French institutions and that powerful interests resist the truth when the truth threatens them.

At Cambridge, Giles has been most fortunate to be able to attend the course on the History of European Philosophy given by Bertrand Russell. It had given him a wide frame of reference to all European history and politics. The men of politics, armies, and churches had been imbued with the thoughts and perspectives of their time and their actions could only be understood by knowing how they thought. It was an essential backdrop for understanding the Dreyfus affair and much else, up to present times.

Giles has written essays for his tutor once a week. His command of English is equal to those of most English students and his speech is virtually indistinguishable from his English fellows. Greatly to his satisfaction, and to the fulsome praise of Joey and Charles, his translation of *La Folle de Maigret* has been published and he is receiving royalty payments from its sale. Earning his own money and banking and spending it, though carefully, and enjoying it all, he feels marks a major step forward into adulthood.

Giles is rowing number three in the Clare College second boat and finds a new depth of pleasure in being one of a team and in the camaraderie of the crew. Very literally, they all have to pull together, precisely and strongly, to be a success. In the next term he will row in the first boat and the coach has told him that the selection committee for the university boat has him on their short list. That would be incredible! To row in the Cambridge boat against Oxford on the Thames in London!

He is playing Rugby on the Clare College team as the reserve scrum-half and finds a quite different pleasure in the rough and tumble, and the skill too, of the game. They play on grass fields that often are muddy. At the end of a game they can look like chocolate soldiers. The big baths in the club houses hold six to eight men at a time. They all jump in stark naked amid the steam and soap bubbles with bottles of beer in their hands. Giles experiences male bonding, not as a boy at school, but as a young adult. It is fun and joyful while being serious too. He is making friendships that can give him entry later on to the circles of power and influence in Great Britain.

Now he is back with his mother in Criselles. He had wondered, rather anxiously, how Sophie had taken his visit *Le Coq*. Well - - it had ended in his being hailed a hero yet again, for saving Juliette and her maid from falling into the sink hole. Even so, he had gone home quite expecting his mother to scold him. But not at all!

"I am French, like you are, Giles!" she cries, as she takes him in her arms and kisses him. "Tell me everything, my dear boy! But what a disaster!"

"Yes, it was, *maman*. But luckily everyone escaped without harm."

"No, no! As Mec has told me, you could not be intimate with the girl. What frustration!"

Giles collapses into a chair. "*Maman*! You are something else! How could I have a better mother! I love you! I love you! But, you know, I wasn't frustrated. I had met a beautiful girl who had put herself out to be something special, just for me; and then she had shown me she was brave and courageous and that her first thought was the safety of her maid."

Sophie smiles at her boy. "So? What have you done? I saw her at the Gala. She is indeed beautiful. Be a man, my son."

So Giles writes to Juliette and invites her to dine with him at *Le Pré aux Clercs,* reputed as the best restaurant in Dijon. Julie has sent her acceptance back to him via Mec.

* * *

Unknown to Giles at that time is that Mec, after chatting with the *maître d'* at *Le Pré aux Clercs,* Henri Malan, has Henri assure him that the young man, a decorated hero of the resistance and recently in the Dijon news and, besides that, a scholar of Cambridge University in *Grande Bretagne,* will have a premier table and that he and his young lady will be given every attention. Mec will take care of the bill.

Henri goes to his office and phones the local paper, *Le Journal de Bourgogne,* that the young French hero and scholar of international repute at Cambridge University in *Grande Bretagne,* will be dining at the restaurant with his lady. The age of the *paparazzi* has begun and Henri is ever on the lookout for favorable publicity. Right after Henri puts the phone down, it rings again. The secretary of Mendès-France informs Henri that the minister will be dining at the restaurant on that Thursday evening. "Have a table for eight prepared, *monsieur,* for the Council Minister and his party. And you will remember, *monsieur,* the well known habit of the minister to have a glass of milk available to him."

Henri Malan is, of course, delighted at the prospect. At the time Mendès-France is in the political news almost every day. He is offering an alternative both to DeGaulle and to the ineffective Fourth Republic, the center-right government in power. It seems unable to solve any of France's many problems, including the costly and losing war in Vietnam. Henri goes to the phone again to report this second event to *Le Journal de Bourgogne.*

* * *

Giles has finished his lunch when Sophie returns home. "*Maman,* you remember I'm driving the Mouse into Dijon?"

"Yes, of course. Just drive carefully and leave plenty of time. My Mouse does not go very fast. I have filled the tank for you. You told me you are seeing the girl again. Whatever happens, you must treat her with every respect."

"Of course, *maman*. That is my intention."

Indeed it is. If intimacy occurs . . . well . . . if it did occur, he hopes it will grow out of knowing each other better. But Giles has not centered on that. In the sink hole drama, she had shown real guts and her caring for her maid had been genuine. He is sure Juliette is much more than just a courtesan. Though she is deliciously good at that!

Giles has his hair cut at the barber shop in Plaignes, then bathes and shaves at home. He puts on the English tailored suit he had bought in Cambridge, at considerable expense. He feels handsome as he looks at himself and his white teeth in the mirror and ties his crested college tie round his neck. But he can't help being just a tad tense. He grins as he recalls what Mec had told him: "When you reach your death bed, Giles, do not be a victim of regrets, of what might have been."

Chapter 22.

Coincidences.

The Mouse chugs its way to Dijon to arrive at *Le Pré aux Clercs* in good time. The *maître d'* informs Giles he has a table for two for him with *banc* seating.

Giles, asserts himself politely, but firmly. "Be sure *Mademoiselle LaPerle* is greeted at the door," and hands the *maître d'* a 50f note. "I'll have a *coupe de champagne* while I wait."

"Certainly, *monsieur*, everything will be attended to."

The doorman of *Le Pré aux Clercs* opens the door of the shiny black new-model Citroën sedan and watches as the black chauffeur, in his chauffeur's suit and cap, hands out the fashionable young lady. At the door she is greeted by the *maître d'* himself. He speaks with polished suavity. "*Bon soir. Monsieur* Martin has arrived, *mademoiselle.*"

The two young people are openly stared at as they are ushered to their table. A few of the diners recognize Giles and are aware who Julie is from their pictures in the papers from their sink hole adventure. Possibly a man or two there could know of her as a *Le Coq* hostess. In any event, not a few raise their glass to the young couple.

After the *maître d'* had handed her lynx fur coat to the cloakroom girl, Juliette, taking advantage of the moment, poses herself in her Dior dress, then ensconces herself gracefully on the *banc* against the wall. She takes a cigarette from a silver case and places it in a holder. The *maître d'* lights it for her. The whole room seems to be watching. Juliette and Giles turn to each other and the hum of conversation resumes. Julie soon puts the cigarette down. She really doesn't like smoking.

A fashionably dressed woman asks the *maître d'*, "is she in films? What a beauty!" Julie overhears it and was later to chuckle that it was her start in the movie business.

Giles is determined to take it all in stride. "Juliette, I think we have made an impression. I hope you don't mind. I hadn't foreseen anything like this."

Julie smiles at him confidentially. "Call me Julie, Giles. That is my real name. But no! I do not mind a bit. I am with a famous and handsome young man. I am proud to be here with you." It was at that moment that Julie decides that the last man she serviced in *Le Coq* would be the last man she would ever service as a prostitute. Her new life began right then and there.

Giles orders a bottle of *Veuve Clicquot* champagne. They are sipping the champagne when a commercial photographer comes to their table. There is no escape for them. The flash bulb goes off, then another and another. Julie moves in close to Giles for more shots. The photographer changes to a Polaroid and takes an instant picture. "It's complimentary," she tells them as she hands them the developing print.

Julie is smiling, her self-confidence up, enjoying the attention they are getting.

Giles asks the photographer who she is. "They call us *paparazzi*. We take shots of celebs like you. I expect you will become quite used to it." She disappears as quickly as she had appeared.

Giles shrugs his shoulders. "Well, Julie, that was unexpected!"

"Oh, I just love being with you, my hero!" She looks at the menu. "I am going to start with the escargots and then have the *filet mignon*. Oh!" she looks at him, "I should say, if I may? That's what a girl is supposed to say, isn't it?"

Giles determines a principle right away. If they are going to be friends, then he will say whatever he feels and thinks.

"Only if she likes to conform to a convention that is falling out of date, Julie. Perhaps my mother did that once, but not now. Each of us should make up our own minds for ourselves. But it can be good manners to ask for advice. Anyhow, you've made a great choice. I'll have the same. We'll need a red wine. I think a *Nuits St. George* would be good. But I'll ask the *sommelier* for a recommendation."

"You are quite the man of the world, Giles. You must have had some good teachers."

"Well, I suppose. A man called Mec, a sort of an uncle to me, has taught me a lot."

"Oh, I know Mec. I like him."

Giles is a little nonplussed. Julie must know an awful lot of men.

"Will you tell me something about yourself, Julie? Excuse me. I - I - don't mean to pry. Perhaps you would like to hear a little about me."

"Yes, tell me about yourself, Giles. I'd love to hear it." Julie settles back in the *banc* with her flute of champagne. She has listened to countless men spilling out their life stories, with almost all having difficulty with other people, like wives, and sex. She'd heard that was what psychologists did, tell the person to spill the beans and listen. Sounds pretty easy. Perhaps she'd become a psychologist.

"I don't quite know where to start," Giles begins. "What would you like to hear about?"

Julie turns toward him so they are close together. "*Oh, dis donc!* (Golly gosh!) Giles! What do you really like doing? Doing just for yourself?"

Giles blushes, just a little. "Well, it's really nothing. Do you really want to hear about . . . nothing much . . . "

"Certainly I do. I want to know you."

"All right. I like being out in the fields, running and walking, then standing still. One time a red fox ran right in front of me."

Julie enthuses, "Oh, that's so romantic, Giles! I sort of did the same when I was a young girl in Avier, a little village in Aisne next to Belgium where I was born."

"You will tell me about it, Julie. Actually doing what I did was useful during the war. I was a messenger for the *Maquis* and had to know the countryside very well. I sort of darted around. I helped to blow up a German train too. "

"Did you have a *Maquis* name. I know some did."

"Yes, my name was *Lutin*. The men saw me as an imp, sort of mischievous, I guess; that is, against the Germans."

Julie is staring at him. She can hardly believe her ears.

"Wait, Giles. They really called you that - *Lutin*?"

"Yes. Most of us had a name. That was to stop the Germans knowing who we really were."

"Oh, Giles! *Mon Lutin!* It must be some sort of fate between us. My nickname was *Lutine*. We are like twins!"

For some seconds they are just mutually astonished and about to burst out with more exclamations. However, at that moment the *maître d'* brings a waiter, with two plates of *escargots*, to their table. The *maitre d'* first sets down the *pinces et forchettes d'escargots*. Another waiter places the serving plates and the bread cut from a fresh *baguette* on the table. Then the plates of sizzling *escargots* are set down, each one in its shell, swimming in garlic and parsley butter. Following a long tradition, *escargots* are cooked and served with finesse in Dijon.

"Bon appétit, mademoiselle. Bon appétit, monsieur," the *maître d'* wishes them.

Giles manages to say *"merci"* while still trying to collect himself. "Really and truly, Julie? We are both imps?"

"Yes! Really and truly. It was my nickname among the girls, too. Ask Colette or any of them."

"I don't know what to say . . . except let us eat these *escargots*! Set to, *ma lutine!*"

"Oh, I will!" Julie cries. She has a good appetite and the pleasure of the occasion has only amplified it. Julie says, "I'm sure this will ruin my lipstick, but I don't care. I've never had better ones."

"Me neither," Giles tells her as he sops up the buttery sauce with a piece of bread.

The waiter comes to take away their plates and give them fresh napkins. The *maître d'* refills their wine glasses. They sit there together, trying to assemble their thoughts. Julie renews her lipstick.

Their occupation with themselves is interrupted by a major stir in the restaurant. Mendès-France, his wife, and six others have entered. Many are standing and applauding. He is smiling, nodding his head to people, shaking hands. The *maître d'* leads the party to a reserved table a few paces away from where Giles and Julie are seated.

Giles recognizes him, of course. "He is Mendès-France of the Council of Ministers, an important man, Julie."

The photographer has returned and Mendès-France gives his permission for his party to be photographed.

"I bet one day you will be as important as he, Giles. I just know you will," Julie asserts.

"Oh, come on, Julie!" Giles grins. "Well, maybe. Who knows?"

"Trust a woman's intuition, Giles. I'm a very French girl. Don't mistake me for anything else. I know some things very well, but what I don't know would fill the oceans. One thing I do know is character when I meet it. And you have character. Truly!"

Giles takes her hand. "Julie! I am a young Frenchman and very proud of it, that's true. I am also an international man, living and learning in the greater world that contains France and many other countries of importance. Like you, I am French. Never doubt it. I was born on Bastille Day, July fourteen. There!" And he gives her a big smile.

Julie is so astonished that she chokes on the piece of *filet mignon* in her mouth. Her eyes are popping and tearing and she has to spit it out. The waiter who had been hovering nearby, rushes over.

"*M'amselle! Oh, m'amselle!*" he cries out. People are looking.

"No, no. I'm all right," Julie gasps. "Give me some water." She breathes heavily and sips the water from the glass the waiter gives her. In a minute she has recovered herself.

"Oh, my! Forgive me, Giles. It is simply too much!" She takes Giles's face in her hands and kisses him full on the lips. It is his turn to gasp.

Julie stands up and raises her glass. "Attention everyone, please. Excuse my fit, but you all must know something."

The diners stop what they are doing to look at her. The photographer is at the bar and readies her camera.

Julie speaks out strongly. "I am a French girl, born on July fourteen. And this wonderful young man, this many-times young hero of France, is also French to the bone, born on July fourteen. I am quite in love with him. Raise your glasses and drink to all things French. *Hé! Les Français!*"

A few people in the room cheer and most raise their glasses to toast 'Les Français.' At first some are hesitant, likely shocked by the breach of decorum. But that soon disappears. A man starts to sing the *Marseillaise*. Everyone stands. It is automatic in France. There is a piano in the room and a woman rushes over to it. All there then belt out their national anthem, Mendès-France leading his group. It's a blood curdling anthem and they do it justice. *"Aux armes, citoyens, Formez les bataillons, Qu'un sang impur, Abreuve nos sillons!"[38]*

At its end Giles clasps Julie in his arms, and she him, and they kiss each other rapturously. People gather around The photographer records the scene.

Mendès-France leaves his table and comes over to them. "Dear young people! I am overwhelmed! We French must be proud of ourselves. As proud as you are! Your name, *mademoiselle?"*

"Julie Rossinger from Avier in the department of Aisne, *monsieur."*

"You must have had a hard time during the war."

"Yes, we did. My parents were killed during Rommel's advance through us. But I survived and am proud of it."

"Well done, young lady. Your generation will lead France to a better life, a decent life for everyone in France. That is what I believe. And you, young man. Your name?"

"Giles Martin, monsieur."

"Giles Martin, eh? Haven't I seen your name in the papers?"

The *maître d'* is standing next to Mendès-France. *"Monsieur* Mendès, if I may. Giles Martin was decorated for his bravery during the resistance. Lately he distinguished himself by saving two women, one of whom is the *mademoiselle* here, from certain death in a sink hole that formed during our recent flooding. He is quite our local hero."

---

[38] *To arms, citizens, Form your battalions, Let's march, Let's march! Let an impure blood, Water our furrows.* The anthem dates from the early 1790's when armies from Germany and Austria were trying to defeat the French revolution. During and after WWII, when Germany had invaded and conquered France for four years, the anthem was sung with great fervor.

"So, young man, you go from adventure to adventure! Do I recall correctly that you were the shooter at St Cyr that saved a squad of British boys from a madman there?"

"*Oui, monsieur.*"

"You are at university now?"

"At Cambridge university in England, *monsieur*. I am studying Political Science. I have read your treatise on the economic policies of Poincaré."

"You have? You must be a diligent student! Remarkable! When you find it convenient, come and see me in Paris. My secretary here will give you the details. I am glad to have met you both. Oh! If by chance you intend to marry, I wish you the best,"

Mendès-France smiles, shakes their hands, and returns to his table. The secretary speaks with Giles and hands him a Mendès-France card and some papers. Then Giles and Julie sit down, Julie again gracefully, Giles with a bit of a thump.

Giles expostulates, "I can hardly believe it!"

Julie takes both his hands in hers. "Oh, yes, you can, Giles! Believe it!" A quick smile runs over her face. "You see! Anything can happen when you are with me!"

"It seems so, Julie. And perhaps anything can happen when you are with me!" Giles bends down and produces his wrapped present for her from under his seat. "I had thought to give it to you before. Then it had to be salvaged from the sink hole. So it has had quite an adventurous life."

"*Oh, mon Dieu!* It is too much for a girl to bear! What can it be? It is all wrapped up. I need scissors to open it."

Their waiter, as if by magic, produces a pair of scissors. Julie deftly opens the package to find the gleaming silver and wood Turkish tea caddy.

"Oh . . . oh! It is gorgeous, Giles. How can I possibly thank you?" She holds it up in the light and people are looking at it. The photographer shoots the scene.

"I bought some tea in Paris. It's inside," Giles tells her.

The waiter clears away the wrapping paper as Julie finds the tea. She looks up at the waiter. "*Monsieur*, would you be good enough to take some of this tea and have it brewed and served to us?"

"Certainly, *mademoiselle*."

The waiter goes off with tea in hand.

They sit together, making small talk. The tea returns on a tray with an English tea service. The tea is well brewed and delicious. They sit enjoying it.

Julie is silent. Giles recognizes that she is preparing herself to say something of import. She turns to him. "Giles, please understand. I do not want to go back to *Le Coq* tonight. I want to stay with you. Take me somewhere. I don't care where."

Julie is controlling herself, but is clearly emotional in her appeal to him. Almost tearful. Giles does not hesitate for a second.

"Right! Say no more!"

Julie goes to the ladies room.

Giles asks for the bill. The *maître d'* waves it off. "It is taken care of, *monsieur,* no charge." Giles gives him a 100f note. The evening has been too full of surprises for Giles to be any more surprised. He imagines it was Mec's doing.

The valet has gone to tell Blackie to bring the car around to the front door. Julie and Giles settle themselves in the rear seat.

"Where to, *Monsieur* Martin?" Blackie asks.

Julie has reclined back in the seat, clearly tired.

Giles leans forward. "Blackie, I must take you into our confidence. Julie does not wish to return to *Le Coq* tonight. Can you suggest a good place where we could go for the night, a hotel away from Dijon?"

Blackie is unfazed. He has done similar things before. "I suggest the Laneloise hotel in Chagny, *Monsieur* Martin."

"How far is it?"

"Less than an hour."

"Very good. Let us go there."

"Before we leave, *monsieur*, I will phone the hotel to tell them of our late arrival. It won't take a minute."

Blackie mentions Colette Saludin's name to an assistant manager at the hotel, who then says he has just the right room for the young couple. Yes, he has heard of Giles Martin and they would be glad to have him and his lady stay at the hotel.

Back in the car, Blackie informs Giles that it is all set and that the restaurant at the hotel is one of the multi-starred restaurants in France. "The food is superb, even at breakfast!"

Giles sits back in his seat. Julie opens her eyes and then closes them again. She folds herself into the corner, closing the lynx coat about her shoulders and neck. Giles looks at her. Heavens! She is so beautiful!

Chapter 23

Exodus

The assistant manager meets them when they drive up to the hotel at eleven o'clock. Giles explains that in their hurried departure they had no opportunity to bring anything with them. Could the hotel help them?

"By all means, *Monsieur* Martin. We have a shop here and I will open it for you. You will find all you need for the night, I believe."

Giles is thankful for the man's tact and helpfulness. But such is usual in France. They do indeed find all they need in the hotel shop, rather expensively, but no matter. Giles cannot resist buying a beautiful peignoir and night gown set for Julie. She sleepily chooses the other things she needs. Giles buys underwear, a shirt, pajamas, tooth brush and shaving gear for himself. He will be all right with that until he gets back home.

Their room is fashioned in romantic Louis XV style, including the oversized double bed. A maid comes in carrying a tray of drinks, biscuits, cheese, and fruit. She turns down the bed and shows them around the room and bathroom. Giles feels he would have no trouble living in this style.

Julie undresses and uses the bathroom first; then flops into bed. In a minute or two she is asleep.

In the bathroom Giles considers shaving again to have his face completely smooth. But he is tired too. Would that be the right thing to do? No, he decides. In the morning there will be time enough. Perhaps Julie will make love with him in the morning. Sometimes he has erections in the morning. He knows that these erections are normal and possibly aided by a full bladder pressing against bits of the nervous system. That sure isn't very romantic! But he hadn't designed the human body!

Well, there is nothing more to do that night. One look at Julie tells him he must not disturb her. Then, realizing with a bit of a grin that it is his first time, he slides himself into the free side of the bed and lies down beside a beautiful girl, albeit that she is unknowing of it.

In another five minutes Giles is fast asleep.

* * *

They are awakened in the morning by a smartly dressed young man who knocks and then enters with a waiter pushing a breakfast tray on a trolley.

"With the manager's compliments, *monsieur*. I am Jules Verne, assistant manager. There are boiled eggs, scrambled eggs, sausages in the dishes; coffee, orange juice, *confitures* and breads on the tray. If you should wish anything more, I will tell the kitchen."

Giles takes one look at the abundance on the large try and can't imagine anyone wanting more.

"No, no. That is certainly enough. Please thank the manager."

"The newspapers are on the tray, *monsieur*. The manager wishes me to tell you that there are several news reporters in the lobby who wish to interview you and *mademoiselle*."

"Good God! Really?" Giles surprise is total.

"Yes, *monsieur*. They will not leave. We have no legal power to force them to leave, the manager would not wish to do so, in any case. The manager wishes to know your intentions. You may phone him from the phone on the desk."

Julie, still half asleep, has heard the conversation. She sits up, pulling the sheet up to her chin. Giles looks over to her. But she just opens her eyes wider.

"Did the reporters say what they want of us?" Giles asks.

"No, not specifically. If you will look at the papers, *monsieur*, you will see that they wish, no doubt, to follow up on the stories there. Please phone the manager when you are ready."

The assistant manager withdraws. Giles grabs the papers. On the front page of the first one is a large picture of them with Mendès-France. Giles looks at Julie. "We have a problem." Giles reads the article quickly. They know everything about him and describe Julie as a hostess at *Le Coq*. He reads bits of it to Julie.

"La vache! Nous sommes dans la merde!" (Oh, hell! We are up shit creek!) Julie wails. "What are you going to do, Giles?"

Giles smoothes his mind, refusing to be rattled. He sits down to consume his breakfast. "What I'm going to do right now, Julie, is eat some scrambled eggs, drink some coffee, and think what is best to do. Don't worry, we are going to get out of this. Why don't you have some breakfast too? It will make you feel better."

Julie comes over and sits next to him. After a minute or two of munching and drinking, Julie, now calmer, queries, "What shall we say, Giles?"

Giles wipes his mouth with his napkin. "Nothing, Julie, nothing. Not a damn word. I'm not going to have you put upon in the slightest. Nor me, for that matter. We'll decamp at the back of the hotel. We have a car and a chauffeur to make our escape. It's just a question of doing it properly. Let me think about it some more as I finish this splendid breakfast!"

"Oh, Giles! I'm so glad it's you," Julie tells him, now smiling and gaining some of his confidence, piling butter and strawberry jam into a *croissant*.

"Well, we'll have to see about that," Giles smiles back at her. But he feels confident that his life experience will lead him through their present problem. He phones the manager.

"What are you going to do?" The manager asks him hurriedly. "May I tell the reporters you will be down to talk with them."

"Yes. You can say that."

"Oh! You plan that?"

"No. My plan needs your cooperation. We won't talk to the reporters. But tell them we will. Keep them waiting. Cooperate with me and I will be pleased to wire you 1000f in two days time. My guarantors will be Colette Saludin, whom I believe you know, and *Madame* Sophie Martin, a merchant and well-known resident of Criselles near Plaignes."

"Very good, *monsieur*. And what is it that you wish?"

"I want a house maid's uniform of a size to fit *mademoiselle* and a waiter's uniform to fit me. Have them delivered here to our room. Give us a suitcase to put our own clothes in. Please have your kitchen prepare us a hamper of food and drink for the coming day. You have a back stairs in the hotel?"

"Yes, back stairs, *monsieur*."

"We will come down by the back stairs. You will tell our chauffer to have the car ready to depart, parked close to a back door. Do not inform anyone of our plan. Have your staff do everything as usual. Just let the reporters sit there with the expecation we will come down. OK?"

"Very good, *monsieur*. I understand your predicament with *mademoiselle* and, in the tradition of *La France,* I am happy to help."

Giles finds him a bit pompous, but is thankful he will cooperate.

Giles's plan proceeds smoothly. He tells Julie she will have to tie up her golden locks. The maid gives her a maid's cap that she can pile her hair in. In their disguises they can pass perfectly well for hotel staff. But, in fact, no one other than the few staff people involved see them. They reach the kitchen and a *sous-chef* presents them with a hamper that Blackie takes to the car. He has parked the car, close to a back door. It is near a water outlet and he has been hosing the car down. No one has paid any attention, as far as he has seen.

Giles and Julie, walking between the building and the car in a normal way, as if they are members of the hotel staff, take the suitcase to the car. They are followed by Blackie carrying the hamper. Blackie tells them in a low voice. "Down! Flatten yourselves on the floor of the back seat, out of sight."

Blackie opens the back of the car and places the hamper inside. He closes the back and says in a loud voice to where a *sous-chef* is standing watching the action by the door, that he is going off to fill the tank and that he will be back.

Blackie drives down the back drive to reach the main road that traverses the town. He drives slowly on the road going south, whereas Dijon is to the north, and the road going south is a main road with a garage with petrol pumps.

"If anyone is suspicious, it may help to put them off if we go away from Dijon," he tells Giles and Julie. "I will continue down this road until we are sure we are not being followed."

After a couple of kilometers Blackie says, "You can sit up in the back seat now. I can't see anyone in my rearview. But we will keep a look out until we are sure."

* * *

Blackie's caution is just as well. A pair of reporters had been kicking their heels in the front lobby of the hotel. One says to the other, "do you really think they are going to come down. Perhaps they will hole up in their room all day."

"Ya, I suppose," the other says. "But they could make a run for it. I will go round the back. Their car is there. I'll see what I can see."

From a little distance he sees the chauffeur hosing down the car and then a maid and a man servant putting a small suitcase into the car. Then he hears the chauffeur say he is going to fill up the tank and sees the apparently empty car proceed down the back drive.

He goes back to the lobby and tells his partner what he'd seen. "We'd better check it out. See where the car goes. Tell our motorcyclist what we are doing. He can stay here with the others. We can talk to him on our walkie-talkie."

They go to their car, parked in the front of the hotel, and set off through the town. "If he's going for fuel, he would go this way and take the south road to the garage there."

But they don't see the car at the garage.

"Perhaps he's scrambling to get away. Maybe he's trying to put us off the scent. Who knows? We'll check down this road. Speed up."

They increase their speed. "Goddam! What do you see ahead. Isn't it their black Citroën?"

"It damn well is! I'll radio our motorcycle man to join us. Between us we will be sure to track them."

On their radio their man at the hotel tells them that one of the reporters has sneaked up stairs and found the room empty.

"OK! They're in the car. We'll get them. Join us as quick as you can on the road going south."

* * *

Giles was looking through the back window of the Citroën. "That's torn it! We are being followed. Do you see them, Blackie?"

"You're right. Listen, the both of you," he tells them as he speeds up the car. "I've done many things in my life including smuggling goods along French roads in souped-up cars. We were chased by the *gendarmes*, some in cars and some on motorcycles. A little south of here the road straightens out and widens and I will make this car go as fast as it can. I think it capable of close to 200 kilometers per hour (125 mph). They will have a hard time keeping up with us. Then I am going to turn off on a country side road and hide ourselves."

Giles is enthusiastic. "Good plan, Blackie. Let's go!"

Blackie puts his foot down and grins as he says to Giles and Julie, "Americans say I'm pressing 'the pedal to the metal!'"

"Hey, Blackie! Go for it!"

Giles can see the speedometer needle turning in its dial. It goes through 100 kph (62 mph) without hesitation and continues climbing. Blackie has arched his shoulders forward, intent on steering the car along the mostly straight road, with some curves on it, but no sharp turns.

Giles, looking back through the rear window, sees a motorcycle with the car chasing them. "Do you see that bike, Blackie?"

"*Bien sûr!* (Damn right!) I think it's a BMW, a very fast bike. It will take all this car can do to outrun him. The rider is flat on the tank. He knows what he is doing."

Their speedometer is increasing more slowly now. The wind roar around them is deafening. Julie has never been in anything like this in her life. She clutches onto Giles, exhilarated, but white faced.

The speedometer needle goes through 160 kph (100 mph) and keeps going. Blackie mutters to Giles who is leaning over the back of the front seat, "We're losing the car, but that damn motorcyclist is hanging tough. We've a little more to go. This Citroën is some car!"

The needle hangs at 200 kph (124 mph). Blackie has his hands full when they hit any slight bump in the road, but the car is handling well. They are owing their lives to the

Citroën engineers. They can hardly hear themselves from the wind roar. Blackie shouts to them. "The motorcyclist is losing ground on us. Our turn off to the right is coming up. I will be braking. Get down on the floor. You will be safer there."

Giles knows he is right. He pulls Julie down with him on the floor at the back of the front seats. "Brace yourself. We will be thrown against the front seats," he tells Julie.

Blackie brakes the car at maximum, while being careful not to lock the wheels. He plays the brake pedal like a musician playing a difficult passage. It will be a sharp right turn. He drives over to the far left lane. No traffic is coming there. The car slows enough. Being a skilled driver Blackie turns and accelerates at the same time. The front wheel drive car pulls the car through the turn better than a rear wheel drive car would. But it is a close run thing. They are nearly in the ditch. Blackie straightens up the car and accelerates up the narrow country road.

Blackie looks in the rearview mirror and sees the motorcyclist overshoot the turning. "Good. He's overshot. It'll take him a bit to turn around and come after us. Giles! Put your head up! Our car can go faster than the motorcyclist on these twisty country roads that are all turns and dips. But you and Julie stay down. You'll be safer and your weight low down will help the car. Just hang on."

Blackie knows the road. He pushes and skids the car round hair pin turns masterfully. They come down a sharp descent to a hump back bridge. The car is airborne. It lands well, just in time so that Blackie can make the sharp turn on the other side. Blackie thinks the motor cyclist will have a hard time if he takes the humpback too fast. Blackie looks back after they have climbed the hill on the other side. There is no sign of the motorcyclist behind them.

"Giles! Sit up! There is a farm two kilometers ahead. We will take the short dirt road up to the barn there. I know the farmer and have been here before. As we approach the barn, you jump out and open the barn doors and I will drive in. We will close the doors as quickly as we can and lie low. Get it?"

"Yes, Blackie. Good man!"

As the car slows Giles jumps out and thankfully finds the barn doors easy to open. Blackie drives the car in and turns off the engine. The two men rush to close the barn doors. They all exude sighs of relief and then smiles and chuckles.

"We have done it?" Julie queries.

"So far, Julie. But be quiet. Listen."

There are the sounds of a motorcycle and a car on the road. They stop 50 meters away, where Blackie had turned off to go to the barn. The wind is blowing in their direction. They can hear the voices. Giles puts his eye to a crack in the wood. A sudden flash in Giles's memory bank puts him back in the barn when the Germans had searched it. Well, he had got through that. He looks around, seeing if they can hide anywhere. He only sees a door at the back through which they could retreat, if necessary. The men are still there, talking.

"I think we've had it," one says. "Up the road there is a cross roads with roads leading off it and further up there are more roads. They could go anywhere. If they went through this gate to go cross-country, they could be anywhere by now. We might as well go back to Dijon."

"*Putain de merde!*" (Fuck it!) the motorcyclist expresses himself. "I thought I had him. Whoever was driving that Citroën was damn good!"

"Another time, Antoine! Anyhow the girl is just a whore. Once a whore, always a whore, that's what my father told me."

"Well, I wouldn't mind fucking her. A nice dish!"

The men go to their car and motorcycle and go off down the road.

Julie has heard bits of the conversation. She is stressed out from the car chase, hurtling along the road, being thrown side to side on the floor of the car, and now these words are too much to bear. Her face crumples, she turns away.

Giles goes to her quickly and takes her in his arms. "No, no! You must never be ashamed of surviving as best you could. I am here with you now. I . . . I . . . love you, Julie. You will be safe with me."

Giles had no expectation of saying these words. They burst forth from him as if they were inevitable. He holds Julie to him and kisses her gently.

Julie looks up to him. "Oh, Giles! I love you too! You are my prince!" she gasps back. She also is being totally surprised at her words.

"Hey! You two. What do we do now?" Blackie inquires.

Julie is the first to speak. "I am not going back to *Le Coq*, not ever!"

Blackie smiles. "Well, that's one thing settled."

Giles mind is racing. He knows full well that it is up to him to decide what to do.

"All right. We are not going anywhere near Dijon. We will go to my home in Criselles. I will phone my mother to make sure the coast is clear there. We will stay the night. Blackie, you will park the car behind the house and we'll throw a canvas over it. We have a big one, I know. The car won't be seen and draw attention that way. That should do it for the night. Then we will think through our next moves. OK?"

Blackie nods his head in agreement. "Yes. A good plan."

Julie just looks at Giles thankfully.

"OK, Julie?"

"Yes! My prince!" and she blows him a kiss.

"OK, Blackie. We need a route. I suggest we make for Chablis and then turn east to Plaignes."

"Yes, that would be a good way to go. I know the roads pretty well. I will go and see my farmer friend here and explain what has happened. Not that he will mind when I say it's a romantic affair!"

Giles goes to Julie, "let's open the hamper and see what the chef has given us."

Julie jumps up, quite revived now that she has something to do. She'll be the woman, Giles's woman, in charge of the food and drink. The last time anything like this had happened was when she was with the German soldiers. When the time is right, she will tell Giles about it.

They eat and drink and laugh about their get-away. Julie grabs a knife from their picnic hamper and runs out into the field. She finds a holly tree laden with red berries in the hedgerow. It has begun to snow, but that does not deter her. She cuts off several sprigs and runs back with them. She wraps them in napkins and splashes them with the end of the bottle of champagne they had found in the hamper. Giles is enraptured.

That evening, after a long slow circuitous drive through the snowfall, they stop at a bistro in Chablis, 30 kilometers from Criselles. While the other two sit at a table with coffee cups, Giles phones his mother.

"Giles! You are alive! Where are you? What has happened?"

"It's a long story, *maman*. Have there been any people at the house?"

"People!" Sophie exclaims. "Half of France has been here! There was a police car here with two *gendarmes*. I told them I was alone in the house and to clear off. What have you done, Giles?"

"Really nothing, *maman*, believe me. I was having dinner with Julie and Mendès-France was there and talked to us. Then we went to Chagny and there were reporters who wanted to speak to us. But we eluded them and now we are in Chablis. I want to come home, *maman*. Have the people gone?"

"Yes, they are all gone. I wouldn't let them in. I shouted 'good riddance' after them. Those people! Prying into our private lives! Disgraceful!"

They drive along the Plaignes road that Giles knows well. They turn left in Plaignes, go over the bridge, and pull up at the back of the house. Sophie flies out and clasps Giles.

"Oh, my boy! I was so worried."

"It's all right, *maman*. I'm fine. We're fine. Now I want you to meet Julie." He takes Julie's hand and gently brings her to his mother.

Julie is reticent. She doesn't know how to relate to Giles's mother. She has never met anyone's mother before.

Sophie takes one look at the hesitant girl and quickly knows what to do. "You must be completely worn out! I have a hot bath waiting for you. Come! Julie, eh! A good name! What are you doing in a maid's uniform? We'll soon have you cleaned up, in some decent clean clothes and fed like a girl should be fed, with good country food!"

At that Sophie takes Julie's arm and whisks her away into the house, leaving the two men looking after them.

Blackie grins. "You know, Giles. I think Julie may have found a mother."

"Oh, good heavens! I suppose so," Giles agrees, his face acquiring a serious look. Things had been happening so fast that he hadn't found time to think about the consequences of bringing Julie into his life. He half-smiles. Yes, life is not simple.

Chapter 24.

A New Beginning.

Giles sleeps in his own room, Julie sleeps in the large double bed with Sophie, and Blackie makes do on the long couch in the living room. Sophie gives Julie a flannel night gown. Julie had carefully kept the luxurious peignoir and gown in the little suitcase they had acquired in the Chagny hotel.

Sophie is up first in the morning and sets about things while the rest are still asleep. Then Blackie stirs.

"So what's your name?" Sophie asks him.

"Everyone calls me Blackie, *madame*."

"I'm not *madame* to you, I'm Sophie."

"If you wish . . . Sophie."

"What is your real name?"

"Raoul Poingard, Sophie."

"Raoul the Dagger!" Sophie laughs. "A good name for someone who has looked out so well for my son, as Giles told me last night."

"Yes . . . well. . . we did have a little excitement," Blackie grins.

"I'm just glad you are all back safe. What are you going to do now?"

"I'll wait for your son to come down and then I will drive the car back to Dijon."

"To *Le Coq*. Is that right?"

"Yes. That's right. The car is *Madame* Saludin's car."

The phone rang. Sophie picks it up. *"'allo!* Yes?"

"Sophie ... Mec."

"Mec! Thank the good lord!"

"Is Giles there?"

"Yes. All safe and sound. With Blackie and a girl called Julie."

"Very good, Sophie! Keep them there. All of them, out of sight. I will drive to you as fast as I can. But I'll take a back route, just in case someone wants to follow me. Where's the car?"

"Behind the house under a tarpaulin."

"Good. That's good for now. Keep it out of sight."

"What's happening, Mec? There were a horde of people here yesterday."

"I'll tell you when I see you. Just stay inside the house and don't tell anybody anything. I'll be with you soon."

As Sophie puts the phone down, Giles enters the kitchen, hand in hand with Julie. Sophie greets them. "My boy! You're looking good! That was Mec on the phone. He's coming here as quick as he can. And good morning, Julie! As pretty as a morning flower!"

Julie has to smile at that. Sophie and she are close to the same size, except Julie, with her long legs, is a bit taller. That morning, while Julie was still asleep, Sophie had found every stitch of her clothing and taken it down to the basement utility room and the clothes washer and dryer that Mec had put in for her. Sophie had put the lot, the whites first, into the washer; all but the night gown and peignoir. She had washed them by hand.

The country clothes that Sophie had found for Julie, fitted her well enough and she didn't mind a bit being in a white blouse and a denim skirt reaching over her knees. They reminded her of when she was a girl in Avier. She had bathed the night before, washed her face that morning, and not put on any make-up. In the rustic surroundings it didn't seem necessary and, she reflected, being natural was the right way to start her new life. She had tied up her golden hair with a blue ribbon she'd found and put simple pearl studs in her ears.

Sophie sat them down at the big wooden kitchen table and served them breakfast. There were eggs, cheeses, slices of ham, apples, various breads and butter, all to be washed down by *café au lait.*

"Well, Giles," Sophie addresses her son, coming behind him and clasping his shoulders," I hope you have been behaving yourself, in spite of whatever this fuss is all about."

"*Maman*! As I've told you, I have done absolutely nothing wrong! Ask Julie or Blackie! We went to Chagny because Julie . . . well, Julie wanted to go there. We fell into bed at the hotel and went to sleep. In the morning there were reporters downstairs wanting to talk to us. I didn't want that. We eluded them and came up here. That's all."

Julie nods her head vigorously. "It's the truth . . . er . . . "

"Call me Sophie," Sophie smiles at her.

"Thank you. Yes. It happened just as Giles has told you. I swear it!"

"You don't need to swear to anything when you are here, Julie. We are family here and we tell the truth and are honest about things. I will speak to all of you. I have known *Madame* Colette Saludin during the war and since. Now she is one of my customers, buying my fresh produce. I have always liked her and I admire her for what she did during the war to help the resistance and since then, too, for what she has accomplished. She is a business woman and, before that terrible Marthe Richard came along, she ran a perfectly respectable and legal business and looked after her girls very well. That she continues in business is hardly surprising, given the needs of men in this country. Now . . . ," Sophie looks at Julie, "that Julie has been a hostess there is, first, none of my business. Second, Julie, you are clearly a beautiful and brave girl. You must have come through some tough times during and after the war. You will tell us about it later, if you so wish. You are now, very obviously, a personal friend of my son. Good for you both. You are a guest in my house, Julie, and I will hear no word against you. Oh! There girl! Don't cry!"

Julie rose impetuously, tears streaming down her face, and threw her arms around Sophie. "I . . . can't help it! Oh! Oh!" and she buried her head in Sophie's shoulder. It was, Julie thought afterwards, the first wonderful crying and sobbing she'd ever had in her whole life. It cleared away all doubts and problems. Whatever happened from now on, she would manage and win through.

They are recovering themselves and having another round of coffee when Mec appears at the door. Clearly he is furious.

"That shit of a Police Commissioner! His head is full of Gaullist crap. Did you hear what he's done? He claims there was riot last night at the restaurant, led by Mendès-France! Just because Mendès is a socialist! He's closed the restaurant down while he investigates, so he says. Now he is saying that a black driver, no doubt an Algerian insurgent, that's you Blackie, abducted a girl, that's you Julie, with another man, that's you, Giles. Jesus Christ! What's happening to France? Give me a cup of coffee."

Giles cries out, "That's absurd! Can't we just tell someone what really happened? Like a newspaper!"

Mec laughs sourly. "The papers are having a field day. They know who you are, Julie. They want to drag you through the mud and do the same for Giles. Fucking hell!"

Sophie says, "sit down, Mec, and let's try to be calm. Have you thought of what to do?"

Julie looks aghast. "All my things, all my papers, everything is at *Le Coq*! All my money! I have to go back."

Mec goes over to her. "No, you can't go back, Julie, but I can. Don't worry. Colette and I will see you have everything of yours. I mean everything. Incidentally I know a thing or two about this fucking commissioner. I know what he does in Paris. I have my connections there." And Mec holds his finger against his nose.

Sophie says, "I thank God you are here, Mec. Let's all sit down. I have some cognac. We'll each have a glass and then we'll see what is to be done."

Sophie pours five glasses of cognac. Giles seats himself next to Mec. Giles is worried. "I can't leave Julie here, I just can't."

"What then?" Mec asks pointedly. "Where are you going, back to Cambridge?"

"Yes, I have to. I suppose . . . oh, my! . . . Julie will have to come with me."

Mec pauses for a moment. "Has she a passport? She'll need a passport."

"I don't know, Mec. Julie, have you a passport?"

Julie is sitting with Sophie. Sophie has been saying to her that they will find just the right thing to do. At Giles's question Julie looks up. "No, Giles. I don't. I've never needed one." Then Julie is struck by a devastating thought. "Marie! She's my very best friend, my maid at *Le Coq*. I can't leave her. I have to look after her. She must come with me! She must!"

Sophie takes her hand. "We'll have to see. Perhaps you can talk with Marie and find out what she wants."

Blackie, who had been silent, interjects. "I know Marie quite well. We've been talking. I think it would be best, when I go back to *Le Coq*, to let me explain things to her."

Julie nods. "Oh, yes! Thank you, Blackie. I know she thinks well of you."

"Yes, Julie, and I think well of her."

After a while they drink their coffees and settle themselves, Mec pronounces. "As I see it, our first job is to get Julie out of here and, at the same time, retrieve her possessions. Next, Giles has to go back to Cambridge in England. Julie can go with him. To do that Julie has to have a passport. I think I can help her out. You have French papers, Julie? You are a citizen?"

"Oh, yes! It was done in Paris."

"All right. You can give me the details. I'll get your papers from Colette. In Paris I will see the right people."

Giles is not much surprised that Mec knows people of significance everywhere and can work minor miracles. It is his forte.

"Giles! How soon do you have to leave?"

"In a week, if that is possible."

"OK. There is a lot to be done and little time to do it. Blackie, you drive back to *Le Coq*. I'll be right behind you. Don't stop. I doubt the police will hold you up. But they may. Play innocent. Tell them, if you have to, that you let the two people off in Chablis or somewhere and have no idea where they are. OK?"

"Yes, Mec. OK!"

Mec sets about his tasks with expedition.

Colette is his ally. "Of course the girl must have her stuff. The easiest way to do that is for me to drive there with everything of hers out of the safe and her clothes and other possessions. If anyone begins to come after me for what I'm doing, I'll just let them know that I keep exact records at *Le Coq* and I can blow the lid sky high, from the mayor on down! There will be no trouble."

Mec smiles. "We are birds out of the same nest, Colette."

The person in Paris who is of most help to Mec is Risé Mayon. She is now running an *Agence Accompagnatrice* (Escort Agency). She remembers Juliette very well and is glad to hear of her. She tells Mec exactly what to do. After that it is plain sailing for Mec. However he has to rush back to Criselles, put Julie in the car, and have her in Paris early in the morning to be first in line at the *Passeport Bureau*. They meet Risé there. Mec and Risé get the French bureaucratic system to turn unaccustomed cart wheels and they get the passport.

When Colette comes to Criselles with Julie's things, she and Sophie meet as old friends. Blackie had fixed a trailer behind the car to hold the boxes containing Julie's possessions. Colette had Julie's furs, in particular, carefully packed knowing how she likes and values them. Colette has put all Julie's papers in a divided folder. They go through them together to check that it is all there. In addition, Collette has Julie's current cash money and she has drawn out in cash Julie's Dijon bank account. It was a joint account. Colette has been scrupulous in maintaining her accounts. She never cheats her girls. The result is (expressed in the US dollar of the time) that Julie has $45, 000 in cash and close to a million in her bank accounts and securities. The Japanese investments in particular have paid off like gangbusters. She is wealthy young woman. Colette has brought a security waist band for Julie to use to put her cash in. "Just be as careful as you can, Julie. Don't tell anyone about the money. When you settle down somewhere, put it in a bank as soon as you can. You can say it's an inheritance, if anyone is curious."

"Thank you, thank you, Colette. You've been just like a mother to me. I love you! I am so happy!" and she clasps Colette to her.

Marie has come in the car with Colette to Criselles, sitting next to Blackie in the front seat. Now Julie and Marie go off and sit talking together. Julie tells her she is going with Giles to England. "And I don't speak a word of English except '*darleeng*'." That makes the two of them laugh. Marie tells Julie she has a secret.

"What is it?"

"Blackie has asked me to marry him!"

"No! Really and truly?" Julie is surprised, but all smiles for her. "Are you going to do it?"

"Yes, I am, Julie. You going away makes it easier for me. Blackie is a good man. Colette has told me he has a lifetime job at *Le Coq*. I don't know if I love him, but I certainly like him and have come to rely on him. We've never has a cross word. I'll love to keep house for him. Will you give me your blessing, Julie?"

"Of course I will. I'll try to come to your wedding. We must keep in touch. I'll write to you and give you my address in England."

Giles writes to Mendès-France assuring him that he thinks the behavior of the Police Commissioner in Dijon was . . . Giles cogitates about the word and settles on . . . *insultant*. Giles describes the courses he is taking at Cambridge and says that his tutor believes he can sit for the Tripos (examination) in Political Science in three years. If he chooses to write a thesis, he could be awarded not only the Bachelor's degree, but a Master's also. After that, Giles writes, he will return to France and look for a government position, possibly with an intelligence or security agency. "I have read," he writes, "that it is collectively called the *Deuxième Bureau*." He gave his college address in Cambridge and hopes that Mendès or his secretary will reply.

The week is up. With Mec's help they have foiled the reporters, secreting themselves quietly away with Sophie. Mec has had one of his men drive Sophie's little car to Criselles so she has her Mouse back.

Julie and Giles are packed. Each has a suitcase. They will travel light and inconspicuously. Julie has worked hard packing her possessions into boxes small enough to be sent by post. She has numbered them and given money, actually more than required, to Sophie to post them after they have settled in England. Some of the money is from the tips her last two customers had given her at *Le Coq*. Julie smiles about it, knowing that her new life has started. She is through with all that. It had served its purpose, saved her skin, made her wealthy, and for all that she is thankful. She has the feeling that her period is coming on. That doesn't surprise her. She never knows when they'd come. She knows from long experience that a working girl's periods come on irregularly. But still, hey! She supposes she can have babies! Will Giles want to have babies? She scolds herself mildly. It's far too soon to think about that, for heaven's sake!

Mec drives them to Paris where they stay the night. Julie goes to their bedroom first. Mec and Giles sit in the lounge of the hotel having a nightcap. "My boy! Have you done it?" Mec asks.

Giles has to grin. "No, Mec. Not yet. I'm still a virgin. We just didn't get around to it in my mother's house. You can laugh if you like, but that's how it has been."

"No, no! I won't laugh, Giles," Mec assures him with a companion grin. "I can only sympathize with you. The gods have been against you. It will happen and I hope it will be wonderful for you and for Julie too."

"Thanks, Mec. I hope so."

Upstairs, in their room, Giles discovers Julie fast asleep. He doesn't wake her.

In the morning they take the *Golden Arrow* train from *La Gare du Nord* in Paris to Victoria Station in London on the first class tickets that Mec has bought for them.

Once on the train to Calais, Giles is as much at ease in speaking English as he is in speaking French. That astonishes Julie. She has never heard Giles speak English. She doesn't understand a word.

"Oh, Giles," she moans," how will I ever get on in England? I'm scared."

"It'll be all right, Julie. First stop in London is with my guardians when I was a boy in England. Joey is a French lady and Charles, her husband, is English, but has lived in France and speaks French fluently. His mother was French. He is an important man, a top general in the British army and often acts as a diplomat in international affairs. Later on there will be French people in Cambridge and you will go to school and learn English."

"It will be so hard, Giles. I didn't go to school after I was thirteen. I will be so stupid."

"No, you won't! And never use that word again about yourself, Julie. You are not stupid. You are a smart girl who knows a lot about life. The other students will soon be looking up to you and asking you to join in with them and advise them with their problems. Believe me. It will be so."

At Calais they walk the short distance from the train to the ferry boat, carrying their small suitcases. Julie has never seen the sea. It is a little rough and she is glad Giles is there to hold her as they stand on the pitching deck and see France recede behind them and the white cliffs of Dover appear before them.

"Oh, Giles! I can't help but be a bit anxious. You will stand by me, won't you? What will Joey and Charles think of me?"

"They'll think you a wonderful girl. Now don't worry, please!"

"I'll try. And it is wonderful, too! A whole world out here that I never knew about. I am going to be the best girl for you that any man ever had. I promise you. Kiss me, Giles. Hold me tight."

Chapter 25.

London and Cambridge.

The steam engine, not yet replaced by diesel or electric engines, chuffs its way into Victoria station. Giles allows a porter to carry their two suitcases, as all of the first class passengers do, telling him that they will take a taxi. Giles tells the taxi driver to go to Belgravia via Whitehall, the Mall, Buckingham Palace, and Constitution Hill.

"We are in the center of London, Julie, and the Mall is rather like the *Champs Elysées*, but without shops. After a few buildings and a small palace called St. James where the kings used to live, there are parks on either side and we will see Buckingham Palace in front of us."

"Will we see the king and the princesses, Giles? I'd love to see them."

"No, Julie," Giles smiles. "They are not usually on public display."

The taxi driver slows down at Buckingham Palace so they have a good look and see the red coated soldiers standing guard. "Aren't they handsome!" Julie cries. "And look at their hats! So tall! But the traffic, Giles! They drive on the wrong side of the road here!"

"They all do it, so don't worry!" Giles grins. "The soldiers wear tall hats to make them look taller and more fearsome. They are meant to scare the soldiers on the other side," Giles tells her. "I suppose it may have done occasionally. Psychological warfare!"

Joey is waiting for them. Giles has wired he is coming, but has failed to say a word about Julie. Joey hops down the front steps of the house and opens the taxi door. She welcomes them, though surprised to see Julie. "Giles!" Joey bursts out in English. "Giles, why didn't you tell me you were bringing a girl?"

Giles blushes. "I'm sorry, Joey. We had to leave in a bit of a rush and it was a sort of last minute decision." Giles breaks into French. *"Elle s'appelle Julie. Elle est mon amie française."* (Her name is Julie. She is my French girl friend.)

Joey's face clears at once. *"Ah, ma chère! Bienvenu. Entrez. Je suis très heureuse de te rencontre. Viens, viens. Tu es belle, ma chérie."* (Oh, my dear! Welcome. Enter. I am very happy to meet you. Come in, come in. You are beautiful, my dear one.)

As she'd told Giles, Julie was jittery about meeting Giles's guardians. Joey's warm welcome comes as a big relief.

"Thank you, *madame*. I am happy to be here with Giles."

"Call me Joey, Julie. Everyone does. Giles, where have you been? What have you been doing? Charles told me you were in some sort of fracas with Mendès-France. He read about it in the paper when he was in Paris. Well, you can tell us about it later. When Charles comes home this evening. You are staying the night?"

"Yes, if we may, Joey. Both of us."

"Well, of course. You really are a naughty boy not to tell us about Julie. Did you come over on the *Golden Arrow* train? Charles and I took it the last time we were in France. Very comfortable! Let's have some tea and crumpets. I would rather think that Julie has never seen a crumpet. I hadn't until I came to England. Julie! You must need to freshen up. Come upstairs with me. Bring your suitcase. I'll show you your room."

In the bathroom Julie is horrified, she has started to bleed. There are spots of blood on her panties. And she hasn't any tampons! She sits on the toilet and tries not to cry. But the tears well up.

In a minute or two, Joey knocks on the door. "Are you all right, Julie? May I come in?"

Joey peeks around the door. "Oh, Julie, what is it?"

"It's . . . it's . . . the blood . . . ," Julie tells her and grabs some toilet paper to dry her eyes.

"Oh, my dear child. Here, use this towel. Have you any tampons?"

"No, no. We came away so quickly, I didn't think about it . . . "

"Now don't worry. There's a chemist almost next door. I can run over and be back in no time." Joey thinks for a minute. Giles couldn't be a part of this. "Stay here, Julie. I have a French magazine in our room. You can read that. Now, dry your tears. All will be well in a jiffy."

Joey tells Giles to stay put in the front room downstairs. "Look at the television. It's not much of a picture. They say it's going to improve. Julie is upstairs with her things. Just let her be. Everything is strange for her here."

Joey returns with the tampons and Julie fixes herself up. Julie has been through far more awful things, but this is different. Her life is now a matter of acceptance by decent people who live ordinary lives. She has to fit in. Right then and there, she tells herself, she has to pull herself together, be strong. She must not let down Giles by appearing to be a silly girl, easily upset. Julie combs out her hair, does up her face, but not too much, and goes downstairs with a straight back.

Tea and crumpets await her. Giles looks at her a trifle anxiously. She smiles back, then looks round the room and says it is charming. Which, indeed, it is. Joey had taken a lot of trouble over the décor and furniture.

Giles says he will go upstairs. Joey tells him, "take your old room on the third floor. It hasn't changed much at all since you were here last. Julie will be in the room next to ours."

Well, that settles that, Giles thinks as he takes his suitcase upstairs. Then it is good to be in his room again at the top of the house, with the books in the book case, including his translation of *La Folle de Maigret* next to the original. The publishing house has contacted him and offered him another translation contract. The money will be a substantial increase, though still hardly enough for a church mouse to live on. He is set to do it and he will have to find the time somehow amid his studies, and they are demanding enough. And he must keep up his athletic life and now he must look after Julie. That means he must earn money. Oh, boy!

Giles sits on the bed, locks his hands behind his head, and rocks to and fro. Is there any realistic alternative to marrying Julie? Quite apart from sex and love, could they do anything else? Giles knows they cannot live together and be accepted as respectable, without being man and wife. It simply isn't done in the England of the 1950's. Particularly at a place like Cambridge. He cannot start off his adult life by being an outcast from civilized society. He has his career to think about and, later on, a young government man in France should be properly married or be an eligible bachelor. Not that a breath of scandal is all that deleterious in France, even might help. He grins at the thought.

So what does he feel about Julie? He really doesn't know her beyond the obvious. Certainly there is an immediate visceral attraction. She is beautiful and very much alive and, no doubt, knows more about sex than he would ever know. She is bright, forthcoming, brave and knows how to look after herself. Everybody likes and admires her. And he is drawn to her like an iron filing to a magnet. What does 'love' mean? Not just in general, but in his case. Shit! He doesn't know. Giles supposes that all young man faced with this decision knows it is a bit of a gamble. Does he have faith that they can make it work, stay together, let their youthful bonding grow into a deep affection and a feeling of responsibility for each other? He would say "God alone knows" except he doesn't believe in god. It is up to him.

Downstairs Joey, though she knows she really shouldn't, is sizing up Julie as a possible daughter-in-law. Not a real daughter-in-law, like she would have had if Geoffrey had lived. Julie, or whoever Giles marries, would have to be an honorary daughter-in-law. Joey's face creases into a half-smile. Geoffrey, she is sure, would like her to have a daughter-in-law and then grand-children.

The girl is a beauty. No doubt about that. Joey could easily see any young man falling for her. She has a strong spirit along with a soft side to her nature. She speaks a good French and is quite candid in saying that she'd had no schooling since she was thirteen. The war had killed her parents. She was alone and had survived by being a waitress and things like that. It is not surprising that she has a worldly air about her. The few clothes she has brought with her are in excellent style, quite expensive, and she walks and moves her body gracefully. They are getting along together very well, seeming to have a natural empathy.

Charles enters the house, earlier than usual. "My, my! Who have we here?" he says, looking at the beautiful girl sitting with Joey.

"Charles," Joey says in French, "this is Julie Rossinger. She has just come over from France with Giles. He is upstairs in his room."

"Well, well! How charming! Welcome young lady to London. What brings you here? I bet it's not our climate! It's turned rainy, foggy, and cold outside."

Joey gives Charles a sharp look. "Charles! Pay attention! Julie is Giles's girl friend. They are going to stay the night here. I have no idea of their plans. Giles hasn't said anything yet."

"Take it a day at a time then, Joey. I think I'll skip tea and go straight to a whisky and soda," and Charles goes over to the silver tray holding bottle and glasses.

Joey continues talking with Julie. "We'll wait for dinner and then have some wine. You left Paris this morning? How was it? Charles and I lived there for a while. Like here, there is so little sun in Paris. You didn't have time to see any of the exhibitions, I suppose? I love the new *Jeu de Paume*. Have you been there?"

"No, but Giles has. He told me about it. His . . . well, sort of uncle . . . really he is an older man who was with Giles during the war . . . "

"Oh, I know who you mean," Charles interrupts. "I met him. He was Giles's captain in the resistance. Quite a fellow, I believe. What is his name?"

"Mec. He's called Mec," Julie smiles. She is of course aware that the word *mec*[39] means a real man. "Yes, quite a fellow!"

Giles comes downstairs to join them. "Come on in," Joey tells him. "Charles has just arrived. Julie and I have been having a lovely time getting to know each other. Charles is having a whisky. Perhaps you will join him."

Charles gives Giles a manly clasp around the shoulders. "Yes, have a whisky . . . that is if you like whisky."

"Thanks. I think I will."

The evening is spent with them all talking French in deference to Julie. These days Joey has a live-in cook with her husband, an old but not too old man, looking after the pantry and doing odd jobs. He also serves as the butler at dinner. A middle-aged London woman who had lost her husband during the war also lives in and is their all-purpose house-keeper.

Thus Julie, knowing nothing different, thinks this is the normal English household. It makes her even more determined to be accepted and to fit in.

---

[39] A near equivalent word is *macho*.

After dinner they repair to the drawing room and chat and look at the grainy black and white television. Julie is clearly tired.

"Come on , Julie, I'll put you to bed," Joey tells her.

They go upstairs together. "Have you brought a night gown with you, Julie?

"Yes, it's kind of . . . rather swish. Giles gave it to me with a peignoir. He really shouldn't have. It was very expensive."

"Men do that. Don't worry about it, Julie. It's more important that you've brought your tooth brush and things like that. Have you everything you need?

"Yes, I have. Oh! Thank you! Thank you. I don't quite know what to say. I . . . Giles . . . perhaps you can see . . . "

"Oh! I can, Julie. Don't worry about that either. I'm very pleased he brought you here. Have a good sleep and we will be all together in the morning. Good night, my dear."

Downstairs Charles is yawning. "It's been a long day. The Germans want to rearm. The Americans are backing them. France is scared stiff. The Russians, as always, know we are plotting against them. I'm tired, I think I will turn in. Good night."

"Good night, sweet heart. Have a good sleep. I'll be up shortly," Joey tells him. They hug each other and have a quick affectionate kiss. Charles climbs the stairs, rather wearily.

Joey turns to Giles. "Stay down here with me on the sofa, Giles, we need to talk." They sit together, Giles disconsolate, Joey worried. "So . . . what are you going to do about Julie, Giles? For the moment I don't want to know anything more about her past than she has told me. I am only concerned for her future. What is she to you? Just a friend or something more? You must tell me! Is she staying here or is she going back to France?"

Giles shoulders slump. "I . . . I . . . don't really know."

"You are making me guess. Is there something stopping her going back to France?"

"Yes, there is. But I don't want to tell you about it. It's something personal to her."

"All right. You know she loves you?"

"I know. It's just awful!"

"Do you love her?"

"I . . . I think so. I don't know. What is love? Nobody seems to know."

Joey looks at him seriously. "Giles, you had better find out and quickly. It looks to me you are responsible for her being here." Joey pauses. She has to know what is going on in Giles's head. "Did you think, Giles, that by bringing her here, we would look after her?"

Giles hadn't thought that at all. Julie was his responsibility. "Oh, no! Not at all!" Giles sits up, then stands up and paces up and down. "Joey, I need your help. Your advice. Should I marry her?"

Joey stands up with him, tense herself and now anxious for Giles. "Good lord, Giles! Have you slept with her? Is she pregnant? No, she can't be! She started her period just after you had arrived. Well, have you slept with her, had sex? We'll start there."

"No. Actually we have not had sex. And it doesn't matter right now, Joey. Tell me what I should do . . . please . . . my mind just goes round and round."

"Oh, my poor lovelorn Giles!" Joey embraces him. "I can't tell you what to do. Nobody can. You have to decide for yourself. Or, rather, you two have to decide for yourselves. But we can talk about it, if you wish."

Giles sits down, still tense. "I have to make a plan, Joey. She and I have to be respectable. You understand that. And all I can see to do is to marry her. But it's such a huge step to take and I have a full life at Cambridge and it will be difficult for her because she doesn't know any English and . . . well . . . you see . . . "

"All right, Giles. Sit down. Take some weight off your mind. I have heard enough from her and you for the moment. Your term at Cambridge starts in a day or two. Right?"

"Yes. And I don't want to miss anything."

"You shouldn't. So right now Julie will stay with us here. You go on to Cambridge. It's late at night and you must be exhausted. You need a good night's sleep without worrying yourself to death about Julie."

"But, Joey . . . . "

"No 'buts', Giles. The matter is settled for the next few days. Julie stays here with me and Charles. Now, off to bed with you, my dear boy!"

Giles, ever thankful for his good fortune in having Joey as his second mother, goes to bed and is soon asleep.

Chapter 26.

Up to Cambridge. 1952.

In the morning Giles starts early. He goes in to see Julie and gives her a hug and a kiss. "Just relax and recover yourself, Julie. Joey is a wonderful person and she'll take care of you. I'll be in Cambridge, working things out. I'll phone and tell you what I think best to do. All you have to do now is to stay here and try not to worry. Talk with Joey. Let her know the truth, but do it gradually. I know she will accept you and love you. Don't be afraid. I know things will work out for the best. And . . . and . . . I love you, Julie."

"Oh, Giles! I love you, too! It's all so amazing! My head is still in a whirl. I'll try to be brave and sensible, too."

"I must go now and catch my train, Julie. I'll be back soon. We'll talk on the phone."

So, after another hug and a kiss, Giles leaves and takes the tube to Liverpool Street station. Cambridge trains leave every hour and he catches the 9.05 train. It will take an hour and fifteen minutes to reach Cambridge. The first thing to do will be to find accommodations for Julie and himself. He will give up his room in Clare Memorial Court and find something in the town.

After Giles has left, Joey looks in on Julie. "When you are ready, come on down to breakfast, Julie. Take your time. No hurry."

Julie almost wants to cry. Joey's friendliness and acceptance of her is almost too much to bear. But what will Joey think of her and the truth? Giles has said to tell the truth. But will the truth be too much? Thinking about it makes her subdued. She goes down to the dining room to join Joey.

"Come and sit beside me, Julie. As perhaps you know, breakfast is more of a meal here in England than we are used to in France. My cook decided you should have some scrambled eggs and bacon. But help yourself to what you would like."

Wishing to be polite, Julie helps herself to a spoonful of scrambled eggs and a piece of bacon along with a brioche.

"Now, Julie. You have not brought many clothes with you. We need to go out and get some things for you to wear. We can walk to Harrod's, one of the best stores in the world, and I told my cook that I would return with some haddock from the fish market there for dinner this evening."

Julie tries to restrain Joey from buying too much for her. But to little effect. "I am not going to have a beautiful French girl staying with me and being poorly dressed, Julie. It's cold here in winter time and you need warm clothes that you will look good in. Long skirts and jackets made of fine wool to start with. So here we go!"

After some strenuous shopping they are having lunch in the restaurant at Harrod's on the top floor. Joey points out the sights of London they can see, starting with the dome of St. Paul's.

"It survived the war, Julie, but only just. The Germans bombed all around it and at one point the roof caught on fire. Some brave men put it out. You survived the war too. Where were you when the war was going on?"

In spite of anticipating that such questions would be asked, Julie hardly knows how to answer. She blushes, raising her serviette to her mouth, struggles to find the words.

"I . . . I . . . was there when the Germans came. My mother and father were standing by the door of the house. Then the bomb came down at their feet. Then they were no more."

"Good God! Julie! That must have been terrible for you. If you don't want to talk about it, I'll understand."

"No, it's all right. It was a long time ago. The Germans came from Belgium. There was no one left. The house burned down." Now Julie was calm, deadly calm, her face drawn and white. It was all coming back to her.

Joey held out her hand to her. "You don't need to tell me more, not anything you would rather not, Julie."

"Then I was raped. Though I was too young to understand. Ernst, a German soldier, was kind to me. He was gay, though I did not understand that at the time. I traveled with them. The sergeant made love to me. They took clothes from the ruined and empty houses for me. Then we came to Paris."

Joey sat very still, with her face drawn tight too. By then, in 1940, Charles had taken Joey to England. Charles had gone back to fight in northern France in the rear guard action leading to the evacuation at Dunkerque. He had been wounded, shot through the shoulder. He had stayed with his men. He and the remains of his Guards company were some of the last to leave. He had told Joey a little of the terrible sights he had seen on the roads and in the villages. The strafing by German planes with their machine guns of the refugees on the roads. They had cleared the roads in that way to allow their tanks and vehicles to speed along them. But this was the first time she had been told of what it had been like for a young girl, raped and made to have sex with the Germans.

"I was not quite fourteen. My birthday is July 14th." A fleeting smile crossed Julie's face. "I am a very French girl, you see."

"My dear girl, Julie! How did you ever survive? You needn't go on. It must have been totally awful for you."

266

Another half-smile ran across Julie's features. "I suppose it was. But in another way it wasn't. I had to survive. That's what I told myself. Giles told me before he left this morning that I should tell you the truth. He said gradually. But I don't know how to tell you gradually. And he doesn't know the whole truth. I would want you to know the truth, but... I am sure you'll never want to see me again. My life, up to now, has been ... well ... disgraceful."

"Julie, I can only tell you that, in time, the truth always comes out. Then it will seem that you have deceived people if you have not faced up to the truth about yourself. And if you keep it all to yourself, it will continue to harm you. And when you do tell someone it will seem less awful than you are thinking now. It's a hard lesson to learn. Think about it. We can go home now."

"No, Joey. No! Stay here and hear me out. I told myself I had to be brave and I'm going to start now. If you don't want to ever see me again, I will understand and stay away from you and Giles."

"Oh, my poor girl! It won't come to that. I assure you. It won't come to that!"

Julie sips from her water glass. "I am a young but experienced woman. What you have just said is the truth. There is no substitute for honesty. When we arrived in Paris in the summer of 1940, the German soldiers who I had been traveling with dumped me by *Porte St. Denis*. I went to a bistro. A woman was there. She saw I was destitute. She took me to the house where she was a manager. I became a prostitute, a brothel girl. I survived. Even now I don't know how else I could have survived. You must be shocked, I know."

"I suppose I am. But I have no right to be, Julie. I wasn't there. You were. As you say, you survived."

"Yes, I did!" Julie relaxed a little. "Actually, I am proud of myself. I became a top-notch girl. They had to pay the highest price in the house for me. It was *Les Poulets* on *rue*

Blondel in the second *arrondisement*. Then I became a spy for the resistance. My top customer was a general in the German army. He told me things that I passed on to the resistance. Other German officers told me things too, about the defenses on the Atlantic Wall."

"I have heard of that, Julie. My goodness!" Joey smiles to her. "You should write a book about it. No! Perhaps not. It's very obvious you are a different person now."

"I certainly wish to be, Joey. And I think I am. Anyhow, I had to move to a house in Dijon, *Le Coq*. I was the top girl there too. I really didn't have to work too hard. That's where Giles met me. So you see he has been a bit disgraceful too!"

Joey grinned with Julie. "Well, you two! What a story! In spite of everything, Julie, you have not just survived, but you are a charming young woman with whom Giles is madly in love! And you have retained your health. Having a period proves that, I think. But, with your permission, I will take you to my gynecologist for a check-up."

Julie felt a huge weight had been lifted off her. "Thank you, thank you, Joey. I have been so anxious about coming to England. I want to start my life anew. It will be easier here, away from France. But I'll always be French, too!"

"Like me, Julie; just like me. And Giles too. Well, thank goodness that's over. Now we can really begin planning on what to do for the best."

That evening Giles called. Joey told him that Julie had told her everything and that she was a sweet wonderful girl. "You have to be as resolute as she, Giles. That girl has more guts in her than you or I would know about."

"I know, Joey. Listen. I have had a busy day and I believe I've found a solution for us. It just so happens that two flats, quite small but nice, have become available in a house on Bridge Street, just by St. John's college. I have checked with the office at Clare and they told me the apartments are on the list as suitable for students. So I have put down a hold on both of them."

"Heavens, Giles! You are a fast worker! You mean that Julie and you can be respectable neighbours."

"Exactly. And the Clare office says there are special courses in English available for foreign students. Everyone rides bicycles here. We'll bicycle out to Grantchester, it's just three miles away, and have crumpets and honey for tea!"

"I think you have been reading the poems of Rupert Brooke! Have you, Giles?"

"Yes. You've found me out. I'll see if the church clock still stands at ten to three and if there is honey still for tea in Grantchester. You know the lines, Joey?"

"Yes, it's a beautiful poem. Rupert Brooke was 27 when he was killed in World War 1, the Great War, the war to end wars. Oh, at times I despair of the times we live in. But my courage always returns. Just like Julie's. She's a courageous girl. Never doubt it, Giles."

Joey could tell that Giles was riding on top of the world. He certainly was a capable young man. When he set his mind to something, it happened!

Chapter 27.

Cambridge. 1952-54.

In retrospect, Giles thinks, as he crosses the Channel yet again, this time to go to Paris and join the government, it was astonishing how quickly time had passed and how full that time had been. Most days had been a packed 16 hours of activity and then a flop into bed to fall asleep until the alarm clock sounded.

What lay ahead, he could only vaguely visualize. It was June 1954 and Mendès-France would become the premier of France in the next few days. Mendès and he had remained in touch by letters. On one occasion, when Giles had been in Paris with his mother, he had visited Mendès at his office. Mendès had asked him to join his group, when he had finished at Cambridge, in trying to put France back on the right track. Now Mendès had pledged that he would start the process of getting out of Indochina within 30 days, give up Tunisia, and revitalize the French economy. A huge program! And he wanted Giles Martin and his young, fresh brains with him to do that. Mendès personally had phoned him at Cambridge. It was a huge opportunity for Giles and, of course, he had accepted.

Giles leans on the rail at the stern of the boat and looks

down, mesmerized by the orderly, but yet chaotic, turmoil of the wake of the boat. The wake was continually being left behind. The propeller was driving the boat across the sea and through the passage of time. For Giles it seemed a metaphor for life; the relentlessness of time and his own urgency to fulfill the gift of human life given to him by the evolution of the earth over 14 billion years and then of *homo sapiens* in the last four million years. Thinking like that gave him the most basic of perspectives on his place in the universe; or, as the advanced cosmologists were now thinking, the multiverse, where our universe is only one of an infinite number of universes. In one sense that meant that anything or anyone was an infinitely small and insignificant object; but, on the other hand, it meant, it seemed to Giles, that everyone was a kind of universe in themselves; that the big and the small were equally significant.

Giles closes his eyes. These thoughts were sometimes just too much of a challenge. Giles breathes out in a long slow breath and closes all his doors of consciousness except one. He lets recollection flood into him.

* * *

Joey and Julie greet him at the front door. Joey gives him a brief hug, then says, "now kiss your wonderful girl." Not waiting for him to do it, Julie launches herself into his arms, like a young kid would do. If ever there was an unmistakable sign that Julie loved him and wanted him, this was it. He hugs her back and they kiss as if Joey is not there.

"Come on, my love birds, lunch is waiting. Charles will join us later," Joey tells them.

Even in the short time that Giles has been in Cambridge, much has happened with them both and needs talking through. Joey sets the stage.

"Julie and I have seen some of the sights of London, starting with Harrod's. She now has some warm English clothes. February and March can be bitter here, as you know, Giles. We have been to my lady doctor and she found Julie a healthy young woman, fit in every respect for life at Cambridge with her boy friend - or, dare I say, lover!"

Giles blushes and even Julie does too, just a bit. Then they all laugh.

Giles says, "I think at Cambridge we will be close friends - at least to start. We'll see how we get on together and then decide."

"That will be best," Julie nods and takes Giles's hand.

Giles tells them about the digs he's found. "The address is 35 Bridge Street. There is a door with a lock on it leading from the street into a narrow passage. That gives us extra security. The two flats are actually on top of one another. We leave our bicycles downstairs in the entry way by the front door. It's covered by a tin roof, so the bikes will be safe and dry."

"Bicycles!" Julie cries. "I am to ride a bicycle?"

"Oh, everyone does in Cambridge, " Giles tells her in an offhand manner. "It's the only way to get around."

Julie looks terrified. "But I . . . I . . . have never ridden a bicycle! Never! I will fall down!"

Joey reassures her, while comprehending that, in the life that Julie had led, there were no bicycles. "Oh, Julie! I'm sure Giles never thought of that. You really won't fall down! I know. I had to learn to bicycle myself when I came over from France to live here. During the war there was no petrol, and bikes were our main means of getting around. So, if I could learn, you certainly can too."

Giles tries to amend for his lack of understanding. "I'll help you, Julie. Don't be afraid. You'll soon be an ace on the bicycle, I'm sure. I have not bought the bikes yet. We'll do it together in Cambridge. There's a good bike shop just up the road. Then we will go to somewhere quiet for you to practice."

"What about furniture, Giles? Are the flats furnished?" Joey asks.

"Yes. After a fashion. However I told the rental agency that we would probably put in our own furniture. They are agreeable to that."

"In that case, I am certainly coming to Cambridge with you to give you a hand."

That makes Giles a little tense. Mothers! He has two!

Julie is delighted to hear Joey say that. In the shops in London she couldn't even read the signs, let alone understand anybody. "Oh, thank you, Joey. That would be wonderful." She will be thankful for any and all the help Joey can give her, woman to woman, to find her way in this new country.

Joey exclaims, "if I know anything about furnished rental flats, the mattresses on the beds will be all lumps! And another thing, Giles. We should get both of you on the National Health scheme and find the right doctors. I know you have the French national insurance, but that's no good here. I should have done it before for you, Giles. But it slipped through and you have been the picture of health all the time."

"*Merde*! I hadn't thought of health insurance," Giles admits. This new life of his is looking to be full of responsibilities that he has no experience of. No, life is not simple.

Joey tells them, "I have stayed in Cambridge before. I will put up in the University Arms. I promise only to help and leave you two alone to start up your lives there."

Charles phones and tells Joey he has to be in Berlin that evening. "How are the young people making out?"

"Just fine. A bit overwhelmed, I think. I'll go up to Cambridge with them tomorrow to help get them started."

"Now Joey!" he ribs her, "just keep your maternal instincts in rein. Don't be too much of a mother hen."

"I know. I know, dear heart. Thanks for reminding me. But I do love them both."

"As you should, my dear."

* * *

With little else to do at first, Julie spends much time making her tiny flat as nice as can be. And she takes on Giles's flat too. Giles has to study so hard and for such long hours, way into the night! She determines after the first week or two that she has to be busy too. The language school is a little more than a mile away, just off Trumpington street. She can walk it in 20 or 25 minutes. She often chooses to go through the market square and see all the garden produce and clothes and kitchen things on sale there. But she can't do anything about it. No one speaks any French and the money is so confusing with shillings, florins, half-crowns, pennies, and six-penny bits! However, she has got as far as saying "good morning" to the fishmonger and pointing to the fish she wants to buy. Then she gives him her purse and he carefully counts out the money. He returns the purse, gives her a sort of respectful hug, and says, "Julie, eh! You'll be all right lass," with a comforting smile. After a number of attempts, Giles manages to understand what the fishmonger is saying to her as Julie repeats the sounds. It's the first bit of English that Julie understands. Soon she is doing the same at the other market stalls and can come away with plenty to cook.

Her English teacher knows some French and that helps. The other students are from everywhere in the world. *Grâce à Dieu*, Françoise, a fellow student, is French from Compiègne and knows quite a bit of English. They will be fellow students. The teacher approves of that. "Yes - you - help - each - other - ," she pronounces to them slowly and clearly. Julie tries to say other, but it comes out as "udder." That makes Françoise laugh. "I have looked up 'udder' in my dictionary. It means *une mamelle!*" So they both laugh.

Françoise is in Cambridge as an *au pair* girl living with an English family, looking after their children. It means that her time to study with Julie is limited, but they make the most of it, working together at a coffee shop for an hour after their morning class.

"The spelling is horrible!" Julie cries one morning.

"I know! You have to learn the words first and then the spelling. Crazy stuff!"

In the evenings when Giles and she have dinner, almost always in her flat so she can cook for him, he helps her for an hour with her lessons. Then they always make time for one another, when she can just speak French, not thinking about it, sitting together on the sofa. They hug and kiss, but don't go further than that. It puzzles Julie, but she sees that Giles is shy about it. When the time comes she will be very careful to make sex an expression of their love together. Then Giles leaves to go to his flat to continue his studies.

Most of their time together is on the weekends. Saturdays are Giles's Rugby day and Sundays his rowing days. Sometimes the coach calls for other practice days when the whole crew can make it. They ride their bikes together to the Rugby field and to the Boathouse. Other girls come to see their men play and row and soon Julie knows some of them and they help her with her English.

It is now May. One day in the middle of a week Giles says, "we are going to ride our bikes to Grantchester and have tea there tomorrow."

"Oh! Why, may I ask?" Julie's mind is busy with other things.

"Because I want to make love with you."

Julie blushes, then quickly agrees. Rather to her surprise she has welcomed the respite from physical sex. She hasn't felt frustrated. She has been occupied with too many other things. And Giles has been so diligent in his studies, as he has to be. She admires him for it. Now she is delighted that they are moving on and about to fit sex into their lives.

She has the good sense to look for her package of condoms. They will have to agree about pregnancy and having children. During all her working life she had not become pregnant, like so many of the girls did and had to have abortions, nor had she contracted any disease. She had been careful, probably lucky, and it had paid off. The doctor in London had told Joey, who had passed it on to her, that she could have babies. She had wondered about that and was relieved to hear it. She was getting older, but was still at a good age to have babies. But that wouldn't last forever. The biological clock was ticking.

For Giles, with so much on his mind, the evening hug and a kiss had seemed to suffice. But now it didn't. His erections were returning full force. He needs, once and for all, to break his luck! He could never go back to Mec and tell him he was still a virgin!

Julie has become confident and adept on her bicycle. On the front and back she has baskets for her books and the groceries she buys at the market and at Sainsbury's. She has developed a real liking for bicycling and sometimes going as fast as she can. That was best done along King's Parade where there always seemed to be students dashing to their classes on their bikes, with their short gowns billowing out behind them. She could almost keep up with them if they were boys and she could beat most of the girls. With the exercise she was very fit, with a great figure, and still quite small B-cup breasts. It seemed to her that every male along the way ogled her, some more covertly, but none the less obvious to her. She enjoyed it, but was never tempted. Giles was her man and that was that.

Giles prepared for the occasion. He has bicycled out to Grantchester and found a place near the river bank by an oak tree that will be a good spot for them and enough distance away from the path that people walked and biked along. At least, he hoped so. They just needed a sunny day in the spring time and, now, the weather had obliged.

On the rear carrier of his bike, Giles strapped a box to hold the blanket they would spread on the grass under the tree, a bottle of champagne and glasses, the Kodak camera he has bought, plus a small jewelry box. Julie will bring their picnic in the front and rear baskets of her bike. Both of their bikes have three-speed hub gears and Julie has become quite the ace in changing gears when she encounters the few hills around Cambridge. On cold days she appreciates the bike design for women, with no cross bar, so that she can ride easily in her long warm English skirts.

They go out through Barnwell and are soon on the path by the river leading to Grantchester. Being a weekday, there are only a few people about. Julie loves being away from the town and the flat land reminds her of the fields around Avier. They come to Giles's oak tree, dismount, and lean their bikes together to keep them upright.

After spreading the blanket and dumping their things on it, they stroll about. Julie picks a few of the wild flowers. Giles tells her she really shouldn't, the flowers there are for everyone to enjoy, but he adores seeing her do it. Anyway, no one is there to see her.

They return to their spot and Giles uncorks the bottle of champagne while Julie opens the packages of food she has prepared.

"*A notre santé!*" (To our health!) Giles says.

"Oh, indeed! To you, Giles! To us!" Julie responds and comes to sit beside him. They pucker their lips and kiss. They laugh. They drink the champagne and eat the sandwiches and fruit. Then they are through and look at each other as if to penetrate their souls.

Right at that crucial moment, a young man with his girl ride their bikes to be beside them and dismount.

The young man greets them cheerfully. "You've pinched our favorite spot! But don't worry. There is just as good a spot on the other side of the tree. Marvelous day, isn't it? Are you up at the university? My college is Trinity."

"Yes, at Clare," Giles tells him.

"Ah, you have the most beautiful court in all of Cambridge! But ours is jolly impressive!"

He is a chatty soul and Giles wonders, after a while, if he will ever stop. However, in time he does and he and his girl ensconce themselves about ten yards away, on the other side of the tree, but still in view.

Julie is giggling behind her hand. "Well, there goes our grand romantic moment, Giles! And you tried so hard! It's a kind of repeat of what happened to us at *Le Coq*, don't you think?"

Giles looks glum, but then grins. "It sure is!"

"Now don't worry yourself, Giles. I can't say I had anticipated this exactly. But I was doubtful about making love in the fresh air. I have never done it, so it would be a first for me. We'll have to do it another time. But I've prepared my room back in Cambridge to be our love-nest for this evening, so all will be well that ends well. There!"

At first Giles had thought that, as Mec had said, the gods were against him. But being there in the countryside is just right for what he truly wanted to do that afternoon, to undertake the most important event in their lives.

"Stand up, Julie!"

He kneels before her. "Julie, this is the first and last time I will ever do this. I love you with all my heart and need you with all my body. Life without you seems impossible. I can only promise you I will try to be your prince in every possible way. So, please marry me, Julie," and Giles produces the small jewelry box and opens its top to reveal the diamond ring in it. It had sunk his bank account down close to zero.

Julie, overwhelmingly grateful, takes the ring, admires it, and places it on the third finger of her left hand. "Giles! I thank you with all my being. I love you. I promise to be the best wife I can possibly be to you and for you. I will be your princess. I swear it!"

She kneels with him and gives him some of the flowers she has picked. "May these flowers, in their beauty, be an emblem of our love, Giles. Kiss me."

Their eyes are teary with happiness as they embrace and kiss. The sun shines brightly on them, making Julie's golden hair glow. Giles has saved the last of the champagne to fill their glasses. They drink to each other and their future.

Giles looks up at the sky. Clouds were forming, with black clouds to the west.

"Well, my love, I think it's back to reality. It's going to rain. We'd better start back."

And that's how it finally happens. In spite of all his attempts to start his sex life with a casual fuck, Giles's first copulation happens in an ocean of mutual happiness and love with his fiancée.

* * *

Their decision, after much wrenching around in their hearts and minds, is to marry in England. The deciding factor is their fear of publicity. Because of Giles's "heroics" it is all too likely that somehow a journalist will find them out, discover Julie's past and blazon it across the tabloids in France, quite possibly in England too. But a quiet wedding in Cambridge, at the Unitarian church, will be fine. Of course, some French people would be coming, starting with Sophie and Mec, and Marie and Blackie.

* * *

At their wedding Sophie, Marie, and Colette Saludin sit in the front with Blackie. Françoise is Julie's brides maid. Mec is Giles's best man and has the ring. Friends that Julie has made at the language school are there. Joey and Charles are up front for Giles along with some friends Giles has made at Cambridge. Julie wears a long sleeve dress and a little hat. Giles has on his best English suit and wears a Clare College tie. In the simple ceremony Giles and Julie say the vows they have written to each other, in French, their native tongue. They both have tears in their eyes.

Cars drive them to Clare college for the reception. The most startling moment for Giles and Julie is when Charles calls Sophie and Mec, and then Marie and Blackie, to come up front with him. He announces their betrothals. The couples are surrounded and embraced and congratulated.

Giles has to make a speech. He uses *entente cordiale* as his theme and then announces they must come and see Julie and himself go off down the Cam. The happy couple get into a gala draped punt, with the punter clothed in Italian costume. They punt away down the river, reclining on cushions, to the cheers of one and all.

For their honeymoon they go off to the remote southwest corner of Wales and stay in a cottage in a small haven on the coast called Dale. "It was here," Giles tells Julie, "that Henry Tudor, a Welshman, landed from France, where he had been living in the court in Paris in 1485, and went on to become king of England, Henry VII. Notice how similar some Welsh words are to French words, like *eglwys* in Welsh and *eglise* in French for a church. A bridge is *pont* in both languages. I was studying it when I was learning about the centuries of tangled affairs between France and Britain. So, you see, down here there is quite an affinity between our two countries."

Giles's scholarship is something that Julie is getting used to. Like most women she is more taken with the here and now. She is thrilled when they take the little boat from the small harbor and set out across the windy straits to land on Skomer island. The island is a bird sanctuary. They are in the midst of countless cute puffins and watch the gannets fold their wings and dive straight down like dive-bombers to catch their fish. Julie is enraptured. That Giles has brought her here, far distant from modern civilization, makes her love him even more.

* * *

For both Giles and Julie time seems to be in such a hurry. No sooner have they settled into some sort of routine as a married couple than Julie is pregnant and Giles has been chosen to row three in the Cambridge university boat. As far as they can quickly find out he will be the first Frenchman to row for Cambridge. Oxford is notorious for importing professional rowers from America and passing them off as scholars. So now there is much comment about Giles being a 'foreign' rower to boost the Cambridge boat. No matter that it is rubbish, his picture appears on the sports pages of the British press. Giles wishes it hadn't happened, but he can't do anything about it. The coach and the Cambridge crew stick by him and enlist a reporter from the London Times to say that Giles won his place in the boat fair and square being both a genuine student at the university and a damn good oar.

Julie now has a number of friends and acquaintances who help her understand the importance of rowing in the university boat and becoming a "blue." The Boat Race between Oxford and Cambridge on the Thames in London is watched by tens of thousands of people on the banks of the river and millions more hear the commentary on the radio and, now, it will be seen on BBC television. For the rowers it is a prime life event, to be forever remembered and celebrated.

For Giles the training is intense. His tutor arranges with the coach a sharing of Giles's time. Charles and Joey come up to Cambridge for a few days and watch the university boat going through its drills. Giles makes a particular friend of James Thirks who rows number four, just in front of him in the boat. James is also a Clare man, in fact the son of the master of Clare, and intends to go into the British Diplomatic Corps. James is reading modern European history and tries to speak French, German, and Italian, but gets them mixed up. It is the era when being gay is a crime in Britain. They are called fags or fairies or queers. So James keeps his orientation well hidden. Actually, it is Julie that senses it and tells Giles. He is quite amazed. Julie says he must not even hint that they know. "Invite him to tea with us, Giles. That is the proper English thing to do. You see! I am learning everything!"

Joey organizes having Sophie and Mec come over from Criselles to watch the race from the Ranelagh Club and, after the boats have rowed out of sight, to watch the race on TV. Beforehand, Joey has been their tour guide to the city and, among much else, takes them to the Tower of London, built by William the Conqueror in 1066.

"He was French, eh!" Mec responds to Joey's account of the tower.

"And he became the king here," Joey reiterates.

"Sounds like a big rascal to me! But I am proud for him. It was good for the English to have a French king! Teach them a thing or two."

Giles tells Mec about the boat race and how, because the Thames river can become rough when a west wind blows, there had been a number of races when the boats became swamped and sunk. "If there is a strong west wind you may see me swimming for the shore!" Giles jokes.

"How fast do the boats go?" Mec asks.

"About 22 to 23 kph." (kilometers her hour or about 14 mph.)

"That's fast enough for automatic bailers, Giles. They invented them during the war for the rubber boats. I have carried them for delivery to boat clubs. They are valves that only allow the water to pass one way. At the speed your boats are going the water would be sucked out just fine."

"I'll tell the coach. I don't think we have them on our boat."

The coach hurriedly looks up the rules for the race and finds nothing to stop him having automatic bailers installed on the boat. Mec rushes back to France and overnight brings half a dozen of them back. The riggers at the boat house put a couple in the Cambridge boat. They think the disturbance to the water flow along the hull will be minimum and a quick trial shows that they work well to remove any shipped water.

Sure enough there is a strong west wind along the Thames on race day. The crews, according to the punters, are evenly matched with Oxford the slight favorite mostly due to the Oxford crew being heavier. It's a long course, 4.2 miles, and stamina is needed. Heavier oarsmen are supposed to be able to pull the heavier oar for longer times. Cambridge win the toss and choose to start on the Middlesex (north) position on the river.

Their coach gives his crew their last briefing. "I don't care about weight. I care about strength and guts. You will go out fast at the start, as we have practiced again and again. Make those first strokes really count. Cox, you are going to call for 'ten' after three minutes. (A 'ten' is ten strokes at a higher rate with maximum power.) That will make you men feel desperate. Don't worry. You are very fit. Cox and stroke! Between you, do everything you can to be ahead at Hammersmith Bridge, that's just before halfway up the course. Then row her in. Remember at Barnes Bridge, just before the finish, you have the curve in your favour. I'll see you at the finish. Good luck men."

Giles, being the lightest man on the crew, by a pound less than bow, traditionally the lightest man, feels his aim must be to be as strong from start to finish as any man on the crew. He tries to relax as they paddle their boat out to the staked boats at the start of the race at Putney. *Merde alors!* That Oxford crew seem a set of determined giants! They have four hulking Americans on board.

Then they are off. The Cambridge eight start off with their eight short, rapid, maximum power strokes, their lighter weight making them more agile than their heavier Oxford counterparts, and their boat picks up speed quicker. Cox immediately calls for ten. They have practiced it. They row to the three minute mark, even with the Oxford boat. "Ten, men!" the call comes from the megaphone strapped to the cox's head. Gile's puddle at the end of his oar is as deep as any. Giles can see out of the corner of his eye that he is equal with the bow man of the Oxford boat. They are ahead by two seats. So far, so good. "Settle, men" the cox tells them. They settle into their longer rowing strokes at a slightly lower pace. Oxford attacks with a 'ten.' The Cambridge cox holds them steady. He lets Oxford gain about six feet. In another minute the Cambridge cox cries "Crew! Stroke! Give her ten!" They gain back the six feet and then another ten feet. Giles is now well ahead of their bow man. Both crews settle into their rowing rates.

On the shore, watching on the new television sets, Julie and the others can hardly contain themselves. Giles has told her, "we have to be ahead at Hammersmith bridge." They are! Whenever the Cambridge boat is shown her eyes are glued on Giles. *"Allez, Cambridge! Allez, Giles! Allons-y!"* she cries out, Sophie and Mec joining in. They watch the Cambridge crew maintain their position slightly ahead with baited breath.

The boats round the long bend with Oxford slowly evening up. Now the wind is strong and the waters rough. Both boats are taking on water. But there is very little below Giles, he can see. In the stormy waters and high wind both crews become ragged. The Cambridge cox rallies them. Shouting out the time, "huh . . . huh . . . huh . . . " and at the same time beating the wooden nub on his steering cord against the hull of the boat with sharp cracks. All the crew know the importance of being exactly on time. Stroke sets a constant cadence. They come back together.

The river straightens out and the curve to Barnes Bridge is in front of them. For the moment neither has the edge. Cambridge has a lead of a few feet. Both boats want the center water. It's up to the coxes to play fair and not come too close to the other boat to entangle their oars. The umpire in the motorboat behind them shouts at each cox to steer clear.

Now they are in the start of the Barnes Bridge curve. Cambridge has the inside lane. "Pick up the stroke," the cox cries to the stroke and the crew. They gain, going ahead slowly on the Oxford boat. But Oxford is not beaten yet. They give her a solid ten and then another. They are back almost even. The commentators are mad with excitement. As is Julie. They can hardly watch. There are 200 yards to go.

"To the finish!" the Cambridge cox cries. He is beating out the time, working with the stroke, picking up the cadence. "Huh . . . huh . . huh . . ." He throws his weight forward with each stroke adding what momentum he can to the boat.

Giles rows as he has never rowed before. He gives his all. His eyes are half closed. His concentration closed to that pinpoint in time. His body cries out to stop. But that makes him all the more determined.

With each stroke he goes up on Oxford's bowman; then he is equal to the point of Oxford boat's prow. "The last ten!" their cox shouts to them. Oxford is doing the same. It's a race to the line. Oxford is gaining on them. But not enough. Cambridge wins by half a bow's length.

Giles leans over his oar. His head spins. He can hardly breathe. James in front of him collapses back over Giles's legs. He is white in the face, there is foam around his mouth. He had given his all and then some. Giles takes his head in his hands and encourages him. They both slowly recover.

Giles looks toward the shore. He can hear the cheering. Every bit of space is occupied by the crowd on the wharf and along the bank. Hundreds of the light blue pennants of Cambridge are being waved furiously. The Oxford crew is a little way off. They exchange waves. It has been a splendid race, each crew giving of its best. Giles almost feels sorry that one crew has to lose. But, the next day, Oxford, the loser, will give the challenge to Cambridge to meet again next year on the Thames.

When they gain the wharf and have got out of the boat they go through the ritual of throwing their cox into the water. Then they all jump in after him. They laugh and cheer and splash about. Then it's time to get out and do the formalities of the day.

That evening, as pre-arranged, Charles and Joey have four of the Cambridge crew, James Thirks among them, and the cox, who did as much as any of them to win the race, to dine with them. They invite Mec and Sophie to be there too. It had been seen that the Oxford boat had more water in it than the Cambridge boat at the finish. The automatic bailers had helped keep the Cambridge boat lighter than its rival. So Mec is toasted as one of the heroes of the day. The young men are exhilarated. One of them was at Eton and learned his rowing there. So, with him, they all sing the Eton boating song[40].

Julie is almost due. Joey insists on Julie staying with them in London and have her Ob/Gyn attend to her. Giles is not averse. He will be down every weekend and, during the week, will be able to devote himself full time to his studies in preparation for the examinations in May. With any luck Julie will recover quickly and they will be able to attend the college May Ball at the end of May. Giles asks Joey if Sophie can stay with them for the birthing. After a quick meeting with Charles, Joey invites Sophie to stay on. A year back, Sophie had engaged a man to be her manager; they would stay in touch daily by phone while she was in London. Sophie had never been anywhere, except locally in France, and had never taken a vacation.

Sophie, determined to see things for herself, sets off, with phrase book in hand and, by pointing and gesturing, manages to enlist the aid of whoever is there and find her way around.

Julie gives birth to a healthy boy. Giles is there at the birth and they name him Charles Mec Martin. Julie will stay in London with the baby at the Marlis house. She recovers from giving birth quickly and assures Giles she will be with him for the Clare College May Ball and dance the night away.

Soon after sitting the examination for his Tripos, Giles learns he has won a 'first'[41] in Political Science for his Bachelor's Degree. For his thesis on *"Intelligence and Security Operations in France from Dreyfus to the Present"* he is awarded his Master's Degree.

Julie buys a long gown at Harrod's for the ball, Giles his first tuxedo. He has reserved a room in the old court for them. The old court is where the marquee is put up to house

---

[40] The chorus of the song is: *Swing, swing together// With your bodies between your knees,* sung twice.

[41] A 'first' is the highest order of degree that is awarded for the bachelor's degree and is much coveted.

the band and the dance floor. They do indeed dance the night away and have coffee and scones in the dawn on the Cam in punts.

In the course of waiting for her baby to appear, Julie decides to stop Joey paying for everything by confiding to her the truth of her fiscal estate. She wants money transferred to a bank in London. Charles and Joey have a chartered accountant to look after their monies, so the man does the necessary for Julie. He advises her about her considerable estate and the investments she should make for the long term. The stock exchange broker that Charles and Joey have will help her with her short term investments.

Joey is totally astounded. "My God, Julie, you are a wealthy woman! Does Giles know?"

"No, and please don't tell him. He wants to be the provider for me and baby Charles. I'll just say I had put some money aside and can pay my way. That sort of thing."

"All right, Julie. Tell me what you intend to do. Where will you live?"

"Well, Giles is going to be in the government in Paris with Mendès-France. We will live in Paris. And I have a secret that I have not told Giles about."

"Oh! Another secret!"

"I don't want to make too much of it, Joey. But one of my friends in Cambridge was a model in the fashion business. She told me that as long as I could keep my weight down, I had just the right looks to be a model, you know, fairly tall and slim. She gave me introductions in London and some of those would work in Paris as well. She said the single most important thing about being a model is self-discipline. I think I have tons of that. So, what do you think, Joey?"

"And be a mother and wife too! My goodness, Julie! How can you ever do it?"

"I'll wait for six months, get things arranged, and then go for it, Joey."

"All I can say is, good luck! Charles and I can give you an introduction to the *Madame* Dionnelle Fashion House in Paris."

Charles invites Giles to have lunch with him at the Army and Navy Club on Pall Mall. Although the exterior of the building has been modernized, the interior retains much of its 19th century character. They dine in the large paneled dining room.

"I wanted to talk with you, Giles, about the French situation and the government of Mendès-France. You will be taking up your appointment there, I believe, in a few days."

"Yes, I'm looking forward to it."

"You realize you will be moving into a very difficult situation. I don't know how long Mendès-France can last or for that matter any government under the present political set-up. The French situation in Vietnam is desperate. I don't believe they can hold on there.[42] I've seen it coming for some time and I have been over in Paris to give the British government's point of view of what's happening. I've told

---

[42]France suffered the worst military defeat by insurgents in a European colony at Dien Bien Phu in Vietnam on May 7, 1954. The cost was 13,000 causalities among the defenders of the outpost. Many of these were soldiers enlisted in Algeria and other French colonies and protectorates, rather than men from mainland France. The Vietnamese had been directly aided by communist China and, more indirectly, by communist Russia. Hence, throughout the west there were shivers of fear that communism was becoming predominant in the world and all the Far East would shortly fall into communist hands. Furthermore, it was seen by the fearful Europeans and the anxious US that all insurgencies were communist in nature and had to be beaten back. There was almost willful misunderstanding that even more powerful was the motivation for peoples to be their own rulers.

The Algerian insurgents were given a boost in morale and in their intentions. If the Vietnamese could defeat France, so could they. Algerian soldiers returning to Algeria were demobilized and many, bitter and disillusioned, unable to find employment, drifted into the ranks of the, as yet, largely covert insurgency. They brought with them their military training and battle experience.

them that the example to follow is what we have done in India and Burma. Get out of there as gracefully as they can. But it looks, as far as Vietnam goes, they are going to be kicked out."

"Is it really as bad as that? I read the French newspapers here. Some say we are just about to bring peace to the country."

"Wishful thinking, Giles. Sheer wishful thinking. The French will be out of there whether they want to go or not. The Chinese will see to that. And, I believe the fact is, that most of the French people want France to be out of there. The war there has been draining France's economy. However, what I really wanted to chat with you about is the situation in Algeria. By the time you are installed in the government, the Algerian situation will be center stage. I know some of your studies in Cambridge have covered French colonialism. Now make Algeria the focal point. Learn all you can. Mendès-France will need a clear head in his staff to understand what's happening there and to devise a policy to meet it. You can be that clear head for him."

Charles pauses to take a good long drink of his whisky and soda. "One more thing, Giles; DeGaulle is waiting in the wings. He offers the strong man answer to France's troubles. The guess here is that he will be in power soon; not exactly to our British liking. But, we'll live with it. Be prepared to join him. In my view, if anyone can save France from going down the drain, he can. Be on the winning side, Giles. Then, in time, when DeGaulle has run his course, you will be in a position to move the country forward and to create, one can hope, a unified Europe with a strong France in a center position. Now let us enjoy our lunch and be thankful that each of us has a wonderful and beautiful wife."

Part 4.
Paris and Algeria.
Team Work

Chapter 28.

Paris. 1954.

The housing question in Paris is quickly settled. Charles Marlis had been leasing out their apartment on *rue Ste. Dominique*. Fortuitously, the lease for the last couple was up, so Giles, Julie, and baby can move in. Charles has a décor company give the apartment a complete renovation, including turning a small room, adjoining the main bedroom, into a nursery with a door between them. At the same time the bathrooms, toilets, and kitchen are torn apart and then modernized with the latest styles, fixtures, and appliances. Joey tells Julie, "you will want new curtains, carpets, and wall paper too. We inherited stuff from the 30's and it has had a good life with us. But you must start out fresh."

They all stay at a nearby hotel along with a nanny they've hired, a Welsh woman called Maggie Davies who had lived in Paris for 30 years, but still speaks French with a Welsh accent. Having a nanny will let Julie get out and about more. Maggie has many tales to tell of Paris during the German occupation, including working for a member of the Rothschild family and watching the Germans steal their art from off their walls. But now, they have nearly all of it back. The children she cared for are grown up and have taken their place among French high society. However, they keep in touch with Maggie and are fond of her. She had been like a second mother to them.

Maggie has a servants room on the top floor. Charles makes sure of the plumbing and electrics and installs a shower in the corner of the kitchenette. Maggie is quite satisfied with that and, after consulting with her, Joey and Julie see to the décor and furnishings.

Julie insists on paying the costs out of her own money, while swearing Joey to secrecy about it. Joey sits beside her and takes her hand. "I understand, Julie. I do. I really do. It will be our secret."

However, Julie can't stop Joey buying the most exquisite cot and baby clothes for young Charles at *La Samaritaine;* "the same stuff at a lower price," she tells Julie. Sophie and Mec join in with Sevres china and silver ware and cutlery. No doubt some of it fell off one of Mec's vehicles.

Giles likes what's happening to the extent that he has time to take it in. He is much preoccupied with his new job and Julie doesn't bother him with domestic details. Charles and Joey love being the grandparents of Charles. Giles tells Julie that he sees it as a gift back to them for all their caring of him.

* * *

Giles's meets briefly with Mendes-France at the Elysée Palace. Mendès tells Giles that he wants him as a special aide. "I want a young, fresh mind to cut through the fog about what is really happening in Algeria. I believe in *Algérie Française.* We are responsible for all the people there. That is your commission. But first," Mendès smiles, "you will have to swim through an ocean of red tape to come on board. Are you willing to take on this task?"

"Yes, my premier. I will endeavor to discover the truth."

"The truth, eh? Truth is a slippery eel. I hope it won't evade or entangle you. But I need it. That is all. Oh! Did you marry that beautiful girl from Dijon?"

Giles smiles. "Yes, I did. We have a baby boy."

"Well done, I am happy for you."

Giles phones Mec and finds him in his apartment by *Les Halles*. Mec tells him, "come and have some food and drink with me, Giles. You sound tired out with your big government job. You can tell me about it." Giles laughs. "I really can't do that. I am sworn to secrecy. They still have the guillotine, you know!"

They meet in the *Le Loup* bistro, a place where all sorts gather, including Algerians. Mec looks up to see some of them coming in. "You should pay attention, Giles, to what France is coming to. You see those *beurs*.[43] They come here expecting to have all the good things we have and then they plot against us. They send half their money back to Algiers and a good bit of that goes to the rebels who want to take Algeria away from France."

"You are interesting me, Mec. As a new member of our government, I do indeed need to be aware of what is happening. You mean that those Algerians over there could be supporting the rebellion in Algeria?"

"And supporting their families too. I give them that. They leave their wives and kids behind to come here and make money. Unemployment is high in Algeria and those that do have work are underpaid by the *pieds noirs*. Most of the *pieds noirs* are fascist bastards who think the Algerians should only exist as their servants. I have Algerians working for me, so I hear a lot of their shit."

"Really, Mec! What sort of things?"

"Well, it's a lot of whispering behind their hands. So, where are we now? June coming into July. Something is supposed to happen in the autumn, October-November time. And another thing. I have a couple of Algerian drivers and they ask me to put them on the runs to Switzerland."

"Why do they do that?"

---

[43] *Beurs* is a derogatory name given to Algerians.

"Maybe to meet their friends there, maybe to carry money there. What I do know is that I have consignments of machinery in boxes to take from Switzerland to Marseilles. It is a good business for me. Giles, I know a bit about Marseilles. I was born there. It's a good place for smugglers, if you have the money. You can make the customs officers look the other way for enough *baksheesh*.[44]"

"What is this machinery, Mec?"

Mec chuckles as he swallows a slug of Pernod. "I was curious about that, too. Not too curious, you understand. So I had one of their cases accidentally fall off one of my vehicles and crack open."

"And what did you find?"

"Rifles. The Swiss army for a long time was equipped with the K-31 rifle. A damn good rifle too. I should know. We had a couple of them during the war. But they have re-equipped with new rifles, so they are selling off their old K-31's for a song."

"And you think these rifles are going to Algeria, for the rebels there?"

"No doubt about it, Giles. It's only just started, so it will take time for them to arrive. You can tell that to your people."

Giles is quite amazed at this windfall of information. "Mec, my first assignment is to look into Algerian affairs. Please tell no one that you have talked to me. But keep your eyes and ears open. We'll meet like this, quite informally, and you can tell me whatever you have heard, anything at all."

"For instance, about the meetings they are having here in Paris?"

"What meetings?"

"There's a café on the left bank near the *Odéon* where they were meeting, perhaps they still are; more likely they've

---

[44] *Baksheesh*. An Arab word meaning bribe.

moved on. These people are not stupid. They know the *flics*[45] of the DST [46]are after them."

"Do you know any names?"

"I overheard the name Boudiaf. He's a big cheese in the organization. His outfit calls itself the FLN[47]. I heard other names, but I wasn't paying much attention. Thousands of the *beurs* living here support these groups and give them money."

"Anything else, Mec?"

"Some big man in their movement has gone to Cairo to enlist the aid of Nasser."[48]

"I am very glad to hear of these things. We French must find our way in this post-war world. I believe colonies will be a thing of the past quite soon. So we must prepare for that."

"But Algeria is a part of France; not a colony. Isn't that right, Giles?"

"That's our pretense, Mec. But the Algerians outnumber the French there ten to one. Something has to be done about it and I'd prefer it not be a war. So help me, Mec. You were my captain, wise and courageous. It's my turn to be wise and courageous as a grown man. Help me be that for France, our mother country."

At the end of the week, Giles reports back to Mitterand, the Minister of the Interior. "My impression overall, sir, is

---

[45] *Flics* is a slang term for policemen, similar to cops.

[46] DST stands for *Directoire de la Surveillance du Territoire*. These letters were spoken as *deest*.

[47] FLN stands for *Front de Libération Nationale*. The FLN became the central and controlling group for the Algerians throughout the war.

[48] Gamal Abdul Nasser was a revolutionary who overthrew the monarchy in Egypt and by 1954 was in control of the country. He was a socialist who seemed to promise support for the Algerians but, in fact, did little to nothing to help them. Representatives of the FLN were stationed in Cairo and the French authorities thought, quite mistakenly and for a long time, that the uprising in Algeria was being run from Egypt. They could not credit the native Algerians to put together an organized revolt and use sophisticated tactics.

that Algeria is a powder keg ready to explode. I have learned from a private source in Paris that there are meetings happening here in Paris and that an uprising in Algeria is planned for the October-November period. A conduit for money exists between here and Switzerland. The money is being used to buy rifles, send them to Marseilles, and smuggle them to Algeria."

Mitterand is listening intently. "How long has it taken you to learn of these things?"

"Actually, sir, only a couple of days. I had to be busy with all the formalities at the start of the week."

"You say you have a source in Paris?"

"Yes, sir."

"Is he or she reliable?"

"Yes, sir. Absolutely reliable."

"Human intelligence . . . we call it HUMINT . . . is nearly always the best; unless we are being purposely misled. Would you want to disclose your source to an intelligence agency?"

Giles didn't have to think before he replied. "No, sir. I would not."

"Why not?"

"If my source knew that talking to me was known by many people, he would just clam up. He is not the sort to trust our government to hold information securely."

"I think I may agree with him. We'll keep him just between ourselves. On another matter. A young man called James Thirks has joined the British Embassy staff as a junior military attaché. That position has traditionally been a cover for espionage. I would like you to get to know him."

"There's no problem there, sir. We already know each other. We were both at Clare College in Cambridge and we both rowed in the Cambridge University boat. But, and I must say this, I can only be an honest friend to him."

"Quite so. Be that honest friend. That's all I ask. And you won the race too! I watched it on television. Well done.

All right. I am astonished what you have been able to find out so quickly. I will have it checked by my contacts at SDECE.[49] I have to be careful with those fellows. They have their own agendas that they keep to themselves. I am relying on you to use every discretion and find out what you can by any and all means about the Algerian situation. Be imaginative, young man, and use that splendid brain of yours.

---

[49] SDECE stands for *Service de Documentation Extérieure et de Contre-espionnage*. It is responsible for Foreign Intelligence.

Chapter 29.

Paris and Algeria. 1954.

Charles tells Julie she should read *Le Monde*, everyone does and it covers all the important news. Julie finds the paper tedious and dull. She goes to a news kiosk and finds *Le Canard Enchaîné* (The Ugly Duckling.) It is a well written tabloid, interesting and wonderfully irreverent, making fun of politicians and all sorts, and carries whatever is modern and lively in Paris. In the advertisements she comes across one put in by Risé Mayon. As Julie had learned when Mec and she had met Risé briefly when she was helping them obtain her passport, Risé is running an Escort Service. The advertisement reads: *Monsieur - belles accompagnatrices pour toi et plus*. The advertisement is in good taste, directed toward men of means, and its location is in a district of high prices for everything. "Well! Good for you, Risé!" Julie exclaims out loud, genuinely glad for her.

She puts it aside, but not entirely out of mind. She is tempted to go and see her, but is hesitant. If she ever did that, she muses, it would be best to meet somewhere out of the way, at some restaurant or other.

Julie is a devoted modern-style mother to young Charles. Her son and she develop their bonding. She holds him and talks to him every morning and puts him to bed in the evenings. When she can she greets him when nanny brings him back from taking him out to the *Champ de Mars* in his splendid pram. There, she knows, nanny meets with other nannies with their prams and children. They sit on the benches and gossip to their hearts' content. Nanny is full of insider news about the families for whom they work. She meets up with the next generation of Rothschild kids and their nannies. Soon Julie knows about the gossip of the extra-marital affairs of François Mitterand, the Minister of the Interior. She passes it on to Giles.

"Good god! Mitterand is one of the people I report to!"

"Well, of course I don't know how true it is, Giles. It's just gossip."

Giles grins. "It turns out, Julie, that gossip is a part of what I'm doing. Though not the gossip about Mitterand, for heaven's sake. I have to steer clear of that!"

"Can you tell me more, darling? You are so obsessed with whatever it is. It's affecting you. Nothing can be that dreadful . . . can it?"

"It's got to be just between ourselves. Not a word, not a hint to anyone else. Understand?"

"Yes. You can trust me, as you well know. I only wish to help, if I can. I want to see you less anxious."

Giles grimaces, but then smiles. "I would like that too. As a matter of fact I believe we will soon be able to let down a bit. Part of the information I have been putting together is about the Algerian resistance movement. They now call themselves the *Front de Libération Nationale*. I believe they are planning to attack government buildings in Algeria soon. I've seen part of an early draft of what looks like a proclamation they will be putting out. They are demanding sovereignty for Algeria. Like to know where I got that from?"

"Yes, I would, I suppose."

Julie is having second thoughts about whether she really wants to know more. Giles hurries on, relieved to be able to share with her his apprehensions, even though it is a breach of security. "Mec. He's my man."

"Mec? How does he get into it?" Julie is completely surprised.

"Yes, Mec. He has been very helpful, but not directly. He employs some Algerians. One of them is a driver who takes consignments to Switzerland. He meets other Algerians there; goes into their homes. This man found a scrap of paper with handwriting on it in a wastebasket. It starts to set out the goals of the Algerians. So the Algerian gives it to Mec who, a couple of days later, gives it to me."

Julie puts in, "Mec is quite an operator, isn't he?"

"Yes. He is." Giles reflects for a moment. "You know, he's also one of my fathers. I lost my true father in 1940 and now I have, sort of, two substitute fathers, Mec and Charles. They couldn't be more different! I love and need them both. I have been very lucky."

Julie nods her head thoughtfully. Risé Mayon had not been much of a mother to her at *Les Poulets* but, nevertheless, she had put her on track to success. "Like you, Giles, I had people to help me. One of them is in business in Paris now. Perhaps I'll look her up."

"Why don't you do that? We should be enlarging our social set."

Julie looks away, with a bit of a smirk. Risé would not fit in very well with their 'social set.' "Tell me more about the scrap of paper, Giles. I envy you getting into this cloak and dagger stuff. Sounds very exciting. What was on it?"

Giles grins wryly. "Usually my work is to sit at my desk, a very large desk in a quite small office. You'll have to come and see it sometime. I'll squeeze you in. I try to make sense of hundreds of bits of information. Not very exciting, except to the brain. Anyhow, this bit of information looks really hot. Actually, I copied it on one of our new American copying machines. I'm not really supposed to do that, so don't tell anyone. But Mitterand wanted the original. Here it is. It's top secret. OK?"

"Yes. OK, Giles. But please don't get into any trouble and I'm not sure I want to know what I shouldn't."

"This is an exception, Julie. Very likely, if I'm right, the whole world will know soon enough. Anyhow, you see it's torn at top and bottom. That's all we've got."

Goal: National Independence through:

1. Restoration of the Algerian state, sovereign, democratic, and social within the framework of the principles of Islam.

2. Preservation of all fundamental freedoms, without distinction of race and religion.

Internal objectives:

1. Political house-cleaning through the destruction of the last vestiges of corruption and reformism, and other causes of our present.... "

Julie reads it with her eyes widening. "*Merde alors!* It's dramatic, isn't it?"

"Drastic is what I call it, Julie. They are planning a rebellion. In effect a civil war. And civil wars, wherever they have been, are always bloody and cruel affairs. I can see absolute disaster ahead for Algeria."

"Does the government understand that, Giles?"

"All I can tell you, Julie, is that they don't seem to. Mendès and his advisers are deluding themselves, I think, by saying it's just another group, and there have been plenty of them, ventilating their hopes rather than their actual plans."

"And you don't think so?"

"No, Julie, I don't. There is too much else going on. It reminds me of when we were a few days off the invasion in 1944. The Germans did not understand that all the resistance groups were planning to act together and do as much damage as they could. I sense this FLN group is doing exactly the same and we have our heads in the sand."

"You have told Mitterand what you think?"

301

"Yes. He's worried, but he's afraid that if nothing much happens he will be accused of raising a false alarm and not having sufficient trust in the army and the police to take care of these things, as they have done in the past. Often with great brutality, I might add. I don't like any part of this," Giles finishes, looking grim.

"Oh, my poor Giles," Julie cries, coming over to sit by him. "What are you going to do?"

"Wait and see. That's all I can do. I told Mitterand my guess."

"What is your guess?"

"They will go on November first, All Saints Day. The day celebrates the resistance of the early Christians against their Roman oppressors. The Arab and Islam mentality is very conscious of history and precedent. I didn't study history and cultures and politics for nothing, for heaven's sake! The Algerians could well think All Saints Day propitious for them. Their build up, what I know of it, points to that day."

"What did Mitterand say?"

"He talked to me more about Mendès-France and the problems he faces. Mendès has a lot on his plate just now, closing down Vietnam, coming to terms with Tunisia, and our miserable National Assembly being impossibly fractious. Mendès doesn't like guesswork. He will only move when he feels certain about something. That's what Mitterand told me. It was his way of saying that whatever I find out and want to communicate, better be water-tight. But for people in the intelligence game, like I am now, you can never be really certain of the future. The future is always open to something else."

"Do you think it will be very violent, Giles?"

"Probably. Very violent and nasty. But it could misfire, too. Large scale coordinated operations are damn difficult to pull off."

Chapter 30.

Paris and Algeria.

That the Algerian uprising on All Saints Day[50] largely

---

[50] As early as April 1954 the French governor general in Algiers knows about the formation of rebellious groups, later brought together as the FLN. But the information is not acted on. In August, Ferhat Abbas, a moderate leader of the Algerian movement is in Paris and warns Mendès-France that unless promised reforms are implemented, then Algerian liberals like himself will be overtaken by events.

In Algiers information is reaching the *Sûreté* of camps in Libya where Algerian guerrillas are being trained. The *Sûreté* director comes to Paris to warn the government, but only sees low level functionaries. He tells them that he thinks the insurrection will start in December. So that gives the French time to waste.

More information is steadily coming in, including the location of the main bomb depot of the Algerians in the Casbah of Algiers. It is only put under loose surveillance, leaving the munitions to be used later.

French army intelligence in Algiers does not take the warning signs seriously until the last week in October.

Mitterand is the only Frenchman in high places who is seriously anxious about the Algerian situation. He goes to Algiers in mid-October and returns to Paris clearly disquieted, but doing little. He can put the security forces on an emergency footing, but he doesn't.

Mendès-France is preoccupied with international and European affairs. He's flying around, paying visits to Germany and England. The EDC (European Defense Community) is a primary concern. He is also in the fails is due, not so much from the French quelling it, as the ill-discipline of the Algerians.

Everything is supposed to start at midnight. But trigger happy Algerians begin firing well before that. Slowly the French police and army realize, because of the geographical scatter of the incidents, that it is a general uprising. Alarms sound up and down the coast. Thus, by the time more concentrated attacks occur, the French are ready for them. But their response is almost as muddled as the Algerian attacks. The truth is that very little actually happens. A few buildings are damaged by explosions and a few guns and some ammunition are captured. The Algerian leaders and their men retreat back into the mountains, angry and disappointed. The reaction by the French in Algeria is, predictably, violent and brutal. Thousands of people are rounded up, jailed, many executed, others tortured. As seen by the French, it has been no more than a large scale scuffle led and directed by an Algerian cabal in Cairo. The French, having done their worst to the Algerians, believe the country is cowed and pacified.

Mendès calls Giles in to see him. "Well, you were right about the date, All Saints Day. You were about the only one to see that clearly. Well done. But you were wrong about the uprising. Those people can't organize. As we well know,

---

throes of planning a state visit to Canada and the USA. Algeria is not a top priority. He knows the English disapprove of his policy there, seeing it as a retrograde attempt to hang on to colonies.

Algerian affairs are not occupying the French mind. The population is absorbed by a spate of flying saucers, the death of Matisse, the painter, the award of the Nobel prize to Ernest Hemingway, the publication by a young woman of *Bonjour Tristesse* (Good-day Sadness). Then there is an earthquake in Orléansville, in the western mountains of Algeria, killing 1400 people and distracting everyone. The earthquake, too, disrupts the preparations of the FLN contingent there. It is already a weak arm of the insurrection and, when the time comes, is ineffective.

a large-scale attack needs solid planning and skillful staff work. Those people are not up to that."

Giles shifts in his chair. "Sir, may I speak frankly?"

"By all means."

"We now know the uprising had been planned for some time and was well thought out. That it failed was due to the lack of discipline among the Algerians in the actual attack. Cairo had nothing to do with the planning. It was an Algerian effort, through and through. Their leaders will have learned from their failure. They are back in the mountains, licking their wounds and, I believe, more determined than ever. We have their manifesto in full now. They are in this for the long haul. This early defeat will not dissuade them, in my estimation."

Mendès frowns. "Did you hear my speech to the Assembly?"

"I read it, sir."

"Then you know that I believe in *Algérie Française*. Algeria will be French, no matter what."

"Then it must be reformed, sir. The Algerians are planning to come back at us, better prepared and even more determined."

Mendès sits still in his chair, his face a study in gravity. He looks up. "You are an honest voice, Giles Martin. I need you. I will tell you a secret. In spite of what I said in the Assembly, I believe that within ten years Algeria will be an independent country with, we must hope, strong ties to France. We must lay the groundwork for that to happen. It will take a long time and we probably will go through hell before it happens."

"Yes, sir," Giles replies, surprised at Mendès words

Mendès relaxes a little. "So be it. What will be your part in this endeavor, Giles?"

"I serve at your pleasure, my premier."

"Not good enough, Giles. Tell me, should I send you to Algiers or take you with me to Canada and the USA, or both?

You are fluent in English. I am also sure that you know the mind of the English very well. You speak with General Marlis from time to time?"

"Sir, I don't want to be put in a duplicitous position with my family or friends."

"No. Quite right. But being well informed is not being duplicitous. I propose this to you. I will give you a warrant to go to Algiers and to speak to people from the top down as my personal aide and emissary. They will be surprised, they will see you as too young, I'm sure. But I want your eyes and your brain to see what is going on. The people I have there, and here too, are good, but often too set in their minds. I'm relying on you to be an intelligent camera. You understand?"

"Yes, sir."

"All right. You will go in three days time. Mitterand and his people will have things set up for you by then. You must have a government passport. Any questions?"

Giles, trying to straighten out his whirling mind, has the good sense to say, "no, sir. I will do my best."

"Good man. Then, all being well after you return, you will accompany me to Ottawa and Washington."

* * *

One of the many things Julie does to settle back into her homeland is to retrieve her parceled-up clothes from Sophie. Most of them have stayed with her in her house in Criselles, in store in her attic.

Julie drives herself to Criselles in their Citroën DS. The roads are improving rapidly. France is putting serious money into creating a new infrastructure. French high speed trains are already the best in the world.

Julie has great faith in Citroën cars ever since their dramatic drive on leaving Chagny to escape the reporters. This new Citroën of theirs has a modern suspension and rides smoothly. It levels itself when the engine is turned on. Julie finds that cute. The car is also one of the first to have disc brakes to go along with its powerful engine. Julie goes to a driving school and passes her license test. Even Giles says she drives well. She avoids driving in Paris as much as possible, preferring taxis, the Métro, and busses. The traffic in Paris is crazy! Even so, that morning she manages the crowded streets very well and picks up the road going to Sens, and then on to Plaignes and Criselles, with no trouble. She thinks of going into Dijon and visiting *Le Coq*. Then thinks better of it. However, she does phone Colette Saludin and is glad to find her well and prospering with her escort business.

Julie spends delighted hours with her clothes and furs. Oh! She has missed her furs! Though they do smell of the moth balls she had put in with them. She will have them all cleaned in Paris.

Sophie, of course, wants to know all about Giles and young Charles, her grandson. Julie has brought pictures with her. She invites Sophie to come and stay with them in Paris.

Sophie cries. "Paris! Oh, my God! What a place! So noisy! Everything going so fast. Just like London. Who can live there? And the trains in the ground!"

"I will look after you, Sophie. You'll be all right."

"Oh! I can do for myself, my dear girl. Never fear! Like I did in London. And in Paris I can speak to the people!"

Back in Paris, Julie decides it's time she sets about becoming a model. Following the advice of Charles and Joey and, taking a big gulp, she phones the house of *Madame Dionnelle* and asks for an interview. She reaches an assistant and tells her she has ambitions to be a model. She mentions the name of the British Diplomat General Marlis whom *Madame* Dionnelle knows. Julie quite understands that who you know opens doors and she is thankful for the introduction. However, Julie can't help but be a little nervous about something else. *Madame Dionnelle* is where General Max Edelman took her to be dressed during the war. Will someone remember her?

Shortly Julie has an appointment scheduled with *Madame* Dionnelle. "Oh, god, Giles! I'm not a young chicken anymore. I mean I'll be . . . "she counted on her fingers . . . "actually 29 on July 14. *Mon Dieu*, I hadn't thought I was that old! She will think me ridiculous."

"If you go in with that attitude, Julie, you will have failed before you have begun. I don't know anything about the modeling business, but I bet there is a place for you. You are beautiful with a great figure and you are sensible and know that work is work. And you have a nice smile, too!"

Julie almost blushes. "Maybe. But those girls never smile. Their faces are all ice cold when they are on the runway."

"I think that's all part of the show. They must smile at other times. Anyhow, do it, Julie! I think you'll be great. And don't worry about being a bit older. As far as I'm concerned you are a beautiful young woman, whom I love, and you have the world and your life spread out before you. Neither you nor I had any responsibility of when, where, and to whom we were born. We are responsible for how we live our lives now. That's all that needs to be said. Now go out and do your thing, Julie!"

With that push from her husband, Julie keeps the appointment. *Madame* Dionnelle greets her graciously. "I was glad to hear from General Marlis and his wife. They did much to help France. And how is that handsome boy, Giles? He's quite grown up now, of course. He is your husband?"

"Yes, he is and he's very well, thank you. He's in the government here, a special aide to Mendès-France, the premier."

"Well, well. I'm glad to hear it. Time does fly by, doesn't it? So you want to be in the fashion business, be a model. What experience have you had?"

Julie had prepared herself for the question and hoped she could get by with saying that she had always been interested in clothes and that she had been a hostess in a club in Dijon. "It meant always to be at my best and wear good clothes. I am afraid that's all I can offer. Except that I am willing to learn and to work hard."

"Get up, my dear, and walk across the room and back again."

Julie did it. *Madame* Dionnelle nods her head. "Very good. You are a beautiful and graceful young lady. As you say, you need to learn. An American, John Robert Powers, has opened a modeling school here. It has quickly become the place for aspiring models. I'll phone John and make sure he has a place for you. Graduate and then come back to see me. I will take you on as a *débutante*, provided you still wish it and you have taken to heart your training. Now, let us be candid. You were here, were you not, during the war with General Max Edelman?"

"... yes ... yes ...," Julie drops her eyes.

"All right. Just so we both know. But don't worry. You and I were in it together."

Julie feels a gleam of hope. "What . . . what do you mean ... together?"

"Don't doubt it. I stayed alive and well by dressing you girls to please our masters at that time. You did the same. You survived just as I did. So we are equal. And we won't think of it anymore. The war is long past. Our business now is to get on with our lives."

Julie is now smiling. That big cloud had blown away. "Thank you, thank you, *madame*. I will do my very best to bring credit to your house. I owe that to you."

"Oh, nonsense, girl! We'll work together. That's the only way to do things."

Back with Giles that evening she tells him of her acceptance to be a *débutante*. Giles can see how enthusiastic she is. "I bet it will be hard work. Paris is the center of the fashion world. You'll have to be good."

"I know I can be. A long time ago, Ernst told me to be the best I can be. I have followed his advice ever since."

Thinking about Ernst unexpectedly makes her teary. Giles takes her in his arms and kisses the tears away. Julie wipes her eyes and says, "what about this rowing club you were telling me about and the 1956 Olympic Games. Could you really be in a crew?"

"I think it possible, Julie. I have been to the Paris Rowing Club clubhouse. It's on the Seine by the *Ile des Vannes*. They welcomed me with open arms. I have to work out a schedule. To row in competitions you have to keep in shape and devote time to it. I'll see about the rowing machines you can have on the floor. Then I can row here! Of course, I must train with the other crew members. It will take a bit of doing. Before rowing in the Olympics a crew has to compete in qualifying rounds and be the best boat in the country."

* * *

Once Julie learns of Giles's Algerian mission, she finds a briefcase and a suitcase made of good leather for Giles to take and has his name embossed on them. She whisks him to *Jacendo* in the Marais at *38, rue de Poitou*, possibly the most elegant men's store in Paris, and in a day Giles has a Givenchy suit altered to fit him. It is cut in a distinctive French fashion, rather square and loose, quite different from the English suits Giles has. Julie instinctively knows that being clearly French will help Giles. She understands these things better than he does. Julie recognizes the shop's neighborhood; it's not far from *rue Blondel*, where *Les Poulets* was. She thinks it might upset her, but it doesn't. One of these days she will go back to *rue Blondel* and see how it has fared.

"You remember, my darling," she say to Giles," that I said in Dijon that someday you would be an important man. I was right. Here you are, doing something really important. For heaven's sake be careful and don't get yourself killed."

"I'll try not to," Giles says with a grin as he kisses her goodbye.

Giles boards the plane at *Le Bourget* airport to fly to Algiers. He sits back with the whisky the *hôtesse de l'air* has served him. The whisky seems appropriate, it's the iconic drink of men of affairs. Then he chuckles to himself. He is hardly there yet! Yet he now finds himself, quite extraordinarily, as an aide to the Premier of France and the Minister of the Interior, and given the name, in his mission statement, of *émisaire*. Giles had tried to find out where the word placed him in the ranks; who was he superior or inferior to? With no luck. It would be up to him to claim whatever privilege he needed. In effect, he is on his own. Thinking about it, sipping his whisky, Giles reckons that is precisely what Mendès intended. Mendès wants to see what he is made of.

Giles opens his briefcase, takes out a detailed map of Algeria, and studies it. He has been briefed in Paris on the state of the war and the names of generals and others who he may meet or hear about. The active insurgency is based in the mountains east of Algiers, in the *Massif de L'Aurés*. Giles memorizes the names of the towns and the roads. He studies the latest reports from General Spillman, the area commander in that region. The general complains that he is fighting a guerrilla war with troops only trained in conventional WWII-type tactics. All they can do is hold the roads and villages while they are there, but have the Algerians move back in as soon as they leave. Ambushes are killing his men. There is no discernible progress in quelling the insurgency. He asks for elite "Para" troops to be sent in. They had been in combat in Vietnam and know how to fight guerrillas: take away their means of existence by destroying the villages that support them and the food crops that feed them; interrogate the native people with advanced techniques; chase them tirelessly and mercilessly into their lairs and kill them.

Giles sees that the report has been endorsed by the army commander in Algeria and by the Governor General. He looks up from the papers in his hands and shudders. It is a policy of deprivation, starvation, torture, and death for the Algerians. How can the future possibly be built on that?

None of this appears in the French press that continues to belittle the rebels and champion the French forces defeating them. Truth, as Giles has seen many times in his studies, is the first casualty of war.

Giles is met at the Algiers airport by a young army lieutenant, George Jody. He has been ordered: "Keep *Monsieur* Martin away from anything important. Take him to the beach rest camps where he can see our soldiers in rest and recuperation. Let them tell him of the awful things the Algerians are doing to their own people."

The lieutenant warns Giles that the Governor General and his generals are not happy about Paris sending "spies" down into their territory or doubting their words in describing what is happening. "Keep your head down, Giles Martin. They feel insulted by having you here to report on them. They think you too young and lacking in experience. I'll try to keep you clear of them. I have a Jeep for us with a driver, an Algerian fellow who knows the city and countryside."

Giles nods his head. "That's pretty much what I expected. I will go about the business the premier has sent me here to do regardless of them. First, I will spend a day or two here in Algiers. You and your driver will show me around. Then I'll go east into the Aurés."

"That's not exactly what I've been told to do, Giles Martin. Tomorrow you are scheduled to go to a Rest and Recuperation camp on the coast."

Giles says sharply, "cancel it. I will make my own schedule."

Lieutenant Jody was not expecting such determination, but he likes it. He knows things are going from bad to worse in Algeria and threatening to become worse still. "I must warn you. There may be hell to pay for you going your own way. But I'll go along with you. You should be your own boss. Otherwise you will only see what they want you to see."

"Good man, lieutenant. We'll get along just fine. I'll take all responsibility. Don't worry. Just help me do my job."

They shook hands on it.

Jody told him, "today things are quiet here in Algiers, but many fear it is the calm before the next storm. A couple of days ago a civilian bus was machine gunned going to Dellys, on the coast, just east of here. Several people were killed. These things go on sporadically all the time."

"Did they catch the men who did it?"

"No and we seldom do. And they are not all men. They have women fighters too." The lieutenant shrugged his soldiers. "They are guerrillas and fade away into the villages and hills. They avoid any confrontation with our troops."

The driver is Abu, an educated Algerian who is doing the only work he can find. Even though, he tells Giles on the side, it puts him in bad with many of his fellow Algerians.

Jody takes Giles into the Casbah. "The only way we are going to eradicate the rebels from this warren is to kill most of them and destroy the buildings; and we will probably do that unless things improve. That's what I hear."

It is the first time that Giles had been in anything like the Casbah. The maze of narrow streets and the sights, noises, and smells astonish him. Only Arabic is spoken. The lieutenant and he are met with blank looks. The street merchants try to ingratiate themselves in order to sell them their goods. Wherever the two of them go, whatever is happening becomes subdued. The Arab men look and mutter. The covered-up women in their *burqas* turn their backs and disappear into the jumble of buildings. The only signs of acceptance are from the children playing in the street. They pay little attention, but some do look up and smile. But otherwise, Giles sees fear and resignation laced with hate and anger all around him.

The next day, Wednesday, November 10, Giles wakes up, along with everyone in Algiers, to find many walls covered with nationalist Algerian slogans. One of them is LA VALISE OU LE CERCUEIL (the suitcase or the coffin) a reference to the choice the FLN proposes to give Algeria's Europeans, the *pieds noirs*. Giles takes photographs. Then he photographs the men, guided by the police and soldiers, who are scrubbing the words off the walls. Later he records Algerians being herded into police stations with their hands over their heads or tied behind their backs. The French civilians around them are approving of what they see. An older well-dressed Frenchman says disdainfully, "they should shoot the lot."[51]

"Maybe they will, God help them," Jody tells Giles. Looking around Giles suspects that security police are mingling in the crowd and keeping an eye on him and the lieutenant.

Departing before dawn, hoping to escape notice, Giles, Jody, and Abu drive into the Aurés mountains. They see signs of the war; burnt out cars, charred and ruined buildings. They come to a control point manned by a French sergeant and soldiers. Lieutenant Jody shows him his orders to accompany the emissary from Paris. The sergeant lets them through with the warning that there is action along the road ahead. Soon they are at another check-point. This time a captain in the French army is in charge. Jody salutes and explains their mission. The captain is reluctant to let them go further. Giles shows him his credentials and orders as an emissary from Mendès-France that require French authorities in Algeria to provide every assistance.

The captain tells Giles. "Our outposts at Pasteur and Makouba up ahead have been under attack. We are withdrawing our forces. We've heard there have been many casualties."

A staff car pulls up behind them. A major gets out and joins them. After salutes are exchanged, the major inquires what is holding them up. The captain repeats what he has said before. He adds, "these actions, sir, seem to be targeted at gaining weapons and ammunition by the rebels."

Giles puts himself into the conversation. "Gentlemen,

---

[51] Records indicate that about 1200 Algerians were killed at this time by the police, army, and the *pieds noirs*.

such information is exactly the type of intelligence the government needs to know and is why I am here, to report back first hand. I see these Algerians coming down the road toward us. What will you do with them, captain?"

"The usual. We send them to the camp over there, where they are interrogated."

"What happens to them then?"

"They are held at the camp. They all side with the enemy. So if we put them back in their villages, all they do is continue their sedition."

Giles puts his binoculars to his eyes. He sees a camp surrounded by barbed wire. It has raised sentry posts with armed soldiers in them. "It looks like a prison or a concentration camp. I see women and children there. Their condition seems deplorable."

The major butts in. "That is enough. *Monsieur* Martin, you should leave here and continue on your mission. My orders are to proceed down the road toward Makouba to see what is happening there. I suggest you proceed before us. We will be right behind you to give you protection."

Giles sees that the major is not about to let him do anything else. In any event, he has seen enough. "Very well, major. We will proceed."

They start off down the road toward Makouba. Once they are along the road a bit, Jody turns to Giles. "I doubt the *wogs*[52] have mined this road, not yet, at least. But I know there has been sniper fire around here. Let's hope we don't run into any or - even worse - an ambush."

Looking back they can see the major's car behind them. Ten kilometers down the road they are hit by the first bullet. It comes from somewhere ahead and shatters the windscreen in a spray of glass. Abu is cut about the face and is bleeding.

---

[52] *Wogs* was a derogatory word for Arabs used by the British. The French took it over.

Giles hauls him out of the jeep and lays him on the ground. Jody joins them. The major's car has stopped down the road.

Giles looks around carefully. "Jody, we are pinned down. I was in the *Maquis* and been in these situations before. For the moment just stay down."

"OK. It's the first time I've been under fire. I am glad you are here."

"Don't worry. We are going to get out of this. Where did you put that rifle I saw you with?"

"Under the seat, at the back."

"Get it for me and some ammo. I learned to be a good shot when I was in the *Maquis*."

Giles lies on the ground behind a rear wheel of the jeep and scans the low ridge in front of him. Every minute or so a shot comes down, pinging the jeep or kicking up dust by it.

"I am pretty sure he's a solitary sniper, may be sent to hold us up while they retreat," Giles says. "The light has come round to illuminate that ridge very well. He will make some movement before he shoots again. See if you can spot it, Jody."

The shot comes in. Both Jody and Giles see the prior movement in a cleft on top of the ridge. Only the sky is behind it. The shooter was etched out clearly "The idiot!" Giles remarks. "He makes a damn good target against the sky. I don't have to see much of him. I am setting the range sight at a hundred meters. Agreed, Jody?'

"Yes. A hundred meters."

"OK. He is shooting at about one minute intervals. We'll let the next shot go by. Then we'll time up to the next minute. I'll line up on the cleft."

The shot comes in. Jody starts to time, calling out every five seconds. Giles wraps the rifle strap round his arm and settles himself, breathing deeply but carefully, as if he is shooting Germans again.

The sniper moves out from behind the cleft into view just enough. Giles can see his rifle as he takes aim. Breathe . . . aim . . . take up the trigger slack . . .fire!

The sniper in the cleft jerks up and then falls back out of view. Jody slaps Giles on the back. "Good shot!" he exclaims.

They are in the process of standing up at the back of the Jeep when Giles lets out an "Ooooh!" and his hand flies to his right buttock. He falls to his knees. He is bleeding. He is wounded. "There must be another of those bastards," he cries.

Jody drags him round to the side of the jeep. "The jeep has a medical kit, Giles. Don't worry. I think it's only a flesh wound. I have dressed wounds before. Abu! Come here and hold down on the wound. Apply pressure."

The major's car comes up. The major jumps out, but takes no cover. "How's he doing, lieutenant? Is he dead?"

"Oh, no. It's a flesh wound. The bullet went through the right buttock. Not serious, but painful, I'm sure."

Giles agrees with that. When the bullet went in, it seemed like a red hot needle.

Jody tells the major he has completed a course in field aid. "I have the bleeding under control. I'll give him a morphine shot. Abu here picked up the spent bullet. Here it is." He shows it to the major. "I'll give it to the emissary as a keep sake."

They carry Giles into the major's car. The morphine is taking hold. The last thing Giles remembers is Jody talking with the major. "Where the hell did that shot come from? It had to be from somewhere behind us, not from the ridge. Did you see anything, major? It must have been from somewhere in your direction . . . very strange . . . very strange . . . "

* * *

Mendès-France was at his desk in the Elysée Palace early the next day when his secretary brought in dispatches.

"Sir, that young man you sent to Algeria has been shot."

"What! Is he dead?" Mendès is truly shocked.

"No, sir. Wounded, but not seriously. He is being flown to Paris on a medical evacuation flight to arrive *Le Bourget* at noon."

"All right. Tell Mitterand. I want a colonel at least to meet the plane and expedite matters. Make sure about the ambulances. There will be other wounded on the flight. Giles Martin must be given the best possible treatment. Get me his wife's phone. I will talk to her."

It was still early in the morning. The only one up was Sophie who was staying with Julie and making sure that nanny was doing all the right French things for her precious grandson.

"*'allo - qui est là?*" (hello - who is there?)

"Am I speaking to *Madame* Giles Martin?"

"No. I am the mother, Sophie. Giles's mother. Who are you?" Sophie, as is her wont, is nothing but direct.

"I am Mendès-France, the premier of France and I wish to speak to *Madame* Giles Martin."

"Huh! You don't say! Well, I'll fetch her. Just a minute."

Julie was up, putting on her bathrobe.

"Julie! There's some prankster on the phone saying he is Mendès-France, the Premier of France."

"OK - I'm just coming."

Julie picks up the phone, "Yes?"

"*Madame* Giles Martin. We met in that restaurant in Dijon, before you were married. I am Mendès-France. You remember?"

Julie blanches. "Yes . . . yes . . . I remember . . . " Could it really be the Premier of France calling her? She stands up very straight as if the premier was right there.

"You are surprised to hear from me, I'm sure. I have some news for you. Steel yourself, *madame*. Your husband has been shot in Algeria, but he is only wounded and I'm told it is not serious."

"Giles . . . shot! Oh, no! It can't be true!" Julie was aghast. Sophie was beside her, hearing the conversation, now with her face too as white as snow.

"Yes, it is true, but the wound is not serious, so I hear. Pray listen. I am sending a car to your house. The medical plane will land at *Le Bourget* at noon. The car will take you there. You will be in the charge of an officer who will arrange to have you meet your husband. You must be as brave as your husband. As I'm sure you will be. He was wounded in service to his country. No man can do more. So, wait for the car."

The two women look at each other and collapse into each other's arms, gasping and crying. Julie fights to recover herself. "He said it is not serious, Sophie. But what does he know? I must phone Charles and Joey. They must know. Let us try to be calm, Sophie. We must dress properly so Giles will be proud of us, as we are of him."

"Good God, Julie!" Charles exclaims. "Giles shot! In Algeria! What was he doing there for heaven's sake?"

"Mendès-France sent him there, Charles, on a mission."

"Are you sure?"

"Yes, I'm sure."

"At *Le Bourget* at noon. Is that right?"

"Yes, that's right."

Charles calls the Air Vice Marshall he knows at the Air Ministry in London. "Yes, just the two of us. Something small will be fine. We'll be in Hendon in 45 minutes."

"Joey. I'll put on my field uniform. You wear a hat . . . and something else suitable. Hurry."

All that Joey can think of is Geoffrey, her war-killed son. Oh, God! Let it not be again!

Julie chooses one of her London suits from Harrod's and a neat little hat. She decides on a short overcoat rather than one of her furs. It's a smart fashionable outfit. Choosing what to wear steadies her.

The government Citroën comes to their door on *rue St. Dominique*, flanked by two motorcycle policemen. A small crowd gathers. A police officer escorts Julie and Sophie to the car. He takes the front seat. The motorcycle sirens are turned on and they set out for *Le Bourget*, running the red lights, the traffic making way for them.

Julie, in spite of herself, starts to cry. Sophie comforts her. "You must be strong, Julie. Your husband will not want to see you crying."

"I know, I know. Help me. Give me some tissues."

They come to the entrance to the airport. The roads are cleared. There are police and soldiers everywhere. "Good God, Sophie! Is this all for us?"

The police officer in the front seat is on his radio, evidently hearing instructions. He turns round to Julie. "The premier is coming to meet the plane. There will be other wounded aboard. The plane will be parked in a special place. We are going there along with the ambulances. The premier will greet the soldiers." He holds his radio to his ear again as more messages are coming in. "Air Traffic Control reports that a flight authorized by the Royal Air Force in London is bringing a British general to *Le Bourget*. "*Alors!* It is an affair, this!"

Mendès-France sees that this occasion gives him another opportunity to declare that Algeria is French, a part of France, and that the country must be brought to order. To acknowledge and honor the service of the wounded soldiers is always good publicity. He has some service medals to hand out.

At the same time he is avid to hear what Giles Martin has to tell him about the situation in Algeria. His government is holding on only by a hair's breadth in the Assembly. The next vote of confidence could go either way. Mendès suspects the generals he has in Algeria are trying to fight WWII again, rather than fight the guerrillas on their terms. Make them suffer! If Giles confirms this impression he, Mendès, will go to Algeria himself and replace the generals. Brutal or not, the war must be won.

Giles hops down the steps from the aircraft on one leg, helped by a burly sergeant. Julie has been standing in a group, held back by a rope. When she sees Giles she lifts the rope, goes under it in a flash, and runs to Giles. All the cameras and the News Reels pivot to her as she is in full flight, like a blonde bird.

She almost knocks down Giles as the sergeant gives him his crutches. The two are standing there embracing and exclaiming to each other as Mendès-France comes up to them flanked by an entourage of people and security men. He has told the security chief, "you have to look after my young man. He is valuable to France."

Mendès takes Giles's hand. "How are you?"

"I'm really fine, sir. I got hit in the rump. It just stops me sitting down except on a rubber pillow," Giles says with a wry grin.

"I want to hear from you as quickly as possible. Can you drive back with me into town?"

"Certainly, sir."

Mendès turns to Julie. She drops a curtsey as he takes her hand. "Excuse me, *madame*. I have to steal your husband for an hour or two. I am so happy that you two are wed. And, may I say, you are as beautiful as ever!"

"Thank you, *mon premier*. I'm very glad to find my husband alive."

"So am I! He and you, I think, are both soldiers of France. I am proud of you," and Mendès embraces her cheek to cheek.

The cameras are flashing and clicking in a tempest of photography.

Some of the close by reporters hear their conversation and see that the premier knows her.

At that point General Charles Marlis comes striding up in his British general's red-tabbed uniform. He salutes the premier.

"Ah, General Marlis. I am glad to see you again. You were the guardian of this splendid young man when he was studying in England, I believe."

"Yes, premier, he is like a son to me."

"He is fluent in English and, if he is fit by then, I will have him accompany me to Ottawa and Washington. He told me before he left for Algeria that he is preparing his doctoral thesis on French foreign policy for the last 100 years. He is a gifted fellow."

"I quite agree, sir. I believe I will be in Washington when you'll be there. Perhaps we can arrange a dinner with our ambassador in the Embassy there."

"We'll see about it, general. Now I must be off. Time and tide and politics and war wait for no man!"

Before he leaves Mendès awards each of the wounded soldiers, Giles included, an Algerian war medal. Giles is helped into the car and the line of cars and motorcycles head for Paris.

The reporters descend on Julie in a frenzy. "*Madame, madame*, how do you know the premier? When did you meet? Did you know your husband was on a special mission for the premier? Your husband is the same man who shot the maniac who was trying to kill the British boys at St Cyr? What is your vocation? Have you any children? Do you think we will in the war in Algeria? Will your husband be there again?"

It was a cacophony of noise and Julie could hardly understand a word. A woman reporter came to her side and held up her hands. "Gentlemen, gentlemen, give *madame* a chance to catch her breath. Her husband has been nearly killed. Be respectful." The men quiet down. "Now *madame*," she continues, "may I ask you just a few questions. You are Giles Martin's wife?"

"Yes. We were married in Cambridge, England a year and a half ago. Giles was studying in the university there."

"But you are French?"

"Oh, yes. I was born in Avier, a small village in the department of Aisne. By a coincidence our birthdays are the same, July 14, so Giles and I are both very French, you see."

Julie's charming manner and good looks are being eaten up by the reporters. She feels confident in herself.

"May I ask, *Madame* Martin, what do you do now?"

"I look after my husband and try to be the best mother in the world to our son."

"I see. Anything else?"

"I have met with *Madame* Dionnelle on *rue St. Honorée* and will be a model there."

"Will we see you in the next show?"

"I really don't know. That will be up to *Madame* Dionnelle."

There are more questions. Then Julie holds up her hand. Quite to her surprise the reporters hush. She beckons Sophie to her side. "*Madame* Martin here is the mother of Giles Martin and both she and her son are heroes of the *Maquis* in eastern France. Now we must go and see to my son, her grandson. Thank you. Thank you."

They are driven back to their home in the police car, this time without a motorcycle escort.

"Oh, Sophie. I am so happy and relieved. Giles is going to be all right. What luck to be hit in the rear end, eh! And not somewhere else. All's well that ends well, eh!"

They laugh together. "That's true, Julie. But where's the end to this business in Algeria?"

* * *

That, in essence, is the same question that Mendès-France asked Giles.

"Sir, I can sum up the situation in three phrases. First: the insurgency is deeper than has been thought; they will outlast us. Second: we are using out-dated and counter-effective tactics, torture among them. Third: the only hope we have of retaining Algeria, or having Algeria our ally, is to overcome the resistance of the *pieds noirs* and implement reforms in the political structure and in the economy."

Mendès looks glum. "Maybe, maybe. I have thought much the same. You saw enough in Algeria before you were wounded to come to these conclusions?"

"No, sir. I have studied the history of Algeria. On my trip I saw what is happening now. Although we have done much for the country, we have done very little for the Algerians. We are now reaping what we have sown."

"You seem to have a biblical sense for what is happening."

"Maybe I do. But I think of it more in Greek classical terms, as in Oedipus Rex. The powerful king blinds himself because he cannot bear to see what he has done. Algeria is a tragedy we are inflicting on ourselves."

"That is a heavy thought, Giles Martin."

"Yes, sir. It is. I have one more thing to report. They, the Algerian authorities, in the form of an army major and the two men under him, tried to kill me while I was undertaking the mission you sent me on."

"What? What did you say?" Mendès expostulates.

"They only wounded me." Giles takes the spent bullet out of his pocket and shows it to Mendès. "This is the bullet they wanted in my brain. Instead it went through my right buttock."

Giles explains that the only possible source of the bullet was the major or one of his men. "They were behind us. The rebel fire had come from the ridge in front of us. There were no rebels behind us. I was crouching. That's when they took aim. Then I stood up. The bullet went where my head had been. If you can find the rifle, we could match the bullet and tell for sure if it was fired by the rifle they had."

Mendès is furious. He calls an army adjutant into the room and has Giles repeat the story. Mendès says, "have it written down as a legal affidavit. Have Giles Martin sign it. Then we'll see. I've had enough of those fucking generals!"

Giles could only say, in retrospect that, for Mendès, having his emissary shot in the ass by his own army, was the final straw. He replaced those generals, but the war continued with increased intensity, killing, torture, and calamity on both sides with no end in sight.

In their bedroom Julie spreads ointment around Giles's wounded buttock. It has healed rapidly and he no longer limps. He will just be left with an honorable scar. The doctors say he is fine to go to Ottawa and Washington. Julie jokes, "before me I have the most significant buttock in the whole of France, responsible for the dismissal of generals, no less! Perhaps its bearer can also be the savior of Algeria!"

Giles chuckles. "Could be. One of these days the war will stop. Then a political solution will have to be found. I hope to be a part of the start of that when we go to Canada and the US. The Algerians have representatives over there. I think we should start to talk with them, but I don't think anyone else thinks that. If I have the chance I will talk to Mendès about it."

Julie says, "just take care of yourself, Giles! Don't be too ambitious. You're flying out tomorrow and I'll be going to see *Madame* Dionnelle. She has asked me to come round as soon as I can. I suppose she wants to know if I still want to be a model."

"Do you?"

"Oh, yes! I think it will be fun before we settle down to be an old married couple. But, as I told you, I have to go to modeling school first."

"Well, good luck, darling. I'll phone you as often as I can. But I expect to be busy. The youngest fellow on the team, that's me, is given all the chores to do."

"I bet you will do them very well, my sweet. Now turn over so I can kiss you before I turn out the light. You must have a good sleep before setting off across the Atlantic."

Chapter 31.

Julie on the spot. Giles too.

Julie arrives at the Fashion House and enters the 200 year old building through its newly installed tall glass doors. *Madame* Dionnelle, looking most elegant, but clearly dismayed about something, meets her. "You will hardly believe this, Julie Martin, but the secretary of the premier, that is Mendès-France, just called. She said the premier trusts I will give you, *Madame* Giles Martin, every chance in your career and wishes you good luck. What next, eh?"

Julie is startled. It must be a hoax. "I didn't have anything to do with that, *madame*, I assure you I didn't."

Madame Dionnelle gives her a wry smile. "No, no. I believe you. The man who came on first told me it was a call from the *Elysée Palace*. I believed him. You know what's in the papers. Your husband has been feted as the hero for being shot in the ass and now you, my dear, have the Premier of France telling me how to run my business! I have enough trouble with journalists and reporters, who I hate and love about equally, and sewing machines that suddenly won't sew, without the Premier of France calling me!" *Madame* Dionnelle adds a few more choice words, then sits back with something of a grin. "Well, *Madame* Martin?"

"I'm so sorry, *madame*. I apologize most profoundly for causing you this trouble. I will leave now." Julie feels dreadful about it.

Madame Dionnelle slams her hand down on her desk. "*Zut*! You will do nothing of the sort! I have to compete with Dior, Fath, Chanel and the rest! Oh, no! Don't you walk out on me! Hey! You're here and we'll teach you everything you need to know. Now, my dear," *Madame* Dionnelle, changing her manner completely, sweeping her arms around as if quelling a rough sea, instructs Julie, "absorb the ambience, feel it like an aroma from the open mouth of a flower!"

"But... but... "

"Oh, no, my dear girl! No, no. I do not deal in buts! I have done my homework. Your husband is away across the Atlantic. You have a baby son and a nanny to care for him. You have your mother-in-law from Criselles and another who is often here from London. You are a fortunate young mother! Commit yourself and I will make you a star shining like lustrous satin ... in this otherwise pretty filthy world!"

Julie is in shock! But in delight too. She grins. She is reminded of when *Madame* Guyton, long ago, was inducting her into being a *fille* at *Les Poulets*. That hadn't turned out so badly! There was this actress in her still impelling her forward. Very much the same impulsion, she surmises, as the one that drove *Madame* Dionnelle.

Madame Dionnelle goes on in her grand manner. "You will say, no doubt, as people do, that you need time to think it over. No! Do not do that! Absolutely not. That is for the *midinette*[53] who is too afraid to trust herself. Such girls find every doubt and reason to dissuade themselves! So! Do what you have to do and then come back here in the morning, at nine, ready to start. I will pay you as a *débutante*. Later, we'll see. Now go! And let sunshine illuminate your soul!"

---

[53] *Midinette* - seamstress, shop girl

Julie has to smile. *Madame* Dionnelle is a character. All right! She will be a working girl again! Actually it feels natural to her.

Julie gets through to Giles that afternoon on the telephone. He is in Ottawa with the Mendès-France party. It's not much of a connection on the radio telephone, fading in and out and buzzing, but they manage. She tells him that *Madame* Dionnelle has confirmed her as a *débutante*. "Good for you," he encourages her. He reminds her that after the war *Madame* Dionnelle's tailor had outfitted him with boy's clothes. "She remembers you, Giles. Thinks you were handsome."

Checking the Métro map, Julie discovers she can take the Métro to the *St Philippe du Roule* station with only one easy change and then have only a short walk to the fashion house. Promptly at 9 o'clock the next morning she arrives and is told that *Madame* Dionnelle wishes to see her *tout d'suite* (immediately.)

Madame Dionnelle foregoes formalities and starts right in. "I forgot yesterday. It must be done. I wish to assure myself for myself. Take off your clothes, Julie."

"My clothes off?"

"Yes. All of them. It's for the bikinis and the lingerie. You wouldn't believe what I've seen; girls disfiguring themselves with tattoos and piercings. But more often it's the skin condition and medical things." Julie undresses. "Ah! Most beautiful, my dear. Now raise your arms."

Julie finds it curiously exciting to be nude and have someone inspecting her. Recollections flood back, combining with her previous thoughts about *Madame* Guyton and *Les Poulets*. It almost seems that *madame* is a man. She has the same eyes as the men had, appraising her as an object, assessing whether she is satisfactory for the purpose. Automatically, without any thought, Julie poses herself as she had done thousands of time. Sensations tingle through her body like quick-silver. Momentarily she has that sinking feeling of possible rejection. Not to impress, not to be bought, would be horrible! "Oh, come on," she scolds herself, that's in the past, she is beyond all that.

Madame Dionnelle has her turn round. "I don't even see stretch marks from you giving birth. You know how to pose, I see. You can put your clothes back on."

Madame Dionnelle resumes her seat at her desk and begins writing notes.

"The small mole on your left thigh - our doctor will take care of it. Your breasts and nipples are firm and not too big. Nothing to do there, thank goodness. Now, as to shaving, depilation, and waxing. By far the best way to go is to decide once and for all, no hair below the neck. I am sure you take good care of your skin, but you will go to our cosmetologist for advice. Your golden hair is *envie du monde* (envy-of-the-world) quality. We must keep it that way. You will lose two kilograms (4½ lbs) in weight. You will work out and watch your diet. Now I am going to hand you over to my Fashion Mistress, *Madame* Guyton. What she doesn't know about girls and fashion you could write on the back of a stamp and have room to spare! Pay good attention to her."

Julie feels the floor giving way beneath her! Could it be? Could the world be this small? "I . . . I . . . shall be meeting *Madame* Guyton?" she asks with her voice quavering.

"Oh, yes! She is not a dragon like some of those mistresses. She has a good understanding of girls. I will have you shown to her office."

Julie says she would like to go to the ladies room. Once there, she sits down in a stall.

Sacré nom de Dieu! (Good God!) *Madame* Guyton! She must keep her calm and think. Does *Madame* Dionnelle know of Guyton's past? Julie thinks about it. If she did know, would she have said something to her? She had mentioned Max Edelman, but then said to forget it. So, even if she did know, it wouldn't be in her interest for that to be common knowledge. Therefore, it seems, it's in everyone's interest to forget the past.

Julie's frown clears. *Courage!* As Julie thinks about it she sees that after the closing of the houses people like *Madame* Guyton would look for positions elsewhere and the fashion business would be an obvious choice. The two businesses, sex and fashion, have much in common: the handling of girls, teaching them the business, and helping them through their crises. Risé Mayon had followed a similar path by getting into the escort business, putting her knowledge of girls and sex to good use. Thinking about that, Julie supposes the two ladies from *Les Poulets* must know each other in the present. They would have to get together sometime.

Julie goes to the mirrors and checks her make-up and hair. Well, if *Mesdames* Guyton and Mayon could be successful, so could she! Julie's determination returns to her.

The young girl guiding her is friendly and advises her to let *Madame* Guyton do the talking. "She is a center-stage person. The girls have to do what she tells them to do."

No change there, Julie thinks.

Madame Guyton does not have a heart attack, just whatever is closest to it, when Julie walks in. The girl closes the door behind them. *Madame* Guyton is speechless.

Julie says, "hello, *Madame* Guyton You are surprised. So am I. Thank you for all you did for me. I have made a success of my life as, I see, you have done. We are going to get along famously, don't you think?"

"*Juliette LaPerle!*" *Madame* Guyton gasps.

"Yes, it's me. We each have our past and we both will let the past stay in the past. Agreed?"

Madame Guyton does her best to recover her senses. She smoothes her gray hair back. "Yes. All right. Very good. What a surprise! So, we'll go from here?"

"Exactly, *madame*, we go from here. OK?"

"Very OK, Juliette," she smiles. "Yes, indeed. So ... "

"Call me Julie. That is my name."

"Of course. You were Julie. It was I who called you Juliette. Ah! Those were the days. But we lived through them, didn't we, Julie?"

"Yes, indeed we did. And now we will continue to live through our days; helping each other and being happy."

"You were always such a determined girl. I see you have not lost any of that."

They exchange brief accounts of what had happened to each of them. *Madame* Guyton looks at her watch. "It's time to move on. You are to go to Yoga class. *Madame* Dionnelle insists on it. You have to be fit here, Julie."

Julie had a vague idea that Yoga consisted of sitting around, taking poses, and thinking about eternity. She quickly discovers how wrong she was. She is in a junior Hatha Yoga class. They go through breathing and stretching exercises, focusing on being "here and now." They do the poses: man-mountain, arm stretching, face-up dog, plank, face down-dog, warrior one, and tree where she has to balance on one foot. Julie begins to sweat. It's hard. Up and down, up and down. The instructor is a man. His hands are gentle as he corrects her poses. He tells her, "it won't all come at once. Yoga is a lifetime practice. You must be patient and let your mind and body develop together."

Julie immediately likes that thought. She will be a whole person, mind and body in harmony, for the rest of her life. She will tell Giles about it and encourage him to take up Yoga. She misses him while he is away in Canada and America, but she is kept as busy as a spinning top at the Fashion House and Modeling School.

The modeling classes start with posture and gait. Julie must learn to walk with one foot placed before the other, keeping perfect balance, and then doing it in high heels. Upright posture is all important. "Keep those shoulders down and back!" Being graceful is equally important. "Think yourself a swan!"

There are classes on cosmetics, perfume, hair, jewelry, accessories, and clothing. "The total image is made of its parts and the parts must agree. Feel and understand the clothing as if it is a part of you."

Julie works and learns. She's going to make it. She loves it. Everything comes naturally to her, as if she was born to be a model. On her own she takes a ballet class early in the morning. "Strength and grace. Grace and strength," the ballet mistress intones as she takes the class through ballet positions at the bar. Julie has a strong sense of what she had missed, but she does not allow herself any regrets. She is just glad that she is still young enough in mind and body to learn and be accomplished in her new vocation.

In the next show, Julie works behind the scenes with the wardrobe mistresses, the cosmeticians, the hairdressers. She is one of the rabbits who fetches and takes away as the models change their costumes. It is hectic work. She sees how the models backstage must be like mannequins, keeping still while being stripped and adorned, stripped and adorned, at each change. Then they come back to life and go out on the runway wearing the next fashion.

At the end of the show, Julie flops into a chair, "Whew!"

Madame Dionnelle is pleased. She already has buyers, incuding for her top drawer. There is plenty of money around. She sits by Julie. "You are ready, my girl. You will do the next show. What name will you take? Any suggestions?"

Without thinking about it Julie blurts out *Juliette LaPerle*. "Excellent!" *Madame* Dionnelle enthuses. Julie wants to take it back, but *Madame* Dionnelle has written it down and insists on it as a perfect name. Oh, well! The name had served her well before. Julie hopes it will do so again.

It did not take long for Julie to see that a good number of the models were playing at the oldest profession. It was happening at a high level and discreetly, but it was an open secret.[54]

---

[54] In describing Paris in this period in his book *Seven Ages of Paris*, Alistair Horne writes: "By the early 1950s the Paris vice squad estimated the number of working prostitutes at around 17,000; they ranged from the

The men were like those she had serviced: top men in industry, politics, government, the professions, the military, with a good few foreigners of every sort and nationality. Different from her past were the sex parties, set up in hotels, with a number of girls. A pretense was made that the girls were there, like the men, to have a good time. But everyone, from the Police Commissioner on down, was aware of the sham. Helping to maintain the deception was that few wished to challenge men standing very high in politics, international banking, and the like. A whistle blower would be given short shrift and quite likely end up in jail. The pay for the girls was very good, especially for those with erotic talents and those prepared to have sex with a dozen men in the evening.

Julie feigns a blind eye, while amusing herself by thinking of the guidance she could give on the finer points of prostitution.

Julie has her first show. She is not given any pride of place. *Madame* Dionnelle makes a point of treating her models as equals. She expects the more experienced ones to help the new ones. She lists the names of her models in the show's brochure to give them credit for their skills. The "stage-door Charlies", as they are still called, can pair, with a minimum of diligence, a face and a name.

A sharp reporter realizes he has seen the face before and pairs up *Juliette LaPerle* with *Madame* Giles Martin. He comes round to write a story about it. *Madame* Dionnelle has no objection to the publicity, of course. Julie finds herself in an unwelcome spot. She doesn't want to refuse and disappoint *Madame* Dionelle but, at the same time, her old

---

blowsy workingman's whores . . . to stunning girls who worked the bars along the Champs Elysées. More discreet, and more distinguished, were the various *maisons de passe*, or *maisons de rendezvous*, such as were so devastatingly portrayed in Buñuel's 1966 film *Belle de jour*, and catering to every taste and perversion. The clients would be entertained by sizzling young models or *jeunes filles bien* in quest for a little extra pocket money and some fun.

fears return. She just has to hope disclosure won't happen. In the interview she glosses over her WWII times, saying she worked as a waitress. She confines herself as much as possible to talking about her luck in meeting her husband, her love for her son, her interest in clothes, her wish to become a model, and her enjoyment in doing the work.

"And where did *Juliette LaPerle* come from, *madame*?"

"Oh, it just popped into my head. I don't know why," Julie says with a smile.

Julie prepares how to talk herself out of it, should she be ever put on the spot. She would say she had a twin sister. With her family dead or disappeared, she hoped she could get away with it, if it ever happened.

* * *

Much of the time of the conferences in Ottawa and Washington, between Mendès-France and the Canadians and Americans at the end of November, is spent on Vietnam and the withdrawal of the French from that theater of operations. Mendès urges that the nationalist aspirations of the Vietnamese be recognized and given priority. Dulles, the American Foreign Secretary, is imbued with the threat of Communism and its spread. Mendès's words fall on deaf ears. Dulles believes the East must be under the sway of America. France should confine itself to its domestic affairs and look to the communists in their country. There is little friendship lost, because there was little there to lose.

Giles, a junior member of the visiting party, only shakes hands with minor people and is occupied with briefings and protocol matters. He has to be immaculately turned out in suit and tie and be quietly well-mannered. It comes quite easily to him. He is also used as a translator and has his first experience of listening in one language and speaking another at the same time. It seems almost impossible at first; but with practice Giles becomes more fluent. It is noticed, even by Mendès himself. Mendès speaks English, after a fashion; at least his English is good enough to know the difficulties of going from one language to the other.

Mendès encourages Giles and warns him. "You are doing very well, young man. You heard what Dulles was saying? He's a puritan who sees things in black and white. He doesn't like us, the French. Eisenhower won't help him there. The French, as represented by DeGaulle during and after the war, were Ike's *bête noir*. DeGaulle was seen as always creating dissension. They would prefer me to DeGaulle. I heard one of them calling him 'odious.' But they may have to learn to get along with him. As things are going, I fear DeGaulle will be in power sometime fairly soon. Maintain a professional stance, young man. DeGaulle will do whatever good and harm he can and then pass on. Make them need you and your talents. Work for the good of France. France needs young people like you to take the helm one day."

"Yes, sir. Thank you, sir. I will do my best."

"All right. Now I want you to get yourself up to New York and figure out what the representatives from Algeria are up to there, talking with people at the United Nations and with the Americans in the university orbit of Harvard, Yale, and Princeton. Their long term goal is to have Algeria recognized by the UN as an independent nation. Our consulate on 5th Avenue will brief you. Find out what success they are having. I'll give you the necessary credentials to talk to people. Another emissary commission, Giles. I hope you won't be shot in the ass or anywhere else on this one!"

"I hope so, too!" Giles grins and they laugh together.

Having presented his credentials and statement of mission to the consul in New York, Giles is sat down in a room with a stack of files and dossiers, all labeled SECRET or TOP SECRET. "Read them. Do not take notes. The documents will be collected and inspected before you leave the room."

It takes Giles a day to wade through them and discover that the French know a lot about two men, Yazid and Chanderli, who have set up an office on East 56th Street. One of their activities is to welcome representatives of the FLN, such as Ben Bella, who heads up the FLN cabal in Cairo,

Egypt and put them in touch with the left-leaning politicians and university "egg-heads" such as Senator John F. Kennedy and Professor J.K. Galbraith.

As a representative of France, Giles has entrée to the UN and can attend some of the council meetings. In this way he meets by chance James Thirks who rowed in front of him in the Cambridge boat. He had been sent to the UN on a somewhat similar mission to that of Giles from the British Embassy in Paris.

They have dinner at the Jubilee French Bistro on East 54th Street and 1st Avenue. It is a joyous reunion and they discover they are both doing well in their new diplomatic positions. They go through a bottle of Chablis with their *hors d'oeuvres*, switch to a Châteauneuf-du-Pape to accompany their steaks, and sip port with their coffee and *petit fours*.

James confides that he is to report back to the ambassador in Paris and then to the Foreign Secretary in London on what the Americans think of the French and the response to the address that Mendès-France was to give to the General Assembly. Giles tells him that Mendès is pretty glum about the outlook in Algeria. The French are sending in their best troops. "Mendès has told me, James, that if the rebels try to meet them head-on they will be decimated. The rebels best hope in the long run is to make France so disgusted with the war there, that the French will give it up."

They take no notice of a dark complexioned man sitting at a table opposite to them and they welcome the attentive service provided them by the waiter.

They talk over a range of subjects and agree to meet again at the bistro after Mendès has addressed the UN.

Giles hears Mendès give his address and thinks it is good in a general way but, frankly, full of platitudes about peace and lacking specifics. Mendès only mentions Algeria in terms of it being a domestic French issue that has to be resolved by France. Thus, by implication, that the UN has no business in France's internal affairs.

John and Giles meet at the Jubilee restaurant as planned. They briefly discuss what Mendès had said and agree on its implications. Having done that they talk about what they think about America and its people. They are impressed overall, but amazed at the contrasts between America's ideals and its actuality, and dislike the arrogance. It's a typical European reaction.

Giles takes a taxi back to the Lex Hotel in central midtown where he is staying. He has taken off his clothes and is brushing his teeth when there is a knock on his door. Giles looks through the spy-hole to see a waiter's face and shoulders. "What is it?" he asks.

"Manager's compliments, sir."

Giles unlocks the door. After that Giles is too surprised and caught up in the rapid action to realize what's happening.

The man and the woman are an expert pair at their variation of the "Murphy."[55] The waiter dashes into the room with his trolley and pushes the almost nude Giles next to the bed. The good-looking blonde in a wide-necked blouse follows him and stands next to Giles. She pulls down her blouse to expose her bare breasts and, at the same time, says "hold this." She puts a wad of money into his hand while still retaining hold of it. The waiter uses a multi-shot camera. The photos seem to show Giles giving the girl money as she exposes her breasts to him. It's all over in 15 seconds. The waiter goes back through the door. The girl follows him out. She says, "thank you for your cooperation. Have a nice evening." Then they are gone.

---

[55] A Murphy, generically, is a con game or scam. There are many variations. The so-called "classic" Murphy is for a man to be lured into a hotel room by a floozy and then to be robbed by her tough guy accomplice. Its name has been attributed to the Murphy fold down beds used in some hotels.

Chapter 32

Giles is propositioned.

At first Giles, entirely surprised, thinks it a robbery. The camera flashes had semi-blinded him. But nothing is missing. He phones downstairs. "Had the management sent two people to his room?" No, they hadn't, the man says, and asks if they were friends of his? Had he seen them before? Oh, there was a woman. Well, sir, the man says, his voice heavy with implication, when that happens it is usually because the woman has been invited up.

Giles is getting nowhere with the hotel people and is beginning to realize what has happened. He reconstructs the rapid chain of events. Someone wants to have his photograph. Why? His mind is tired and he can't imagine why. At least he can't imagine it until the next morning when having breakfast at the buffet downstairs.

The dark-complexioned man who, Giles vaguely recollects is the man who was seated in the Jubilee bistro, asks Giles if he may share the table with him. Giles thinks it strange because the buffet is not crowded. Before Giles can reply the man sits down and puts a large brown envelope on the table.

"You will forgive me for pressing myself on you like this, Giles Martin, but we have some matters to discuss. Let me introduce myself. I am Felco. I go by one name as a matter of security," he says in French.

"What . . . what . . . are these matters, Mr. Felco? I do not know you."

"No. We have not met until now. Though I will mention I was sitting in the Jubilee bistro yesterday evening when you were having an intimate conversation with James Thirks from the British Embassy in Paris. Of course it would be natural for you to meet with your friend from Cambridge. Although, as I'm sure you must realize, certain French security services might be concerned with you divulging Mendès private views to a foreign diplomat. I took the trouble to photograph your meeting so that it might be documented."

Giles is angry. "I don't know who you are, Mr. Felco. But I shall certainly report this meeting to my superiors. I do not wish to continue speaking with you. Good day."

Giles starts to get up. Felco says, "I must advise you to stay and hear what I have to say, Giles Martin. If you go now you will encounter unpleasant surprises very soon."

"What surprises?"

"Please sit down so we may continue pleasantly."

Giles collects his wits. He sits down. "Very well. Who are you acting for, Mr. Felco?"

"We'll come to that, Giles Martin. You've had a remarkable young life and we wish it to continue and for you to prosper. To do that you need to make certain accommodations."

"Really! Such as . . . ?"

"Nothing that would endanger you. We just need to be up to date on, for instance, the views of Mendès-France on the short term and long term prospects for *Algérie-Française.*"

Giles is now attending closely. "Even if I knew his views, I would not tell you anything about them."

"On the contrary, Giles Martin, we know you have one-on-one talks with the premier and that he likes you, treats you like a son, in fact."

"I hardly think so. But even if he did I would not betray any confidences of his."

"We know you quite well, Giles Martin and you live up to our expectations of being a loyal Frenchman. That is why we decided to approach you and to take some extra steps to help you decide to help us. If you will look at the photos in the envelope ... "

Giles takes the large 10x12" photos from the envelope. The first ones show him seated at the Jubilee with John, with their faces turned to one another, evidently in deep conversation. Attached to the photos is a sheet with notes on the topics they were discussing. The next set of photos show him in his underpants with the girl with her bare breasts close to him and giving her money.

"That's a dirty trick No one will believe it!"

"That's not quite to the point, Giles Martin. Certain papers in various countries would be interested in publishing these pictures. Here in the US, you can be sure that a foreign diplomat having sex with a call girl in a New York hotel would be a delicious tidbit. The State Department here could very well ask for your recall to France and demand you never set foot here again. In England the career of your friend James could be compromised even at the suspicion that he was talking out of school with a French diplomat. Of course your wife would be dismayed at the publicity of her husband having sex in New York with a call girl. Not so much for herself, I suggest, knowing her past, as for the long term interests of your son."

Giles face whitens as the monologue goes on. "You beast!" he spits at Felco.

"Oh, maybe so. But that also is not to the point. To avoid the contingencies I have alluded to, all you have to do is provide us with reports on anything that comes up in the discussions of *Algérie Française* here or back in Paris or at other times. We realize this comes as a shock to you. You need to mull it over and the implications for you, your wife, your son, your friend, your standing in the government, in France and, indeed, in the world at large. Let us meet again here at breakfast tomorrow and you will give me your answer then. You may keep the photos. They are just copies. You asked who we are. Clearly we are an interested party. Our intentions, we believe are good and we use the methods that suit the problem. We are champions of France! That is all you need know."

At that Felco stands up, says *bonjour*, and leaves.

Giles sits there, appalled, in a daze. They would go after his son and his wife! The waitress comes round and fills his cup with coffee. What to do? What in the hell to do? His brain almost stops functioning, overtaken by the hot and cold flushes racing through his body.

Giles goes upstairs to his room and washes his face in cold water. There! That's better. He steadies himself and sits on the bed. He puts his head in his hands and tells himself to think.

After a while it works. He begins to assemble the facts. First, he has a day to do something; second he has been in dangerous situations before, but never like this one; third, he has a brain and he must use it.

Who were they? Had he any clues to their identity? He goes back over the conversation, word by word, from start to finish. They are well informed about him. They must have an organization, probably some inside people in the government. Felco had twice said *Algérie Française*. They were focused on Algeria. They wanted to know what French Government policy might be concerning Algeria. Giles nods his head. There were basically only two sides now: the Algerian nationalists wanting their own country and the French elements wanting to keep Algeria French, headed by the *pieds noirs* in Algeria. Not that it meant much, but many of the *pieds noirs* were swarthy, he had seen that for himself. Their watchword, indeed their war cry, was *Algérie Française*.

OK. That's who they were. Would an approach to him make sense for them? Giles knows that the *pieds noirs* suspect Mendès-France of being against them, in spite of his sometimes encouraging words of keeping Algeria French. He would reform Algeria, knocking them from their all-powerful position. It made sense that if they knew what Mendès was thinking, they could take appropriate counter-measures.

Giles rises from the bed feeling better. In fact, he smiles. He is, and would be, smarter than them, the bastards. He knows about moles and counter-spies, the arts of deception and much else, starting with what the Germans had done to them in the *Maquis* and what they in the *Maquis* had done to them, the Germans. The *pieds noirs* were trying to recruit him in the role of a mole. Fine! He would be that and provide them with delicious information . . . that would be false.

Giles looks at his watch. Mendès is due to leave that evening on a flight back to Paris. Giles grabs up the envelope with the pictures and high-tails it to the French consulate on Fifth Avenue. He goes to the consul who he had dealt with before. "Where is the premier?" he asks peremptorily.

"Steady on there," the consul tells the breathless Giles.

"It's important, very important. I have to see the premier before he leaves."

"What's the nature of this importance, Giles Martin?"

"It's . . . it's . . . I really can't tell you. It's a plot against France."

"Are you sure?"

"I'm damn sure. I've just been talking with one of the plotters."

"All right. Mendès is having lunch with the mayor of New York. A low-key meeting. They are at Gracie Mansion, the residence of the mayor, way up on the east side of

Manhattan. He will leave there in a limo to go to Idlewild airport[56] to take the flight back to Paris."

Giles sets himself to see the situation as objectively as possible. For all he knows, he may have been followed to the consulate and they may try to follow him when he leaves. Giles reckons he can get himself to Gracie Mansion by taking the subway. But he'll take steps to throw them off his scent, if they are trying to follow him. At Gracie Mansion he'll find the limo waiting for Mendès. He will tell the consul to alert Mendès that he'll be there with important information.

Having convinced himself of the plan, he tells it to the consul. The consul agrees and shows him how to get to Gracie Mansion. On a map of Manhattan with the subway trains and stations on it he traces the route. "You can take a 4, 5, or 6 train going north on Lexington. Get off at 125th street and walk east. It will take you right to Gracie Mansion. Here is a picture of the house. It's unmistakable, standing on a bluff above the East River."

Giles has been forming a mental map of Manhattan in his mind. He leaves the Embassy and, instead of going east to Lexington Avenue, he heads west into Central Park. Once inside the park and somewhat covered by the trees and bushes, and the undulating land, he runs around the small lake there and then goes back to Fifth Avenue and continues to Lexington. He looks back a couple of times, but sees no one who might be following him.

He finds Gracie Mansion with no difficulty and the limo, flying the French *tricolore* flag, is right there by the gate.

Mendès has received the brief note saying that Giles Martin has information for him and will meet him at the limo.

After Mendès has bid goodbye to the mayor, he comes up to Giles. "You want to see me? You have something to tell me?"

---

[56] Idlewild was renamed J.F.Kennedy after the president's death.

"Yes, sir. I believe the *pieds noirs* of Algeria are infiltrating your organization to learn of your intentions. They have tried to enlist me in their scheme."

Mendès smiles. "It's no news that the *pieds noirs* don't like me. But what is this about a scheme, Giles?"

"Sir, I would like to show you some photographs and explain. I think it would be best if we sit in the car."

"All right. But you may have to come to the airport with me. I don't want to miss the flight."

"No problem, sir."

The limo drives away with them and a couple of staff members inside.

Giles provides an exact account of all that had happened and shows the photographs. Mendès is a little amused. "Giles Martin - - you do get yourself in some scrapes! Well, what are we to do?"

"I can be a double agent, sir. I'll provide them with false information while reporting back to you what I can learn about them."

Mendès asks his two staff people what they think of the idea. After only a brief discussion they approve of it, while saying it will take a good bit of working out.

"That's what you are paid for," Mendès tells them.

Chapter 33.

Julie is propositioned.

After the show the models congratulate Julie on her good start. It is late in the evening by the time most of them get to the *L'Arome* restaurant close by the Métro station that Julie uses. Only a couple of the models are accompanied by their boy-friends, so it is really *les girls* among themselves. For Julie it is very like being back among the girls of the two houses she worked in. The difference being that here the talk is about the fashions and what they liked and did not like, while before it was mostly about the men and their vagaries. Everyone smokes which, to Julie, is unpleasant. She can only not smoke herself. Most of the models think that odd. It is at a time when 85% of adults smoke in France.

The room in the restaurant is spacious and the other tables have the usual assortment of diners.

Natalie, a classic north European blonde from Germany, though she hates to admit it, is chatting with Julie. "Did you know you have an admirer? He's over there by himself."

"What do you mean, an admirer? That rather swarthy fellow? I've never seen him before. Anyhow I'm not interested."

"Just thought you should know," Natalie tells her. "He was talking to *Madame* Guyton and told her he thought you were the most beautiful girl in the house and all that stuff. But they all say that."

"Oh, I know! Men are so stupid! They think flattery will get them into your knickers. In my experience only two things do that, love and money," Julie laughs, knowing it's mostly true, with exceptions, of course.

"You are a bit of a cynic, Julie."

"I suppose. I think of myself more of a realist than a cynic."

"You have a husband, but if a man offered you a fortune to go to bed with him, would you take it?"

"A fortune, you say. How big a fortune?"

"Oh, I don't know. Just a hell of a lot of money."

"Would you, Natalie?"

"Sure. If I was sure he was disease free and would use a condom. Just fucking is not much, frankly. But I'm not married. What are you going to do about your admirer?"

"Nothing. I'm through with all that. I have a husband and a son. That's really all I want or need." Though there was this furry animal in the back of Julie's brain that appeared sometimes in her dreams and made her uneasy.

"I'm sure I agree with you, Julie, and glad to hear it. But, you know, that makes you different from most of us."

"Yes, it does. But that's OK. Go off and play the field, Natalie. Just don't expect too much of men. Good ones are few and far between."

They chat on and then break up. Julie chats with the others until it is time to go home. She glances over to see the man still there, he is an older man, but still quite handsome. He is reading a book while he smokes a cigar and has his coffee and cognac. Julie leaves, walks to the Métro, and goes home.

The next morning, shortly after Julie arrives at the Fashion House, the receptionist calls to tell her there is a *Monsieur* Alexis Finisterre wishing to see her.

"Who is he? I don't know anyone of that name."

"Well, he looks all right, quite distinguished looking, could be an Italian or a Spanish. Well dressed and polite. I think you should see him. He says it's about business."

Julie goes down to the lobby, vaguely disquieted.

In the lobby Julie recognizes the swarthy man, the one supposed to be her admirer.

The man stands up. "*Bonjour, Madame Martin*," he says politely.

"*Bonjour, monsieur*. You wish to see me?"

"Yes. My name Alexis Finisterre. I wish to speak to you about a certain matter. Rather than talk in this place, allow me to invite you to lunch at, shall we say, twelve thirty, if that would be convenient."

"That's kind of you. But what in the world is this about?"

"It concerns you and your family. That is why I wish to speak with you privately."

"I would rather you speak to my husband. He's returning from America in a day or two."

"Ah, yes. But the matter concerns you, *madame*. I do think it best that you agree to have lunch with me. That would avoid any consequences occurring."

Julie does not like it. But, reflecting that she is better off knowing whatever the man has to say than not, she agrees to have lunch with him.

Alexis Finisterre is in the lobby to meet her at 12.30. They walk the short distance to the restaurant *L'Angle du Faubourg*. The *maître d'* seats them at a good table, evidently knowing Alexis.

Alexis Finisterre is the perfect host, offering her a champagne cocktail to start and advising her about the dishes; all the time making pleasant small talk. Julie thinks that if he is preparing to proposition her, he was doing a good job. She has been with such men many times, though not so much for propositioning as for fucking. Alexis reminds her of General Max Edelman. He might have brought her to a place like this. What a lover he had been! The thought makes her quite wistful for a second or two. If this man, Alexis Finisterre, invites her out again she would wear her fox furs for him, just like she had for the general. It would remind her of him and how kind and generous he had been to her.

"Now, dear lady, we come to the point of this occasion. It is this. You are a true French woman, born on July 14. You contributed your services during the war. Yes. We know about it. Now France is again in need of true nationalists to preserve her integrity. The Department of Algeria is threatened by communists and Muslims made mad by their preachers. The valiant French there, who have done so much to make Algeria a garden of Eden for all to live in, are being threatened and even killed by the mad men. Are you following me?"

Julie hears his words, but almost the only ones with real meaning to her are those that meant he knew about her past. She nods her head, "yes, *monsieur*, I have heard your words. But the troubles in Algeria do not interest me. Let them sort it out." Julie looks at her wristwatch. "I have enjoyed this lunch. Thank you. But I must go back to the Fashion House. I do not think we'll meet again."

He lays a restraining hand on her arm. "I ask you to stay and hear me out, *madame*. I can assure you it will be to your advantage. It won't take long. I will talk and you will listen. There is a man called Henri Bourstelle. It's possible you have heard of him. He is a general who had an illustrious war record with DeGaulle and is well thought of in government circles. Very likely he will be appointed by our premier, Mendès-France, to a high position in Algiers. As you may also know, Mendès-France is being two-faced about his Algerian policy. Sometimes he says that Algeria is forever France and then says it must be changed. True Frenchmen, of course, know Algeria will be forever *Algérie Française*. The French people there must be supported by all honest and true Frenchmen."

Julie does not have to pretend to be impatient, she is. "But all that, *monsieur*, has nothing to do with me."

"Ah! There you are mistaken, dear lady. Henri Bourstelle is married, it's true, but he has a roving eye and a strong *esprit de sexe*. His wife is content to be away in the country at their *château*. We intend to introduce you to him."

Julie, even though she subsequently thought she shouldn't have been, is genuinely shocked. She takes a deep breath and tells him, "that certainly will not happen! I refuse to be part of some shoddy scheme! I am a wife and a mother. I consider you no Frenchman to not respect the sanctity of motherhood!"

Julies is surprised at herself for finding these words. She glares at Alexis and is about to rise again.

"Oh, my dear lady! You do touch me. At *Les Poulets*, where you were quite the star, I add with my felicitations, you were, quite understandably, not much engaged with the sanctity of motherhood. Nor, for that matter, when you were at *Le Coq* in Dijon. So please resume your seat and relax. My proposition is this, and I do not expect immediate acquiescence. You meet the general and become his mistress for a while. During that time you will ascertain his views about Algeria and what he intends to do there when appointed. When I say mistress, I mean a person he meets for perhaps two hours, perhaps more, perhaps less, with every discretion, of course."

Julie is now staring at him, her brain awhirl. Alexis thinks she is about to say something and holds up his hand. "Let me finish. In the case of your agreement to this proposition we will be as silent as the grave about your past.

Furthermore, we will pay you a good sum for the information you provide. I know you did exactly this for the resistance during the war, except that you were not paid then. So now you have that advantage."

It was as well that Alexis spoke slowly while he made his proposal. It gave Julie time to think. Giles was in the thick of the Algeria business. Could she, in some way, using this man, aid her husband? It is only an idea hanging in the air, but it is there.

Julie turns herself into a business woman. "OK. It's possible you may interest me, Alexis. If I go forward - and I only say if - I must have professional treatment and reimbursement. Professionals are paid up front and in cash. My past is sufficiently known. Anyone who is interested can find it. It is no secret to my husband or family. I worked legally and responsibly at that time. So that has little impact on my decision. Your talk of true French people hardly impresses me. There were more people working and collaborating with the Germans during the war than there were resisting them. That's how true French we were! As for Algeria, I don't give a shit! I'm a business woman and you should talk to me on that basis and no other. I will have my terms."

Alexis is impressed. Julie Martin promises to be a better agent than he had expected. "Your terms, *madame*? What might they be?"

Julie sits up straight, her confidence restored. "First, this man going to Algeria. What do you want to know about him? Be brief and to the point, *monsieur*."

"You know the term *pieds noirs*?"

"Of course! Do not take me for a school girl, *monsieur*!"

"We wish to know, whatever his words are, whether he will support the interests and positions of the *pieds noirs* in Algeria to the full. Or, alternatively, whether he is another of the two-faced sort who say one thing and then do the opposite. Do you understand?"

"Of course."

"We feel the only way we can know for sure is what he may divulge in his intimacies with a woman."

Julie chuckles. "That is the French way, is it not?"

"That is why I am here talking to you, *madame*."

"Very well. I will not give you my answer or my terms now. I need to think about them. However, I am favorably impressed. You have been honest with me. I need a day or two to think it over. Today is Tuesday. Meet me here for lunch on Thursday. I will only say now that, if I agree, you have put your trust in a woman of experience. In that you have been wise."

At the Fashion House Julie begs off early. She goes home and puts in a call to Giles at the New York consulate. It happens he is there and for once the connection is clear. First they assure each other that all is well and she tells him that baby Charles is in fine shape. They both go on to say they have a lot to tell each other and it is critical that they are not overheard. "How secure is this line, Giles?

"I think it's secure. But it's an open line, not scrambled, so you never know."

"I think it best we wait until you are back here. Then we can really talk."

"You sound very mysterious, Julie. Is everything all right?"

"Yes. I promise you it is. When will you be back?"

"Tomorrow morning, that is Wednesday morning. These time shifts can be confusing. We get in at *Le Bourget* at six o'clock."

"*D'accord.* I'll meet you there."

Chapter 34.

Julie plans.

Giles sleeps on the plane and is fresh when they land at *Le Bourget*. He steps down the ramp and, seeing Julie waiting behind the restraining rope, rushes over to hold her in his arms. "Oh, my darling," he breathes. Julie strokes his face and kisses him.

"Come on, you two love doves," the official in charge of seeing government people through the entry procedures tells them with a big smile.

Giles drives their car into Paris from the airport. "Julie, you will never believe what has happened. It's all terribly secret. But I don't care if they guillotine me. I have to share it with you. You have to know the truth and then you will understand how I've become a double agent for Mendès in this Algerian business. I'll outline it to you as we drive in and then we'll go into details at home. You know about the *pieds noirs*?"

"Yes! I sure do, Giles. I will tell you about them when we are home."

"You will?" Giles was surprised.

"Yes, but go on with what happened to you."

"A trick was played on me that made them think I would tell them about Mendès and his plans for Algeria. I told Mendès about it and suggested we play along, give them only dressed-up pap, and learn as much as possible about them. That's what we are doing. I'm the go-between. It's exciting, isn't it?"

"Yes. It sure is. You will have to be careful not to be found out. What was the trick?"

"I'll tell you when we are home. Let me concentrate on driving through this traffic. As usual it's ghastly. They really must do something about it."

At home Giles is delighted to pick up baby Charles. The two of them are all smiles for each other. Charles recognizes his father. For ten minutes they crawl around the floor together playing some sort of game with shrieks of pleasure from Charles. Julie thinks it couldn't be better. She has the best husband and the best father for their child that there could possibly be.

They sit down to enjoy coffee and croissants. "So what was the trick, Giles?"

"I hate to admit it to you, but I was taken. Here, look at the pictures."

Julie looks at the pictures taken in the hotel room in New York and bursts out laughing. "That's one of the oldest tricks in the book! Giles! You didn't see through it?"

"No, I didn't, not at the time. It happened so fast and they were expert at it."

"So they thought it would embarrass you and make you play their game?"

"Yes, that's it, in a nutshell. But, without them knowing it, we'll turn the tables on them."

"Splendid!" Julie exclaims. "Now you have to hear my story."

Julie relates what had happened. As she tells the story, Giles becomes upset. "That's terrible!" he gasps.

"No. Not really, Giles. You must understand that I know about men and what they do. To me there's nothing at all extraordinary about it. In fact, as the man said, I had done exactly that during the war."

"But . . . but . . . that was then. Everything is different now. You can't possibly do . . . well, do that."

Julie pours him another cup of coffee. "Now calm down, dear, and listen to me. You are helping France in the ways you are. Let me do my thing for France too, with your cooperation. If this man is two-faced, then Mendès should know about it. He wouldn't want to send a man on a mission and then have him do the opposite. So what the scumbags want to know is exactly what Mendès would want to know. Understand?"

Giles, in spite of himself, nods his head. His wife, Julie, is as sharp as a cracker. He had always known that. But to do what she is describing is impossible! "What do you mean, be his mistress!" he asks, aghast at the thought.

"That's only what Alexis said, Giles. Of course I wouldn't be his mistress. Far from it. He will be my dupe. Just as you are turning the tables on those guys, I will do the same with this man."

"But what does that mean? What will you do?"

"You have to leave that to me, Giles. Listen up, my dear. You are of immense value to France because you are smart and have had one hell of an education. Now you are putting that to use. Just think about it. I had a very different education but, like yours, it was a very thorough one. I know about men and women and their innermost needs and feelings in intimate detail. That's my asset and now I have the opportunity to serve my country using that asset."

"Oh, Julie! Do you really mean that? It will be, well, awful . . . " Giles turns away and puts his hands over his face.

Julie goes to him, pulls him up, and gives him a big smile and a kiss. "Giles! We have each other. Never, never doubt that. We love each other and are faithful to each other. At the same time I am my own person, just as you are yours. Now I have a chance to play a part in an adventure on behalf of my country. I very much doubt that anything like this will ever happen to me again. I am uniquely experienced and skilled to do it; probably better than almost any other girl in the country. So I am going to do it and you will help me."

Giles tries to come to terms with what his wife is telling him. "But, I mean, well . . . he will want to . . . won't he?"

"Oh, I'm sure he will, Giles. My answer to that is, first, quite likely I can play him so that he doesn't actually get that far." She laughs. "Girls can be very rotten about that, you know. Lead a horse to water and not let him drink. And second, my dear Giles, if it has to happen, absolutely nothing changes. We are the same two people, committed to each other and loving each other. Face reality, Giles! I have had a lifetime of casual sex. I have been fucked by literally thousands of men. Casual sex means just that, a casual encounter, very little more than shaking hands. And think back too, my dear Giles. You were hell bent on having casual sex and would have had it except for a sink hole and being chased by reporters and circumstances piling up to prevent it. If it had happened, what would the consequence have been? Damn all! You would have just gone on. However what actually happened was that we met as two people and in no time, without any sex, were in love with each other. Just think about it. Incidentally, one of these days, Giles, I think you should have casual sex, fill in an empty hole in your experience."

Giles drinks his coffee. He looks up with a shy grin. "Frankly, Julie, I have no answer to that. Let us just say that we expect this to be your last adventure of this sort. OK?"

"OK. But I'll also say that we're not gods and don't know what the future may hold for us. Anyhow. We'll go on from here. Let's begin by seeing what we have to do. First, what does your work, with the addition of being a counter spy, require of you?"

Now that they had established their positions, they began working as a team. They were both concerned that nothing must impact on baby Charles. "I think, Giles, that when we both have to be away of an evening or overnight, Charles must go up to Nanny's room and be with her. That should happen too if we have to have people here. It's just contingency planning. We'll only do it when necessary."

"Yes, Julie, I agree. Until we see what our adventure entails we should keep my mother, Sophie, and Joey and Charles away. It will be enough to let them know about it after it's finished."

They sit down with pads of paper and begin planning in detail. Giles develops a plan for gaining the information, making sure that it would be plausible to the *pieds noirs*, and then how to pass it to them.

Julie 's plan covers the presentation of herself to the man, how to wheedle information out of him, and then how to pass it on both to the *pieds noir* and to their side. The obvious way to do that is to have Giles pass it on. She thinks of Mec being her security guy.

Julie still hadn't completely unpacked all her boxes from *Le Coq*. Now she does so, indulging herself in nostalgia and a few regrets. She has a fabulous wardrobe to be the vamp, especially in her furs. She holds them to her face, loving the feel. It excites her.

She goes to a theatrical shop in the *Marais* to pick up some of the cosmetics she will need, along with eyelashes and facial skin tighteners. Some of these are available at the Fashion House, but she doesn't want to raise any suspicion there that she is up to something.

Julie checks the time. It is four in the afternoon. *Rue Blondel* is just along the way, a few minutes walk up *Boulevard de Sebastopol*. She is sensibly dressed, her hair in a chignon under a simple hat. She is no different from many other everyday women to be seen in the *quartier*. When she reaches the turning onto *rue Blondel,* she hesitates. She looks along the street and sees where *Les Poulets* had been. The door is gone, but the building looks much the same. She can almost see the car, loaded with her cases, that she entered, gorgeously dressed and in her furs, with Marie, to be driven to Dijon and *Le Coq*. That was the last time she was here.

Julie shakes her head, comes back to the present. She sees the girls, the prostitutes, lined up on either side of the narrow street. That hadn't changed at all. In front of her, two middle-aged women turn down the street, talking to each other as if being there is the most normal thing in the world. Probably it is for them, Julie thinks. She follows them, trying to seem as unconcerned as they.

The street is crowded with men strolling and stopping. The painted prostitutes, some in eye-catching wigs, present themselves openly. They pose themselves in their high heels, revealing costumes, and sexy furs. They eye the men passing them. The trade is brisk. As Julie strolls along behind the two women, she sees men talking with the *fille* of their choice and then enter into one of the doors with her. She hears a *fille* entice a man with the traditional , *"à votre service, monsieur?"* Julie feels her breath coming in pants. Dammit! Her genitals itch! She must be wetting.

She walks on, half annoyed, half thrilled, that the sight of it has stimulated her. Then she grins. There was no reason why she should not find enjoyment when looking back at what she had been. She had been a top girl!

* * *

Fully prepared to talk business, Julie meets Alexis at the restaurant as planned. She has come from the Fashion House and is well dressed in a plain way. They sit down. Again he is the perfect host. They both enjoy *coupes de champagne*. "So, *Madame* Martin. What is it to be?"

"An agreement, in effect a contract between us, *monsieur*. I will vamp, seduce, and listen to the secrets of this man's heart for money. Then I will let you know what he says. I, of course, cannot guarantee what he'll say. Therefore the money must be assured beforehand and be payable irrespective of what he says. I trust you agree."

Alexis sits back. "I am surprised to find you a business woman with such a clear head. But also pleased. How do you propose we proceed?'

"In my presence you will place in cash in a bank vault box twice the sum we agree that you will pay me. The box will be only openable by two keys, yours and mine. Thus at the end of our business we will go to the bank and open the box together. You can be accompanied by whom you wish. I will be accompanied by a personal guard. You will take half the money, I the other half. You see, Alexis, that way you pay me my fee for sure. So, provided you are an honorable man, you gain the information you want from me for the fee agreed on and nothing more nor less. If you should be tempted to be dishonorable, you will lose twice the fee you were to pay me and have no information. If either of us fails to come to the bank, the bank will be instructed that after, say, one year, they are to open the box and donate the money to a charity that I will choose. This contract will be written out, by a lawyer, witnessed and signed by you and me. If you fail to abide by this arrangement, the bank will give the money to the charity."

Alexis looks at Julie with respect. "That is an ingenious plan. We have to trust each other."

"Exactly, *monsieur*. We must trust each other or the money is lost to us both."

"Let us order lunch and enjoy it while I consider your proposition."

"Certainly. I will have their *escargots* to start, followed by their *sole meunière*. The wine to go with my lunch will be a premier cru Chassagne, domain Cailleret, 1950."

Alexis has to smile. "I couldn't have chosen better myself, *madame*."

"I hope you will say the same for my proposal, Alexis," Julie replies with her own smile.

As they enjoy the lunch, Julie tells Alexis, "I should say one more thing. Any gifts of any kind, including money, that this man gives me, will be mine alone. Do you agree?"

"Certainly, *madame*. We have no interest in that. You can put it in your contract, if you wish."

"Oh, I will."

The follow up proceeds quickly and smoothly. A lawyer draws up their contract. They sign it. It is cast iron.

The only negotiation is the size of Julie's fee. She is firm that it has to be ten thousand dollars US[57]. Alexis at first baulks. Julie is firm. Alexis agrees.

Julie has Mec with her at the bank as a bank clerk places the certified $20,000 dollars in a bank vault box. The clerk gives her one key, Alexis the other. The clerk demonstrates that both have to be used to open the box.

* * *

It takes a few days to get Giles on track as a purveyor of information to the *pieds noirs*. The meeting place is set up, the restaurant *Le Versance* by the *Bourse*. The restaurant is always full of stock brokers from the Exchange working out their money dealings. That appeals to Giles. He will be paid too, though as a double-agent. Giles works with various trustworthy people on Mendès staff to decide what to say.

Mendès is clear he would like the *pieds noirs* to trust him. "They are French, they must stay in Algeria. We must guide them to an understanding that more integration with the Muslims is in their long term interest. We must educate them. You fellows work out how to reassure them I have their interests at heart while preparing them for the future."

The first response to come back is a request to know the army units that will be sent to Algeria. They will give them the name of a battalion and no more. The battalion

---

[57] In today's values, the sum would be worth four or five times as much. It may seem a large sum, however it is now known how much spies were paid at the time. This amount would not be unusual.

had been notified to leave some months beforehand so nothing is lost by passing on this information and, the team hopes, it will reassure the *pieds noirs* and gain their confidence.

Chapter 35.

Julie meets her mark.

This Saturday Julie sits cross-legged on her bed in an old bathrobe reading Henri Bourstelle's file. Baby Charles is playing with some wood blocks on the floor. Nanny has the afternoon off. Giles is off rowing as he will be tomorrow, Sunday; and Sunday is the day; the day she will meet Henri Bourstelle for the first time.

Julie is not entirely happy with the plan for their meeting that Alexis has set out. She thinks it may alert the man that he is being set up. Alexis has gathered the essential information, its thoroughness impresses Julie, and he has set up a scenario to ensnare the man without too much difficulty. Alexis is a clever bastard. Her identity will be as a model and a journalist for a new fashion magazine, **Modèle**, featuring models and their lives.

General Henri Bourstelle has an apartment in Paris in the 8th arrondisement on Avenue George V. On Sundays he makes it a practice to walk over to the nearby *Brasserie La Fermette Marbeuf*, with its mosaics and décor of *La Belle Epoch*, to have a leisurely lunch. He is a late riser on Sundays and comes to the *Brasserie* to read the Sunday papers. Sometimes he meets a fellow officer there. More usually he is alone. He never has a lady with him. His habit is to reserve those assignations for the evening.

At the *Brasserie* Julie is to wait until he arrives and is settled. Then she will ask the *maître d'* to deliver a note to the general in her handwriting, requesting an interview. Her card will accompany the note. Alexis has had a new business card printed for her with her name, Juliette LaPerle, and her occupation as Model and Journalist. It is a beautiful card in a delicate shade of maroon with curvy scrolls framing the writing.

Julie asks herself how must she look. She knows very well, as the saying goes, that there is no second chance to make a good first impression. Her life in the business had proved that to her many thousands of times. She has to be the "fly" that a fisherman casts on the water to catch the eye and stimulate the appetite of the fish. Her head and face will be all important for the first glance. She will have her blonde hair fall in a soft wave to her right shoulder in an off-set style and wear a small "fascinator" hat on the left side. Pearl earrings and necklace. A narrow waist, of course. For clothes: a blouse and ankle length skirt with a trim little jacket. Gloves and a good handbag. OK. She knows how to do all that very well.

Julie turns back to the Bourstelle file. In the war he was a brave and brainy fellow. He had worked in intelligence in London and back in France had been one of the first to lead a motorized infantry squad into Paris in 1944. He had been in Vietnam and studied guerrilla warfare there. He'd had quick promotions and now, at 45, is the youngest general in the French army.

Julie studies his picture. He is a fine figure of a man, slim, tall, handsome, good strong facial features. He's credited to be something of a hawk in his views, believing in peace and well-being through power. But some see him as more a cultured fellow with an understanding of history, one who knows that military power has its limitations. No one doubts his loyalty to France. What she has to find out is how his loyalty to France will be worked out in practice in Algeria. She smiles as she realizes again that she is working both sides of the fence, the *pieds noirs* in Algeria and Mendès here at home.

Julie phones the *Brasserie La Fermette Marbeuf* to ask if she needs to make a reservation for tomorrow lunch. No, she is told, but they will take her name and will be glad to see her at one o'clock. She sits back. Yes, there is a thrill to this job. She's enjoying the sexual atmospherics and the machinations. And the man? With his experience in dalliance he must be an expert lover. She really wouldn't mind finding out, if it ever came to that. One thing she absolutely must do is not endanger her health in any way.

The next day, Sunday, the *maître d'* at the *Brasserie La Fermette Marbeuf*, has the pleasure of escorting the exquisite *Mademoiselle Juliette LaPerle* of **Modèle** magazine to a table in a small alcove set around by colored glass panels. She had given him her card when she entered. He is reminded of both Grace Kelly and Marilyn Monroe and he says so to the head waiter.

The head waiter decides that it is his duty to wait on *Mademoiselle LaPerle* and discover what he can about her. He brings the *sommelier* and a waiter bearing the *amuse gueule,* a mini tower of fig slices with goat cheese, with him to her table. Some of the people in the Brasserie have turned their heads. Is she a film star?

He presents the menu to her. She waves it away. "I shall start with some shell fish. What are your choices, *monsieur*?"

"May I suggest the thinly cut lobster slices with a terrine of avocado and capers? A specialty of our chef."

"I will take your advice. With it I wish your *sommelier* to serve a *Puligny-Montrachet Blanc*, preferably from *Domain Joseph Drouin.*"

The head waiter swivels to look at the *sommelier*. "Do we have it? " he mutters. The *sommelier* blanches a little. "I think so, sir."

Julie sits back, then tastes the *amuse gueule* and sips the tiny glass of sherry served with it. Thinking back she thanks Max Edelman for being the first to teach her how to behave and impress in these situations. If her plan works, she won't need to send any note.

General Henri Bourstelle enters, well dressed in a suit and tie, and is shown to his usual table. It is angled across from the alcove where Julie is. She recognizes him from his picture. He is alone, with the Sunday papers under his arm. He sits down, arranges himself, accepts the glass of Scotch whisky that a waiter brings him, and sits back. Casually he looks around.

Only out of the furthest corner of her eye does Julie see him. She busies herself, elegantly of course, with the *amuse gueule* and the small notebook she has brought with her in her bag. The notebook is equipped with a gold pen and she writes some brief notes with it.

Henri Bourstelle cannot help himself. He stares at this vision. Then corrects himself. The last thing he wants to be is rude. He looks away and catches the eye of the *maître d'*. He beckons him over. "Who . . . who is that?" he asks, nodding towards Julie.

The *maître d'* takes Julie's card from his pocket. "Her name is Juliette LaPerle, general."

"Have you seen her before?"

"No. I haven't."

"Well, well. Have you any idea who she might be?"

"No. By her card she is in the fashion business. The head waiter tells me she knows her own mind. She has expensive tastes."

"Thank you," the general says. "Bring me paper and pen, will you?"

"Certainly, sir."

When Julie receives the note the general has written her, she looks up to see him looking over to her. She nods her head and raises her hand with a small beckoning motion. The general rises and comes to her table. She raises her hand so that he may take it, with a little bow. "*Madame*, allow me to introduce myself. I am General Henri Bourstelle and I am at your service."

Julie smiles. "I don't think I need your service, general. If you wish to sit down, please do so. And I am not *madame*. At least not yet. I am still young enough, I hope, to be *mademoiselle*." Julie blesses herself for remembering to take off her wedding ring.

"A thousand apologies, *mademoiselle*.

"Not at all. Our French customs sometimes trip us up and are a mystery to foreigners, are they not? You may call me Juliette, Juliette LaPerle, general. Here is my card."

Henri takes her card. "Have you finished your lunch, *mademoiselle*? Do you mind? I have ordered my lunch, a *filet mignon*. May I enjoy it with you? Have you had dessert?"

"No, I have not. By all means enjoy your lunch here, general. What would you suggest for dessert?"

"I recommend the *crème brûlée*. It is very good here."

"Thank you. Tell me about yourself, general. Are you stationed in Paris?"

"Not exactly. We are exiled to our staff buildings in Rocquencourt, twenty kilometers out of Paris, near Versailles. But I have my apartment here and the drive there and back is not too bad."

"Before we continue, general, I must ask you something. Are you married?"

Henri frowns. He hadn't expected the question so soon. Oh, well! Better get it out of the way, for better or for worse. This young lady was engaging him, from his mind to his cock and all stations in between.

"Yes, I am. But we live separate lives. Why do you ask?"

"Because I find you attractive. Not that a wife would be an absolute bar; but a complication. In your case, if I am hearing you right, a very little one. I fancy an Armagnac with my coffee."

Henri orders two Armagnacs with their coffees. He is silent, wondering how to proceed.

Julie sips her Armagnac. "You are full of ardor, are you not, Henri?"

Henri stifles a gulp. "You are forward, Juliette!"

"I know. I have been since I was a young girl. Now I find truth and honesty to be the only values that truly count. Much may be important in our lives, but ultimately everything is secondary to truth and honesty." Julie looks out the side of the window next to her. "I have been inside long enough. It looks to be a fine day outside. Let us take a taxi and go to the *Jardins du Luxembourg* and watch the children sail their boats on the round pond."

For Henri it is a totally novel suggestion. He insists on paying the bill, including the equivalent of $100 for Julie's rare bottle of wine, and is glad to do it. He has never met a woman like this Juliette.

Julie goes to the ladies room and takes her time to pee and attend to her looks. So far, so good. Her plan, that the general discover her as if by chance, has worked. Much better than her writing a note to him. She is one up on Alexis for that! At this point the general seems a fairly easy "mark." At the same time, she has begun to like him. But she isn't being paid to like him. Just the same as, she reflects, a prostitute is not paid to like the men.

They stroll in the gardens that, on Sunday, are full of people and children. Henri tells her that he had been in London during the war. He had missed the hardships in France. She tells him she had been a student in Cambridge. While she divulges very little, Henri says quite a few things about his feelings for France and the transition they are in.

"Henri, I'm getting tired. Let's go to a spot I know at the end of the park away from all these people."

Julie finds the spot she remembers, up by the *Avenue de L'Observatoire*, and they sit on a bench. The bench has a back to it. They relax against it. Henri puts his arm around her shoulders, the familiar opening movement before kissing. However Julie backs off, just a little. "I don't think so, Henri. What you need is pressure relief, not more excitement."

Julie places herself more to his front and, using herself as a screen, unzips his fly and hands out his half-erect cock. "Sit back, Henri."

From her bag Julie deftly produces KY Gel and a towelette. She rubs up Henri to perfection. She folds her hand into a tube so that it feels remarkably like a vagina to the man. She times her actions to be in synch with his rising tumescence and catches the stream of spunk neatly in the towelette so that none goes on Henri's suit.

"There, Henri. I'm sure you feel relieved. Now," Julie looks at her wristwatch, "I really must be going. I have stuff to prepare for tomorrow at the Fashion House. Thank you for the lunch and a lovely afternoon."

Julie stands up and is buttoning up her jacket. Henri, still in some disarray, bounds up. "Wait! Wait! For heaven's sake, give me a moment. You are the most glorious woman I have ever met! Please sit down, just for a moment. I must see you again, Juliette. Tomorrow evening! Could we meet tomorrow evening?"

Julie pauses as if considering the possibility. "I don't see why not, Henri. We seem to get along very well. You are an interesting man. Let us meet at the same place, *Brasserie La Fermette Marbeuf,* and enjoy *coupes de champagne.* Choose a place to go on to where they have the best *escargots.* I like Paris at night. I like to dress as a night girl too, so all the men will be envious of you! And I will seduce you!" She laughs lightly as she gives Henri a kiss on his cheek.

"May I see you home?" Henri asks.

"No. Just get me a taxi. My home life must remain my own affair."

In the taxi Julie says, "just drive ahead. I'll tell you where to go in a second." She waves her hand to Henri as he recedes from her view.

Julie sits back in the taxi. Two thoughts predominate. The first is that Henri is a decent fellow, torn between being the soldier, all set to do his duty and enforce his country's will, and his own self, a man of culture, reason, and vitality. She is sure he will be conflicted by the situation in Algeria. But what he would do is another matter. The second thought, or, rather, feeling is that she likes him. If she has sex with him, would she regret it? It would be quite distinct and separate from her life as a wife and mother. Rather it would be a service to her country. It would just be the actress in her that would be involved, not her true self. That's how it had been, especially at *Le Coq*, when she had played scenes for the men. It would be nothing more than a self-indulgence, provided she enjoyed it, which she thought she would. Content with that thought, she is happy to hop out of the taxi, go rapidly inside, and kiss baby Charles as he sleeps in his crib.

She hears the front door opening. Quickly looking up the passage way she sees Giles coming in. She rushes to him. "Giles! Giles! My darling man! I love you. Don't speak. Just come to our room."

She throws Giles down on the bed and kisses him voluptuously. They tear off their clothes, their bodies pulsing. He is as aroused as she. "Fucking hell!" he shouts, the tempest inside him breaking out into the open. He fucks her and she him like they have never done before.

Chapter 36.

Julie's one night stand: the force of habit.

The next day, with the sober white light of morning coming through the windows, Giles and Julie bring each other up to date. Giles tells her the messages they are receiving back from the French in Algeria, the *pieds noirs*, in return for the information they are sending them, are not hopeful. Any peaceful solution between them and the Algerians seems impossible.

"They are a hard-nosed bunch, Julie. All they seem to want is for us to send them men and arms, the latest stuff, to wipe out the Algerian nationalists. Mendès is pessimistic. The Algerian French reject even the idea of sitting down and talking with the rebels. My under-the-counter opening with them only confirms their declared position. They take it as a settled truth that Algeria is eternally French and the French in the country will rule there as they please. If there are any moderates within their ranks, it is hard to find them. Whoever we send there is going to have a hard time. So, what news have you, Julie? How's the modeling going?"

"Fine, Giles. I'm finding my feet, learning the business. For all the glamour the outside world sees, it's grinding hard work when you are in the inside. But fun too. Some of the girls are great. I am making friends."

"Good for you, Julie."

"Oh, I should tell you, Giles, I have met the man who may be going to Algeria. He's a general. I had lunch with him and we went for a walk in the park. Just talking. A nice fellow. He may have a hard time of it with the French in Algeria being as hard as you say they are. I'll see him again to have him open up his mind a bit more. He seems to like me, which helps. I am not exactly a Mata Hari, Giles," she smiles, "but I rather enjoy being a spy, if that's what I am."

"Sounds good, Julie. Listen. There's a conference about to happen in Geneva, Switzerland. It's mainly about Vietnam, but on the side Mitterand or someone, is going to talk with representatives from the Algerian rebels, the FLN. It's possible that Ben Bella himself will be there. Their top man in Cairo. Anyhow, I have to be there."

"How long will you be away, Giles?"

"I don't know yet."

"I'll miss you, my darling. Especially after last night! You wiped me out!"

"Me, too, sweetheart. I had never known it could be like that. We'll save up for another when I come back. I have to pack my things. We are leaving this afternoon. Going by train. Our really fast trains are in the planning stage. But even the trains going to Geneva now are fast and comfortable. It's something that we French seem to be able to do better than others. So we can celebrate that!"

"OK, darling. Take care. I have to go to the Fashion House now. I'll just check with nanny first. Baby Charles is growing up so fast!"

Nanny was hardly surprised that Giles should be off again to another foreign country or that Julie would be tied up with the fashion shows. The people she had always worked for did those things. That was why, in good part, they hired her. "At any time, nanny, you can get a message to me at the Fashion House," Julie tells her.

"Certainly, *madame*. Just leave it to me. Charles and I will be fine together. Mostly I will have him up in my room, except when I take him out in the pram, of course. So, don't you worry, *madame*. I'll take good care of him."

* * *

At the Fashion House Julie is working at fitting a show gown for Lollabrigida to wear at a film festival. Julie is wearing a dark wig so that *Madame* Dionnelle can see how the colors are working out. Wearing the wig puts Julie in mind of having her hair done for the evening with Henri. She is glad that Giles will be away. It leaves her free to concentrate on how best to fulfill her contract with Alexis and be paid. It is possible that she will have sex with Henri that evening, if that will encourage him to tell her more about his inner thoughts and feelings. But it could be enjoyable just for its own sake. Should she scold herself for having such a thought? Hardly, she decides. As she well knows, sex can be enjoyable and quite impersonal. And no one need know.

Through with the fittings, Julie is eating a *Croque Monsieur* (ham and cheese sandwich), at her desk. The phone rings. She is told that General Henri Bourstelle is on the line for her.

"Oh, it must be something to do with my husband," she tells the girl downstairs at the switchboard. She picks up the phone. Henri says, "Is that you, Juliette?"

"Yes, it's me."

"I had to call you because I have received my posting. I am speaking to you from a phone outside the base. I don't trust our army phones not to be tapped."

"What is so serious, Henri?"

"I am to go to Algiers and be in charge of the Parachute Regiments there, leaving tomorrow. I am to use all means to quell the rebellion. You told me that truth and honesty are the ultimate values, Juliette. Well, the truth is that I believe the Algerians deserve to live peacefully in their own country and that we should help them do that. It's complicated, I know. But that's what I said to my commanding general."

"Oh, my! I take it he wasn't thrilled."

"He's a stickler and, as far as I can make out, wants the army to be in charge there and to back up the *pieds noirs* in keeping Algeria French. The general told me orders are orders. I know that very well. I told the general that orders are always to be carried out in the light of circumstance. He puffed and huffed and told me he had no choice but to send me, though he now had doubts whether I had my heart in carrying out my orders. I have to go, Juliette. I have to obey orders. I know we have known each other for only a few hours. I suppose it's foolish to confide in you; but I felt I must. I would like to keep our date for this evening, even if it's a farewell for the moment."

"I can tell by your voice, Henri, you are stressed out. Relax. I feel it my patriotic duty to give you a great send off. You need the girl of your dreams. I know the place to take you after we have had a wonderful dinner somewhere. I'll meet you as we arranged. Just be there, my handsome fellow."

All right. She would have a one-night stand with Henri. It wouldn't be more than what she had done thousands of times before. It could be the last time she would ever do such a thing, so she would make it the best; prove to herself that she was still as good as she had ever been. Quickly she writes notes about what she must do that afternoon.

From Natalie she needs to know the details of *la maison de passe* behind *La Madeleine* where Natalie had told her she had been with a lover. "Delicious," Natalie had said. Natalie gave her the phone number after Julie had told her she wanted to give her husband a thrill; which could be true, at a later date. Julie phones and sets up the arrangements for later that evening, just saying her name is Juliette.

Julie phones Alexis. "I have the scoop. Everything you could possibly need to know. I will meet you at the bank." She quickly writes down the essentials she would tell Alexis. Basically that General Henri Bourstelle will be going to Algiers to command the Parachute Regiments in suppressing the rebellion, but he would look for ways to pacify the situation.

She phones Giles. He hadn't left for Geneva yet. She tells him the same news about Bourstelle. She has found out because the general had phoned her. "Pass it on to your people, Giles. It sounds to me as if the army is taking matters into their own hands and, maybe, by-passing the government."

She phones the *Salon de Beauté* she uses and makes an appointment to have her hair and face done.

She phones a limo service to pick her up at the *Salon de Beauté* and to be at her disposal for the night.

She looks at her watch. She must leave to meet Alexis at the bank. She phones Mec. She finds him in his office. Of course he will accompany her to the bank.

At the bank she tells Alexis about General Henri Bourstelle. "I am afraid he will be a weak reed for your people, Alexis. He is an honest and straight-forward man. He will do his duty, but only as he sees it. He is flying out tomorrow."

"Right!" Alexis tells her. "You have done well. That's all we need to know." He looks at her and smiles. "I hope your foray into espionage had some rewards for you, beyond the money you are about to have."

She smiles back. "You will never know, will you?"

With Mec standing with her and following the bank clerk's instructions, Julie puts her key in the box and Alexis does the same. The box opens. The bank clerk takes out the two wads of $10,000 dollars. Julie puts her money in her bag. Alexis puts his in his pocket. She and he shake hands. They both leave.

Julie goes upstairs in the bank with Mec and changes $2000 into French francs. She deposits the rest in her account. She tries to give Mec some of the francs, but he refuses. "Whatever it is, Julie, enjoy this money with Giles."

* * *

At home Julie finds Charles is upstairs with Nanny. OK. She looks over her G-strings and chooses a silvery-red satin one; then puts out the matching garter belt and half-bra, with some under padding in it to help her prominence. She adds two surprise items with a grin on her face. She finds her long black satin skirt, a left-over from *Le Coq*. It folds over and clings tightly to her legs on either side. When she parts her legs it becomes a split skirt reaching to her belly button. She will top it with a satin blouse with a wide-neck and low décolleté. She chooses black lacy stockings and black shoes with three inch heels. She selects her most luxurious silver fox fur stole, styled in a fulsome swoop falling from her shoulders to her buttocks at the back and closing with a clasp at her waist. The marvelously plump pelts date from General Max Edelman and she has had the stole fashioned from them to her design. To go with it is a silver fox fur muff with a capacious pocket. It is large enough to hold the items she anticipates needing, if all goes to plan. She likes wearing muffs and feels sexy with them. A man had told her that when she put her hands into a muff, it reminded him of a cock going into a pussy.

Julie reclines in a hot bubble bath. She shaves herself, being meticulous, especially of her pudenda. It must be baby smooth. Then she creams her body. What she is doing is force of habit. She's on a business assignment. Therefore she preps and dresses accordingly.

Julie puts her clothes and jewelry choices into a suitcase. She will dress at the *Salon de Beauté*. Once there Julie has her hair washed and then glistened with the latest concoction to give her hair a glossy shine. Her hairdo is a theatrical whirl high over her head, with wispy ringlets falling by her cheeks. The girl uses a *Super-Set Finishing Spray* to hold it in place for the evening. An Asian girl has been doing her manicure, glueing on the long nails and painting them a glistening red. Julie has her favorite little man, Basile, glue on eyelashes and colorize with blues, mauves, and purples around her eyes. Then he gives her face a professional *maquillage*, a powdery pale complexion highlighted by rouges to go with her eyes. Basile is so enthusiastic! So skillful! Daringly she allows him to inject her lips to plump them out. It's the latest thing. They are being called "Paris Lips." Basile reminds her of Ernst. She reminds herself that one day she must go looking for Ernst.

Julie looks at herself in the mirrors. Yes! Done! Henri will be turned on. Whatever men say, or whatever they may want in a lifetime wife, a prossy look erects their cocks. Those Egyptian women in the Louvre knew it 4,000 years ago. *"Plus ça change, plus c'est la même chose."* (The more things change, the more they stay the same.)

Julie dresses. She scans herself critically in the mirrors. OK! An elegant courtesan. The limo arrives. *Madame* helps her into her furs and wishes her *"bonne chance."*

Henri is at the *Brasserie*. He comes quickly to her with his eyes aglow. "Juliette! I can't believe it! You said a girl of my dreams! No! You are the girl I have never dreamed of! I couldn't, because I had never met you. Thank you! Thank you!"

They sit together, sipping champagne. "Henri, you must cast all your cares aside for the evening. For all we know this may be the last time we meet."

"Oh, don't say that!" Henri implores her.

"You're off to the wars tomorrow. You may be killed. I may very well not be here if and when you do return. I have reasons to tell you that, but I won't explain why. So let us just be here together tonight and enjoy each other to the full. Agreed?"

"Yes, agreed! I will be your Romeo for the evening - - and we won't die from it! That's what they did, you remember,

Romeo and Juliet. Die from being in love." Henri chuckles, a little grimly. "We live in desperate times, with desperate people. I don't know what's going to happen. Nobody does!"

Julie takes his hand, gives it a gentle squeeze. "We'll live just for ourselves this evening, Henri. I have a limo. Where will you take me?"

"You said the best escargots. You showed me you have an educated taste in wines. In Paris there is only one place to go for both and I have booked us in. Shall we go?"

Henri directs the chauffeur to take them to *Le Tastevin* on the *Ile Saint-Louis*. The place is authentically French, with dark wooden ceiling beams that have been there for some hundreds of years. Its impression is intimate rather than luxurious. The wine cellar is well stocked and the restaurant has the reputation for having the best escargots in town.

Henri and Julie spend two hours there enjoying the food and wine, the atmosphere and, most of all, themselves.

"Now I take over, Henri. We are going to a *Maison de Passe*, the best one in Paris."

Outside the restaurant they see other limos. Their chauffeur tells them it is a popular place with limos always there in the evening. As they drive off they see one limo pulling out and another pulling in.

The *Maison de Passe* is on *rue Castellane* behind *La Madeleine*. They are held up on the narrow streets there, just by *Fauchon*, the ultimate grocery store in Paris. Henri jumps out to purchase one of their sumptuous boxes of chocolate.

While she waits Julie has a view of *les motrices* on *rue de Sèze*. She has heard of them, but never seen them. Their parked, over-sized, American convertibles fill the sidewalks. The vixens sit with the tops down, under the street lamps, in full view. Their dramatic coiffures and showgirl *maquillage* are seductive beacons for the male eye.

A convertible drives in. Its top opens to reveal its driver. The young *professionnelle*, 22 or 23 Julie judges, is slight in build, with a cool polished aura. Her creamy shoulders are framed by a luxuriant white fox fur. Her ash-blonde tresses are stacked over her head with a deep fringe reaching to her thin arched eyebrows. Her long eyelashes and lightly rouged cheeks are perfection. Clinging to her svelte body is a silvery mini, with her bowl breasts bursting out of its top. Her arms are sheathed in white satin gloves, her wrists are glittery with rhinestone bracelets. She settles and poses herself.

Julie smirks; it takes one to know one. She could be that girl, even to the pout of their swollen Paris lips. She had turned herself out for her evening with Henri in a very similar style, as an elegant whore. She had to have *l'air juste* (the right look) for what she was about that evening, just as the girl had to have *l'air juste* for her business. They could be twins! A well-dressed man comes up to the blonde. She puts her hand out, looks up to him with a questioning look, and touches his crotch. He bends over and says something. She laughs. The deal is made. The car top is lowered. They drive off.

Julie moans, "Oh! God!" She's smoldering. Sex is alive and well in Paris. She herself is part of it, inescapably. A hot wave flows through her. She has a sense of desperation. Like the man had said at the farm, "once a whore, always a whore."

Henri rejoins her. Julie calms herself. At the house they are met by a man who takes them to a room just off the courtyard. A woman sits at a table. Julie tells her of the reservation she has made. "Certainly, *m'amselle*. We require that the gentleman pays now."

Henri takes out his wallet. Julie stops him. "No, Henri. My treat."

The woman gives them the key to the room. "Take the elevator to the top," she instructs them. The spacious room is on the top floor, with windows having a view of the rooftops of nearby Paris, with the Eiffel tower in the distance. The room's decor reminds Julie of the rooms in the houses where she had worked, red velvet wallpaper, etc. It's just right for the business at hand. Wine and p*etit fours* are on a table. A phonograph has an assortment of records with it. To one side is a bathroom with a toilet, bidet, and shower. It is well supplied with towels, soaps, creams, etc. The oval bed is huge with many pillows. All in all, Julie considers, looking around with a professional eye, very well done.

"I bet you'll find a robe in the bathroom, Henri. Undress and be comfortable. Take your time. I have a few things to do."

Julie is intent. She grabs her muff and finds the things inside. She replaces her shoes with shiny-black platforms with soaring high stiletto heels. Quickly she puts on a little black satin bustier and arranges her breasts to show well. She attends to her make-up, making her dramatic coloring sparkle and gleam afresh, her complexion powdery and flawless, plumps up her hair, fixing it again with the spray. She has to do it, she has no choice.

She pulls on shiny-black satin arm gloves and adorns her wrists with red-rhinestone bracelets. She fastens a matching choker round her neck and dangle earrings in her ears. *Voilà!* She spritzes herself with perfume. She puts condoms and KY gel by the bed and finds a record with strip music. She arranges the lighting and sets an arm chair for Henri to sit in. She goes to a dark corner of the room and puts on her furs.

Henri appears in a bathrobe. She has her back to him. "Sit in the chair, *monsieur,*" she tells him, as if he has just arrived. *Oh, bordel et putain!*[58]she swears to herself. It feels so good to be in action again! She has spent most of her life becoming and being the perfect whore. It's her *métier* (skill, vocation.) She needs it. She needs to fuck.

Julie sets the phonograph to play a record of strip-tease music. She turns around, comes forward into the light, lingers, then parades on her high heels. She slinks. She grinds.

---

[58] Literally the words mean brothel and whore. But they are used as general exclamations, like goddam.

She eyes the man, then looks away as if he isn't there. She darts her arm in and out of the muff. Henri, at first amazed and silent, soon gets into the act, clapping and yowling. Her rhinestones flash beams of light into his eyes as she teasingly discards the muff and the fur.

Julie parts her skirt, slowly dividing it higher and higher up her thighs. After teasing him with 'will-she-or-won't-she,' she discards the skirt to show her garter belt and G-string.

She wiggles in front of him. Henri beckons to her. He puts his finger into the top of her elastic G-string and tucks in a 100f note.

"*Oh - - la, m'sieur!*" she coos. She hadn't expected the money. She spins around and presents her quivering loins to him again. Henri's wallet is full of cash for his trip to Algeria. He tucks 100f notes into her G-string and the tops of her stockings as she slinks and gyrates for him. Henri is doing exactly the right thing, rewarding her for being an accomplished prostitute. Sure! She will give him her best! She wobbles her ass in front of his face. He slaps each cheek, at first gently, then hard, stinging her, making her yelp.

"Yeeks!" she cries out. "*Oh, chérie,*" she moans, "*je t'aime, je t'adore! . . . darleeng . . .*" (I love you, I adore you) She bends down. Her breasts are before him. "*. . . et maintenant, après le zizi, également pour les doudones . . .* " (and now, after the hole, the same for the tits.)

Henri tucks money into her bra. She takes out some of the notes and kisses them. "*Oui, oui! Il faut que la garce travaille pour son lucre!*" (Yes! Yes! The bitch must work for her money!)

Henri sees she is wearing shiny red pasties with tassels. Julie had put them on as her surprise item. She loosens her bra. He takes it off her. The tassels from the pasties fall down and sway in front of him. She grabs the money falling from the bra. She's a money girl! She flaunts her breasts to him, twirling the tassels as she used to do at *Les Poulets* and *Le Coq*.

"*Donc? Juliette LaPerle te plaît, m'sieur? Tu veux la baiser?*" she questions. (So? Juliette LaPerle pleases you, mister? You want to fuck her?)

"Damn right! I am a man, you fucking bitch! I have a cock!"

"*Et moi! J'ai mon zizi à argent. Tu l'as acheté et je baise bien, m'sieur!*" (And me! I have my money hole! You've bought it and I fuck well, mister!) It's one of her well-used business lines, coming out like a conditioned response.

Julie's hands go down and, with a "*Hoorah!*" she pulls out his erect cock. She falls to her knees. Her head goes down. Henri's cock is in her mouth

"Oh, God! You are a devil woman, Juliette!" he groans.

He is as stiff as a general's baton, but thicker. He lifts her up and carries her to the bed. Deftly, with him hardly noticing, she unrolls a condom down his rod. She pushes him down on his back. Swiftly she scoops up her silver fox stole and puts it round her shoulders.

"You can fuck a fur slut tonight, Henri, if that pleases you!" she tells him, panting, starting to straddle him. Her genitals are dripping wet. She has to have his cock inside her. It's madness, delirious! Henri is panting as much as she. He grasps her furred body. "You crazy witch! God almighty! I love you - - you fucking fur slut!"

Julie thrusts her tongue into his mouth. His cock is at her portal when the commotion starts. They both hear loud shouts and noises from below. The sounds carry up the stairwell. They stop and listen. They hear *pfft, pfft.* Henri is startled. "Those could be shots through a silencer, Juliette. Stay there. I'll find out what's happening."

Henri retrieves his bathrobe and goes to the door.

Julie finds another dressing gown in the bathroom. "What is it, Henri?"

Henri looks down the passageway. "Come over here with me, Juliette." She joins him by the door.

They hear the elevator stop, just along the passageway, and someone coming out of it. Henri peers round the side of the door to be greeted by a *pfft* and a slug embedding itself in the wall by him.

He pulls his head back quickly. "He doesn't like us. He has a pistol with a silencer. We need to lure him forward so I have a chance to tackle him."

"OK. Hold on, Henri." Julie goes to the bathroom and finds a white towel. "I think this will do, Henri." She goes back to the door, slipping out of the bathrobe and picking up her fur. She holds it in front of her. With any luck she can put it to good use.

At the side of the door she waves the white towel. "*Monsieur, monsieur.* Don't shoot me. I am a working girl. I'll show myself to you."

"OK. No tricks."

Julie eases herself into view, with her fur held in front of her. "You see, I am just a girl. I hardly know the man here. He seems nice. What have you against him?"

"He's a traitor. He has to die."

Julie shakes her head. "I can't hear you very well with the music going on. Come closer so we can talk without shouting. Come along the wall. The man can't see you there. You said something about a pie? You look a good fellow. I am here on business."

"What are you, girl? A fucking whore?"

"Yes! And I fuck well! I'll bring you off like you've never been done before! I bet you have a marvelous cock. Here! I'll show you what you get."

Julie puts one of her legs forward in its black stocking, tipped with her sky high stiletto heel, and then, trusting she will not be shot, steps out from the doorway. She lets her fur drop to the floor. She poses herself, wiggles her breasts, making the tassels fly about. She gives the man a bump and a grind in time with the music.

"What the hell are you playing at, girl? Come out here."

"No. I don't think I will. Someone might come up in the elevator and see me." She stoops down and picks up her fur, glancing back into the room. She can just see Henri behind the door. She turns round more and peers around the room.

"Oh!" she cries out loudly, "he's gone!"

The man comes toward her. "*Des clous*! (No way!) What do you mean he's gone?"

"I don't know. Perhaps he's in the bathroom. There's a window there. Perhaps you frightened him away. And he hasn't paid me! Not a *sou*! That's the worst thing to happen to a girl and it's all your fault, whoever you are."

"*Merde alors!*" the man swears coming up to Julie, pushing her aside, looking round the apparently empty room with his gun in his hand.

No doubt in another second or two he would have discovered Henri behind the door. But Julie doesn't give him that chance. She holds the fur in front of her and throws it over the man's head, pulling it down over his face and neck. She leaps on top of him. The man falls to the floor under her, enveloped and struggling in the fur.

Henri swiftly comes out from behind the door. He grabs one of the man's hands and twists the arm back into a lock. Then he twists some more, dislocating the man's shoulder. The man lets out a howl of pain. Henri gives him a hard karate chop on the back of his neck.

"Juliette! Give me your stockings."

Julie quickly takes off her shoes and rolls her stockings down her legs. She gives them to Henri. Henri ties the man's wrists together with them, saying, "stockings make damn good handcuffs. I learned that when I took a class in Unarmed Combat. Never thought it would be useful! But hey!"

Henri picks the man up and throws him into a chair. He sits there limply, dazed.

Henri smiles at Juliette. "In my next fight I want you right by my side! You were magnificent!"

"Who is the scumbag, Henri?"

"I can guess, but I don't know. Juliette, put your clothes on and go down in the elevator. See what the shooting was about. I'll see what I can get out of this would-be assassin."

Julie throws her clothes back on, in her haste not bothering to take off the breast pasties. Downstairs, to her horror, Julie finds the man and the woman, the ones they had met when they entered, dead. Both have bullet holes in their heads. She hurriedly takes the elevator upstairs again and tells Henri.

"The bastard! He's an Algerian *pieds noirs* killer. After my interview with that general they must have reckoned I wouldn't play their game. So they took what they thought would be the easy way out. Kill me and have someone else there more to their liking."

"They would really do that?" Julie is aghast. Very likely what she had told Alexis had helped bring about this attack on Henri.

"You've seen for yourself, Juliette. OK. Let's tidy up. Go round the room and make sure we are leaving nothing behind. I will take this rat down to where he killed the two people downstairs. Then we will leave. I will tell the police to check out this place. I don't want you, or me, to be involved. I have to go to Algiers and you have to get on with your life."

That's what they do. Julie goes round everywhere with damp towels to clean off finger prints. She puts all the money that Henri had bestowed on the "stripper" in the pocket of her muff. Momentarily she debates if she should give the money back to him. But then he's there. "Keep it, you earned it," he tells her with a grin.

"If there ever is another time, Henri, I will remember."

Henri picks up the gun with a towel to preserve the man's prints on it. They pick up everything of theirs.

When done, Henri takes the man by the scruff of the neck and frog-steps him to the elevator. They descend to the lobby. There's a ball of twine at the desk. Henri binds the man's legs and then hog ties him with the twine tight around his neck and ankles. "If he struggles, he will strangle himself. Maybe he'll die anyway, his eyes are beginning to pop."

Henri dumps the two corpses together with the man and his gun on the floor of the office and locks the door. "That will teach them to send sewer vermin after me!"

Julie's limo is still there, the chauffeur dozing. Julie lets Henri off at his apartment building after they have embraced and said farewell.

Julie tells the chauffeur to drive around the *Bois de Boulogne*. She wraps herself in her fur and, in doing so, feels the pasties still on her breasts. With a smile she lets them stay there, a temporary remembrance of the evening and of the fuck that wasn't. What an evening! She grins as she reflects that, in spite of thousands of successful fucks, she has a penchant for having some important ones interrupted by cataclysmic events.

Arriving home, alone in the house, Julie uses a vibrating dildo. She has to get off. She does. Relaxed at last, she falls asleep. In the morning, in the shower, she finally removes the pasties, gives each a kiss, and puts them aside. "Until the next time," she tells them.

The papers are full of the killings. In the early hours of the morning an anonymous caller had tipped off the police to go to the house. The culprit is obvious. The man was a professional killer. After shooting two innocent victims, things had gone very wrong for him. Speculation abounds about who had tied him up. Hog tied as he was, the man had slowly strangled himself and was dead by the time the police arrived. No one knows who had been his real target.

For the police there are no records of who had been there that evening, just a list of first names. The rooms in the house yield no useful evidence, though a slug from the killer's pistol is found embedded in the woodwork on the top floor. No one comes forward with information. The police close the case.

Nobody calls on Julie, then or later.

Chapter 37.

Julie and Giles have their worries - - that are dispelled.

Julie has her luxurious silver fox fur and matching muff cleaned, as well as her slinky black satin skirt. They have all served her very well, she thinks with a broad grin. When she had checked the muff she had been a little shocked to find so much money in it. Henri had been very generous to the "stripper." This money, too, would go into the fund for baby Charles.

She had hand washed her blouse, lingerie and G-string and had let her thoughts linger as she did so. Damn! The build-up to having Henri make love to her had been perfect! By the time she was straddling him and had his cock entering her, she had been as horny as hell! Playing the strumpet is something she is loath to give up. But she genuinely adores and loves her husband and their child. Humph! The light dawns. The solution is staring her in the face. She will introduce her husband to *Mademoiselle Juliette LaPerle*, the hussy, and have him take her as his mistress. Otherwise he might become just a stuffy diplomat! She had to save him from that!

The thought buzzes around her brain like a firefly. She has the money to do it. She will find a studio apartment somewhere and do it up. Then her husband will receive invitations to visit *Mademoiselle Juliette LaPerle* when she knew they could both take the evening and night off. Or, in time, she imagines, he would demand his rights of her and have her service him in whatever way he wished. If he wanted to tie her up and paddle her bottom, she would have to let him! Wow! Could it ever come to that? And the muff! Why not have draw strings put in round each opening of the muff? Then, when he wished, he would have her put her hands in the muff and tighten the draw strings around her wrists. She would be "muff-cuffed" and subservient to whatever he wished to do with her. Oh, God! That made her wet, just imagining it. There were so many possibilities. What would he like? How can she "give" herself to him utterly and completely?

Julie lies back on the bed and contemplates it all. For her *pied à terre* she would choose somewhere central in the city that she could use to rest up in or have it as a retreat where she could write the book; the book that Joey had suggested to her about the houses in war time. At the same time it would be where *Mademoiselle LaPerle* entertains her lover, *Monsieur* Martin, and services him as his mistress in fabulous scenes.

Then the next idea breaks through. Natalie had told her that the *Hotel de Passe* that a man had taken her to had been shoddy and dirty. She hadn't liked it at all. Why not rent the apartment out on some of the many days when she would not be using it? Not that she exactly needed the money, but it would be a source of revenue that she would put aside for something special, like the fund she was starting for baby Charles.

The whole idea made her buoyant with happy eagerness. Yes! There would be all sorts of details to work out. But she is good at that. She muses on in her ever creative mind. It could be a first step to becoming a realtor in Paris. She would buy up apartments and rent them out to visitors, like wealthy Americans. Wow! What a life she had before her!

And not only that. In the last fashion show she had worn designs similar to those that Grace Kelly had worn in her films. Julie knew she looked good in them. After the show, a man had approached her and asked whether she would be interested in having film tests. She had no idea what these were. The man explained she would go to a studio and be photographed to find out if her face was friendly to the camera. *Madame* Dionnelle had overheard it all. "So you are trying to steal another of my girls, Jean?"

"Only if she accepts being stolen, *madame*. But I hardly think it is stealing to uncover a beauty who is, from what I have heard, also most intelligent and charming!"

* * *

Giles is required to sit at the back of the French delegation at the Geneva conference. The hours are long and mostly boring. All the representatives set out their well-prepared and well known positions at inordinate length. Giles, being at the back with no one behind him, can slip a paperback into the large and thick files and dossiers under discussion. By this means he is reading Simenon's *Le Chien Jaune* (The Yellow Dog). The story starts with a stray dog always being at the site of the murders happening in a windy seashore town.

Giles admires Simenon's inventiveness and finds the book a page turner. As he reads the French he is busy turning the sentences into English. He will translate the book, following up his success at translating the previous Simenon book. The money is still not big, but he has established his reputation as a translator. He can expect to get commissions. He has begun his own book, *Un Garçon dans Le Maquis* (A Boy in the *Maquis*) and has a French publisher keen to buy the rights. He has begun to feel that he has to have private time and a private place where he can concentrate on his writing and literary career. He will have to approach Julie carefully about it, and assure her he is not deserting her or baby Charles in any way. He will make ample time to be with them both.

In the evening, after dining well in Geneva, Giles walks back to his hotel room. His lonely hotel room. He thinks of masturbating as a way to relive the last love session with his wife. But turns away from it. He had felt he was satisfying Julie by his response to her almost out of control gyrations, heavings, cries and moanings. Her orgasms were something else! But, at the same time, he suspects she is missing the drama that she had shown him in their sink-hole aborted event at *Le Coq*. He thought back. Yes! He had been frustrated! He had loved the artistic build-up she had developed just for him. She was - - Giles thought about the proper word and decided on - - a "sex-artist." Yes, that was his wife's flair. But now she was without the means to create her *tableaux et scènes*. And, perhaps, she was doubting that her properly-married-scholar-and-diplomat husband would participate in such sex revels. Well, that had to be corrected. Yes indeed! That had to be corrected.

The next day, with Giles again sitting in the back row, the French delegate describes the events unfolding in Algeria. He is saying it is an internal French affair and that a new army commander, General Bourstelle, has arrived on the scene with strong instructions to bring the rebellion to an end. The government in Algiers is complementing the army effort by setting up local Algerian groups to advise the government on needed reforms.

Giles looks down. He feels deeply disappointed. It is the same old stuff, the same repressive measures, the same empty promises. He knows from inside reports that the killing and devastation in the Aurés, where he had been, had grown worse. The French are committing what is close to genocide. The government in Paris is almost certain to change. Mendès is about to lose the next vote of confidence in the Assembly. The talk is of putting a nonentity, a man called Pineau, in charge. Apparently someone has taken a bet of 10,000 francs that he won't last a week.[59]

Giles believes that his place in the government is safe. However, he had been talking with a representative from SDECE *(Service de Documentation Extérieure et de Contre-Espionage.)* They knew he had been involved in the attempt to decipher the true intent of the *pieds noirs* in Algeria. Of interest to them, too, was that he knew England well and spoke English perfectly.

Giles had told Charles about it. Charles thought he should go for it. "That outfit, Giles, knows everything that's happening in France as well as the world. It is equivalent to the British MI5 and MI6 combined, that is both domestic and foreign stuff, and the American FBI and CIA. They do covert operations, no doubt some dirty tricks, but that is in the nature of intelligence operations these days. When DeGaulle comes back to power, and he surely will, you had better know about all that's happening. You will need to play your cards right. DeGaulle might very well look at someone like you, not strongly affiliated and knowledgeable, to come into his group." So Giles had that in his mind.

* * *

Julie is excited. Giles is on his way back from Geneva. She has so much to tell him. But she is nervous. First and foremost Giles must be sure she will be the devoted mother of Charles and his loving wife for as long as they both shall live. How will he take her plans? Will he be shocked? Should she be so daring?

And there was this nag in her mind now. She understood all too well what had happened, and why, with Henri. The whore that she thought she had killed was still there, driving her. Why had the image of the young blonde in the convertible struck such a chord in her? Because, given

---

[59]The story may be apocryphal, but Pineau actually lasted for only 6 days. So the bet would have been won.

the chance she could do all that the girl had been doing, maybe do it better, maybe enjoy it more. The girl had laughed with her customer, just as she used to laugh with many of her men. Her personal truth was that she could not discard her past, as if it had never happened. It had to be expressed in some form; else it would overwhelm her.

If she couldn't be the mistress to her husband, what else? Could he ever be a cuckold husband and allow her to go off and do her thing? Cuckold husbands were not all that rare, she knew. Married girls had worked at *Les Poulets* and at *Le Coq*. They worked out arrangements with their husbands. She knew one of them, a real nice guy, not a dud at all and proud of his wife. Did she want that? No! She could never impose that on Giles nor, even more, on their son. Unless, of course, Giles wanted it. Was that totally unthinkable?

Julie fell back into the armchair she was sitting in. To really know oneself was so damn difficult, let alone knowing the inner workings of someone else. She couldn't know what was in the future for her, for Giles, for baby Charles. OK. She was a practical girl and a realistic one. She would work it out, one way or another. Right now her mission was to sex up her husband. Good! That was resolved. Now all she had to do was to get on with it.

* * *

Giles sits in the train clasping his hands together anxiously. He has so much to share with Julie. First and foremost he wants her to know categorically, without a shadow of a doubt, that he will be the best father he can be to Charles and the most caring husband to her for their lifetimes. But he has much to confess, starting with crying out to her in the loneliness of his room and wanting her as a prostitute. And then when Mec had taken him to see the *filles* on *rue Blondel*, he'd had a huge, almost painful, erection. If Mec had not taken him away he would have chosen one of them and fucked her. He had hidden too much from Julie. She, who had shed her past so wonderfully, would hardly countenance her husband wanting anything except loving copulation. But he must be open to her. He mustn't be like other men, frustrated with their wives and seeking sexual and erotic excitement elsewhere.

* * *

Julie has come to meet him at the *Gare de Lyon*. She runs to him as soon as she sees him. They embrace, with their bodies and minds in a free fall of emotions.

"Julie, I love you, I love you, I love you."

"Giles, I adore you, I adore you, I adore you."

They hold hands all the way home in the taxi, every now and again kissing lightly. At the house nanny has Charles, brightly dressed in a new blue suit to greet them. Nanny likes to cook and she had prepared her Welsh cakes with strawberry jam and clotted cream.

"Oh, Julie! I think we are the most fortunate people in the world!"

"Giles, I think we are. I have lots to tell you and I have some propositions to make."

"Julie. We have to decide who goes first, you or me. I suppose I can say I too have some propositions for you and, well, some confessions too."

That evening, after they had kissed Charles in his crib and he had closed his eyes, they walk to the bank of the Seine, sit on a bench, and hold each other as lovers do.

Giles says, "let's say this together, Julie: 'we are going to have a wonderful life together'."

So, together they say, looking into each other's eyes, "we are going to have a wonderful life together."